Kerry Tucker
Learns
to Live

BOOKS BY LOUISE VOSS

His Other Woman

The Last Stage

The Old You

The Venus Trap

Games People Play

Lifesaver

Are You My Mother?

To Be Someone

With Mark Edwards

Forward Slash

Killing Cupid

DETECTIVE LENNON THRILLER SERIES

From the Cradle

The Blissfully Dead

One Shot

KATE MADDOX SERIES

Catch Your Death

All Fall Down

Kerry Tucker Learns to Live

LOUISE VOSS

bookouture

Published by Bookouture in 2022

An imprint of Storyfire Ltd.
Carmelite House
50 Victoria Embankment
London EC4Y 0DZ

www.bookouture.com

ISBN: 978-1-80314-153-4
eBook ISBN: 978-1-80314-152-7

ONE

JUNE 2020

She wouldn't have admitted it to anybody because it sounded weird, but Kerry loved her sorting frame. It looked so daunting when empty, but it was so *satisfying* to fill, slotting each piece of post into its rightful place with the speed of a skilled card dealer in a casino. She just wished it was as straightforward to sort out her own head. If only all the questions tormenting her could simply be popped into the correct answering slot, gathered up into the trolley and then taken out on a round, leaving behind a clean and empty frame ready for the next day. Instant ordered catharsis.

If only life were that simple.

For the past six weeks, since her mother's funeral, lunchtimes were when she did her grieving. She would park the post van somewhere quiet and pretty on her rural round, stick in some earbuds, navigate in her music app to something choral and really loud and whack it on at top volume.

Then she'd open the doors at the back of the van and perch on the tail, unwrap a foil package of sandwiches and take a huge bite of the top one (grief never seemed to affect her appetite, more was the pity). Peanut butter and bread would stick to the roof of her mouth as tears rolled down her cheeks and she allowed herself to fall deep into the distracting embrace of Elgar or Mozart or Vaughan Williams.

Her sister, younger by two years, teased her for liking choral singing after being such a Goth in her teens. Now that Beth – aged forty-one – was the singer in a local covers band, belting out 'Play That Funky Music' and the like at sixtieth birthday parties for drunken middle-aged men in golf sweaters, she seemed to look down her nose at Kerry's love of classical music even more. Kerry found this confusing, since Beth was also always having a go at her for not being cultured enough. Just because she didn't like reading or opera! Beth often made her feel like she couldn't win.

Still. Beth wasn't there now. Kerry felt relieved that she had a job in which she could be alone, in beautiful countryside, with nobody judging or criticising. Nor was she in some grim office canteen making small talk with colleagues she didn't like. Fresh air, gorgeous views, loads of walking, peace and quiet. Plus, when she did see her colleagues for the morning sorting ritual, they were a kind bunch, on the whole. They'd given up inviting her to nights out because she hardly ever came to anything, apart from the Christmas party, but they were easy enough company.

The lunchtime weep had become a comforting daily routine. Although she would never use the words 'self-care', if she stopped to think about it, they would be appropriate. Far more wholesome than some of the other habits she was sorely tempted to edge into – drinking too much, not going out, eating crap food and staying up all night playing computer games or binge-watching TV.

It *was* getting easier though, she thought. She only cried once or twice a week now, instead of every day. Plus, out of Mum's death was going to come something so momentous and so wonderful that Kerry knew she needed to be a grown-up to rise to the challenge: she would finally be moving into the 'big house'.

Funny that at the age of forty-three she still had to remind herself that she *was* a grown-up, but the move would be equally nerve-racking and exciting.

Kerry had lived in the annexe of her childhood home since her and Beth's dad died in 1993, when she had just turned seventeen and Beth fifteen. It had been his darkroom, a converted garage, and she did still love it, even though it was tiny and cramped. Besides, it had been worth putting up with because she had always known that one day she would move back into the big house. Now that day was almost here.

Her mum had told her years ago that she would make sure 'you'll be taken care of, Kerry love,' and not left with nothing when she died; that Beth was already sorted financially, so it was only fair Kerry should be allowed to stay in the house until she chose to sell up. Especially when she became her mother's carer, to all intents and purposes. It was all agreed. Kerry would rent out the annexe and Beth could have the income from that, in lieu of splitting the proceeds of the house sale. Everybody happy.

Today Kerry couldn't stop wondering: had her mother enjoyed her life? Did she die feeling as if she had lived well; been happy; achieved good things? Kerry realised that she really didn't know and this upset her. They had literally never spoken about that kind of stuff. Everyone thought her parents had been blissfully happy, and they certainly seemed to have been – despite the evidence Kerry once found that seemed to suggest otherwise...

But her dad had been dead for over a quarter of a century. What of all those years of widowhood? Had they been blighted by her grief? Kerry had practically lived with her mother for all of them – well, across the driveway in her garage – and she genuinely had no idea.

Beth had moved out as soon as she finished her A levels and gone to uni, and Kerry always suspected that their mother wished it had been Beth who stayed and she, Kerry, who left – although that could have been her own projecting. Kerry was at least emotionally articulate enough to realise that. She should have talked to her mum more, she thought miserably. Asked her about herself, her feelings, her state of mind. She missed her mother, but it was only now she realised that she had been missing her for years *before* she died too.

Kerry just hadn't been able to confide in her. She didn't know why. But she was left with an overwhelming feeling of having failed her mother, despite having been the one who technically was 'there' for her. She'd checked in with her from the annexe every day, done her shopping, eaten meals with her most nights, organised repairs, paid the bills... all still with a nagging sense of inadequacy, that she wasn't Beth.

Kerry had also thought that her mum would be around for a lot longer. Seventy-five felt far too young to die these days.

These were the sorts of dark thoughts that scrolled through Kerry's head on a repetitive loop. Today, they were at odds with the perfect summer weather, warm and breezy, with bright fluffy clouds scudding past the sun. She wished the contents of her brain would drift past like that too, and not keep going round and round in tedious, tear-soaked circles.

Rotund sheep grazed lazily in the field around her, and a tiny baby bunny hopped across Kerry's eyeline. Rolling patchwork hills stretched to the horizon. It was proper English countryside. But she couldn't enjoy it, not properly. All she could think of was her mum, and how she would never again be able to listen to music with her. It had been their own private indulgence, a secret passion shared by no one else in the years since the death of Kerry's dad.

Kerry's forty-minute lunch break was currently being spent in the grounds of Lord Buckley's country estate, her preferred lunch venue whenever the sun was out. She always felt her shoulders slowly slide back down from where they'd been hunched around her ears. Unless it was raining, when she usually sat in the van in a lay-by. Not nearly as bucolic, and her tears felt more bitter when she couldn't shed them freely – worried as she was that some well-meaning dog walker would stumble across her crying and make unwanted enquiries into her mental state. Nobody wanted to see a weeping postwoman.

Her favourite spot was on the brow of a hill, just off the mile-long private driveway towards Dunsmore House, about halfway along, parked up where the views were at their best.

Having never seen a soul along here before, Kerry almost jumped out of her skin when, over the top of the angelic chorus in her earphones, she heard a jolly voice call out, 'Hello there! Everything all right? Have you broken down?'

She was mortified when the actual lord of the manor strode up beside her, cocked shotgun in the crook of one arm and two gun dogs at his feet. She hadn't heard him approach at all.

She managed to swallow the cloying lump of sandwich, sniff unbecomingly and wipe her eyes.

'I'm so sorry, sir, I mean, Lord Buckley, sir,' she gabbled, jumping to her feet, practically curtsying and tugging at her forelock. Well, fringe, technically. 'I was just having my lunch. I'll be off straightaway.'

He was a gimlet-eyed, white-haired old chap, a proper country gent in tweed jacket and actual plus fours. Kerry recognised him from the large portrait she passed every day when she delivered his post. She felt as if she was in the presence of a celebrity.

Every day she had to key the code into the automatic gates at the end of the long driveway, drive right up to the house and round the back, let herself in through the servants' entrance by inputting another code, walk along a couple of hundred feet of flagstone corridors, then leave the household mail on a huge, highly polished hall table. It made a change from the rest of her round. In fact, it was the highlight of her day – particularly when the housekeeper, a rotund, elderly Mrs Tiggy-Winkle-type lady called Virginia, spotted her and lured her into the kitchen for a quick coffee and a freshly baked biscuit.

'Don't be silly, stay as long as you like!' he barked, while the dogs milled around hoping for a scrap of sandwich. 'Cracking view, isn't it? Never get tired of it myself.'

'It's beautiful,' she agreed. 'I can't think of a better spot for lunch – as long as you really don't mind?'

'Of course not. I'm sure you could do with a rest after all the walking you posties do every day. May I?' He gestured to where she was sitting and before Kerry knew it, he had joined her on the tail of the van, with a great sigh as he lowered himself down. 'The old back's giving me all sorts of gyp.'

'Sorry to hear it,' she said, quashing a ridiculous urge to offer him one of her sandwiches. She knew that he was divorced, or widowed, and entertained a brief fantasy that he would fall in love with her, whisking her off her sensible-shoe-clad feet to make her the third (fourth?) Lady Buckley. I'd love to live here, she thought.

Could she overlook Lord B's inch-long eyebrows, spindly legs and plummy voice?

Sure, she decided. Then she wondered, would she *really* love to live here? The thought of having so many rooms to over-see, and acres of grass to cut... Obviously there were plenty of staff, but... she was happy in her garage. Even the prospect of moving into the big house was slightly intimidating. All those carpets to hoover!

'What's your name, Ms Postie?' asked Lord B.

Kerry was glad of the question, as answering it meant she didn't have to tell him that she'd just been daydreaming about marrying him and coming to live in his house.

'It's Kerry, sir. Nice place you've got here. This is my favourite part of my round. It's just so... different.'

'Glad you like it. And please, call me Charles.'

Gosh, she thought. First-name terms with a lord!

They grinned at each other. 'I used to come here with my family when I was a kid,' she said. 'My sister and I couldn't get enough of the adventure playground, and we loved the llamas...' She hesitated. 'You did have llamas, didn't you?'

Impulsively she did offer him a sandwich after all, holding out the three remaining quarters in their opened foil wrapping.

'No thank you, Kerry, I've recently had a large piece of cake with my coffee. We did. Two – Bertie and Bertha. Both long gone to the big llama farm in the sky now. So where else do you go on your round?'

Kerry gestured into the valley below. 'Great Dunsmore, Little Dunsmore, Chewton Magna and all that area.'

'Goodness me. That's a fair few houses.'

'Yup.'

'Do you enjoy it?'

She glanced at him, unsure if he was saying it like Beth did, as in, 'Surely you can't enjoy doing something so dull?'– but he seemed genuinely curious.

'I do, actually. I like chatting to people I wouldn't normally get to meet – like you, for example. And I enjoy routine. It's been weird during lockdown of course, though. I miss bumping into people on my round – I like feeling part of the community.'

'An important part,' he chipped in, looking serious.

Kerry felt embarrassed. 'Oh no, not really... You're very nice, for landed gentry.'

He threw back his head and brayed like a donkey, a literal 'hee-haw' of mirth. Then he stood up, still chuckling. 'Well, must crack on. It's been lovely to meet you, Kerry, and please feel free to have your lunch here whenever you wish. Stay safe!'

He strode away, with a brisk wave behind him and the spaniels trotting obediently at his ankles.

Crikey, thought Kerry, flustered. That was different. It had been such a novelty to actually chat to someone new. Since lockdown she hardly saw anyone outside of the sorting office. It was also quite refreshing that they hadn't had the inevitable tedious conversation about Covid, which seemed to have replaced the weather as the principal topic of small talk. Who was disinfecting their groceries, whose auntie was on a ventilator, whether dogs could get it, how long this lockdown would last, and so on.

Life wasn't all that bad, she thought, feeling slightly cheered. Of course she was sad about Mum; that was normal. But she'd be OK, given a bit of time, especially once she moved into the big house. All the other bad stuff was way in the past. She needed to let it go. That was what all the self-help books said, wasn't it?

Easier said than done though, she decided, glancing at her watch. Six more minutes of lunch break left, so she spent them finishing her sandwich and imagining herself in different scenarios, as she gazed out over the countryside. She could be a Lady, eating truffles and venison, like one of Charles' former wives. Or she could be like poor old Bev in a council house in Chewton Magna, unhappily married to an abusive lout, with five or six kids she couldn't afford to feed properly. Or even like Beth – she wouldn't want Beth's life either, she thought. It must be so stressful, trying to make everything so perfect all the time.

Swallowing the last mouthful, she screwed the tinfoil up into a ball, chucked it into the back of the van with the parcels and slammed the doors shut.

In spite of the fact that she wasn't a Lady, things could be a lot worse.

TWO

Delivering mail during lockdown was the weirdest experience, Kerry reflected, once she was back on the early-afternoon part of her round. Almost no cars on the roads, everybody hidden away inside their houses. The only people she occasionally passed were joggers and cyclists, who invariably ignored her, and dog walkers, who sometimes nodded before scurrying off as if scared she'd breathe on them, even though she was wearing a mask.

She missed the raft of old ladies who always used to stop to chat to her – they were all sequestered away, terrified of catching the virus. Everyone seemed suspicious and worried. And the silence! No aeroplanes in the sky. No trains rattling past, no traffic, no gaggles of little girls skipping to school, or groups of boys at the bus stop grunting at and shoving each other. It all felt a bit post-apocalyptic. Though she did very much enjoy seeing hedgehogs and hares scuttle and skitter across the empty country lanes far more frequently, even as she silently implored them not to get into the habit of assuming they were no longer about to be squashed flat, like their forefathers regularly had been...

Would she still be delivering the mail if the virus was worse than Covid and had wiped out half the population, she wondered? The roads would be overrun by wildlife; it would be like that Welsh town, where the herd of goats wandered into the marketplace, only everywhere. Britain reclaimed by the countryside. Probably not, she thought. Squirrels didn't get mail.

Some days she realised she hadn't spoken to anybody at all after she left the depot. But it was OK. She felt proud of being a key worker. Of course, delivering the post wasn't on the same scale as being a nurse or surgeon, but Kerry felt she was doing her bit to keep things going; to keep up at least a pretence of normality.

Stuffing a flimsy pizza leaflet and a frumpy underwear catalogue through the letterbox of the last thatched cottage on the road out of Great Dunsmore, she sighed heavily. Somehow it made such a difference when it was interesting-looking mail she shoved through doors, like exciting-looking packages and handwritten invitations in thick envelopes. Wondering what they were and how they'd be received always seemed to make the round pass faster, and there was no mystery whatsoever in a takeaway menu or a cheap envelope marked 'To The Homeowner'.

Kerry had hoped that lockdown would herald the comeback of the actual handwritten letter, but sadly hadn't noticed any real increase. Even eighty-year-olds just emailed these days, it seemed.

Thinking about eighty-year-olds made her recall her mum's funeral. It had been awful. Just herself, sitting alone on one side of the tiny crematorium, and Beth's family across the aisle on the other. Beth had arranged for it to be live-streamed on Zoom, but there were only seven people watching. While old people were a whizz at emailing, the new technology of Zoom had clearly been a step too far for most of them.

Kerry always imagined that when her mum finally went –

in her head this hadn't been for at least another decade –they would have a massive party in the big house with the wine flowing and lots of lovely anecdotes about Mum and Dad told through laughter and tears over the vol-au-vents. Instead, she had gone straight back to the annexe and played online Solitaire for four solid hours, getting up only to top up her glass with wine. She wasn't even able to go to Beth's, because the government had decreed you could only be in a so-called lockdown bubble with one other person, and Beth's elderly father-in-law had claimed that position.

But Kerry didn't really care about that so much. Her relationship with Beth had taken an inexplicable downturn over the last few years. She had no idea why – they used to be so close. She couldn't shake the feeling that she had somehow disappointed her younger sister.

This reminded her that she was going over there for lunch on Sunday, for the first time all year. If she was honest, she hadn't massively missed them…

Her phone rang. She wasn't supposed to take personal calls on the round, but by this time she was in the middle of nowhere, stomping along under the weight of her postbag, down a leafy single-track lane, trees forming a canopy over the top of her, heading to some farm buildings just round the corner.

'Hi, Sharon.' Kerry knew it was her even before she looked at her phone's screen – Sharon was about the only person who ever phoned her during the day. 'You OK?'

'Lockdown ends next week. We can go oooooouuuuuut!' she squawked, and Kerry held the phone away from her ear, wincing.

'Must we?'

This was her standard response to Sharon's relentless socialising, of which she, Kerry, was the focus, mainly because Sharon didn't have any other single friends.

She and Sharon had known each other since they were in

the same year at college, but they'd been mostly in different classes and their paths never really crossed until their early twenties, when Sharon joined the Post Office shortly after Kerry had. They became mates then and had been ever since, on and off.

Sharon's own career as a postwoman only lasted a couple of years, when she was fired for lying. She'd hotly denied dumping a heavy bag of free magazines she was supposed to be delivering, but the thing was, everyone knew she'd done it. She'd been spotted stuffing it into a skip, and someone complained, but to this day she still denied that it was her and said that 'someone' had nicked the bag of magazines to get her into trouble. When asked who would do that, she was unable to be any more specific than 'kids, probably'. Even though the witness's description of the offender had been a tall blonde woman in a Post Office uniform. With a name badge bearing the name Sharon Waters.

Once, about ten years ago when she was drunk, after years of outraged kvetching about unfair dismissal, she finally admitted to Kerry that it *had* been her – and then promptly forgot she'd told her and continued to insist she had been set up, years after anybody else cared.

That was the thing about Sharon. She was a dreadful fibber. Kerry spent about the first three years of their friendship saying, 'But that's so *weird*,' with furrowed brow, as Sharon told tale after fantastical tale, usually painting herself as a victim of some injustice or another, until Kerry finally twigged that it was all completely made up.

Kerry strongly suspected it was the reason that none of Sharon's relationships ever worked out. Blokes initially seemed to be taken in by her big eyes, quick wit and slim figure, but they always went off her over the next few weeks, months and, very occasionally, years. She had been ghosted more frequently than a haunted house – and it was always, *always* their fault, when she came to explain what had happened.

'He behaved appallingly.'

'Turns out he's still hung up on his ex.'

'I can't believe I fell for it – the man has no idea how to have a relationship.'

Kerry diplomatically always agreed with her that she had the worst luck, and that she would eventually find a good one, but privately she had her doubts. Nobody wanted to be shackled to a compulsive liar.

Beth was always nagging her to challenge Sharon: 'You're not doing her any favours by going along with it!'

Sharon never did it with any sense of malice, though, not like some of the horror stories you heard about lying narcissists. She *was* a liar, and a narcissist, but she was good fun, when she wasn't being a victim, and Kerry knew that if she confronted her, she'd lose her as a friend.

She didn't want to do that, since Sharon was pretty much the only friend she had.

'I know it's ending, but I'm not sure it's all going to be back to normal. If we go to a pub, we have to eat a meal. You can't move around without a mask on. Table service only. Doesn't sound like a barrel of laughs... you could just come to mine?'

Sharon groaned. 'No offence, but I've been inside my own flat for months. Now that I can finally go out, I don't want to be sitting in someone else's. I want to be in a bar! With cocktails and hot men!'

Kerry laughed. Sharon always had a massively over-optimistic vision of their nights out. Although they did sometimes feature an overpriced Day-Glo drink with an umbrella in it, they were rarely troubled by any hot men. At least not ones without equally hot girlfriends in tow.

'OK, I'll come to the pub with you. Can we make it next

Thursday? I'm staying in town that day to go shopping with my sister. She wants a dress to wear for her band's gigs.'

Sharon snorted. She didn't much care for Beth. The one time they had met, in a pub garden where they had stumbled across each other when Beth and Jitz were out for an anniversary drink, Beth had very obviously looked down her nose at Sharon, and afterwards Sharon had referred to her as 'That stuck-up cow... no offence.'

'No offence' was one of Sharon's favourite expressions, but on that occasion, none was taken.

'Next Thursday then. Six thirty. Can't wait!'

THREE

As Kerry cycled to Beth's two days later, she couldn't help wondering again if Beth had always thought of her as a failure, or if it was a more recent thing. She had forgotten how the four-mile ride to her sister's house always made her feel quite philosophical – and nervous. She couldn't shake the feeling that Beth and her family only ever invited her out of a sense of obligation, and the fact that they'd chosen to be in a bubble with someone else during lockdown only served to reinforce this notion. Jitz's dad was a very sprightly and independent seventy-year-old with lots of very close neighbours and, besides, couldn't Jitz and his dad have been in one bubble while Beth and Kerry were in another?

Imaginary conversations reverberated around Kerry's head as she pedalled through still-quiet villages, past closed-down pubs and shuttered local shops (even though lockdown was being eased, many places had not survived). She imagined her nephew Roddy groaning, 'Do we *have* to have Auntie Kerry for lunch?' Beth's reply, 'Be nice, Roddy, we haven't seen her all year and we're all she has.' 'But it's soooo boring...'

She honestly didn't understand why Beth seemed so disappointed in her, though. It must be because she, Kerry, was so resolutely single, she decided. It annoyed her – what was wrong with that? She didn't want a man! She liked her life. She had a good job, her own home, a social life, of sorts. She'd soon be moving into the big house.

Kerry chained the bicycle to the railings on the driveway, hoping that the lengthy gap since the last lunch didn't mean it was going to be even more awkward than usual. Removing her helmet and wiping the sweat off her face, she tugged at the iron bell pull – which always reminded her of flushing an old-fashioned toilet. Chimes reverberated ponderously inside their hallway.

The house was enormous, a rambling Victorian ex-rectory on the edge of town that Beth and Jitz had pooled their resources to buy when they got married four years ago. It would be fantastic once they'd done it all up, but it seemed they had got used to the tired 1960s decor and threadbare carpets, as nothing much ever appeared to get done. Despite Beth not working, Kerry thought, bitchily.

Beth opened the door and ushered her in with a more fulsome hug than she'd given her in years. To her surprise, Kerry found herself sinking gratefully into her sister's arms. The unexpected joy of physical contact with another human hit her so hard that tears welled in her eyes.

'Kerry! Long time no see.'

'It's been a while. Sorry I'm late.'

'Come in, we were about to start – it's on the table. How's work?'

That brought Kerry back down to earth. She had forgotten that Beth pretty much always asked her this as soon as she got there, with an air of polite bemusement, the tone of which managed to encompass everything from astonishment that she was not yet bored rigid delivering mail, to disappointment that she hadn't done anything better with her life. As if success in life was measured by waist size and prix fixe bottomless Prosecco lunches...

'Great!' Kerry replied, with over-compensatory enthusiasm. 'No complaints at all. So glad I've been able to keep working throughout. Weather's been fab. I met Lord Buckley last week, and he was so nice to me. I can eat my lunch on his estate whenever I want. And one of the old ladies on my round gave me a box of homemade brownies yesterday, which was lovely.'

Beth wrinkled her nose as if Kerry had said 'a box of turds' instead – anything with sugar in it had become her absolute sworn enemy, she'd mentioned on the phone recently – and ignored what Kerry had said about Lord Buckley.

'What about Nasty Nige, is he behaving himself?'

Kerry sighed. She didn't really want to have to think about her horrible line manager.

Nasty Nige had started off on the rounds, same as her, although he joined the Royal Mail a few years after she had. Via a stealthy route of intensive sycophancy to management, snitching – which he interpreted as 'keeping up standards' – and dogged persistence, he kept being promoted way above his abilities, until now Kerry had the misfortune to have him as her actual boss. He was the only real fly in the ointment of the otherwise unchallenging job, because he really didn't like her. As with Beth, Kerry had never quite figured out why.

'I don't think he knows the meaning of the words. Still a massive pain in the neck. Hi Jitz, hi kids,' Kerry said, taking the seat across from her niece and nephew.

'Hi, Auntie Kerry,' they chorused, including Jitz.

'Oh dear,' Beth said sympathetically, then nodded at the roast chicken on the table. 'Breast or leg? It's organic, of course.'

As always, they were in the formal dining room. It was a grand room with elaborate cornicing and a huge marble fireplace with a tiled insert, although gloomy; its once-white ceiling now a murky nicotine-yellow. The faded dark-red flock wallpaper didn't help, either.

Jitz was at the head of the huge, polished oak table – handmade by Beth's first husband Larry, who'd been a cabinet-maker – slicing into the chicken with one of those very retro electric carving knives, the ones with two blades that swished together very fast.

'Leg, please. The seventies called,' Kerry added. 'They want their carving knife back. Didn't Mum and Dad have one of those?'

'Oh, ha ha,' Beth retorted, grinning. 'Yes, they did – and this is it. I found it the other day. Mum gave it to me a few years back, said she didn't trust herself not to saw off one of her fingers.'

'It works a treat,' said Jitz. 'I can't imagine why they went out of style, it's like a knife through hot butter.'

'The chicken smells delicious,' Kerry said, her stomach audibly rumbling. 'And those roasties – yum.' Beth's cooking was definitely the best part of the family Sunday lunches – Kerry rarely cooked for herself.

Beth piled food onto everyone's plates, handing the kids' out first. Roddy and Opal, eight and six, tucked in immediately, unchallenged by their parents. The children both had thick mops of bright sandy-coloured hair tinged with red, and Roddy was at that unfortunate massive-toothed stage when you wondered if their new adult front teeth were ever going to stop growing. Sweet kids, but Kerry couldn't say she had a brilliant relationship with them. They were the most independent children she had ever met, recoiling if you tried to give them hugs and talking to you only if spoken to first, as if you were the local mad old lady and they'd been warned to keep away from you.

It made her pretty sad, if she was honest.

Beth handed Kerry the last full plate and she was about to

steam into it, a forkful of potato halfway to her mouth, when Beth stilled her hand.

'*Never* do that,' she said, as if Kerry had tried to eat the cat.

'What?'

'You must always start with a couple of mouthfuls of protein,' Beth said earnestly. 'It stops your insulin shooting up, which it does when you eat carbs first. We shouldn't really be having roast potatoes at all, but hey, it wouldn't be Sunday lunch without them, would it?'

'It would not,' Kerry agreed, obediently cutting herself a square of chicken instead. She didn't meet Jitz's eyes for fear of rolling her own. 'Any chance of a glass of that wine I brought?'

'Of course, sorry. I didn't pour it yet because that's the other thing I've recently learned – never, ever, drink on an empty stomach, that also sends your insulin levels haywire.'

Kerry sighed.

Beth took a delicate forkful of chicken and spent an inordinately long time chewing it, before eventually unscrewing the bottle and filling the adults' glasses. Kerry guessed what was coming next.

'How *is* the diet going, Kerry?'

Kerry had made the mistake of saying on the phone that she was going to try and cut back a bit, after the lockdown junk-food bingeing she'd been doing. 'OK, thanks,' she said, 'although I'm having a day off.' She changed the subject. 'So, Jitz, what's it been like, working from home?'

Jitz had recently given up the lease on the serviced office in town from where he'd been running his accountancy business for the last ten years and had set up shop in the attic at home instead.

'It's fab,' he said, although without much enthusiasm. 'No more commuting. No more sharing a kitchen and loo with the guy with BO from the office down the hall. And I wasn't sorry to say goodbye to his PA, either. She always nicked my biscuits, even when I put my name on the tin.'

Kerry grinned. She really liked Jitz. Although she'd really liked Larry, the kids' dad, too. When Beth had kicked Larry into touch five years ago, Kerry had not been able to get her head around why her sister would dump a perfectly nice, funny, normal, kind guy.

'It's about chemistry. Larry's a sweetheart but there was just no chemistry,' Beth had explained, as if Kerry was a backward seven-year-old. Kerry hated it when she talked to her in that patronising way. She may even have added, 'you wouldn't understand'.

Beth would have been right about that, though. Kerry had tried to be sympathetic five years ago when Beth sobbed and sobbed about the pain she was causing Larry and the kids by breaking up the family, but she had already admitted that she was 'sort of' seeing someone else and then, with bewildering speed – or so it seemed – they had sold the family home and she and Jitz had bought this huge new place together.

Kerry *thought* she understood the importance of chemistry but, having never clicked with anyone the way Jitz and Beth did with each other, she did find it hard to understand how someone could blow their family apart for it, or if that could ever be the right thing to do. She just couldn't get it out of her head that their own parents had been the poster children for chemistry, mutual adoration and fidelity – and yet Dad had apparently been sleeping with someone else...

In all these years, though, she hadn't once told Beth her suspicions about their father's fidelity. Beth would have gone ballistic, for one thing, and Kerry knew that underneath any anger, it would really upset her too. Beth had adored their dad as much, if not more, than Kerry had. He died when she was just fifteen – Kerry seventeen – tough ages to lose your father. Kerry didn't want to sully Beth's memory of him the way it had done hers, leaving her feeling marriage probably really couldn't be trusted.

Beth had thought Larry was the One when they first got hitched, which further proved Kerry's thesis. Roddy and Opal had been too little to really understand about their mummy and daddy's divorce, and Jitz had bent over backwards to be accommodating to his new family, but even so it all felt a bit... off. But, as with everything in Beth's life, it all turned out fine in the end. The kids were unscathed and had a great relationship with Larry, who they saw regularly, in the house he'd built for himself and his new wife. Beth and Jitz were like soppy teenagers together. Everyone happy.

Kerry knew Beth just thought she was jealous. And she had to admit, she was, a bit. How did Beth get to marry *two* lovely guys, when she herself had never been able to find anyone to bond with? It was a good thing she loved Beth as much as she did. They drove each other mad, but when they clicked, they really clicked – despite the downward trajectory of their relationship since Beth went away to university. Kerry felt sad that they didn't seem able to recapture the friendship they'd had as little girls. But then she, Kerry, had changed so much.

The table fell silent as everyone tucked in. It felt awkward, but for a while Kerry couldn't think of anything to say. Eventually she tried, 'So, what have you guys been up to?'

Jitz looked up at her in the quirky convoluted way he had of rolling his head round in a circle starting the opposite direction to where you were sitting until his gaze alighted on you. It reminded Kerry of a train engine on a turning circle, or a clock with spinning hands, and always made her grin.

'Not much,' he said mildly. 'Hoping to start the renovations as soon as we can.'

Kerry laughed. 'You've lived here for years! I'd have thought lockdown would be an ideal time for you to get stuck into all that. What are you waiting for?'

She had been trying to project a tone of levity but could see Beth bristling with outrage.

'I didn't mean it as a criticism!' she protested. The kids sat very still, sensing the tension. Crikey, Kerry thought, I've only been here two minutes and I've already pissed her off. That had to be a record, even by her standards.

Beth's fingers tightened around the stem of her wineglass. 'We're waiting to be able to afford it. Mum's will should be through soon, and that'll mean we can start.'

Kerry was surprised, on several levels. Beth was always decked out in what looked like brand-new and expensive leisurewear, the kids went to private school, and Jitz drove a top-of-the-range Lexus, so it had never occurred to her that money was an issue, even though she had wondered why they didn't just get decorators in. She was also surprised that Beth thought she was getting any money from the will. As far as Kerry knew, Mum hadn't had a lot of savings. She opened her mouth to query this but Jitz, ever the diplomat, jumped in and changed the subject:

'Opal, didn't you want to ask Auntie Kerry some questions about working for the Post Office?' Jitz prompted.

Opal laid down her fork in such a long-suffering way anyone would think she'd been told she had to go on a two-week fast starting right that moment.

'We-ell, we have to do a project on careers for home school,' she began, managing to sound both reluctant and dramatic, her dimples deepening as she stretched out the word 'well' as if someone was pushing sharp pencils into her cheeks.

'Being a postwoman isn't a *career*,' Roddy chimed in, incredulously. 'It's only a rubbish sort of job.'

'Roddy, it's not,' Kerry said, in a more heated way than she'd intended, even though he did have a point. Career progression was often limited unless you were so useless on your rounds that management wanted you promoted out of the way, like Nigel had been.

Was she having to defend herself to Beth *and* her kids now? 'It's actually a great career, if you like the outdoors, and meeting people, and a routine, which I do. And I'm a key worker. I think that's pretty cool. It's called the Royal Mail these days, it changed its name from the Post Office a few years ago.'

'Mummy says it's a rubbish job,' Roddy maintained stoutly, and Kerry glared at Beth, resisting a sudden urge to give her nephew a clip round the ear.

'Cheers, sis.'

'Oh Kerry, I didn't say that! Not like that, anyway. Roddy, a career is when you can get promoted and move up in the company, earn more money, so Auntie Kerry's job definitely counts as a career. She just doesn't want to move up. You don't have to if you don't want to.'

'Why not?' Opal asked, swinging her legs and looking bored before she even heard the answer. 'I'd want more money if I had a job.'

Kerry shrugged. 'More money would certainly be nice, but in the Royal Mail, if you get promoted you end up staying in the office all day instead of going out on rounds, and I wouldn't want that. I like being outdoors and seeing people.'

'Even if it's raining and dogs bite you?' Roddy wanted to know.

'I've only been bitten once, about five years ago.' She showed the kids the small scar on the top of her forefinger. 'My finger got stuck in a letterbox and I couldn't yank it out in time before this yappy little terrier jumped up. It wasn't his fault, he was only trying to pull the letter through. I make sure my hands never go inside the letterbox these days. And I don't mind the rain if I have waterproofs on, or shorts. It's only grim when you're not expecting it and you get soaked and have to walk around with wet trousers for hours.'

'I wouldn't like it *at all*,' said Roddy, shuddering.

'Well, I love it. What else did you want to ask, Opal?'

She pondered, chewing. 'How many houses do you go to every day?'

'That's a very good question.' Kerry realised she was enjoying having an actual conversation with her niece and nephew. This almost never happened. 'Have a guess.'

'Thirty-seven.'

'Way more.'

'A hundred and... ten?'

'Nope. Still way out. It's four hundred and fifty-four addresses.'

The kids' eyes were like saucers.

'That's *loads*,' Opal breathed. 'Every day?'

'Yup. Every day that I'm at work. I walk about seven miles a day.'

'That's like walking from Great Dunsmore, where Auntie Kerry lives, to Salisbury *and* back again,' Jitz said.

'Wow! You must be really tired when you get home.' Roddy looked impressed, for once.

Kerry was so used to the routine now that she rarely thought about the physical fatigue. Yes, the tops of her thighs and her feet usually ached when she got in, but she'd have a cup of strong tea – or, more often these days, a glass of wine – a slice of cake and put her legs up on Mum and Dad's old pouffe for an hour or so, watching some crap telly or a Netflix box set. By the time she had done that, she was ready to get on with the rest of her day. Or – as often as not – go to bed.

She saw herself then, at home after work, as if looking down from a great height. The tea's exact shade of brown. The raisins in the store-bought cake. Comfort in talking to herself, because there was never anybody else to talk to in the tiny converted garage she called home.

One way to look at it was that it was just her cosy habit of unwinding after work. But another way, when she considered how frequently that post-work hour stretched itself out till bedtime, hours and hours swallowed up like Pac-Man – well, that was more a picture of a lonely middle-aged woman who had little in her life outside of work. And wine.

She dismissed the vision. She wouldn't be in the garage for much longer. Now Mum had died, she could move into the big house any time. Could've done already but hadn't quite been able to face the place without her in it, and it had felt a bit ghoulish to start relocating while her mother's body was practically still warm. She would soon, though.

It was to be her new start and she couldn't wait. She would have the space to have friends over for dinner. Drinks in the garden! Enough room to put a yoga mat in front of the TV so that she could start Pilates. She had surreptitiously been planning for years what colour to paint the walls and which bits of furniture she wanted to keep. Maybe her niece and nephew could come for sleepovers.

'I am usually a bit tired,' she said. Suddenly the chicken tasted like sawdust in her mouth. 'But it keeps me fit; that, and cycling over here once a month, now we're all allowed to meet up again. I don't need to go to the gym or go running or anything.'

'Lucky you,' Beth chimed. 'That's definitely one of the perks. You'll never get me out of my gym when it reopens next week. It's been awful since it's been closed, I've had withdrawal symptoms. You should've seen how much weight I piled on!'

She patted her flat belly and Kerry had to resist a second temptation to roll her eyes. Beth had never had to worry about her weight, not even after she'd had two kids. Kerry had reluctantly agreed to go shopping with her because, Beth said, she needed a wing woman to help her choose a smart dress for a few wedding gigs her band had coming up. Kerry was dreading it, because Beth was bound to try and force her to try stuff on too.

One of her constant nags was regarding her sister's generally scruffy appearance.

Kerry genuinely couldn't understand it. If she was more comfortable in old jeans and sweatshirts, instead of choosing to teeter round in pencil skirts and heels in her spare time, what did it matter to anyone else? And why? Not to mention the utter torture of being forced into dresses that made her look like a bag of sprouts, while Beth – inevitably – preened and pouted in front of the same mirror, looking like a supermodel.

'Still OK for our dress-shopping trip on Thursday? Those poor retailers need all the help they can get. I'm so excited. It's been years since we went shopping together!'

Nodding glumly and pouring more gravy onto her plate, Kerry wondered if she could claim mild food poisoning on the day. She would swear Beth could read her mind.

The gravy was delicious, made in the old-fashioned way passed on by their mother, in the same tin the chicken had been roasted in, with fat and stock and Bovril.

Kerry had never made gravy in her life. 'Will you show me how you make this one day? It's lovely. Just like how Mum used to do it.' She was going to add, *I'll need to know, now I'm soon going to have a kitchen big enough to cook Sunday lunch in,* but something stopped her. Fear of ridicule, or of tempting fate? Or – with hindsight – a premonition?

FOUR

Kerry still felt a bit fuzzy-headed the next morning when she left home at quarter past five – five minutes later than usual, but she'd hit the snooze button twice. Surely she wouldn't still be over the limit? She had downed a whole bottle of rosé when she got home after Sunday lunch.

She backed her elderly Nissan Micra carefully out of the driveway. The house was on a bend, on a narrow road into the village, and she always held her breath in case something came whizzing round the corner and crashed into her. It was a miracle it hadn't happened before. But she reversed unscathed and set off, twenty miles an hour over the speed limit in order to try and make it on time. She'd been late a couple of times recently so it would be a bit of a disaster if it happened again. Nasty Nige would have a right go at her.

Kerry felt safe in her garage annexe. She loved the village and everybody knew her there. It was full of Mum and Dad's friends, all elderly now, but she was part of a community, even though she didn't often actively participate in it. However, it would undoubtedly be easier to move into Salisbury, where Beth lived. At the moment, Kerry drove from her home to the sorting office, sorted out her mail, got into the van and drove back past her house to the edge of the village. From there, her Point One, she would set off in a loop through Great Dunsmore and back to the van, drive on to Point Two, and deliver through Points Three and Four, the neighbouring hamlets of Little Dunsmore and Crookhampton before ending up back at the van a few hours later. Back to the depot then, and eventually, home again. So it did sort of feel like she spent her entire life on the road between the two places. But she wouldn't be *moving*, exactly, only across the driveway into the big house, so she didn't really give it much thought.

This had always been Kerry's route, and she knew she was really fortunate not to have had it changed over the years, as many of her colleagues had. She'd be absolutely gutted if they did ever change it – not least because being the local postwoman meant that she was able to pop home as she passed her place to use the loo and grab a quick snack.

Her head was pounding by the time she parked in the depot yard and dragged herself into her booth. The empty slots of her sorting frame loomed down at her like the walls of a prison cell and she wanted to go home and lie down again, rather than have to start filling the slots with approximately fourteen hundred pieces of post – tedious for sure, but a task she usually quite enjoyed nonetheless.

'Morning, Kerry lovely, how did your shopping trip go?' called Clarissa from across the office, which cheered her up a little. She adored Clarissa. In her late fifties and with resolutely long pink hair, Clarissa was the longest-standing Post Office worker and would do anything for anyone. Before management put in these towering enclosed booths some years ago, the sorting layout was much more open-plan, and Clarissa and Kerry used to sit next to each other to sort their mail. She missed their daily banter sessions. They had made the time pass so much quicker. These days they were forced to listen to Kiss FM because Nasty Nige liked it, even though the rest of them would far rather have had Radio Four or Classic FM.

'Morning, Clarissa. It's not till Thursday. Plenty of time for me to dwell on the fact that I hate shopping.'

'Are you looking for anything special?'

'No – definitely not. It's for Beth. She's after a party dress so I'm just going along to advise her. Can't remember the last time we went shopping together! Have you got any paracetamol? I've got a bit of a hangover.'

Nasty Nige loomed up behind her from seemingly nowhere and Kerry swore under her breath that she'd admitted to being hungover. She knew he'd be all over it.

'So that's why you're late again, is it?'

She sighed. 'Morning, Nigel. I'm only four minutes late. Sorry. There were some lights stuck on red on Wilton Road.'

Nige frowned and crossed his arms over his seven-month-pregnant beer belly.

'They all add up. That's the third time in two weeks. I've made a note of it, and on top of the tracked stops on your PDA last week, it's not looking good.'

'Wait – what tracked stops? When?'

Clarissa passed her across a sheet of pills, so she popped two out and swallowed them dry.

'There were two ten-minute stops. I left you that Post-it to ask you to come and talk to me on Friday before you left, but you didn't.'

He gestured towards the pink Post-it note on her desk. It said: *Kerry pls pop in to my ofice b4 u go.* Nigel had the worst spelling and grammar of anyone Kerry had ever met; he was unable to write a single correct sentence. She had felt sorry for him for years, assuming that he was dyslexic, until the time his girlfriend Jaye had been laughing about it at a Christmas party. Kerry had been shocked and said, 'but it must be really difficult if you're dyslexic,' to which Jaye replied, 'Ah, no, he's not *dyslexic*! He just can't be arsed.'

The truth was she *had* seen the Post-it before she went home on Friday. She just pretended she hadn't.

'So?' Nigel waited. Kerry noticed he had chocolate crumbs in the corners of his mouth.

'I don't remember any unauthorised stops,' she said innocently. 'Which days?'

He pretended to consult his PDA – Personal Digital Assistant, a.k.a. Big Brother – but Kerry knew he already knew. 'One on Monday and one on Wednesday.'

'Ri-iight.'

She did remember having a long chat with Mrs Polkinghorne in the tiny cottage on the bend, because Mrs P's brother, her only remaining living relative, had just died. Mrs P had been coming out of the house to take her elderly Scottie for his morning walk and Kerry had handed her the three greeting-card envelopes and pizza leaflet comprising her mail. 'How lovely!' Kerry had said. 'It must be your birthday?'

Mrs P's wizened, grey face had collapsed and she'd started to cry.

'My brother passed away from Covid two days ago,' she sobbed. 'They must be condolence cards from people at his care home.'

Kerry had felt so terrible that she'd stopped for far longer than she should, listening to the old lady unload about how she hadn't been able to see him before he died, and how expensive funerals were. She could have kicked herself for not remembering that Mrs P's birthday was in November.

The second transgression, however, was eluding her.

'What time on Wednesday?'

'Eight minutes past twelve,' Nigel said immediately, without needing to consult his electronic private detective. 'And the stop details show your own address.'

She did remember then. She'd had a bit of a dodgy tummy after a takeaway curry the night before and had gone back to the garage to relieve herself. As she sat on the loo, she'd passed the time by playing a new game she found on her phone and *just one go* had turned into a much longer comfort break than she'd planned.

Oops. She'd hoped he wouldn't notice but no transgression, however minor, seemed to escape Nasty Nige's eagle eye at the moment, at least where she was concerned.

'I had a stomach upset, it was an emergency! And I still finished the loop on time!' Kerry protested, which was true. She had absolutely powered through the rest of her round. That was why she'd been so tired when she got home.

'That's as maybe,' he said pompously. 'We'll keep this as an informal warning for now but if it happens again, I'm afraid I'm going to have to follow formal procedure.'

'Ah come on, Nige,' called Clarissa, who'd been shamelessly eavesdropping from her booth. 'Kerry told me about this. One of the old dears on her route was crying on her shoulder and that's how she got held up.'

'Clarissa, I'd advise you to mind your own beeswax,' Nige said, moving back towards his cubbyhole of an office, already removing another chocolate bar from somewhere about his person and unwrapping it. Nigel was ruled by his addiction to sugar – Beth would have a fit if she saw how much he stuffed into his mouth over a typical working day, Kerry thought. But it looked like the lure of a Galaxy bar had got her off the hook, at least temporarily.

She felt herself relax a bit as she got settled into her routine, sorting the bags of already postcode-sorted mail into their slots for individual streets and reflecting again that it was a source of mild distress how rarely she saw a real letter these days. If she did, it was usually in the spidery, shaky hand of an elderly person. Greeting cards, yes; but the long oblong of good quality envelopes stuffed with several folded sheets of lined writing paper were few and far between. She was so sick of franked, logo-ed envelopes with people's phone bills and what-have-you. Even postcards were a rarity, nowadays. She used to deliver tons of those, especially in summer, and always enjoyed reading the messages in case there was something out of the ordinary, perhaps a revelation of undying love, or a smutty joke.

Mostly, I love my job, she thought, as she loaded up a trolley and wheeled it out to the van. It was a beautiful sunny day, she was escaping Nige's malevolent clutches – every job had its downsides – and she was looking forward to walking round the villages and seeing people out and about again, now that lock-down was over.

See the positives, Kerry. She just needed to remind herself that life was OK. And it would only get better, once she moved into the big house.

FIVE

1992

Despite what she'd said to Clarissa, Kerry did remember the last time she and Beth had gone clothes shopping together. It had indeed been years ago – twenty-eight, to be precise. She remembered it because it was one of the last times they ever went out together as a family, before their dad got ill. Beth was about thirteen and Kerry fifteen, so it had been unbelievably thrilling that their parents allowed them to go to Oxford Street Topshop – on their own! Entirely unaccompanied! Let loose in London for the first time, as a summer holiday family treat.

London was a place of myth and mystery to Kerry, home of shops the size of football pitches, and red buses that came once every two minutes instead of twice a day as the village one did. Foul-mouthed tramps living in tents, punks in the King's Road (she wondered at the time why she didn't see any, not realising till later that they'd all died out – or worse, become respectable – a good ten years before that), implacable policemen on skittish horses, pop stars and supermodels diving in and out of members' clubs. She couldn't wait for her senses to be assailed. Being a bit of a wannabe Goth – albeit years after they were

popular – she had her sights set on Camden Market, not realising that it wasn't walking distance from Oxford Street.

It was a day trip organised by the camera club. Families
were allowed to come too, but apart from a few wives and girlfriends, none did, apart from the Tuckers. They had got up
early and Dad had driven them into town, where they all
climbed onto a coach that had definitely seen better days,
with uncomfortable faded tartan seats and rattly windows,
along with lots of middle-aged men sporting cameras round
their necks and hair sprouting out of random places like
nostrils and ears and crawling out of shirt necks. There was
only one really gorgeous guy, in a leather bomber jacket, with
long glossy hair touching his shoulders, and the tightest of
tight jeans.

Kerry nudged Beth, even though she was too young to be
impressed. She liked fashion, but she was still mostly into
ponies. 'He's gorgeous!'

Then she gasped. 'Oh my goodness, look, he's with *Miss
Smith*!'

That got Beth's attention. Their history teacher had a
boyfriend? That seemed all sorts of wrong, and scandalous. She
looked up from her copy of *Are You There, God? It's Me,
Margaret* and gawped shamelessly as they came up the aisle and
slid into seats a few rows in front. Miss Smith clearly hadn't
spotted them, because they could hear her giggling hysterically
as her dishy boyfriend seemed to be teasing her. Beth twisted
round and stuck her head between the seats to talk to Mum and
Dad behind.

'*Miss Smith is up there, with a man!*' she hissed.

Kerry heard their mother laugh. 'Beth, teachers are allowed
to have boyfriends! He's called Jeff. Actually, it was Daddy who
introduced them. They met at a dinner party at our house a
couple of months ago.'

This was news to Kerry, so she turned around too, kneeling

up on the seat to look over the top. 'Miss Smith was in our house?'

Mum nodded. 'We know her from choir. Dad knows Jeff from camera club, and he thought they'd get on. They certainly do!'

'I don't remember Miss Smith coming to our house,' Kerry insisted, as if it couldn't really have happened.

'It was when you two were having that sleepover party at Corinne's.'

'Oh. Weird.' Kerry had wondered why they'd been so keen on her going to Corinne's as well, when Corinne was more of a friend of Beth's. She had felt like a right spare part all evening, listening to them shrieking and giving each other makeovers while she sat in the corner listening to The Cure on her Walkman and refusing to let them come anywhere near her with the lipsticks. Now it made more sense.

'You told me you were having a date night,' she added sulkily.

'We were. It was just with two other people as well,' Dad said.

'Every day is date night for us,' Mum contributed, smacking a big kiss on Dad's cheek. She looked sad, though, and unless Kerry was imagining it, tears sprang to her eyes.

Kerry tutted and turned back to stare out of the window, as the coach throbbed into life and inched out of the coach park with a laborious grinding of gears.

It was a fantastic day. Mum and Dad wanted to go to some boring exhibition at the Royal Academy so they pointed Kerry and Beth in the direction of Oxford Street and told them they'd all meet back at Pizza Express for a late lunch, having first got promises from each of them that they would stick together like glue, ensuring that they had lots of fifty-pence pieces for phone boxes in case of emergency or unforeseen events preventing them making the rendezvous on time – the contingency plan was that they would ring their Uncle Harry and leave a message, then Mum would do the same, if they were more than half an hour late. Kerry and Beth spent the money on Cokes.

As they set off down Regent Street, Beth was subdued into uncharacteristic silence by the sheer cacophony of traffic and the crush of people around her. They had to shout to be heard above the blare of horns and diesel chug of black cabs and buses, and dodge around numerous Japanese and American tourists stopping to take photographs and point at window displays. Kerry felt pretty overwhelmed too, but adrenaline was pumping through her and it felt like being on a completely different planet to their normal rural Great Dunsmore life.

Plus, Kerry reflected, it was also really nice to know that Beth was, for once, deferring to her. Her little sister was no longer the tiny queen of her horsey village domain and Kerry could tell she felt cowed by it. Kerry played up to it a bit by consulting her *A–Z* and giving very firm directions in a tourist-guide voice with more confidence than she actually felt – 'We're just coming up to Great Marlborough Street; if you look to your right, you'll see Liberty's, a very famous old department store...' but inside, her head was whirling a mantra of *ohmigodwe'rein-Londononourownthisissoexciting...!*

'I'm going to move to London when I graduate,' she declared, as they descended the escalators into the bowels of Topshop, the most enormous clothes shop she had ever seen. She felt faint with excitement, even though she'd never enjoyed clothes shopping all that much. Her boobs were too big and her tummy not concave. 'You can come and stay in my flat. It'll be so much fun!'

Beth looked up at her then, her trusting face so full of admiration that Kerry felt overcome with sisterly love. 'Brilliant,' she said. 'I can't wait!'

After about two hours in Topshop they successfully reunited with their parents, had pizzas the size of dustbin lids, and showed off their purchases. Beth had bought a Salt-N-Pepa crop top and some tinsel star deely-boppers that were only seventy-five pence, and Kerry had succumbed to a (in retro-spect) downright strange banana-coloured sleeveless jacket thing with lots of pockets that she literally never wore later, not even once. She'd kidded herself that her Goth phase was over and she should wear more grown-up clothes if she ever wanted to get a boyfriend... but somehow nothing changed. She still wore mostly black – and she never did go and live in London.

Still, it was an excellent day; a stand-out day. Kerry had often wished things could have stayed like that – but they didn't. Couldn't, she supposed.

SIX

2020

'I'll meet you at the sorting office at four! Can't waaaaait!' Beth trilled.

Kerry had to hold the phone away from her ear. Bats recoiled in nearby rafters. Why was Beth's voice so loud? She could have just texted, but Kerry knew that her sister knew it would be easier for her to come up with an excuse via pixels on a screen.

'OK,' she said reluctantly. Now Beth knew she was at work, she couldn't feign illness. 'I've got to go, Beth, my break's over. See you in a bit.' She started to add, 'But don't expect me to try on any clo—' but before she could finish, Beth had hung up.

Punctual as ever, Beth was waiting for her on the pavement by the depot gates at exactly four o'clock that afternoon, wearing a floaty, rose-patterned summer dress with matching lipstick and cork-wedge sandals.

'Hi, sis, you look nice,' Kerry said, kissing Beth's cheek and feeling annoyed that Beth had dressed up when she knew Kerry was coming straight from work.

Predictably, Beth looked her up and down. Kerry had

changed out of her Royal Mail polo shirt but still had her khaki shorts and trainers on.

'Can't you just wear that for the wedding gigs?' Kerry said, trying to pre-empt a comment about her own attire.

'Of course not! Who would wear a tea dress to sing in a band? We don't do Vera Lynn covers.'

They set off on foot towards the city centre, under the bird-shit-splattered railway bridge. It was when Kerry found herself wishing that a pigeon would poo on Beth's 'tea dress' that she thought perhaps she needed to try and adjust her attitude towards her sister. They were in danger of becoming stuck in a grim vortex of mutual disapproval.

'What is a tea dress, anyway?' she asked, injecting a note of cheeriness into her voice.

'Nineteenth-century ladies would wear them to take tea with other ladies, and the name just stuck,' Beth said, although she didn't sound too sure either. 'Let's go to Charline's Closet first, shall we?'

Charline's Closet was Salisbury's most upmarket designer boutique. The name alone had always put Kerry off even setting foot inside it, and from what she saw of the prices of the items in the window, there would have been no point in it anyway.

'OK,' she agreed meekly.

She followed Beth into the shop, which was terrifyingly minimalist. The racks of tops and dresses were spaced out with what looked like an exact number of millimetres between each padded clothes hanger, mostly muted tones of colours that Kerry would never be able to exactly identify – taupe, or ecru or stardust. She had no real idea what any of them were. Much of it just seemed beige to her.

'I don't see many party dresses,' she said, but Beth had already homed in on a more colourful rack right at the back of the shop. A skeletal assistant tottered across with a determined smile on her face.

'Hello, ladies!' she said, very definitely only addressing Beth. 'Can I help you with anything today?'

If she was ever asked this, Kerry always replied, 'No, I'm just looking, thanks,' even if she had come in for something specific, but Beth beamed and engaged the salesgirl in such a detailed explanation of her requirements – right down to most of the set list that her band would be playing at the wedding – that even the assistant blinked and looked slightly nervous.

Beth pulled out a short, backless dress covered in gold sequins before the salesgirl had time to move. She'd obviously had her eye on it since they walked in, so Kerry wondered why she had even bothered with the lengthy explanation.

'Now, this looks perfect!'

'Try it on,' Kerry suggested, more to shut her up than anything else.

The assistant ushered Beth into a changing room and swished the heavy velvet curtain across, then she and Kerry engaged in a sort of reverse mating-ritual dance on the shop floor, studiously avoiding each other's eyes as Kerry browsed through the shelves and racks in a perfunctory way. Some ambient, squiggly sort of music drifted through the store from invisible speakers somewhere. *Wanky music*, Kerry thought. She hated it in here. At least in New Look or one of the high street chain stores, there were other shoppers browsing too, and the assistants didn't give a rat's arse what their customers' appearance or dress size was.

The good news was that there was absolutely nothing in the shop that would have suited her, even if she could have afforded it, fitted into it or liked it, so she felt fairly safe.

She hoped Beth didn't know it, but she was actually borderline phobic about trying clothes on in shops. She never did it when she was on her own – she had a funny feeling the last time might even have been that lovely day trip to London all those years ago – and it would be even worse to be forced to offer her body up for the scrutiny of Beth and a random snooty shop assistant. *She* couldn't look at it herself, so she definitely didn't want anybody else to. The assistant was already regarding her like something horrible she'd stepped in, and that was with her clothes *on*.

When she had a flu jab a few months ago, even removing one arm from her shirt and baring it in front of the nurse had made Kerry shudder with dread. The thought of anyone looking at her bare flesh literally made her want to vomit. She'd had to close her eyes – not to avoid catching sight of the needle, but so that she couldn't see if the woman was looking at her and her terrible arms. She knew it was irrational. There was nothing much wrong with her arms; they were fairly typical forty-some-thing arms, a bit of a bingo wing, but nothing that regular work with hand weights wouldn't sort out if she put her mind to it. But she hated them, and her belly, and back, thighs and bum.

Everything, really, apart from her legs. She didn't actually mind her legs, from the knees down. The baggy Royal Mail cargo shorts were pretty all-encompassing.

She missed swimming, she thought, suddenly feeling sad. She used to love swimming, before...

'Kerry, what do you think?' Beth called from behind the curtain.

Kerry could already hear in her voice that she thought it looked great. Beth emerged into the shop, smoothing the very tight skirt down over her toned thighs. Spotlights caught the sequins in their gaze and her sister shimmered.

'Wow! The search is over,' Kerry said, in genuine awe. 'You look amazing.'

Beth kissed her cheek. The dress had a strong chemical smell to it that hit Kerry's nostrils even through her mask when she got near her sister, and she wondered if it was the metallic sequins or some sort of dry-cleaning fluid.

'I'm not sure, though,' Beth pouted, tipping her head to one side and regarding herself in the vast, gilt-framed, free-standing mirror.

Kerry caught a glimpse of herself standing behind her like Giant Haystacks, and hastily moved aside.

'Why not?' She resisted the urge to roll her eyes as she tried to imagine what she'd look like in that same dress. It didn't bear thinking about.

'I've got to make sure it doesn't ride up when I'm singing. I do dance around a fair bit too.'

Beth gave a totally unselfconscious demonstration, holding an imaginary microphone and having a little boogie on the spot, staring at her thighs in the mirror. The dress was so short already there wasn't really anywhere for it to go.

'No, it's fine,' Kerry said. 'I think you should get it.'

Then she'd have time to go home before coming back in to meet Sharon, without having to traipse round any more shops and with any luck, Sharon might have cancelled by then.

'Let's keep looking for a bit. This is the first one we've tried,' Beth explained to the shop assistant, who wasn't doing a very good job of hiding her disappointment at the prospect of losing such an easy sale. 'We'll probably come back for it.'

The salesgirl forced a smile and nodded. Beth went back into the fitting room, handing Kerry the dress through the gap in the curtains as soon as she'd peeled it off. As Kerry turned it back the right way round to put it on the hanger, she caught sight of the cardboard price tag swinging from the sleeve. '*How* much?' she muttered, aghast.

The dress was £275. Two hundred and seventy-five pounds! That was about the total value of her entire wardrobe. She had never spent more than fifty quid on an item of clothing, and even then, only for a very special occasion.

When they left the shop, Beth graciously thanking the assistant, Kerry said, 'Did you see how much it was?'

Beth nodded blithely. 'Yeah, not the cheapest, but you know, I need nice stage clothes.'

Kerry felt like saying, *You're in a local covers band, Beth, not embarking on a residency at Caesar's Palace in Vegas!*

How could she claim she was hard up and yet be willing to drop that much cash on a single dress?

Over the next couple of hours, Beth dragged Kerry in and out of numerous shops. Shops that she'd never noticed before, down alleys and in courtyards she didn't even know existed. Her feet started to hurt – after all, she'd already walked seven miles that day – and she was getting a headache.

'Isn't this nice?' Beth said at one point, giving her arm a squeeze. 'Sisters, shopping together. We should do it more often! And you must come and see me in action.'

Kerry must have looked either blank or horrified, until Beth clarified, 'With the band! We've got quite a few gigs coming up this summer, if we're not in lockdown.'

'Oh yes, could do. I suppose I could see if Sharon would come with me. She will if I tell her there'll be lots of hot guys in the band... Are there?'

Beth frowned. 'Well, "hot" might be a bit of a stretch.'

Kerry realised she'd never seen any photos of her sister's band. 'Do you have a Facebook page?'

'There is one,' Beth said, 'but the group picture was taken before I joined, so it's just the guys.'

'That's OK. Sharon isn't interested in you.'

'Rude,' retorted Beth, laughing. 'Oh, this is such fun.'

'Such fun,' Kerry echoed, forcing a smile.

SEVEN

In the end, Beth frogmarched Kerry around every upmarket clothing outlet the town possessed. So many, in fact, that Kerry did not have quite enough time to go home and get changed before meeting Sharon at six thirty. Even though she'd specifically arranged the rendezvous early so that she could go straight there, she had belatedly realised that her work clothes probably wouldn't pass muster with the fashion-conscious Sharon any more than they had with Beth.

'I've got half an hour to kill,' Kerry said, looking at her watch, the sound of door chimes of expensive boutiques still ringing in her ears. 'Will you come for a coffee with me?'

Beth narrowed her eyes. She was obviously trying to think of some reason not to but, since Kerry had given up two hours to come shopping with her, there wasn't really anything she could come up with.

'Oh, come on, Beth. We hardly spend any time together just talking.'

'I didn't say I wouldn't!' Beth protested, laden down with so many ribbon- and rope-handled carrier bags that she was practically a trip hazard. She had bought at least one garment or accessory in each shop they'd gone into, including that first gold dress, which again seemed to Kerry to contradict her sister's assertion that money was tight. 'I was just trying to think when my parking runs out.'

They settled themselves at a table outside one of the cafes in the Market Square, catching the last shaft of afternoon sunshine before it slid behind rooftops. There was a chilled, Mediterranean feel to the square, toddlers running around squawking, two guys playing Irish music on a fiddle and a guitar, lovers strolling hand-in-hand or gazing into each other's eyes at nearby tables. Two large iced lattes in glasses stood in front of them, but only Kerry's had whipped cream on top.

'It's like being in Italy,' Beth exclaimed, taking a delicate sip through her paper straw.

'I wouldn't know. I've never been.'

'Oh you must! It's so wonderful.'

Beth and Jitz took the kids to a villa in Tuscany every year and had never invited Kerry to go with them.

'I'd love to, if I ever get the chance,' Kerry said, trying not to sound too pointed. She decided to change the subject lest Beth took this as a criticism. 'Are you pleased with your dresses? I must come and see your band some time. You'll look fab on stage in that gold sequinned one.'

Beth smiled graciously. 'Yes, you must! I'll let you know as soon as we're playing anywhere local. It's funny,' she continued contemplatively.

'What is?'

'That it's me who ended up in a band, not you. When we were kids, you were always the one who'd get up and sing when we used to go to that hotel in Lymington, remember? What was it called?'

'Hilltop Lodge.' Kerry smiled at the memory. 'I only did it once, though, didn't I?'

'No, you were first in line every year, you were mad for it! I remember you blasting out a Jackson 5 song one year when you were about thirteen, and didn't you sing an Abba thing one time? I'm sure you won the kids' talent contest with that. "Waterloo?" I was so jealous.'

'Oh yes! And the Jackson 5 one was "Rockin' Robin". How could I have forgotten that?'

'Mum and Dad definitely thought you'd end up on stage. I was the shy one, back then.'

'Wow.'

It *was* hard to imagine. Kerry really had forgotten – or maybe it was too painful to remember so she'd blocked it out – that she used to be different, that the unfettered child in her had once taken confidence for granted. Until the night it had been snatched away from her, never to return.

She looked across the square at two little girls on roller skates, taking advantage of the empty paved expanse to twirl and glide, shrieking and laughing in the unselfconscious way kids did when they wanted attention.

'You might have been the shy one, but you were definitely the pretty one,' she said, without rancour.

Beth did not disagree. 'Yeah, but you had the personality.'

Had. But Kerry couldn't disagree either. She tried to keep her voice light. 'What happened, eh?'

She knew what had happened: one night on the village green when she was seventeen.

Kerry had never told Beth the full extent of the events of that sultry night. Beth had been present for some of it, although not the worst bits, and she had never asked for any details, and Kerry had never mentioned it. She had a sudden urge to explain, to say *this is what happened. This is what changed me.* Perhaps Beth would be less disapproving. They would become proper friends again, as they had been as kids. Beth would invite her on holiday with them all. Roddy and Opal would finally embrace her, rushing to claim pole position in her lap as soon as she sat down, twining their little arms around her neck and telling her how much they loved her...

Kerry opened her mouth to ask Beth what she remembered about that night – but Beth had drained her iced coffee and was standing up, corralling all her carrier bags so their ribboned handles fitted on her wrists.

'Must dash, sorry, Kerry. I said I'd cook a vegan mushroom stroganoff for Jitz and the kids, and if I don't get home soon, he'll be feeding them turkey dinosaurs and oven chips.'

Kerry thought she could well imagine which option the kids would prefer. 'I'm surprised you allow turkey dinosaurs over your threshold,' she said, swallowing down the words she'd been planning.

'Only the ones from the health food shop. They're actually tofu in an organic crumb coating, but we call it turkey. Anyway, this was wonderful! Thanks, Kerry, you've been a great help. See you Sunday? Bye!'

And she was off, leaving Kerry to pay for the coffees.

EIGHT

Kerry's heart sank when she walked into the wine bar ten minutes later to find Sharon already sitting on a high stool around a converted barrel table, dressed in a tight yellow sparkly top, black bodycon skirt and stilettos, complete with fake eyelashes a baby deer would be envious of. 'Makes the most of what she's got,' her mother always used to say. Kerry was never sure if this had been a compliment or not.

She *did* make the most of it, though. She had a great figure, her round face was always immaculately made up, and Kerry suspected she had hair extensions in all the time.

Kerry had once turned up unannounced at Sharon's flat to drop something off, and when Sharon answered the door without her make-up on, there was a split second when Kerry thought that Sharon's mum must be staying. Fortunately she realised in time, just as the words 'Is Sharon home?' were about to plummet from her lips.

Mind you, she thought, I can't talk. Not having had time to go home first meant that she herself was still wearing the khaki shorts, trainers and Smashing Pumpkins T-shirt she'd had on when she left work. She hadn't brushed her hair, and she suspected that she might even be a tad whiffy about the armpits. It had been hot, trailing in and out of all those shops.

'Oh Kerry,' Sharon wailed as a greeting. Luckily the over-powering clouds of her perfume would definitely win a battle of supremacy with any body odour Kerry may or may not have had, she thought. 'It's girls' night, we're not taking a load of rubbish to the recycling centre. You may as well go the whole hog and put on some wellies and gardening gloves.'

'I told you I was coming straight from the depot! And this is my favourite shirt,' she protested. 'I totally wouldn't wear it to the tip. Besides, I'm not sure that two of us going out for a drink at six thirty strictly qualifies as a girls' night. We could have stayed home and drunk wine.'

'It does count,' Sharon insisted. 'It's just a very *select* girls' night.'

Sharon didn't have many friends either. Kerry felt sorry for them both.

'I need a drink,' she said. 'I've just been dress-shopping with my sister. It was very stressful.'

Sharon poured Kerry a glass from the bottle in front of her. 'Did you get anything?'

'What do *you* think?' Kerry took a large swig and immediately felt a bit better.

'I'm guessing not. Well, good for you for coming out. We'll never meet men staying at home to drink wine. Here, have a gander at the menu, we have to eat something. Cheeseboard looks nice.'

Kerry agreed without looking. Cheese would be OK, although she'd have preferred a burger and chips. To be honest, she'd only agreed to come for the novelty of not being stuck inside, and to placate Sharon. While lockdown had allowed her to indulge her burgeoning anti-social tendencies, even she had got bored eventually.

It was a change of scene, that was all. She certainly didn't want to meet a man. But she really didn't see the point of paying four times more for wine and a few cubes of poncy cheese that tasted the same as it did at home, and she'd rather have had Sharon over to hers to drink it. At least they could've watched something on TV at the same time, and she wouldn't have to get a night bus home.

Sharon was the only friend Kerry had ever allowed in her annexe, which, Kerry supposed, must mean that she was her best friend. The thought was unaccountably a tad dispiriting.

Five minutes in and Kerry's back was already aching from the stool – the barrel table's bulging sides meant that there was nowhere to put her knees, so she had to either spread her legs in an undignified fashion, or sit side-saddle, which twisted her spine uncomfortably.

Sharon did not seem to be having the same problem. She sat upright and alert, legs neatly crossed, eyes fixed on the door to see if her future husband was arriving. She was desperate to meet someone, and apparently this was the most promising route. Internet dating, she claimed, was a waste of time.

In fact, she spent a good fifteen minutes explaining this, even though she had often said it before. It was a good thing Kerry was fond of her, because in a stranger this quirk would drive her mad: Sharon had perfected the art of hogging conversational airtime by constantly saying 'erm' and 'er' in the middle of her sentences, thus preventing any sort of interjection or change of subject from the listener/hostage. It made it impossible to interrupt without sounding really rude – you were trapped until she decided you were allowed to speak. Kerry wondered if this might be another reason Sharon couldn't keep a bloke.

Yet by the time they had been in the wine bar for over an hour and demolished their teeny cheeses – Kerry was still hungry and was contemplating eating the decorative nasturtiums which were all that was left on the platter – not a single man had entered without a woman on his arm already, so she wasn't at all convinced that Sharon's theory even held water.

'I'm not sure that groups of unattached blokes really ever come to wine bars for their nights out, do they?' she ventured, once she finally managed to get a word in edgeways.

Sharon reapplied her very shiny lipgloss. 'Well, no, but they would for a birthday party, or an office night out. This place usually has loads of groups upstairs. We can always go to Wetherspoons later.'

Kerry groaned. 'Oh please don't make me.'

'You're so negative,' Sharon complained. 'We're supposed to be having fun.'

'We *are* having fun!' Kerry said, chinking her glass against Sharon's. 'Sorry. Actually, it's really nice to see you. And thank you for dragging my miserable arse out, I do appreciate it. Sometimes.'

She did, too.

Sharon grinned at her. 'You're welcome, mate. It's nice to see you too after all these months. So, what's new?'

'Loads, as it goes,' Kerry said. 'Nasty Nige's on the warpath. I got an informal warning the other day, for an unscheduled ten-minute stop. He spotted that I'd gone home. But I needed the toilet – I mean, what was I supposed to do? Oh, and he also clocked that I'd stopped and chatted to one of my old ladies, but her brother had just died and she was really upset.'

'He's a little Hitler, that man,' Sharon said. 'Still can't believe he's actually your boss now.'

'Tell me about it,' Kerry replied gloomily. 'And he's so much worse than when you were there. The power's gone to his head.'

'And how are you, er, feeling?'

'Feeling?'

'About your mum.'

Sharon arranged her features into a sympathetic pout and laid one hand on top of Kerry's on the barrel. One of her talons briefly dug into the soft skin between Kerry's knuckles and she flinched, resisting the urge to drag her hand away. She noticed how soft and smooth Sharon's hands were, whereas her own more resembled a seventy-year-old's, craggy with wrinkles and already spattered with liver spots. How was that possible? They were the same age. Must be my constant exposure to the elements, she thought. She should have taken her mum's advice and been more diligent about the regular application of the Pond's hand cream Mum used to put in her Christmas stocking every year. She vowed to dig out a jar from the teetering pile of unopened boxes of them that she had discreetly relocated back into the cabinet in the big house's spare bathroom.

Clearing her throat, she suddenly felt disloyal to her mum for not doing it before. 'Well... still quite bad really, although I suppose a bit better than I was a month ago.'

'Awwww,' Sharon said, her head tipped to one side.

The thing about Sharon was that, although Kerry was sure her sympathy was genuine, she somehow managed to make it seem really fake.

Kerry didn't want to talk about her grief. About the sudden shocks of loss she still got every afternoon when she pulled onto the driveway and Mum wasn't standing at the window waving at her; or the absence of the smell of frying bacon on a Saturday morning hitting her as she opened the front door of the big house. Mum always used to cook her a big fry-up breakfast at least once a week. She hadn't had one since her mother died.

'On the plus side,' Kerry said, forcing into her voice a brightness she didn't feel, 'I guess I'll be moving into the big house soon. I need to book a few days off, do a spot of decorating, sort out what furniture I'm keeping, that sort of thing. I can't wait. I won't know what to do with myself, with all that space!'

Sharon nodded and withdrew her hand to wrap it back around the stem of her glass. She looked very relieved that

Kerry hadn't collapsed into tears. 'It will be amazing! How many bedrooms is it?'

'Four,' Kerry said. 'Three of them bigger than pretty much my whole annexe. I wonder if I'll turn into a hoarder like Mum was, now that I've finally got room to store stuff.'

'You could get some walk-in wardrobes built,' Sharon enthused. 'You know, maybe have a double row of rails down one side, and shelves for shoeboxes down the other...'

Did Sharon not know her at all? Sometimes Kerry wondered. 'Sharon, I have about five pairs of shoes including trainers and wellies, none of which have their own shoeboxes. And I can fit all my clothes on one short rack. I think you're projecting.'

Sharon had the grace to look sheepish. 'Fair,' she conceded, and then: 'You should have a house-warming party!'

Kerry snorted. 'What, you, me, Clarissa, my sister and her husband, and a few other randoms from work? I don't think so.'

'You're always so negative,' Sharon complained. 'Do you know what I think?'

Kerry did not, but suspected Sharon was about to tell her.

'I think that all those years of being cooped up in your tiny garage has made your horizons tiny too. I think that when you are finally able to spread your wings into the big house, your life will completely change. You'll suddenly want to meet people and socialise more, because you won't be embarrassed about where you live any more. It's a whole new future! Happy for you, babes.'

Sharon chinked her glass against Kerry's, as Kerry opened her mouth to argue that she had got her cod psychology completely wrong... but then she closed it again. Sharon probably did have a point. Actually, it was pretty exciting!

'Come on,' she said instead, rooting around in her bag for a mask. 'Let's go and get a kebab.'

NINE

Kerry had been surprised that Beth invited her over for Sunday lunch again the following week – prior to the pandemic it had only been once a month. When she'd accepted, it was mostly because Beth was such an amazing cook – but she soon wished she hadn't, when she realised her sister had an ulterior motive.

The conversation had started innocently enough, once the kids had been allowed to scramble down from the table to go and play, after turning their noses up at the healthy pudding – stewed rhubarb and natural yogurt mixed together.

'Ewww,' Opal said when Beth set it down on the table, and privately Kerry agreed.

Jitz cleared the bowls and excused himself to go and watch some sort of essential sporting event. Kerry was so disinterested in all sports that she hadn't even registered which one. Cricket, maybe. Or rugby. Who cared? For some reason, people on her round always assumed that she was a sports fan and were forever saying things like 'Joe Root out for a duck, can you believe it!' or 'How about those Gunners?' but she had no idea what gave them that impression or, most of the time, what they even meant.

Beth put her elbows on the table and gazed at her, her eyes wide and her expression disingenuous.

'Have you started sorting stuff out in the house yet?'

This immediately got Kerry's back up. 'Give us a chance, Beth. Mum's only been gone a few weeks.' She wanted to add: *and I've got work. You don't.* But then Beth dropped a bombshell.

'Only, I've got a few agents on board, and they're champing at the bit to come round to start viewings.'

Kerry blinked at her. 'Wait – what? Agents?'

For a moment she stupidly thought Beth must mean some other type of agent. Film? Literary? Secret? Her brain refused to accept what Beth was actually telling her.

'I thought we'd go for a multi-agency sale. They charge a teeny bit more commission, but I reckon it's better for them to be in competition with each other; we'll get more viewings that way.'

Beth mistook Kerry's silence for sadness. 'Ah, I know it'll be tough, Ker, but the sooner we do it, the sooner we'll both get our halves of the cash. And of course I'll help you. I was just asking if you'd made a start yet, that was all.'

Kerry hadn't actually planned to get rid of any of their mum's stuff, apart from her clothes. She'd need it all when she moved in, at least until she could gradually afford to replace all the old-lady brown furniture, piece by piece.

Now it seemed like Beth thought she wasn't moving in at all. This was surely a mistake, or some kind of terrible misunderstanding. How could Beth not know?

'Beth,' she said slowly. 'What are you talking about? We're not selling Mum's house. I'm moving in, and we're renting out my annexe. You get the rental money until either I die or choose to sell up. That was what we agreed.'

Beth gaped at her, seemingly in genuine astonishment. 'Who agreed?'

'It's in Mum's bloody *will*! It has been for years!'

Kerry was trying to keep calm, but her leg had begun to jiggle and she couldn't stop her voice rising in pitch.

'I don't think it is,' Beth said quietly.

'What? Have you seen it? It must be! She told me that's what she was going to do years ago, when she gave you and Larry the deposit for your first house. She offered to give me the same amount, but I said that I was happy in the garage, but one day I would love to live in the big house again, and she promised!'

Beth looked aghast. Kerry could not believe that this seemed to be news to her. Admittedly, she and Beth hadn't ever had the conversation, but surely Beth and *Mum* must have done?

She tried again. 'Beth, the house will still belong to us jointly. Just because I'm going to be living in it, doesn't mean you won't get your half, eventually. And you'll get about £600 a month in rent from the garage! For years!'

Beth shook her head rapidly, as if a wasp had flown into her ear. 'No.'

'Yes, Beth. Have you seen the will?'

'I saw it a few years ago. I'm sure there was nothing like *that* in there. I've not seen it since she died. She specifically didn't put her funeral wishes into it, so that we wouldn't have to rush into sorting it all out before the funeral. We have to wait for Uncle Harry to contact us and let us know officially.'

Uncle Harry, Dad's brother, was the executor. He lived up in Scotland and they rarely saw him. Kerry wondered why Mum had chosen him as executor. He was notoriously slow in everything – eating, walking, responding to phone calls. His Christmas and birthday cards always arrived late, if at all.

Then she wondered if this might be exactly why Mum had picked him as executor. She would have known it would cause huge ructions between Kerry and Beth, and she wouldn't have wanted anything to spoil her funeral. Had she really changed her will, or not done what she'd told Kerry she would in the first place? It would be a massive betrayal if she had.

'Well, you might not have spotted that particular clause. Or if it wasn't in there then, she'll have changed it since. I think we should just wait and see what it actually does say before you even think about putting the house up for sale,' Kerry said stiffly, trying not to cry. 'That's only fair.'

Then her voice cracked, and she reached over the table to grab her sister's hand. 'Beth, please don't make me sell; please. I don't want to live anywhere else. It's my home. I've been looking forward to moving back in and making it mine for *years*. And it's your home too. If we sell it, neither of us has it.'

Beth said nothing. Slowly she slid out her hand from underneath Kerry's and picked at a scratch in the tabletop with her fingernail. 'Jitz and I need the money to renovate this place. Things have been tight lately. That's why he gave up his office, and why nothing's got done around here.'

There was a long pause, into which Kerry wanted to howl. Beth was suggesting she give up her future so that she, Beth, could get new wallpaper? Kerry's half of the inheritance, after the mortgage was paid off, would barely buy her a one-bed flat.

'Beth, you spent about five hundred quid on clothes just last week. How do you equate that with things being tight? Why don't you get a job?'

Beth had the grace to look sheepish. 'I only splurge like that once a year,' she said defensively. 'The rest of the time I buy second hand. And I already have a job – full-time mother. I don't want another one, not until the kids are in secondary school. It's important to me that I'm there for them.'

The house fell silent, apart from the sound of sparrows chirping in the garden, and Beth's huge wall clock ticking into the fraught stillness.

'But you're right,' she added eventually and Kerry's heart momentarily leaped, only to sink again when she realised Beth was just stalling. 'Let's wait and see what the will does say. And in the meantime, I'm going to open more wine.'

She vanished into the kitchen and returned with an opened second bottle, sloshing a generous helping of it into Kerry's glass, not meeting her eyes.

'I've been meaning to ask, Kerry, do you know if Mum still had any of Dad's photos? You know, those fabulous landscapes he used to do? I'd really like to get some of them printed up – if you can even still do that these days, from negatives? I thought a framed series of them up the stairs would look amazing after we've redecorated. I should've asked Mum, but...' Beth tailed off, and they might have had a shared moment of mutual recognition of their loss – but instead Kerry found she was gritting her teeth with annoyance.

Maybe Beth hadn't meant anything by it, but her casual mention of their proposed renovation project again, so soon after saying they should wait and see what was written in the will, felt like Beth was just reiterating her belief that Kerry was somehow mistaken about being allowed to live in the big house.

Perhaps it was because her back was up. Because she was upset, because she was a little drunk, because at that moment she wanted to hurt Beth the way her sister had just hurt her – but the mention of Dad's negatives made Kerry decide to tell Beth what she knew, the thing she swore she'd never tell because it would upset her so much.

After years of avoiding thinking about it, she blurted it out, no longer caring what effect it might have: 'You know what? Last time I looked in Dad's photography drawer was just after he died, and I found a contact sheet of arty black-and-white pictures of Miss Smith. Our history teacher. And she was naked. Dad must have been having an affair with her. All those years we thought he and Mum had such a perfect marriage? Guess we were wrong about that.'

The colour drained from Beth's face and for the first time ever, Kerry saw a glimpse of how her sister would look as an old lady. The wine bottle began to slip from Beth's grip as she sank into a chair, and Kerry caught it just in time.

'*What?*'

TEN

1994

Kerry had just wanted to feel close to him.

He'd been dead for nine months but it still felt inconceivable that she would have to spend the rest of her life, decades and endless decades of it, probably, without seeing him or talking to him or smelling the oiled-wool scent of his favourite green winter sweater.

She had shouted and screamed at her mother when she walked into their bedroom a few weeks ago and saw Mum hanging up all her summer clothes in *his* side of the wardrobe. These were the clothes usually kept under the bed for half a year, sealed in plastic vacuum storage bags. Kerry had always loved watching the air being sucked out of the nozzle with the hose of a Hoover, the garments rendered stiff and trapped, as if they'd been frozen in time and space by an alien's ray gun. Now they were all liberated from their cramped quarters, stretching out in the empty space left by Dad's numerous identical short-sleeved shirts and his three suits: the 'good' one, the work one and the funeral one.

'What are you doing?' Kerry had screeched. 'Where's Dad's stuff?'

Her mum had looked both shamefaced and simultaneously defensive. 'I gave it all to the Oxfam shop. No point having it clogging up the shelves when I could use the extra space.'

'All of it? Not his green jumper too?'

She had her back to Kerry, but Kerry saw her nod guiltily. She burst into tears.

'Sorry, darling,' said her mother, but didn't come over and comfort her, just continued to hang up her colourful dresses as if it was no big deal.

Kerry never quite forgave her for that. And now she wasn't sure she could ever forgive her father either, for what she'd just found.

Kerry had been spending a lot of time sitting at the desk in her dad's darkroom out in the garage, crying and listening to The Cure albums on her Walkman. The garage had been Dad's domain including, under its vaulted roof, his tiny darkroom cubicle on one side and an office area-cum-studio on the other.

His desk was under the window with a view over the paddock owned by their neighbours at the back, and Kerry would sit there for hours, staring out at the shaggy little pony and its two manky-looking donkey henchmen who shared residency of the field.

Dad had been a very keen amateur landscape photographer, particularly favouring New Forest and Lake District scenes. One day, bored of staring out of the window, Kerry decided to look through all his photographs.

He habitually chucked them into the huge bottom drawer of the chest of drawers next to the desk, where they all sat in a massive, un-filed jumble, as he constantly grumbled about having to categorise them into folders and then never did.

Never would, now.

She had a vague idea that she might undertake this task as a

labour of love, to honour his memory with a selection of immaculately curated photo albums of his best work, but when she
managed to haul open the drawer, the vast clutter greeting her
made her think twice.

The drawer was probably a foot deep, and filled to the brim
with photos, contact sheets and negatives. Her dad had been
particularly fond of an autumn scene, and many of the colour
ones tended to be of orange beech trees against gorse and green
backdrops. Kerry riffled through the top couple of layers – much
the same. Waterfalls over speckled rocks, quaint wooden foot-
bridges, fords and falling leaves. Barren desolate-looking moun-
tains and vast, empty valleys.

Boring as hell, in her opinion. She was longing for some
human interest, a splash of colour to enliven them, even if it was
just her mother in a headscarf on a hillside. But no, they were
all strictly landscape.

She dug a little deeper, hearing the faint crunch of the cello-
phane-wrapped negative strips in their individual cases,
smelling the familiar scent of old paper mixed with a whiff of
developing fluid. More trees, more spring water bubbling over
rocks, more dead leaves and close-up petals.

No photos of her or Beth. Their dad had taken some, when
they were younger, but they were in albums on the bookshelf in
the living room. Kerry wondered if he got bored of taking their
pictures when they became awkward, galumphing teenagers.

Well, when she became one, at least, she thought. Beth had
always been more gazelle-like than galumphing. Kerry didn't
mind that there weren't any photos of the two of them together.
She hated having her photograph taken and, even more than
that, hated having to look at the results. Bar a few when she was
full-faced smiling at the camera, she was hideously unpho-
togenic.

By the time she'd rooted down to the bottom of the deep
drawer she had reconsidered her thoughts of displaying or cate-

gorising its contents. There weren't even any photos of her father.

Kerry was just about to try and jiggle the drawer closed again when a photo of what looked like a white tube caught her eye, on a black-and-white contact sheet. Intrigued to see something that wasn't sky or mountain she pulled it out by its corner – then dropped it on the floor in shock.

Her heart pounding, she picked it up and squinted at it, horrified. The shape she'd glimpsed wasn't a white tube, it was a long, pale leg, bent at the knee.

Attached to the naked body of a woman whose face she recognised immediately.

She was staring at a sheet of three-inch square images of her history teacher, stark naked, in a variety of poses, all of which showed her breasts and, some, her dark scribble of pubic hair.

Kerry blinked. She must be mistaken. It couldn't possibly be Miss Smith.

But it was. There was no mistake. That was the face she used to see twice a week in her GCSE classes. That sensual mouth was more usually telling a group of bored fifteen-year-olds facts about the Industrial Revolution and the Ninety-Five Theses that Luther nailed to the church door than pouting at a camera lens.

A camera lens that, presumably, Kerry's dad was behind. Miss Smith was in a variety of poses, but mostly reclining on a shaggy rug – the same rug Kerry could see right then, merely by turning her head. She felt queasy.

She forced herself to look closer at the woman's expression, because something about it was troubling, at odds with the proud body language. Once you saw beyond the thrust-out breasts and coquettish dip of the head, there was something not right, something that even Kerry, as a completely naive teenager, could see.

Or perhaps it was *because* she was a completely naive

teenager that she could see it – because Kerry knew what it was like to feel out of place in the world, self-conscious, not happy in her skin. She had seen that same look in her own eyes in the mirror of late, too many times to count; a hollow, bleak desolation that leached out even when she was smiling. Miss Smith was not comfortable with the situation.

It didn't make sense, she thought. There was absolutely no way that Dad would ever, ever have made someone do something they didn't want to; the very thought of making another person feel even remotely uncomfortable was anathema to him. He could get the worst service in the world in a restaurant and he still wouldn't dream of saying anything to the waitress for fear of upsetting her.

What the hell?

Their parents hadn't ever been overly demonstrative to her and Beth – but the one thing that seemed obvious about them was that they adored each other. They weren't out-and-out party animals, although they were big drinkers and very sociable. Kerry's childhood had been punctuated with evenings where the house and/or garden would be filled with shrieking tipsy adults ironically dancing to sixties music, doing exaggerated twists and even quicksteps and waltzes, and she'd always found it a bit overwhelming. Who were all these people in their house? She had not liked it. In fact, she thought, she would go as far as to say that the only good thing about Dad dying was that there had been no more parties for a while.

'Ah, your folks, they give other married couples a bad name!' Kerry remembered Mum's friend Jean cooing, as her mum and dad canoodled at a picnic one summer when she was about nine.

'Get a room, you two!' Jean's husband had bellowed across from the neighbouring blanket.

Kerry and Beth had exchanged mortified and confused

glances. It was years before she understood the meaning of 'get a room' or why that made all the adults crack up.

But, for all their mother's frivolity, and Dad's jovial snogging-on-blankets attitude, the pair of them had been incredibly serious about their relationship. At least, Kerry had always thought they were. They got married young, and had wanted to start a family straight away but remained childless for ten years before she came along, closely followed by Beth – so, as delighted as they were to find themselves parents, they were already wholeheartedly dedicated to their marriage. Kerry and Beth had been added extras, accessories to their happiness.

They never once heard their parents argue or saw either of them sulk in a major way. There was a very occasional snippy comment, usually from Mum, but that was really it, Kerry thought. They used to hear stories from friends on the school bus about the screaming rows their parents had had the night before, and they just couldn't understand it. Why would you ever marry someone you didn't like? they wondered. What would be the point?

Now Kerry wondered if perhaps she'd had an idealised, over-simplified notion of what their folks' relationship really had been.

Dad and Miss Smith must have been having an affair. There was surely no other possible reason for him to have taken pictures of her in the nude. Kerry racked her brain to try and think of one, but simply could not come up with anything which wasn't completely far-fetched and implausible. The contact sheet was now lying on the carpet, but her hands were shaking too much to pick it up. She wanted to stop staring at it but found she couldn't, her eyes inexorably drawn to the twelve little naked Miss Smiths at her feet. Dad hadn't loved Mum after all, he couldn't have done. It felt almost more devastating than his death.

What the hell was she going to do? She couldn't say

anything to Mum, obviously, because her mother almost certainly didn't know. She didn't think she should destroy the contact sheet because, just say, on the off-chance Mum *had* known, then when she came to clear out the drawer and the photos weren't there, she would know that Kerry had found them. It was a minefield.

Kerry thought about what might have happened immediately before or after he took the pictures, and bile rose in her throat. Here, in this room. She couldn't bear it. How could he have done that to Mum? To them? Where had they all even *been*, while Miss Smith was getting her kit off in the garage?

She wanted to track the woman down and smash her fist into her face. She felt vastly relieved that Miss Smith no longer taught her – there was absolutely no way that she could ever have sat in her classroom again, having seen her naked.

Kerry had last seen her at Dad's funeral, where Miss Smith had been crying on a girlfriend's shoulder. She, Mum and Dad had all sung in the same choral society for years, and Miss Smith got up with the rest of the choir halfway through the service and sang a rousing 'Hallelujah Chorus'. Kerry remembered the way her lips were wobbling so much that she could hardly get the high notes out.

Even so, Kerry wouldn't have said that Miss S and Mum and Dad had been exactly friends, more acquaintances. Kerry did recall her coming to one of their Christmas drinks soirées, because that was the first time she had been mortified that one of her actual teachers was standing in their living room drinking wine and, later, disco-dancing on the rug. Kerry was used to seeing Miss Smith at school dressed in puffy-sleeved, complicated blouses tucked neatly into tweedy skirts, with sensible shoes, so to see her in high-heeled boots and a denim mini skirt kind of blew her mind. Especially when one of the buttons straining across her tight velvet top popped off as she danced, exposing a generous cleavage.

Kerry remembered her dad's eyes snagging on it, then hastily looking away when he caught her following his gaze. Miss Smith had been shrieking and giggling like all the girls in Kerry's class did in biology, when it was the module on human reproduction. Kerry had been about thirteen then and thought she had reached peak embarrassment. She could still remember the burning that started in your cheeks and became one of those blushes that crawled into your ears and down your neck too.

But that was nothing in comparison to how she felt now, finding the photos.

Kerry picked up the contact sheet by one corner and methodically tore it into tiny pieces until all the images of Miss Smith's bare limbs, breasts and torso were reduced to monochrome confetti. She swept the pieces into the wastepaper bin, then took the bin outside and buried its contents at the bottom of the compost heap.

ELEVEN

2020

Kerry did not have to wait long for her fears to be confirmed. She saw the letter about the will when it arrived at her sorting frame two days later. It was in a thick creamy envelope with her name and address handwritten in copperplate writing, the sort of letter that always intrigued her when she was sorting. If she hadn't been expecting it, she might have assumed it was a wedding invitation.

She imagined an identical letter landing on Beth's doormat that morning, and wondered, as she had done many times over the past forty-eight hours, how Beth would feel when she realised the house was going nowhere. Her sister would just have to get a job after all, Kerry thought. It was what everyone else had to do, to make ends meet! Being a full-time stay-at-home parent was only possible if the other parent made enough to support them all. The kids weren't babies. They could go to after-school clubs and holiday camps, surely? Beth had her handout years ago, when Mum had given her that huge house deposit. Now it was Kerry's turn.

She still felt furious, albeit guilty about the shock she'd given Beth over the photos of Miss Smith. They'd had a massive row after the revelation, Beth screeching incoherently at her, so much so that Jitz had had to haul himself away from the cricket – or rugby – to see what was going on. Kerry had stormed past them both and slammed out of the house, and they hadn't spoken since. At least it had stopped them having a big row about the will, anyway, she thought.

When she opened the letter, heart thudding in her throat, she saw the lengthy solicitors' name embossed across the top of the page. Winfield, Swallow and Must. Sounded to her like one of the location names you got in that app that was supposed to help emergency services find you if you were stuck on the moors or up a mountain: what3words, she thought it was called.

Glancing over her shoulder to make sure Nige wasn't prowling, she scanned the typed content, too nervous to read it properly at first. The letters appeared utterly foreign, as if written in Cyrillic or Cantonese, and she had to take a deep breath and look closely at them, tracing the words with her finger like a child learning to read.

Dear Miss Tucker,

We have been instructed by Mr Harold Tucker, executor for the will of the late Mrs Hilary Tucker, that you are one of the named beneficiaries. Please see attached a copy of the will, but to summarise, the estate of your late mother is to be divided in its entirety equally between yourself and your sister, Mrs Elizabeth Desai.

No clause allowing her to live there, and Beth getting the rental from the annexe. She flipped the letter over in the vain hope that it was on the back as a PS. Nothing. Then she leafed frantically through the photocopied attachment.

Again, nothing. Apart from notification of fourteen thousand pounds in cash, her half of Mum's savings. Kerry internally sent her a small hug – that would enable her to do up the house, to really make it hers.

Although not if she was forced to sell it.

Was she being unreasonable; ungrateful? After all, she'd just been gifted a sum, on top of the fourteen thousand, that would probably end up being in the region of a hundred and fifty thousand pounds (the house itself was worth about half a million, but Kerry knew that there was still a mortgage on it. She wasn't sure exactly how much it was, but the amount of two hundred grand rang a bell).

But she didn't want the money. She wanted the house she'd been promised. She wanted her home. If it was sold, then she'd lose her garage too. She'd lose the two only homes she'd ever had.

She couldn't let that happen.

Kerry went out on her round, lost in a fog of confusion and bitterness, stomping around the villages in the drizzly rain and avoiding contact with anybody else where possible, until finally it was over and she was able to retreat to the safety of the annexe.

Her mobile rang within minutes of her getting through the door. Beth, of course. She knew what time Kerry got back from work.

Kerry knew there was no point in letting it go to voicemail. Beth would only keep calling unless she switched off her phone altogether. She'd better not gloat or think she's 'won', Kerry thought savagely as she picked up.

'Did you get it?'

But Beth sounded subdued, which briefly made Kerry feel bad for thinking she'd be all Mrs Gloaty McGloatface of Gloatsville.

'The letter about the will? Yes.'

'So...'

'So what?'

Beth sighed. 'You know.'

Kerry had meant to be calm and reasonable, but fury bubbled up inside her like a toxic gas. 'Yeah, I know. But just because it's not in the will that I'm allowed live there doesn't mean we have to sell. You could always do the right thing.'

Kerry heard her sister's gasp of outrage. 'Me, do the right thing? What about *you*? If you move into that house, you're depriving me of a hundred and fifty grand! And yourself of it too! You can't tell me you don't need that money, and I know that I do. Jitz and I have been holding out for it for years!'

'Nice. Waiting for Mum to die so that you can get your hands on the inheritance. Stay classy, Beth. And let's not forget that you got that massive handout from her so you and Larry could buy your first house. *I* didn't – *plus*, I've been paying Mum rent all this time!'

Oh dear. That had escalated quickly, Kerry thought, wincing. Why could she not learn to bite her tongue and not snap? She never did it with anybody else, just Beth.

Beth was livid. 'You can talk! You were waiting for her to die so you could move into her house!'

'*Our* house. I wasn't at all.' Kerry hesitated. 'And I know you weren't either. I'm sorry. We really need to find a way not to fight about this.'

But Beth proceeded as if she hadn't even spoken.

'Yes. *Our* house. Where I get as much of a say about what we do with it as you do.'

Kerry's apology had been flung back in her face and she felt herself getting even more upset. Her voice hardened. 'Not when it's not what Mum wanted.'

Beth was on a roll: 'If Mum had wanted it, then explain why she didn't put it in her sodding will!'

'I really don't know, Beth, because she promised me that she would. And I don't believe that she wouldn't have mentioned it to you.'

'Oh, so I'm a liar now, am I?'

'I didn't say that. Maybe you just forgot.'

Beth snorted. 'As if I'd forget a conversation that important.'

'I don't want us to sell the house,' Kerry repeated miserably.

'And I do. So what now? You're not going to make me take you to court, are you?'

'Surely you wouldn't really take me to court – would you? Mum would be devastated.'

There was a pause. 'But Jitz and I need that money, Kezza.'

Calling her Kezza was Beth's way of trying to win her around. Still, at least she no longer sounded so furious, thought Kerry. She had assumed that Beth would go ballistic at her bringing Mum into it, but it seemed instead to have taken the wind out of her sails.

'How about trying to buy me out, have you thought about that?' Beth's voice was wheedling. 'You could talk to a financial adviser about it. A loan wouldn't cost more than the rent you were paying Mum, and you've got fourteen grand to put down as a deposit.'

'I hadn't thought about that. I still don't think it's enough, on my salary, but I promise I will consider it as an option,' she said reluctantly.

'That would be a brilliant solution! And you could rent out the garage for extra income.' Beth sounded as jubilant as if it was all a done deal. 'Then we'd all be happy.'

'Fingers crossed,' Kerry said.

She was about to say goodbye and hang up when Beth suddenly blurted out, 'Oh, by the way...' as if there was something urgent she'd forgotten to say. Her tone made Kerry feel as if there was an icy finger skittering up her spine.

'Yes?' Kerry replied cautiously.

'That thing you said the other day, about Dad.'

'Yes?' Now there seemed to be a large block of ice obstructing her bowel.

She wondered what Beth was going to say. She, Kerry, had actually been having lurid shame-nightmares about it again, ever since she brought it up – the most recent featuring her walking into a full classroom to find her dad and Miss Smith having sex on the desk at the front while all her classmates jeered at her and her mum looked through the window, sobbing.

When Beth's parting shot came, it was even blunter than Kerry had feared.

'You were definitely wrong about the naked photos. There is no way it could have been Miss Smith. You probably dreamt it. And I really do not appreciate you trying to sully the memory of our parents' marriage when we both know they were extraordinarily happy together. That was such a shitty thing for you to do, Kerry, I don't know what possessed you, but I have to tell you, I am *really* disappointed in you.'

Then she hung up before Kerry could even defend herself.

'Right,' Kerry said, into the ether. 'Bye then, bitch.'

Her fingers were shaking as she threw her phone as hard as she could into the sofa cushions.

TWELVE

Every day in the fortnight since the phone call with Beth, Kerry had got in from work and lain down on the sofa in a foetal position, not even bothering to take off her shoes, staring at the switched-off television, not able to concentrate on anything except the tone of Beth's voice when she'd told her she'd been wrong about Dad and Miss Smith.

She couldn't get it out of her head, and the more time went on, the angrier it made her. Two weeks later and she was fuming. How dare Beth gaslight her so outrageously? She had simply insisted Kerry had been wrong, with the confident steeliness with which Kerry once overheard her telling Roddy off for stealing Opal's birthday five-pound note.

She wanted to have it out with her sister, shake her until she accepted that she hadn't made it up, or imagined it, or misremembered it... but also, she couldn't face another row.

Even now, over twenty-six years later, Kerry could still remember the expression on Miss Smith's face, and her own shock at seeing photographs in Dad's drawer of anybody naked, let alone her *teacher*.

On top of that was what happened to Kerry on the village

green just a few weeks after that. The two events were conflated in her mind and she could not think of one without the other. There was no way she was telling Beth about that second one, though; at least not any more details than she already knew. She'd been there, for at least part of it, and never once afterwards had asked Kerry if she was OK, if she'd got over it. Kerry had always subsequently made excuses for that, since Beth hadn't known the full story and also, she had only been fifteen and that year had been really difficult for her as well...

But now she was thinking that Beth only ever paid attention to what she wanted to. If she was honest, it felt a bit scary having unleashed the truth of the photos out into the world, especially since she hadn't even been believed.

That was when Kerry started obsessing about Miss Smith and what had gone on between her and her dad, trying to make her memory recreate a timeline obscured by decades and trauma, like a cloudy wineglass or smeary bifocals. Had Dad taken the photos before Miss Smith met that hot guy they'd seen with her on the coach to London, or after? Or even during? Kerry tried and failed to remember if Dad's demeanour had changed upon seeing Miss Smith and her boyfriend climbing onto the coach, barely able to negotiate the steps because they were so wrapped around each other.

If only her dad were still alive so she could ask him – if she ever would have had the nerve to.

So many other things had come up over the years that Kerry wanted to ask him, either because Mum hadn't known or because she didn't want to bother her, from the prosaic – why on earth was the gas meter buried in a flowerbed outside the annexe? – to the philosophical: would he have been OK with Kerry never marrying and therefore never giving him a grandchild? Mum used to hint with monotonous regularity at how much he'd have loved to have seen her 'settled'. Kerry always felt like replying, *Well, he's not here so he doesn't know either way. If by saying 'Dad' you actually mean 'you', then just be straight about it, rather than implying I'm such a disappointment to my dead father...*

The memory made her both roll her eyes and wipe sudden tears from them. Complaining about her mother now that she was gone felt horribly disloyal. In her more melodramatic moments (i.e. three quarters of the way down a bottle of Sauvignon Blanc, which was fast becoming her regular next move in the afternoon, once she finally got up from the sofa), she felt like she had lost her whole family; first her dad, then her mum and now Beth. From the first row they'd had after Sunday lunch when it had become clear they had very different ideas about what would happen to the house, and then the distance and suppressed rage in her sister's voice in that last phone call, Kerry couldn't stop thinking that Beth had washed her hands of her. She had a horrible sinking feeling that Beth would have no qualms about gaslighting her about the will in exactly the same way as she was doing about the photos of Miss Smith.

You got it wrong.

You misremembered.

You're mistaken.

It didn't happen.

Kerry shot bolt upright on the sofa so fast that blood rushed to her head and she almost keeled back over in her sudden, overwhelming urge to prove Beth wrong.

Her own naivety over the house, and now the will, meant that it would be nigh on impossible to show that she wasn't mistaken about the inheritance, and she could no longer ask Dad about the photographs – but there was one person who *would* know, who could prove to Beth that she hadn't made it up:

Miss Smith.

If she could track down Miss Smith, she could ask *her*.

And while she was doing that, she could be proactive about

the house. Possession being nine-tenths of the law, and all (or had she made that up? It rang a bell, and suited her purposes, so she decided it must be true), if she began to stake her claim right away then perhaps it would become a fait accompli. She had read an article on her phone recently about creative visualisation and 'manifesting' and dismissed it as bollocks at the time, but now she thought *yes*! She could make this happen, if she wanted and believed it enough.

Kerry decided: she was going to move into the big house, tomorrow. Beth would have to prise the keys out of her cold, dead fingers before she'd let her sell it. And she would find Miss Smith, and drag her to Beth's if she had to, to explain why Dad had taken naked photographs of her in his office, on his rug. Beth would realise she'd been wrong to doubt her about that, and therefore give her the benefit of the doubt about the house...

Possibly. But it was worth a go, Kerry thought, and anything was better than lying on the sofa fuming for the rest of her life.

THIRTEEN

The next day after work Kerry got caught in the sort of rush-hour traffic that her working hours – and the pandemic – had helped her avoid for several years. It took her so long to get home that she'd almost have welcomed another lockdown. Thank goodness she'd managed to book leave for the next ten days, she thought, as she finally got through the roadworks only to get stuck behind a huge farm truck, which was flinging bits of shitty straw and mud from its gargantuan wheels at her windscreen.

Nigel had given her a hard time about taking leave at such short notice, but Bill, one of the other regulars, had happened to be passing and overheard the dressing-down Nigel was giving her. He leaped into the conversation and practically begged Nige to give Kerry's round to his son Kieran, who was looking for extra hours next week, so Nigel couldn't get too mad at her.

Even so, by the time Kerry was twisting the key in the annexe front door she felt tired, grumpy and like a great big fail-ure, as if last night's resolution to stand up for herself had been the wave of a sugar high, and now she was in the depths of the crash.

The thought of making the big house her own had been the only thing keeping her mood from being permanently in the gutter since her mum died. Now that even this one potentially good thing in her life was in jeopardy, she felt a desolation more intense than she thought she ever had before. The determination of her vow to fight Beth on this, the vow she'd made not twelve hours ago to prove her wrong, had not waned, but she no longer felt bullish. She felt afraid now. What if she couldn't persuade Beth to do the right thing? Beth and her family were all Kerry had. Was she really prepared to risk losing that, for the sake of some bricks and mortar?

Then she thought about the way Beth had always ridden roughshod over her feelings and decisions and decided, yes, she was. She needed this, for her. For her future. If she didn't fight it, the house and the annexe would be sold and she'd be homeless with not quite enough to find anything other than a grim studio flat somewhere.

Kerry didn't bother cooking herself any dinner that night, even though she'd had plans to make a healthy stew, part of the new start she was always promising herself (and Beth). That could wait. Today had been rubbish.

Instead, she cut up the least soft and wrinkled of the elderly apples in her fruit bowl – a nod to healthy eating – opened a bottle of wine and a tube of Pringles, and sat down in front of her TV, preparing to binge-watch something about vampires for the next seven hours straight.

Then she realised she had already reneged on one of the two promises she'd made to herself – she'd sworn she would move into the big house today.

She wavered. The wine was cold and delicious and obviously it was impossible to keep her hand out of the Pringles tube. She was tired. Her garage was cosy and warm, and she knew the big house would be stuffy and sad. Apart from emptying the fridge and turning off the electricity, she hadn't set foot in there since the ambulance crew carried her mum down the stairs, strapped into a portable sedan chair thingy. Her eyes had met Kerry's and it was as if they'd both known she was leaving the house for the final time. She'd had a mini stroke, a TIA. Luckily Kerry been there and called the ambulance, but then her mother had another massive one on the way to hospital and even though she'd literally been in the best hands, the crew hadn't been able to save her.

At least it had been quick.

Kerry wanted the house, and she would go all out to get it – but right at that moment, the thought of being in it without her mum's beady presence felt too painful.

Excuses.

It was seven o'clock. She went to bed at nine. How much could she really do, in a couple of hours? Plus, she wasn't that likely to sleep well on her first night alone there.

More excuses.

She drained the glass of wine and turned off the TV, but remained curled up in the corner of the sofa. One thing at a time, she thought as she picked a Pringles crumb out of her lap. Glancing across to the key rack by the door, she saw a set of keys for the big house.

Come on, Kerry. Don't fall at the first hurdle. You've booked it as holiday already, don't waste the time off.

This sort of behaviour was exactly what Beth would expect of her. Putting things off, being lazy, saying she'd do something and then failing to do it.

She'd said to herself – and now she crushed the temptation to use as an excuse the fact that she was therefore not accountable to anyone else – that she would be proactive and move into the house straightaway, so that was what she should do.

Should. More prevarication. No – that was what she was *going* to do. It would be weird at first, but the sooner she did it, the sooner she'd get over it. She needed to get her feet under the table. Literally. It would be a step in the right direction of 'taking back control', one of the anodyne slogans of which politicians were so fond.

Right!

She stood up. Out of the window above the kitchen sink she could see the big house across the driveway, crouching in the dusk.

It wasn't literally a big house, not really; the family had just taken to calling it that after Kerry's father died and the garage was converted a second time, from her dad's photography studio to her home. The term 'big house' was just used to differentiate it from her small one, which was always known as the garage or the annexe.

The big house was a stolid, detached, four-bed, chalet-style house, a new-build when Kerry's parents bought it in the seventies, with an oak porch at the front and a brick chimney stack running up the back. They had been self-conscious, almost apologetic, about it when Kerry and Beth were kids, presumably because it was the only modern house in a road littered with winsomely cute thatched cottages. They did have a five-barred gate, though, which was more in keeping with the rest of the village, and often referred to their home as 'the cottage' which, looking back, seemed pretentious as well as inaccurate.

Kerry remembered asking her dad why he hadn't bought an old house, if he felt they were so much better than their modern one, and he'd laughed and said, 'No way! I think you'd have to be crazy to have a thatched roof. Costs thousands to maintain and replace, massive fire hazard, not to mention all the wildlife you get up there. Spiders, bats, birds... hey, girls, do you know—'

'Yes, we do,' she and Beth would chorus, because this was always where his train of thought took him, literally every single time thatched roofs came up in conversation.

'What?' He sounded hurt.

'You're going to tell us where the expression "raining cats and dogs" comes from, aren't you?'

He'd hold up his hands in mock surrender. 'Might have been,' he'd say, pretending to be huffy, until one or other of them, usually Beth, would climb on his knee and hug his neck to mollify him.

My God, Kerry thought, she missed him. Why was she missing him more than Mum, when it was Mum who'd just died? She'd loved Mum too, of course, but that relationship had been a far more complex beast, fraught with tension and obligation.

But the memory of Dad was what it took to propel her to her feet. In the same way she'd felt close to him by moving into the garage when she was nineteen, now she wanted to be in the big house, to help remember both of them as they had been when she was a kid and life had been straightforward and happy. Before he'd died. Before she found the photos, before that night on the green.

Plus – to be stubborn – because it was what her mum had promised her.

Kerry was already in her PJs and dressing gown, but she didn't bother getting dressed again. She often got ready for bed as soon as she got through the door, even when it was only about 5 p.m., for several reasons: she liked to get out of her uniform as soon as she was home and there seemed little point in another change of clothes when she wasn't going anywhere; because she frequently fell asleep in front of the telly; and, finally, because she never had any visitors so what difference did it make? Her mum used to object when Kerry would pop across the driveway, the sides of her open dressing gown flapping, to check on her in the evenings – but Mum was no longer around.

She gathered up her wash bag, fresh underwear and a change of clothes, put a pint of milk, the rest of the wine and the

Pringles into a carrier bag, then unhooked the keys, stuck her feet into outdoor shoes and let herself out of the annexe.

Her hands were shaking as she unlocked the front door of the big house. She hadn't set foot in there for weeks. The only reason that post wasn't piled up in the entrance hall was because the address was on her round and she knew to return it all to sender, or deal with it herself.

As soon as she glanced at the staircase, she visualised Mum being carried down, the friendly bulk of two green-clad paramedics topping and tailing her uneven progress, the expression of intense sadness in her mother's eyes. What must she have thought, on that final journey? Was she remembering that Dad, too, had made that grim last descent years before? Perhaps she was wondering if they were about to be reunited. She knew her mum had a faith once, although she stopped mentioning it once she and Beth were grown up. Kerry hoped she'd kept it till the end – but that was yet another thing she'd never had the courage to talk to her about.

The house felt chilly and damp, the sort of chill that came from being unoccupied rather than from cold weather. Kerry turned on the electricity and decided to turn on the heating too, if she could remember how. It was July, too warm outside for it to automatically come on and, besides, she'd switched off the boiler the day her mum left for the hospital. Mum had had a habit of carrying the thermostat around with her in her pocket, so it took Kerry a good ten minutes to find it, half hidden behind a framed school photograph of herself and Beth on one of the shelves of the bookcase in the living room.

Beth looked adorable, grinning gap-toothed and winsome with her hair in two skinny braids, and Kerry thought how gormless she looked next to her. Her own school jumper was hand-knitted and stretched-looking (Mum had been an enthusiastic but not very proficient knitter) whereas Beth's appeared to be fresh out of a cellophane wrapper from the uniform shop. That about summed it up, Kerry thought.

She managed to switch everything back on and the central heating lumbered into life with a series of complaining roars, groans, ticks and whooshes whose familiarity instantly made her feel more at home.

Putting the milk in the fridge, she surveyed the shabby kitchen. Mum and her friends had always sent one another postcards whenever they went anywhere, and the long cupboard door was completely covered in photos of Tenby or Porto or Benidorm. Hardly any of those friends had come to her lockdown funeral, and probably wouldn't have done even if numbers had been unlimited – they were mostly too old to drive, or too scattered around the country. Or, perhaps, dead too.

The postcards looked pretty sad, hanging crooked, or dog-eared and stained. Most of them had been there for years. Kerry took a deep breath and began peeling them off until they were in a messy stack in her hands. It felt so strange seeing the cupboard door bare. But it was a start.

She decided it was enough that she was in, and that she was going to start sleeping there. She didn't have to redecorate the whole place straight away. Just stake her claim on it, for the sake of her sanity.

She ventured upstairs and into the main bathroom, where she ran a bath. The garage was too tiny to have anything other than a shower, in the space previously occupied by Dad's dark-room, and she felt gleeful at the thought that now she could have a long soaky bath every night, if she wanted one. It was not a nice bathroom, objectively, still with the original avocado bath, basin, toilet, and a fairly rancid carpet (whoever thought carpeting a bathroom was a good idea?) stained brown from decades of water damage. The grout in the tiles was speckled with black mould.

Kerry had never really noticed how awful it looked before, but without Mum to give it context, it was easier to see it for what it was. It had always just reminded her of listening to the Radio One chart rundown on a Sunday night on a transistor radio propped on the toilet cistern, as she rinsed her hair with the mixer hose, one rubber connector stuck on each tap. It was almost impossible to get the water temperature to be anything other than scalding or freezing.

Doing up the bathroom would have to be high on her list of priorities, then. She visualised the room sparkling white with wood floors – or at least, that lino that looked just like wood. She couldn't wait.

In the meantime, though, as steam and the scent from a generous splash of Mum's Badedas bubble bath filled the air, it was easy to forgive the room's shortcomings and just relax into a lovely hot bath.

In her own bathroom. In her own home. Despite all the hurdles and angst Kerry knew she most likely faced, she couldn't help hugging herself with excitement.

My house.

FOURTEEN

Kerry moved in properly over the next week, trudging back and forth across the gravel drive with armfuls of clothes – there was no need to bother with suitcases – and carrier bags containing anything perishable from her tiny galley kitchen. It didn't take long to remove most of her personal effects from the garage and redistribute them around the big house.

The most time-consuming element of the actual move had been deciding which bedroom she should claim. She didn't want to take the master because it had been Mum and Dad's, and her old bedroom had long ago been requisitioned as a dumping ground for random junk – not that she'd have wanted to move back in there anyway. That would be weird. In the end, she chose the biggest of the spare rooms, which had a built-in wardrobe and a double bed in it, and a view over the paddock at the back.

Setting up her laptop in the 'office' (Beth's former bedroom), she couldn't stop marvelling at the sheer number of steps she was taking to get around the place, up stairs, along hallways, out into the back garden... it was such a novelty after the annexe, where everything was within ten paces. She revelled in it.

Next, there were a few other fairly major – but less physical – steps to occupy her days off: she booked a decorator to come in and repaint the whole place, chose and paid for new carpets and booked a locksmith to come and change the locks. She didn't mind paying for it all, because in the worst-case scenario where the courts forced a sale, she could claim it back then, saying she had added value to the place by renovating.

Kerry was still convinced it wouldn't come to that, though. Beth wouldn't do that to her.

But to be on the safe side, she decided not to advertise the annexe for rent, not just yet. It would be awful to get a tenant in there only to have to boot them out a couple of months down the line.

Beth had gone completely quiet. Kerry was bracing herself to receive a solicitor's letter or to get another bossy phone call, but there was nothing. No more invitations to Sunday lunch either, she noticed.

Still, she didn't care. If Beth's acquiescence meant that she, Kerry, no longer had a relationship with her and the family, then so be it. She couldn't worry about that for now.

To dampen the almost permanent sensation of being on tenterhooks about it all, Kerry decided to put her energies into another important project: finding Miss Smith. Beth had done her at least one favour in not believing her – giving her the incentive to try to get to the bottom of what had happened between Miss Smith and Dad. Somehow, being in the big house made knowing the truth feel like even more of an imperative.

Had Dad crept along this same upstairs hallway, coming in late after a secret tryst with her history teacher? Had he invited Miss Smith over to the garage when the rest of the family were out for the day, telling her to park round the corner so that nobody would notice the unfamiliar car on the driveway? Had they gone on dirty weekends together, glee-fully chinking glasses of fizz in a seafood restaurant somewhere miles away, safe in the knowledge that they wouldn't be spotted?

It made Kerry feel ill. As with the house, the uncertainty of it was driving her crazy. She felt she wouldn't be happy 'moving forwards' in the big house – she hated that expression, but it seemed apposite – until she knew for sure what had or hadn't gone on.

It was a turning point in her life. One which, if it all worked out, would herald a new Kerry, she thought. A homeowner, no longer living in a rented garage in her mum's garden. A responsible grown-up. She'd give up drinking. She might even venture onto a dating app, try and find someone. After all, it would be a lot easier when she had a proper house to welcome them to. She'd always been far too embarrassed to even consider letting anyone other than Sharon see the garage.

Right, she thought, cracking her knuckles. Miss Smith, where are you now?

Where should she even start? Think rationally, she told herself. There was no point in looking at online phone directories or anything like that – there must be thousands of A. Smiths locally. Kerry hadn't known where she lived back then and anyway, the chances that she would be still in the same house were slim. She was also fairly sure that Miss Smith would have got married at some point.

Especially once Dad had died.

Or perhaps she was being hasty again. She didn't know for sure that there had been anything going on between them. After all, that was the reason for her quest; to try and find out. But through force of habit she couldn't help wondering if Dad had been the reason Miss S hadn't come close to getting married before that. She must have been in her mid to late twenties when she'd taught Kerry, the sort of age where most women who wanted a family were thinking of settling down.

Kerry looked up the website of the Salisbury Choral Society, the choir at which her mum and dad had first met Miss Smith. They had a huge number of performance photographs in their gallery page, both past and present, and she spent a painful hour zooming in on blurry faces to see if she recognised anyone. All the choir members looked middle-aged or older and she thought there was a good chance that Miss Smith had stayed in the choir, if she was still local. Mum got booted out about six years before her death – you had to re-audition every few years and she had been devastated to learn that she no longer cut the mustard, as she'd sadly said.

Kerry shook her head to try and dispel the mental image of the last concert she'd taken her mother to, only a couple of years ago. All Mum's friends were singing in it and Kerry remembered asking her then if Miss Smith was still a member of the choir. At that stage she'd been merely curious to see her again, and planned to monitor any interactions she and Mum had at the post-concert mingle. The weird thing, though, was that Kerry couldn't for the life of her recall what Mum's answer had been. Miss Smith definitely hadn't been in the soprano ranks at that event, but whether that was because she'd moved away, or just hadn't been singing in that particular concert, eluded Kerry, much to her irritation.

What she did remember was squeezing Mum's hand under the tartan blanket she'd brought along to keep on her lap in the chilly cathedral. Tears were running down her mother's face as she listened to the music; perhaps regret and disappointment that this part of her life had ended, or because she was still grieving for Dad all those years later. Music always reminded her of him.

Poor Mum, Kerry thought.

She couldn't find Miss Smith anywhere in the more recent choral photos – unless she just didn't recognise her, now that she must be approaching sixty. She was sure she would, though. Her face was etched into Kerry's memory. Not the way she'd

looked at Mum and Dad's parties when she was disco-dancing,
nor standing in front of the blackboard with a piece of chalk in
her hand – but her expression in those naked photos. A veneer
of seduction and pride only barely papering over deep cracks of
shame and defiance.

Kerry felt angry with her father all over again. How could
he have encouraged Miss Smith to do that? Or even, if she had
been the one who wanted to do it in the first place, for whatever
reason, how could he have agreed to let her?

Kerry's back was stiff from hunching over her laptop and
she felt as though her eyes were bugging out, so she took a little
walk around the garden, stuffed a laundry basketful of dirty
clothes into the washing machine, had a stretch, then decided to
try a different tack.

To her knowledge, Miss Smith had taught at her old school
for some years. It had been her first teaching role since qualify-
ing, Kerry remembered her saying once, and she was still there
after Beth left, so that must have been at least a decade or so.
When Kerry thought of her as a teacher she did recall her being
a bit green, actually; afraid to raise her voice to the more rowdy
kids and prone to blushes. Once, Kerry heard on the grapevine,
she'd run out of a classroom in tears when one of the boys made
a lewd comment to her face.

She googled the school and scanned the staff lists without
any expectations. Who stayed working in the same place for
their entire teaching career? Hardly anybody, she'd have
thought, although it wasn't out of the question. If Miss Smith
had been, at a guess, about thirty in 1993, she wouldn't even be
sixty yet.

Unsurprisingly though, there were no Miss Smiths listed.
Kerry tried a couple of other search terms: *Anita Smith History
Salisbury*, *Anita Smith Tutor Salisbury*, before running out of
inspiration.

She typed *Anita Smith + Salisbury* into the Facebook

search engine and was surprised that there weren't as many hits as she'd thought. None of them though, going by the profile pics and ages, looked as if they were the one she wanted.

Finally she tried the school, to see if they had a current Facebook page. They didn't, but to her utter astonishment, she got a result for a group with about three thousand members, Westwood St Thomas Alumni. Because Kerry had neither any nostalgia for her secondary school years, nor any urge to contact anybody from those days ever again, it would never have occurred to her to search for a group like this. It was a public page, so she didn't have to request membership to be able to start scrolling down the posts.

They were mostly along the lines of, *Hey guys, does anyone remember me? I was known as Chunk*, or, *Where has the time gone? Thirty-nine years since we left school! Here's me in Miss Atkins' class.*

Kerry tutted. Did these people not have lives to live?

One post caught her eye:

Does anyone remember old Mr Emory? 'Dick'? Is he still around or has he popped his clogs? He was strict as anything but a brilliant teacher. I'd never have got my O levels if it wasn't for him!!

She read the responses, which varied from rude – *That ancient git? Threw a blackboard rubber at my head once, made me see stars* – to helpful: *His daughter lives four doors up from my mum, I'll find out for you.* But nobody said, *Why do you want to know?* or challenged the original poster in any way.

Kerry could do the same, she thought slowly. People were bound to remember Miss Smith. She'd been so young and pretty. All the boys fancied her and all the girls wanted to be like her.

Kerry didn't want to post under her own name, though,

because she didn't want anybody to remember her, in case they had gone on to the same college and been privy to her later shame. So she created a new Facebook profile under the name Katherine Jones, a deliberately bland surname, and added a profile photo of a boring, cross-looking dog she found on some-one's Instagram. She decided against a cute puppy or anything comment-worthy in case it led to conversation openers. There'd been at least three Katherine/Catherine/Kathryns in her year, she seemed to recall, so hopefully nobody would challenge her. She could just pretend that Jones was her married name and if anybody asked her what her maiden name had been, she was under no obligation to reply. There was no need even to say which year she'd been in.

Kerry felt a swell of excitement and nerves in her throat as she joined the group – you had to join in order to be allowed to contribute – and composed her post.

Who remembers lovely Miss Smith? Anita, I think her first name was. She taught history in the 80s and early 90s, maybe longer. She was quite young and really gorgeous, I seem to recall. Would love to find out if she's still local. Anyone know if she got married and changed her name? I'm guessing she probably did at some point. Would love to get in touch with her.

She re-read it, then edited out the first 'would love to' and the 'lovely'. People might think she was stalking Miss Smith if she was too effusive. Although she left in the 'really gorgeous' as she thought it would jog some memories, probably the boys'.

Then, with her heart in her mouth, she hit 'post', and there it was, at the top of the page.

Kerry sat staring at it for a good ten minutes or so, but nobody commented on or liked it, so she forced herself out of Facebook and into the safer, more reassuring environs of Casino

World, where she allowed herself to be soothed by the turn of cards in Solitaire. It took her five goes before she won a game, but the reward of the Slinky-like graphics of completed card suits bouncing across the screen worked its usual magic. Winning always made her feel that all was, at least temporarily, right with her world. Even better when she muted the irritatingly tinny and jingly soundtrack and put on Vaughan Williams' *Sea Symphony* instead. The music was so stirring and monumental that it almost allowed her to kid herself that playing online Solitaire was a noble activity...

She had nothing else to do except compulsively refresh the Facebook alumni page, so she gave herself permission to keep playing cards instead. She was trying to win in fewer goes and faster times, and once she started she found it difficult to stop, but today she didn't even attempt to, even after she felt herself getting bored with the repetitiveness of it. It was the challenge.

Over the next three days Kerry had a few comments on her post and a smattering of 'likes', but nothing in any way helpful, all the commenters merely saying they did remember Miss Smith and agreeing with her statement about how lovely she had been. Nobody queried who Kerry was or why she was asking. She didn't recognise the profile pictures of any of the commenters – in fact, anybody at all on the site.

It was so strange, she thought. Many of these people must have sat in classrooms with her for five years. They'd have made cheese and onion pies together in Home Economics, parsed sentences in French, sketched vases in Art, and yet she could pass any of them on the street without a clue of their shared teenage experiences. She had the uncomfortable feeling that she had somehow erased her own past. Nobody remembered her, and she remembered nothing of those years. She was only ever recognised because she was a postwoman.

Sharon, on the other hand, had an almost forensic recollection of her school years. She still knew all the words to the school song – Kerry hadn't even remembered there *was* a school song. Sharon could recite the first and last names of all her teachers as well as most of her classmates, which parts she played in every school production, entire verses of poems she'd done in English in Year Nine. Kerry found it weird. How could Sharon's brain have any room left in it, with all that old stuff cluttering it up? Or perhaps her own brain had replaced all her memories with lists of postcodes and names of the residents in care homes to whom she delivered mail.

It was day four of checking Facebook before anything useful popped up. Kerry was beginning to think it had been a waste of time and was on the verge of abandoning it as a line of enquiry, as there was suddenly so much else to sort out at home. She'd never get it all done before she went back to work. There would be no more coming in and zonking out on the sofa in the annexe – she still had a vast amount of cleaning and clearing to do. She was half expecting to find another drawer full of Dad's negatives and couldn't stop wondering if there were other photos of Miss Smith still in there – that would be all the proof she needed to show Beth she hadn't imagined it – but nothing so far, outside of old family albums.

Kerry had just got in from a supermarket shopping expedition, kicked off her shoes and made herself some cheese on toast before she logged in to her Facebook on the iPad (she intentionally didn't have the app on her phone, for the same reason that she didn't have any Solitaire apps either. Too much temptation).

Her heart jumped to see that she had a new comment and she was so distracted to see the notification that she rammed half a slice of the molten cheese on toast in at once, burning the roof of her mouth.

She really should learn to cook, she thought, doubling over with the scalding pain. This was the third time in a week she'd had cheese on toast. There had only been room for a microwave in the garage, so 'proper' cooking had only been attempted on rare, fraught occasions in the big house. Her mother, like Beth, had loved to cook, so Kerry had always let her do it.

No excuses now, Kerry thought as she huffed air in and out of her mouth to try and cool the tender skin. She entertained a brief fantasy that she'd get herself on a cookery course and...

... and then what? Her mood plummeted. What would be the point, if she lost the house? It wasn't as if the inevitably tiny studio flat that would follow would be big enough for her to ever have anybody round for dinner. Her 'dining' table in the annexe had been a metal folding garden table barely big enough to seat two people around, and her imaginary dinner guest would need to be squashed in so close to the wall that unless he or she was the size of a toddler, they'd be pressed right up against the edge of the table. She'd have to take that bloody table with her, if she moved.

Kerry shook away the negative thoughts. She didn't have anybody in her life she liked enough to want to cook for anyway, so it was all moot.

The new comment under her post in the school alumni group said,

Oh wow, Miss Smith! I had a HUGE crush on her. She's living up in Trowbridge these days – my mate Johnny from school (he doesn't do Facebook, so he's not on here) bumped into her last year and she recognised him and stopped to talk. He said she still looks really good. She left WST in '99 when she started a family.

This was so much information in one go that Kerry felt she could hardly take it in – at least it took her mind off her burned mouth. Trowbridge! A family! So Miss Smith's name wasn't Smith any more. And she was still relatively local. Kerry felt dizzy with revelation.

She didn't want to bombard the guy with all the questions

currently bubbling up in her, so she merely gave the comment a thumbs-up, and said *Will PM you.* She didn't recognise the name – Tim Deyes. She was sure there hadn't been anybody by that name in her year, so she thought she'd be safe to contact him. His profile photo wasn't much help; he was just a normal, average-looking, middle-aged guy in a baseball cap and shades, pictured gesturing expansively at the view from the top of a mountain somewhere. She'd never have been able to pick him out of a line-up, let alone identify him as someone she went to school with.

She messaged him immediately, hoping he would look out for it and that her note wouldn't languish in his 'Other' folder.

Hi Tim, could I pick your brains a bit more please? Really want to try and get in touch with Miss S. She was a close friend of my parents.

And she wanted to find out just how close.

I don't suppose she told your friend what her married name is? Or which street she lives in? Any other information, like what she's doing now, or if she's on Facebook or anything? Much appreciated, Katherine.

He replied very quickly, somewhat to Kerry's surprise.

Hi, no worries, happy to help if I can. Been trying to remember what Johnny said about the conversation. She was with her husband and she introduced the husband as Glenn, or Gary – or maybe Greg. Something beginning with G. I remembered thinking, lucky sod, to be married to Miss S! LOL. Pretty sure Johnny said no surname, because I remember asking. The husband's on the town council, or was trying to get voted on. They said something about local elections, and that he was

*campaigning for Labour. I only remember because I had a
vague thought of looking him up but forgot about it in the end.
Might be an idea for you, though, if you're trying to track her
down.*

*So, what years were you at WST? I was only there for GCSEs,
we didn't move to the area until '91. I'm not in touch with
anyone I went to school with. I just joined Facebook to see if I
could connect with anyone I remembered in local groups and
so on but haven't seen anyone I recognise yet! Moved to
London after A levels, like most people did, and only just
moved back here. Trying to find my feet. What are the decent
pubs in Salisbury these days? In my day it was the Pheasant
and the Wig & Quill. Hope you don't mind me picking your
brains in return. Best, Tim.*

Kerry did mind. The 'LOL' irritated her, and she felt almost
affronted that this random guy was trying to make conversation.
Why was he, anyway? He didn't know her from Adam, nor she
him. And it couldn't have been that he was trying to pick her
up, since she didn't have a profile photo. She was tempted to
just write a brief 'thanks' back and ignore his questions, but
then she reluctantly supposed that would have been rude, when
he'd gone out of his way to help her.

And he had really helped – hopefully all she had to do now
was look up Labour councillors, or wannabe councillors, in
Trowbridge, narrow them down by first initial, and then she'd
have Miss Smith's married name. It would be a huge step
forward. She owed him.

Kerry wrote back:

*Hi Tim, thanks so much for that, that's brilliant. I think I'd
have been in the year above you, if you started GCSEs in '91.
I'm also not in touch with anyone from those days – prefer to*

forget about them, frankly. School wasn't too bad, but college was hideous for me, I dropped out before exams. Stayed in the area though. Never lived anywhere else! Re pubs... hm, well, both the ones you mention are still going, and used to be generally pretty lively at weekends, before Covid. Cosy Club is nice for food. My favourite is the New Inn though. If you remember, it became a no-smoking pub in about '89 I think, and all us kids immediately avoided it like the plague, but then when the smoking ban came in it was just the same as everywhere else, and it started getting better again then. Nice old place.

She paused in her typing. If she asked him any questions in return then he'd feel obliged to reply again, and before they knew it, they really would be in an actual conversation.

She did not have actual conversations with people she didn't know, on or offline.

But then she thought, oh, sod it, why not? She could look at it as practice, in the unlikely event that she ever decided to do internet dating. It was just a bit of chatting, to help out someone newly returned to the area.

Feeling a brief frisson of something approaching excitement, she continued. Look at me, she thought, interacting with an actual man! Then it subsided again. When she thought about it, he didn't feel like a *real* man. It didn't feel much different to turning over cards in an online Solitaire game. Passed the time, though, she supposed.

So, what about you? Have you moved back for work? Did you like school, apart from the obvious enjoyment of lusting after Miss Smith?!

She hit 'send' and, while she waited, took the opportunity to browse his profile to which, since he had replied to her message request, the site had granted her access. There were a few other photos of him and she saw that he was bald as a coot without the cap on. He had a nice enough face though, nothing remarkable, just pleasant. His profile was, like Kerry's, fairly minimalistic. Nobody listed under 'Relationships', 'Hobbies' or 'Relatives'.

He replied straightaway. Bit keen, she decided, already thinking a bit less of him for it.

Haha, well, that wasn't quite all I did at school, although it did seem to take up a lot of time :) To be fair it actually wasn't all that enjoyable; the lusting, I mean. At fifteen it was more like the torture of unrequited love! Half the time I was convinced that we'd get married and live happily ever after, and the other half – the more realistic half – was in torment that she had no idea of my feelings, and I couldn't make her see them without making a total tit of myself. Fortunately I managed to make it through GCSEs without declaring myself. That's one thing I have been forever grateful for. But I hated school and, like you, college. I was really badly bullied in sixth form – you'd think everyone would have outgrown the idea of bullying by then, but I must have been a particularly tempting target! I think that's why I stayed a bit obsessed with Miss Smith, because she was so nice to me, even after I'd left school and gone to college. I found out where she lived and sent her a Valentine's card, can you believe it? Embarrassing or what? Hopefully she never knew it was from me.

I've just started a job at Broughtons, the insurance brokers out on the London Road. First week done, but my colleagues don't seem like a very sociable lot. They either seem to have young families, or they're in their sixties with very few social skills. Nobody our sort of age. Even my friend Johnny, the one who bumped into Miss Smith, recently moved to Scotland. It's a little bit depressing. Are you new to Facebook, by the way?

Your profile doesn't say much. Was hoping to see a photo of you, to see if I remembered you. Can I friend-request you?

You won't recognise me, Kerry thought. I am totally forgettable. And then she thought, ah, he really is lonely. She could identify. The bit about the bullying made her feel sad for him – and the part about the unrequited love made her laugh.

She'd had a crush on a boy at work once, about twenty years ago; Craig. He had the biggest chimney-brush eyelashes she'd ever seen on a guy, and the slimmest hips. She used to hang around his frame while he was sorting and they'd have a bit of banter – but then she found out he had a tiny little gorgeous girlfriend and went into a deep funk of depression. She'd always known he would never fancy someone like her and felt stupid for thinking she might be in with the faintest chance.

Craig left the Post Office few months later to retrain as a plumber, but she still sometimes thought of him and what might have been – if she'd had a different face, a different body, a different personality...

Actually this isn't my real profile, she admitted in the next message. *I created it just to message the school group, because I didn't want any of them to recognise me. Just want to forget about those days. I think that's why I've stuck working for Royal Mail all these years, because I do fit in there... at least, I think I do...*

Then she stopped and deleted the last couple of lines. What on earth was she thinking? She didn't know him! She supposed it was because he had confided in her; she had felt an urge to reciprocate. But she didn't want to terminate the conversation either. She was enjoying it. She so rarely got to talk to new people – apart from small talk with people on her round – that somewhere along the line she had decided it was because she didn't like it, when it was probably just that she hardly ever got the chance.

I'll friend-request you from my real profile, she concluded instead. *You won't recognise me, though, even if you did remember me. I look really different. And my name is actually Kerry, not Katherine.*

Then, before she could change her mind, she switched profiles to her regular one and, typing his name into the search bar, found him and sent a request. There weren't a huge number of photographs of her on her own profile either, just one or two, but she'd vetted them first and they were acceptable enough that hopefully they wouldn't put him off their chat. Even so, she literally had to sit on her hands waiting to see if he accepted or not. She was worried he'd look at her photos and change his mind about wanting to continue the conversation.

Kerry went to the loo, to pass the time, and grabbed a beer from the fridge on her way back to the table. She poured it too fast into a glass and didn't wait for the head to settle before taking a big swig, which made her hiccup, burp, then wonder if living on her own was making her lose the few social skills she used to have, once upon a time.

It was a good thing she didn't want a man, she thought. She'd never be able to live with one. The thought of sharing her space with the male equivalent of herself made her shudder. The random smells and noises, bodily detritus and excretions... yuck. Why would anyone want to? Let alone having always to consider someone else's feelings and accommodate their baggage, both emotional and literal. Not for her, she decided.

Yet even though she wasn't thinking of Tim Deyes in any sort of romantic way, she actually punched the air when she saw that he had accepted her friend request. He hadn't dismissed her as soon as he'd seen what she looked like!

It all felt so unexpected and momentous that she temporarily forgot that she was now a good deal closer to finding Miss Smith. She was making a new friend, and the thrill of it felt like a deeper glow than the hit of the beer buzz.

FIFTEEN

Kerry continued to sort and clean all weekend, neither seeing nor speaking to another soul. She had filled twelve bin bags with her mum's dusty old plastic handbags, dried-up cosmetics and elderly underwear to be binned, then another six with clothes and ornaments worth taking to the charity shop. Then she spent hours slaving away with dusters and polish, tidying and re-ordering everything from her mother's stack of copies of *The Lady* magazine to her bookshelves, stuffed full of yellowing Georgette Heyers and ancient P.D. Jameses. It had taken hours to alphabetise all the books, even while she had every intention of packing up the lot and taking them to the tip or to a charity shop at some point down the line. It was just the first stage in the process, she told herself as she flipped through the pages of every book and magazine, vaguely wondering if, years ago, Mum might have tucked that contact sheet of Miss Smiths inside the cover of something and then forgotten about it. Nothing materialised, but Kerry decided it had been worth looking, for her peace of mind.

By Monday morning, the house was looking a lot less cluttered, and Kerry's muscles burned. When her phone vibrated, at around nine, she was sitting on the kitchen floor with her head stuck in one of her mother's kitchen cupboards, trying to extract the lids of all the myriad Tupperware boxes her mum had kept shoved in there in an untidy pile, with a view to matching them up and binning any of the boxes whose lids were MIA. Someone ought to invent a storage system for Tupperware, she thought, to prevent it all sliding out every time you opened the door. Surely it couldn't be hard. She extracted herself and straightened up with difficulty, reaching for the phone on the kitchen table. Beth's name was flashing on the screen.

Kerry stared at it with trepidation, wondering if she was ringing to apologise or to have another go at her about the house – could be either, she thought. She was tempted to ignore it, but knew if she let it go to voicemail Beth would badger her with more calls and texts until she answered. She seemed to take it as a personal affront if you weren't available to her straightaway, and things were so frosty between them at the moment, Kerry didn't want to further antagonise her.

'I know you're at work,' Beth chirruped when Kerry reluctantly answered. 'But I just thought I'd try and catch you before you set off on your round, to find out if you've had your meeting with the financial adviser yet. When was it?'

'Beth, you know that Nige gets his knickers in a twist if we take personal calls while we're sorting.'

This was true, although Kerry omitted to tell Beth she had taken ten days off to get settled into the big house.

'That's never bothered you before!'

'He's gunning for me. I've had it up to here with that idiot.'

'Where are you now?' Beth asked nervously. 'He can't hear you, can he?'

'No – actually, I'm at home. I had some leave to take.'

'So why mention Nige, if he's not even there?'

The edge was straight back in Beth's voice, but Kerry

couldn't really blame her. She was not good at lying. She ought to take some lessons from Sharon, she thought, cursing herself for giving the game away so soon.

'He was just on my mind, that's all.' Kerry bit her lip. 'Anyway. I did some research online and there's no point in me seeing a financial adviser. They'd only say that even if we sold the house – which I have no intention of doing – I'd still have nowhere near enough to buy a place of my own, once we've paid off Mum's mortgage.'

An oven timer beeped in the background and Kerry wondered what Beth was cooking so early in the morning. A sugar-free cake, probably. She was always baking, but because carbs and sugar were her sworn enemies, the results were inevitably joyless and often inedible. Kerry felt sorry for Jitz and the kids. She heard the sounds of an oven door opening, the quick, quiet roar from its interior, and the clatter of a tin onto a cooling rack.

'Kerry, why are you so negative all the time? They might say you do have enough! And you'd have a lump sum to use for rent if not.'

'I've done those online mortgage calculations and I don't. Plus I don't want to rent anywhere else. Can you please stop criticising literally every single thing I say or do? It's really starting to get me down.'

'I don't!' Beth replied hotly. 'I'm just trying to make you look at life in a more optimistic and positive way.'

'All right, Pollyanna, but no, you aren't. You're trying to make me agree with what you want, what you think, and I'm sorry, but when it comes to what Mum said about me and the house, and about Dad and Miss Smith, I know what I was told, and what I saw, and I'm not having you telling me I was wrong about either of them!'

Beth almost shouted, so harsh and sudden that it hurt Kerry's ear: '*Kerry!* What is *wrong* with you? No way was Dad having an affair with Miss Smith, or anyone! The photos must have been of some life model that they had down at the camera club.'

'Beth. You didn't see the pictures; I did. I'm telling you, it was Miss Smith, on the rug in Dad's studio. I've still got that rug! There is absolutely no doubt in my mind. And even if it was at the camera club, are you telling me that *Miss Smith* would have posed naked there, in front of men whose kids she taught? There's no chance! They didn't even ever have life models. I asked Mum once.'

'God, Kerry, you have to let it go. You saw those photos, what – twenty-five years ago? You got it fixed in your head that it was Miss Smith, and now you can't picture it as anything else. But I'm telling you, it couldn't possibly have been her. It *wasn't* her!'

'How do you *know*? We were teenagers – well, you were practically still a kid. Mum and Dad could've had all kinds of secrets. For all we know, they had an open marriage.'

Beth snorted with disgust. 'Of course they didn't.'

'Again, Beth; how do you know? They'd hardly have admitted it, and certainly not to us.'

'Right. So my next question is – why do you care so much?'

This was a good question. Why did she? Kerry took a moment before answering.

'Because it matters to me. If Dad was having an affair, then I want to know. It's important. But more importantly, if there is a completely innocent explanation, then I can stop worrying and accept that our folks really did have the amazing marriage that it looked like from the outside. And you know what else? I'm going to find out. I'm going to track her down and ask her myself.'

Kerry heard Beth actually growl with frustration. There was a long silence before she spoke again.

'I need to go and get this cake out of the tin before it goes soggy. So do a bit of detective work, if you want to. Just don't tell me if you find out that they were having an affair, I really don't want to know. They weren't, and I'm completely sure it wasn't even her in the photos, so neither of us has anything to worry about, do we?'

'Whatever, Beth. If I do decide to see a financial adviser, I'll let you know what they say – but only if it's the news that I can get a mortgage to buy you out of your half of the house. So when you don't hear otherwise, you can assume it's a no and I'll be contesting the will instead.'

'You wouldn't.'

'I damn well will. This is my future home we're talking about. You're always on at me to get motivated and do something. Now that I'm planning exactly that, you hate it.'

'I won't let you.'

The conversation was beginning to veer out of control, like a car skidding across two lanes of an icy dual carriageway. She could feel it going but was powerless to stop it.

'As if I need your permission for anything. Wind your neck in, Beth. I'm sick of you bossing me around the whole time.'

Beth snorted again. 'Bossing you around? Or trying to motivate you to get off your arse and change your life? It's a fine line. Why don't you ever want *more* for yourself?'

There were so many potential replies to that question that Kerry didn't know which one to pick. In the end she plumped for a churlish, 'Have you not been listening? I *do* want more for myself. I want to live in the house I was promised I could, by Mum. Why don't you just fuck off and stop judging me?'

Beth tutted. 'I have to say, Kerry, I'm really starting to lose patience with you. And so is Jitz.'

'Jitz? What the hell has Jitz got to do with it? Anyway, he only ever says whatever he thinks you want to hear, so it's no wonder. You never give the poor guy the chance to have an opinion of his own.'

Kerry heard Beth's outraged intake of breath. 'How dare you insult my husband? You've got a nerve. Just because you're jealous of me and my life, you have to start picking holes—'

'I'm not jealous, you thick cow! Why can't you get it into your vain head that we are two completely different people and what you want is not the same as what I want? I wouldn't want your life for a moment, stuck at home running round after two whiny kids and a husband.'

Kerry's imaginary car was now fully out of control, whirling round in expansive skidding circles, crashing through the central reservation and taking out whatever was in its path.

Beth went quiet for a moment, then: 'What I want is to be happy. And I wish that's what you wanted for yourself too. And please don't insult me like that.'

What Kerry actually wanted for herself at that moment was to punch a wall. Beth wound her up more than any other living person, including Nasty Nige. 'Of course I want to be happy, who doesn't? I *am* happy. I've got a job I like, most of the time and, oh for God's sake, why am I having to go over this again?'

'A job you enjoy so much that you're always complaining that your line manager's got it in for you?'

Again Beth made this sound like it was Kerry's fault. It made her blood boil.

She did feel a bit bad about calling her sister a thick cow. Although not bad enough to apologise, not yet. As she had been after the argument at Beth's house, she would usually be in tears of rage and frustration by now, but today the anger was so ice-white inside her, it compressed into a pillar of resolve and unexpressed bitterness.

'You keep telling me I need to take more responsibility for my life. Now I am, I'm fighting to live in the house I was promised, and I'm going to track down Miss Smith to get some answers to something that's been bothering me for years – and you're criticising me for all of that, too? I can't win!'

Beth could never tolerate anybody calling her out on anything, because she had a firm and unshakeable belief that she was always right. At that moment Kerry loathed her. She steamed on:

'I am so sick of you making me feel like a failure! And I'll tell you this once more to make sure you have really heard it: I am not going to let you make me sell that house. You'll have to take me to court if you want me out because I'm bloody well going to live there!'

SIXTEEN

When Kerry finally managed to winch open her eyelids the next morning, all memories of the rest of the previous day were initially a complete blur. But after she'd staggered down the stairs, the three empty wine bottles on the kitchen counter helped explain her horrifically pounding skull. Thank goodness she was still on leave. How could she possibly have drunk *three* bottles of wine? Surely at least one of them had already been open. It hadn't been more than two and a half, max...

Not that this made it anything to be proud of.

Either way, she didn't feel robust enough to do much that day, other than try and mentally absorb it all. It was a sunny afternoon, so she decided to get the padded lounger out of the shed and lie in the garden, in the jean shorts that she'd accidentally cut off too short to ever be seen in public in.

She lay out on the lawn in the big house's back garden, the hot sun burning her cheeks, lulled by the busy sparrows chirping and the symphony of bees bumping in and out of Mum's foxgloves. She imagined their little feet enjoying the velvety softness and cool interior of the flowers. They also loved the huge spiky mahonia bush next to the patio, ugly as all hell, but bees adored the bright yellow blooms. She remembered her mother telling her this and felt her presence then, reclining in a chair next to her, her bubblegum-pink toenails catching her eye as her toes waggled with pleasure. Mum had loved a pedicure. She'd loved her garden. She'd loved Kerry... hadn't she?

Of course she had, Kerry chided herself. She had no idea why her mother hadn't kept her promise and made arrangements for her to live in the house, but she didn't want to let doubts cloud her memories of her, in the same way that finding the photos had done to her memories of her dad.

Kerry stared across the garden, missing her mother terribly. The grass needed cutting and bindweed wound itself enthusiastically around the bushes in the borders. She vowed not to let the garden go to rack and ruin – she wasn't a particularly good gardener herself, but she'd done enough under her Mum's supervision that she knew basically what was required.

Tomorrow, though. She felt far too wrecked to do anything about it today.

She was just about to drop off into one of those fuzzy bucolic naps which are part-relaxation, part-hangover, when she could have sworn she heard voices from inside the house. She sat up, blood rushing from her head, listening intently. Perhaps the neighbours were out in their garden? But the neighbours were a very elderly couple on one side, who rarely ventured outside, and an old lady called Joy on the other who lived alone. Both their gardens were like wildernesses and not places she had ever seen them enjoy, even in lovely weather like this. Plus, the voices did not sound old and quavery.

One was male, posh and assertive. Kerry couldn't make out the words but judging by the unfamiliar braying laugh, it wasn't anybody she knew. They must be at the front door. Voices sometimes floated over the roof to the back garden – although she hadn't heard a car on the gravel. She stood up slowly, to make sure dizziness didn't make her stumble, and went barefoot into the big house via the kitchen door. The coldness of the tiles under her hot feet made her gasp, but then she heard the voices again – in the hallway. Definitely in the hallway! There were people actually in the house. What the hell? Burglars, knowing that Mum had died?

Kerry was about to grab a knife from the block and confront the intruders when she heard a familiar tinkling laugh, and a voice she did know, very well:

'Well, of course, we'll make sure it looks a lot better than this before you take the photos. A lick of paint out here will make all the difference.'

Sodding *Beth*. Kerry couldn't believe it... and yet, she could. She cursed the locksmith, whose first non-emergency appointment wasn't until next week. She should've found one who could have come sooner.

Kerry burst around the kitchen door into the hall, silent in her bare feet, and they both jumped out of their skins. 'What the hell do you think you're doing?' she snarled, ignoring the man with Beth, an overweight guy in a too-short suit.

He appeared to be in his late twenties, with slicked-back hair and the spongy belly of someone who never exercised. The sight of that belly reminded Kerry that she too must have looked an absolute fright – her way-too-short shorts, bikini top, reddening and equally doughy belly, not to mention her unmade-up face, puce from sun and puffy from alcohol, and her uncombed hair sticking in all directions.

Naturally, Beth didn't have a silky-smooth auburn hair out of place. She was in a crisp white shirt tucked into linen tailored shorts and looked as if she'd just stepped off the set of a catalogue fashion shoot. Her legs were long and tanned.

Kerry hated her.

'You nearly gave me a heart attack!' Beth blustered. Kerry could tell she was dying to snarl back at her but didn't dare.

'I said, what are you doing here? Who is this?'

The tubby guy strode forward, holding out his hand. Kerry didn't take it.

'Hi, you must be the co-owner, Miss Tucker? I'm Henry, from Cavendish and Wells. Your sister asked me to come and do a valuation. I'm sorry if there's been a mi—'

'Did she now?' Kerry said, crossing her arms over her chest; mostly to hide it.

'Kerry, why aren't you at work?' Beth asked. 'I thought you'd be at work, since you were off last week.'

'And my car on the driveway didn't suggest that I might still be on holiday?'

'I thought you must have got a lift,' Beth said weakly.

'So you thought you'd sneak an estate agent in, while I wasn't here, when we are nowhere near agreeing on the best course of action for us and the house?'

Beth spread her arms out, palms up, in a gesture of resignation. 'There's no harm in getting the facts together, is there? We need an accurate valuation to be able to work out the figures.'

Kerry turned to Henry, who was pretending to be fascinated by the hall lampshade, which must have been tricky, because it was a horrible old faded yellow one, probably as old as Kerry herself, with a lace trim hanging off the bottom of it where it had come unglued. She made a mental note to buy a new one ASAP.

'I'm sorry, you've had a wasted journey. This house is not going to be up for sale, not any time soon. Please leave.'

Beth grabbed her forearm and Kerry shook it off. They faced each other, hackles up, like a pair of feral cats fighting over half a dead pigeon.

'Come on, Kerry. We're here now. I would like a valuation. You can't refuse that much. It's not like I'd put it on the market behind your back! I wouldn't do that. I was going to tell you I'd been over.'

Kerry was not convinced. 'You're not legally allowed to put

it on the market without my permission anyway, even if you did want to,' she said, while Henry shifted awkwardly from foot to foot in the hall. 'I thought we were spending some time thinking about what the best thing – the *right* thing – to do is?'

She said 'right' very pointedly.

'We are,' Beth said. 'And we both need to know the value of the house. Could you give us a minute, please?' she asked Henry, as she literally dragged Kerry through the kitchen towards the garden.

Her hand was cool and her grip firm on the hot skin of Kerry's forearm. Once they were outside, Beth turned to face her again, her eyes searching.

'Kerry,' she said urgently. 'Please. I don't want us to fall out over this! Mum would have been so upset.'

The obvious response, Kerry thought, was why then had Mum not made her wishes clear? Why had Mum let her believe for all those years that she could live here? By not stating this in the will, she had allowed Beth to accuse her of misremembering or lying.

'I don't want to fight with you either,' she managed, with great effort. Now that Henry wasn't privy to their conversation, she couldn't stop hungover tears springing into her eyes. 'But Mum promised me, honestly, she did. I wouldn't forget something like that.'

'It's an awful situation,' Beth said.

Kerry noticed that she hadn't agreed with her.

'We have to do whatever we can to resolve it, amicably. Please, let's get this valuation done and then have another chat when we've had more time to think, or get advice? Perhaps Jitz and I can lend you enough to get a mortgage on somewhere better than a studio flat. Let's try and be creative; come up with a solution.'

Beth was trying, Kerry knew, and she could tell she felt bad too.

'OK,' she said reluctantly. 'As long as I don't suddenly wake up one morning to find Henry hammering a "For Sale" board into the gravel.'

'Of course not. Good. Thank you, Kerry.'

Beth sounded massively relieved, even though absolutely nothing was in any way resolved. It reminded Kerry of when they were little girls of about five and seven, and Beth had drawn a felt-tip picture of herself on the bedroom wall because she thought the wall looked too bare. When they heard Mum's footsteps on the stairs, Beth had thrust the red felt-tip pen into Kerry's hand, and their mum believed she'd caught her in the act. Kerry got the blame and a few sharp smacks on the leg, her protestations of innocence going unheeded. The expression on Beth's face now reminded her of that day; mingled relief, guilt and smugness.

The drawing on the wall hadn't even been *of* her. It had clearly been Beth, because the hair had been red and straight, not orange and curly! It always rankled Kerry that their mum hadn't been able to see that, even when she'd been telling her, and it was obvious.

Kerry left Beth and Henry to it after that, crunching back across the gravel to the garage with her laptop. She didn't really want to be around when Beth realised she'd already moved into the big house. It would be obvious as soon as they went upstairs, since the spare bed was unmade, with her pyjamas lying on top of the duvet and her toiletries in the main bathroom. They seemed to have declared a temporary truce, so she thought it best if she removed herself from the possibility of another row.

Not that there was any reason she shouldn't be sleeping over there, Kerry thought defensively. No reason she couldn't enjoy a bit of space to herself while the house was empty. If

Beth did challenge her, she'd say she wanted to spend as much time in her childhood home as she could, while she still could.

The annexe seemed tiny, cluttered and oppressive after being in the big house for a few days. Kerry wondered how she'd been able to live so contentedly there for so many years. Climbing the ladder to the cabin bed was a pain in the neck. The bathroom was minuscule – the shower door only just opened wide enough to let her squeeze in before it ran up against the toilet. If she put on any weight, it would be actually unusable. There was no storage space (not that it mattered to her, since Mum had always let her store stuff in the big house).

For the first time, Kerry saw it through the eyes of a potential and objective new tenant. She had to be honest: a converted garage on the outskirts of a village four miles from town was unlikely to be anybody's idea of a dream dwelling. Perhaps this was part of the reason Beth was uninterested in the idea of a regular rental income, because she knew that Kerry was probably the only person mad enough to want to live there. It was a depressing thought, not least because it made her wonder if everybody did think she was mad. Was she mad? Had she wasted decades of her life – 'her best years', as Beth probably would have said – cloistered away in her garage like a dog in a crate?

She opened a new bottle of wine.

SEVENTEEN

Back at her sorting frame the next morning, Kerry felt hungover and low, deriving hardly any of the pleasure from sorting that she usually did. She'd gone to bed the previous night back in the garage and slept really badly, suddenly no longer feeling at home either there *or* in the big house. She was so unsettled by Beth and the estate agent that everything just felt wrong. Drinking a whole bottle of wine probably hadn't helped either – waking up hungover was starting to become the norm.

Sorting calmed her... usually. It was a sign of great unease that it did not appear to be working its habitual magic, either at home or here at work. Everything was irritating her, from the circulars to the bills and credit card statements in their bland typed envelopes as she shoved them into the correct slots.

'Did you have a nice holiday, Kerry sweetie?' Clarissa trilled from her frame. How on earth that woman was always so cheerful, Kerry had no idea, especially as she suffered from both IBS and a football-obsessed, perpetually complaining husband.

'It wasn't a holiday,' she replied, trying not to sound grumpy. 'I was just sorting out Mum's stuff; the house is a right old mess.'

'And I know how much you hate things being out of place!'

Normally this would have upset her, someone picking up on the fact that yes, she did have a slight tendency towards OCD. She put it down to living in the garage her whole adult life, where there was literally no room for any clutter, not if she wanted to be able to see the floor. Her mother had been a bit of a hoarder, another reason Kerry couldn't have countenanced moving in with her, even if Mum had wanted her to. It had also made it easy for Kerry to 'store' her unwanted stuff in her house. Perhaps that made her a hoarder by proxy, she wondered.

'Yup,' she said, and then swiftly changed the subject. 'Are you watching that new thing with Nicole Kidman in? I hear it's very good, but I haven't seen any of it yet.'

As Kerry knew she would, Clarissa immediately began to give her a blow-by-blow account of the plot and it enabled her to relax slightly, forcing her body into autopilot and her brain into receive mode as Clarissa's words washed over her.

Pick up stack of post, sort by postcode, further break down into road groups, then chronologically by number, then slot into appropriate section of the frame... She could practically do this in her sleep by now.

As always, any interesting-looking post caught her attention, and her hand stilled on a postcard. Glancing at the front of it, she did a double-take – it was her village. A glossy picturesque shot of the green looking immaculate, ducks sailing in obedient circles around the pond as if the photographer had choreographed them, the church and the pub in the background under a royal blue cloudless sky. If the shot had been any wider, the big house would have been in it too.

She discreetly turned it over, checking over her shoulder to make sure Nigel wasn't watching, as she fully intended to read more than the address. The writing was small and squiggly and it was signed 'A'. It was addressed to Mr and Mrs Mann.

Mann... she'd known someone called Mann. Her heart started to beat a bit faster.

'*Hi C&S,*' it began.

C Mann. Could it be *Chris* Mann? Kerry felt sick. She had not allowed herself to think about any of that lot for years. Last she heard he was living in London anyway. The address on the card was for the next village, one of the big detached houses up on the hill. She wondered if it could be his parents, having moved one village over? But she had a feeling that his dad had died soon after they left school; she was sure she remembered Mum mentioning it. And she'd never spotted any other mail with his name on it.

Beth had really fancied Chris. She'd got off with him that night when...

... *No. Don't go there. Don't think about it.*

It was too late; she was already thinking about it. She skim-read the card and started shaking. Her hangover dialled itself up a few more notches as bile rose in her throat and she knew she had to get out of there, otherwise she was going to be sick all over the post.

Kerry stuck the card in her back pocket and blundered out of the sorting office, making it to the weed-choked flowerbed in the car park just in time to vomit into it.

No sooner had she finished retching than she got in the car and drove home, not giving herself time to think about it, the post-card burning a hole in her shorts' pocket. Back in her garage, she texted Clarissa, asking her if she could explain to Nigel that she had left work because she'd been taken ill and if he didn't believe her, he was welcome to go and examine the evidence in the yard flowerbed. She felt bad, because it did leave her colleagues in a bit of a last-minute tight spot but she genuinely couldn't have gone out on her round. Her legs were like jelly and she'd dry-heaved all the way home in the car.

Kerry drank a glass of water with a shaking hand and laid

the postcard on the kitchen counter to examine it again. She
had so many questions about it. Who was 'A'? She couldn't
connect it with a name but it must have been someone who was
there that night.

> *Saw this and thought of you. Hope all well with you and yours.*
> *Happy memories of many a drunken night on this green in the*
> *mid-90s, right? College. White Lightning. Bad behaviour.*
> *LOL. A x*

Calm down, Kerry, she told herself. Hundreds of people
surely had drunken nights on that green over the years.

But what would the chances be of someone she didn't know
writing a postcard to C. Mann when one of the people present
that night in 1994 had been Chris Mann? Kerry racked her
brains to try and remember what she'd been blocking out for
decades. It had been Mum's fiftieth, she remembered that
much. She and Beth had gone over to the green. Beth had got
off with Chris. Who else had been there? Serena Jackson. She
was the one who'd laughed the most. Timothy Alcock, the little
creep. Lee Carlton, weasel, local vandal... even thinking of him
and his mate made Kerry's guts churn again. She didn't
remember anybody with the initial 'A'. The mate's name had
been Mutt, or something equally stupid. She'd definitely tried
to block *him* out of her memory.

 She still saw Lee Carlton around the village very occasionally, a barely functioning alcoholic with smeary tattoos on every
bit of exposed skin, and an overweight Staffy that he didn't look
after properly. His ma lived in a council bungalow up near the
village shop and Kerry was never quite sure if Lee lived with
her or if he lived in town and just visited – he never seemed to
get his own post to that address. On the few occasions they had
been in close-ish proximity they always pretended not to recognise each other (or at least Kerry pretended; Lee probably didn't

actually recognise her at all) and she always felt sick. Fortunately, she was generally only out and about in the village in the mornings, delivering the post, and judging by Lee's pallor and dark under-eye circles, Kerry gleaned he was most likely not a morning person.

Neither did he seem like the sort of person to buy, write and send a postcard of a village green to anybody. From Kerry's long experience of sneaking glances at other people's postcards, the vast majority of them were written by and to women.

Serena Jackson, then? Was the 'A' the initial of some sort of nickname? But even that seemed like a weird thing to do. For a moment, Kerry wondered whether it had been sent on purpose as a way of tormenting her, by someone who knew she worked for Royal Mail and that the village was on her round. Then she dismissed the thought. She knew she had a tendency to be a bit paranoid at times, but she wasn't *that* paranoid. And why would they, anyway? She had never reported what happened that night all those years ago, even though she should have done.

EIGHTEEN

For the rest of that day, Kerry tried to take her mind off the postcard by allowing herself to get sucked into an online wormhole – two, really; the school Facebook group, to see if anybody else had responded to her request for information about Miss Smith, and then a detailed search to work out what the legal position was when a house was co-owned and only one of the owners wanted to sell, something she'd been meaning to do since the estate agent's visit.

By 7 p.m., she'd learned that Beth did indeed have the option to apply for a court order to force her to agree to sell – which upset her so much that she opened a bottle of wine even though she'd sworn she was going to have an alcohol-free day – and discovered that there were no further bites on the alumni page. Although she did spend an interesting hour looking up as many of her classmates as she could recall. Without exception, she recognised none of them now.

Lee Carlton was on there, which surprised her. She wouldn't have put him down as a Facebook user (PornHub, yes, for sure), but his profile was set to private and she certainly had no intention of requesting him as a friend. His profile photo-

graph was of the hideously aggressive-looking Staffy she occasionally saw dragging him through the village.

Sometimes she wondered if her entire non-working life
would end up being lived through a screen. Perhaps she'd eventually quit her job, barricade herself inside the big house and
just never come out again. It wouldn't be too difficult. Grocery
shopping online, sufficient floor space to do exercise classes with
virtual instructors, a big garden to lie in and soak up some
Vitamin D, social media to meet her very paltry need to talk to
anybody else. She hardly ever went on holiday so wouldn't miss
that, and her only nights out were with Sharon – she didn't
think either of them would mourn the loss of those. It would
just be like permanent lockdown.

She found the idea worryingly appealing, even more so
after a bottle and a half of Chardonnay. Beth would never be
able to sell up then! It was when she realised she was actually
beginning to think of it as a serious option that she reluctantly
turned back to the task at hand: finding Miss Smith.

With no further information to go on, she re-read Tim's
original message about his friend's encounter with Miss Smith,
jotting down keywords: *town council, candidate,
Greg/Gary/Glenn (Graham? Grant?), left WSG 1999, had
family...*

Next, she googled Trowbridge councillors, and a webpage
came up, with about twenty names captioning an unflattering
series of posed, serious-looking studio headshots. Eagerly, she
scanned them all, but none of the names began with a G. Obviously, that would have been far too easy. So next she tried *Trowbridge Council Election results* and got a list of the wards –
eight? In a small town like Trowbridge? Searching the page of
each one, she had trawled down to the seventh ward with no
first names beginning with a G, when it occurred to her that
either Tim or Tim's mate – Johnny – said they might have
misremembered. Miss Smith's husband's name might not start

with a G at all, in which case she was pretty much back to square one, apart from knowing which town she and her husband now lived in.

Finally, on page eight, there was a Glen Pickles. He'd been the Green candidate, though, not Labour, and he'd come last in his local elections with a paltry sixty-three votes. The good people of Trowbridge clearly didn't prioritise the climate, she thought, looking him up. At last, an unusual name, something to work with...

She found him on LinkedIn. Glen Pickles, Trowbridge, solicitor. There was a photograph; he looked about the right age, early sixties perhaps. Bit of a silver fox, with a head of white hair gelled almost into a quiff, and a matching white beard. He looked nice; the sort of man who Kerry imagined would not think he was punching above his weight when trying to attract a woman like Miss Smith.

There were a few other hits on the name 'Glen Pickles'. Kerry scrolled down to an article in the local paper dated last year, with the headline PICKLES WANTS A GREEN SOLUTION. It was all about him standing for the local council, and what his manifesto was. Drunkenly scanning the text, black type jumping around like onscreen fleas, nothing leaped out at her – until the final line, which, thanks to a typo in the second word, read more like an obituary than an opinion piece: *Pickles lived in Trowbridge with his wife Anita and their two black Labradors, Skala and Betty. They have two children, both grown up and living in London.*

'I found her!' Kerry shouted into the empty room. With a shaking hand, she searched Google Images for Anita Pickles and, once she'd trawled through a lot of pictures of jars of chutney posted by women called Anita, there she was. Miss Smith. A photograph of her smiling, accepting some sort of award or certificate. Definitely her, no doubt at all, even though her hair was shot through with streaks of grey and cut short and, of course, she looked far older. Same smile, though, same full, curved lips. The lips that had been almost pursed in those naked photographs.

Next, Kerry looked her up on Facebook, and there she was again, her profile pic a snap of her and her now-familiar husband on a mountain in matching Gore-Tex jackets. So now Kerry had a way to contact her, once she was *compos mentis* enough to string a sentence together again.

It felt like a small triumph, a step forward out of the bog into which she felt she was sinking. But instead of doing the sensible thing and going to bed – it was late now and she had to get up for work at the crack of sparrows – she decided to celebrate. Jubilantly, she sloshed the rest of the second bottle of wine into her glass, downed it in one, and about an hour later, fell asleep on the sofa.

Kerry's regular alarm woke her at 4.30 a.m. as usual. At least, it did its best under very difficult circumstances. When she opened her gummy eyes, she felt as if she was dying, so she closed them again immediately, but not before the light split her head, causing pain to reverberate around her skull like a pinball. Her mouth felt like the sawdust at the bottom of a birdcage; and she felt so hot that she was concerned she might spontaneously combust. Oh dear God, how much had she drunk last night? It surely hadn't been two bottles – had it? She decided that the fatal error must have been omitting to have any dinner.

Everything felt impossible, but she really couldn't pull another sickie after yesterday, not without a doctor's note. Nigel would have her guts for garters.

Squeezing her way into the tiny shower, she stood under water as cool as she could bear it, for several minutes, groaning and wondering if she was going to be sick, until eventually she felt very slightly better. And then she remembered – she'd found Miss Smith!

She sincerely hoped she hadn't emailed her last night because it would probably have been gibberish, but a quick check of her Messenger folder reassured her that at least she hadn't done that. She would have to think carefully about how to approach her.

Forcing down a piece of toast and peanut butter, she drove as slowly as she dared to work, aware that she was almost certainly still over the limit. She didn't feel drunk, but she didn't half have a headache. She had a word with herself – this was becoming a bit of a bad habit.

Henceforward, she resolved, forgetting that she had sworn something similar just yesterday, she would only drink alcohol on the nights before her days off.

Of course, the first person she bumped into was Nasty Nige, who was slurping a mug of coffee by the noticeboard.

He hadn't shaved and looked as baggy-eyed and grey with exhaustion as Kerry felt. If she hadn't disliked him so much, she'd have felt sorry for him.

'Morning, Nigel.'

He grunted, barely managing a curt nod. 'All right, Kerry. Feeling better, are you?'

'So-so,' she said, not meeting his eyes. 'Bad prawn, I think. Sorry.'

'You had a big one, then?'

Wait – what did he mean by that?

'No,' she replied, carefully. 'I was in bed most of the day feeling sick, except for a couple of hours in the afternoon when I went out and lay in the sun. Look at the state of my knees!'

Nigel very pointedly did not look at her sunburned knees.

'Oh… you seem like maybe you had a big night last night. Are you sure you're OK to drive the van?'

Kerry tried, and failed, not to sound insulted. 'I'm fine to drive. I drove here. I don't know what you're insinuating.'

He sighed gustily, wafting his coffee-breath all over her. 'You still just seem a little... under the weather, Kerry, that's all I'm saying.'

Shit. He could tell she'd been drinking last night. Kerry blushed, and was then furious with herself for showing that small pink weakness.

'I was ill yesterday, but I'm fine now,' she said firmly, turning towards her sorting frame. It felt like a refuge, its curved edges reaching for her as if to hold her in its wooden embrace.

'If we wasn't so short-staffed, Kerry,' he said, looking at her properly for the first time, 'I would feel it necessary to check if that smell – what seems to me a lot like the aroma of stale wine – coming off of you was real and not my imagination. Because if it was, I would have to send you straight home, you know that, don't you?'

Kerry was momentarily speechless. She knew he had her bang to rights, and that she'd just had a very lucky escape.

'It must be your imagination, Nige,' she said, as breezily as she could muster. 'Nothing to see here!'

She thought it was a miracle she sounded even remotely breezy. At that moment, she could not have disliked Nigel more, and the awareness that he actually had a point made his criticism even more of a bitter pill to swallow.

She would have to sort herself out. It couldn't happen again.

But this was *Beth's* fault, she decided, ramming a batch of envelopes into a slot. How could she, Kerry, live with all this uncertainty hanging over her? It was enough to drive a teetotal *saint* to drink.

NINETEEN

Kerry could not remember the last time she had been to meet a man for an evening out. She was intentionally not using the word 'date', because she and Tim had both been very clear about this: it was not a date. It was a spot of company at a quiz night, that was all.

Although judging by the level of her nerves, anyone could be mistaken for thinking it *was* a date. After closing the front door behind her she had to run back three times to go to the toilet before she finally managed to set off. She'd decided to drive, so that she wouldn't be tempted to drink much, and at every stop sign and red light she checked her face in the rear-view mirror to make sure her sparkly lipgloss wasn't smudged.

'Sparkly lipgloss' – these were not words she had associated with her appearance in about two decades... And nor were the words 'going out to meet a man'. It was both a novel feeling and a completely terrifying one, but Kerry forced herself to stop thinking the latter, otherwise she'd have had to turn the car around. She couldn't shake a worry that she looked like a man in drag, and that she wouldn't know the answer to a single question and he'd think she was a total dunce.

The invitation had come out of the blue. Tim had done some research, he said, found a pub in town that did a pop quiz and had pretty much begged her to go with him. They had been messaging on Facebook for about a week now and, somewhat to her surprise, she found him easy to talk to. He was droll, very dry, and made her laugh every day by recounting the encounters he'd had with his work colleagues and the estate agents he was dealing with (he was in a rented terraced house in town while looking around for somewhere to buy). She noticed that she had barely played any Solitaire that week, so lengthy were their conversations.

Kerry was sure he didn't have any sort of ulterior motive – after all, he'd seen her photos now so he knew she wasn't a looker, and he also knew she worked for the Royal Mail in a role many grades down from his managerial rank at the insurance company in both responsibility and – doubtless – salary, so it couldn't be that he was after her (non-existent) money. He was, like her, just lonely.

She had even confided in him about her troubles, a little. About how she was wondering whether to make a complaint against Nigel for bullying, and the issues with the house. She and Beth still weren't speaking, and Sharon was away on a post-lockdown singles holiday in Capri, so she didn't have anybody else to talk to about it. Tim had proved a sympathetic and non-judgemental ear, offering practical advice and encouragement as to what she should do next.

They were supposed to meet inside the Fox and Goose in the Market Square but, as it happened, they both arrived at the door simultaneously. He seemed to identify Kerry straight away even though she had already put on a mask, but she looked startled when he called her name, because even though he'd said he'd wear a red baseball cap, the man next to her – in the red baseball cap – was much shorter than she'd assumed from his photographs. He was probably about five foot seven, an inch or so taller than Kerry, but she was wearing wedge-heeled sandals, which had the effect of making her tower over him.

'Hello,' she said, her hand flying up to cover her masked mouth out of embarrassment. But then he smiled at her so easily that she immediately felt about fifty per cent less awkward.

'Hi Kerry! It's lovely to meet you.'

They touched elbows, which managed to feel simultaneously both ridiculous and warm. He had such a nice way about him. She discreetly scrutinised him as he hooked the elastic of his own mask over his ears and they entered the pub.

'So weird, isn't it, having to put a mask on to walk in somewhere only to take it off thirty seconds later when you sit down,' she said, and then was embarrassed that he'd think she was some mad anti-masker. 'I don't mean that it's weird having to wear a mask, of course...' she babbled, as they headed for the last free table, a small round one by the window, and removed the masks again.

The pub was filling up in readiness for the quiz, and they discussed for longer than strictly necessary how lucky they were to have bagged their table, and how strange it was to be in a room with so many other people.

'I'll go and register, or whatever you have to do. What are you drinking?' he asked, flinging his cap onto the table.

Kerry noticed, from the dark stubble around the back and sides of his skull, that if he didn't shave his head, he would have a monk's tonsure. Good thing he did shave it, she thought. Fortunately he had a good-shaped head. She had always thought that it must be awful to be a cone-headed guy who lost his hair. He was quite nice-looking, although she didn't fancy him. It felt more like meeting up with a distant cousin or something; someone to whom you felt an affinity but nothing particularly close.

'It's ordering by phone only,' she said, pointing at a sign on the table.

Tim groaned and scanned the barcode to bring up the drinks menu.

'What'll you have? You know,' he said, contemplatively, looking up at her. 'You do look kind of familiar. I think I do recognise you...'

Kerry immediately felt mortified again, imagining the unsaid words ... *from those photos that were pinned up around college.*

He did not say, or think, that, she told herself sternly. And anyway, her face hadn't been in them. He'd never recognise her from them. *Stop projecting.*

'Could I have a white wine spritzer please?' she asked. 'I'm driving, so I'll only have the one.'

'Don't worry,' he replied. 'I wasn't planning on buying more than one at a time anyway. Back in a second, just going to the Gents.'

It wasn't funny but she guffawed obligingly as he put their order through and donned his mask again, heading for the stairs to the toilets with a slim-hipped, easy gait.

A stocky tattooed guy in a dog-face mask came over to the table then, holding a bucket and a clipboard. 'Doing the quiz?' he asked, and Kerry nodded.

'Two of you? A quid each please, and I'll need your team name.' He shook the bucket.

'Um...', she said, blushing. She had no idea. A team name! Immediately she felt put on the spot. Quiz team names were supposed to be clever puns, weren't they? Like John Trivialta, or The Quizzard of Oz, neither of which felt appropriate. She was stumbling at the first hurdle.

Then she had a flash of inspiration: 'Band on the Run!' she announced. It wasn't a pun, but since it was a pop quiz, it felt suitable enough. She hoped Tim would approve.

The quiz guy merely grunted and wrote it down, as she put two pound coins into his bucket. 'You're team thirteen,' he said and handed her some stapled blank answer sheets. 'Hope you've got a pen.'

Tim returned a couple of minutes later, at the same time as a waitress brought over their drinks on a tray.

'We're officially registered and above board,' Kerry said, thanking the waitress, then hastily adding, 'for the quiz, I mean,' lest he should think she meant that she'd suddenly got them betrothed or something in the four minutes he'd been away. 'I took an executive decision and called our team "Band on the Run", I hope that's OK.'

'That's fine! I really like it.'

He was probably just being polite, thought Kerry. Personally, she felt it was a bit rubbish.

'Thanks for the drink,' she said, clinking her glass against his. She didn't recognise him, she decided, but then boys tended to look very different in their adolescence than they did as adults, more so than girls. She hoped he wouldn't press her further as to why he recognised her. She definitely didn't want to discuss it, for fear of where the conversation might lead. They had already agreed that they wouldn't waste time asking each other if they remembered so-and-so, since neither of them cared. That had been Tim's suggestion, and it was what had convinced Kerry to agree to this rendezvous.

Fortunately the quiz started shortly after that, so she no longer had to cast around for things to say. It was, she reflected, the perfect activity to do with someone you'd only just met in real life, because it involved talking only about potential answers to questions like, 'Which eighties band was comprised of two guys called Roland and Curt?'

Tim looked blank and suggested Haircut 100, but Kerry squirmed with excitement in her chair. 'No, I know this one! It's Tears for Fears.'

He slapped his forehead. 'Of course. Nice one, Kerry. Good

start!' He wrote it in the answer box and she beamed, feeling a warm glow of pride. This was fun.

'You have a really pretty smile,' he continued conversation-ally, not looking at her. She felt utterly flummoxed. For a moment she thought he must be talking to someone else, someone at the next table, perhaps? But when she glanced across, she saw the next table was occupied by a group of hairy fifty-something men with beer bellies and biker jackets hanging off the backs of their chairs.

'I wasn't talking to any of them!' he said, grinning at her. 'I think I'd get beaten up if I was.'

Kerry couldn't think what to say in reply, so she just grinned uncertainly back at him.

Nobody had ever said that to her before. What a shame she didn't fancy him.

The rest of the quiz proved quite a lot harder, and they ended up with the second from bottom score. Kerry didn't care, though. She was flushed with the triumph of having got quite a few more correct answers, particularly in the Intros round. She got 'Eye of the Tiger', Prince's 'Kiss' and, to Tim's impressed delight, 'Green Onions' by Booker T. and the M.G.s.

'How on earth did you know *that*?'

'It was one of my dad's favourites.' Kerry's cheeks were aching from smiling so much. 'This has been so great, Tim,' she added impulsively. 'Thanks so much for inviting me, I've really enjoyed it. Even though we did practically come last.'

Tim laughed. 'Well, we'll just have to improve our perfor-mance next time. Practice makes perfect and all that. And thank you for saving me from the fate of being Billy No-Mates. Same time next week?'

Kerry felt an unfamiliar glow of pleasure, beaming underneath her mask as Tim held open the door for her. If this was what a fun night out was like, she might well be tempted to do it more often.

She was so used to only seeing Sharon and Beth socially, and both operated on such a strict transmit-only basis that coming away from time spent with either left her feeling slightly wrung-out, in need of solitude and a large drink. She hadn't realised how knackering it was, to be talked *at* all the time and rarely asked your opinion on anything. She and Tim had had actual conversations! He had been interested in Kerry's views about all sorts of things, holding eye contact and not constantly glancing over her shoulder to see if there was anybody more interesting around to talk to, as Sharon always did. The whole evening had been a bit of a revelation.

Perhaps she didn't want to brick herself into the big house and never come out again, she thought as she drove home. Not yet anyway.

TWENTY

Kerry ripped off her mask and stuffed it in her jacket pocket, looking approvingly around her at the newly decorated saloon bar. It felt great to be back in the village pub after it had been closed for so many months, and such a relief that Neil and Ginny hadn't had to shut up shop altogether. Ginny's auntie had died and left her enough money for them to be able to afford to rip up all the old sticky carpets and have them replaced with blond wood floors, and to paint the previously nicotine-yellow walls a fresh pale green. It was a vast improvement.

The current Covid regulations still stipulated that pubs must only offer table service, but this news did not seem to have reached Neil and Ginny, or, if it had, they were turning a blind eye. Neil, standing behind the bar with a copy of the *Daily Mail* open and resting atop his taut belly, was sporting a mask but it only covered his chin and neck, so Kerry supposed that was his nod at compliance.

Sharon had only agreed to meet at the Cricketer's Arms after Kerry told her it had been done up over lockdown, and Kerry couldn't really blame her. It had been a right dive before; one of the few remaining independent pubs with a constant assortment of elderly morose men with drinkers' noses at the bar, supping from personal tankards, but this had never bothered Kerry. Besides, she delivered mail to all the sullen barflies so if anyone could coax a smile from them, she could. They'd all known her since she was a kid. It was quite intimidating if you were an outsider, though, especially one as glamorous as Sharon, who dressed up to put the bins out.

'It's a gastro pub now!' she'd announced on the phone, to try and entice Sharon over to her neck of the woods for a change. 'What, not a gastroenteritis one any more?' Sharon had replied, which made Kerry laugh. Sharon rarely made jokes.

Kerry spotted her friend's sleek blonde head bent over her phone at a small table by the fireplace, pathologically early as always, even though she'd had to get the bus out to the village. It had taken Kerry all of three minutes to walk across the green and Sharon had still arrived first.

'You'll never guess what,' Kerry said to her, once she'd nodded hello at all the regulars propping up the bar; Double-Chin Kev the shopkeeper, Tom the dairy farmer, wearing the same Fair Isle tank top he'd had since Kerry was a kid, and Jonty the rotund binman, all of whom waved and raised their glasses in response.

She slung the strap of her handbag across the top rung of the chair and plopped down next to Sharon, anxious to get her own news in before Sharon began to hold forth. She did look gratifyingly intrigued at Kerry's enthusiastic conversation opener.

'What will I never guess?'

Kerry placed both palms flat on the table in front of her. 'Not only,' she announced grandly, 'is this the third time I've been out for a drink recently – first time was when you and I went to Maul's – but the second time was last night, and it was *with a man.*'

Sharon pretended to faint, slumping down in her seat and

then perking straight up again. 'No. Way! Details, please. What, who, where?'

Two of the villagers, tweedy spinsters called Peggy and Tabitha, stopped by their table, both clutching books they'd liberated from the pub's new library shelf. This was an initiative that Ginny had persuaded Neil to try, much against his better judgement, but their stock wasn't exactly the best. Kerry noticed the two ladies had nabbed the only two non-Reader's Digest volumes on there, a John Gardner with the rather unappealing title of *The Dancing Dodo,* and an old Stephen King.

She must start reading again, she thought, once she was settled in the big house. She used to enjoy settling down with a good book, but for some reason hadn't done so for years.

'Hello, Kerry love!' said Tabitha, the stouter and chattier of the two. 'How nice to see you out and about and not in your uniform. So sorry to hear about your mum.'

Peggy nodded. 'We'll miss her so much at flower-arranging,' she said, giving Kerry's arm a sympathetic pat.

'Ah, thank you both.' Kerry felt her throat tighten at the sympathy. 'Nice to see you two too. Isn't it looking smart in here now? Ginny's done a lovely job with the decor. I love those picture frames.'

They chatted for a few minutes while Sharon looked bored. The women eventually moved on to their own table, and Sharon glanced up from her phone. 'God, Kerry, do you know *everyone* in this village? Where were we?'

Kerry grinned. 'Yes, I do, actually. So – I got asked out to a pub quiz at the Fox and Goose by a man I met on the school's alumni Facebook page. We had a brilliant time. He was really nice!'

She had already decided not to admit that she in no way saw Tim as a potential boyfriend. For once she had something interesting to tell Sharon. She didn't want to ruin it by confessing that she didn't fancy Tim. Though she realised she had been thinking about him an awful lot in the past twenty-four hours, for someone she didn't fancy at all... Perhaps it would be more accurate to say she didn't fancy him *much*. It was probably just the novelty of going out with a man at all that was making certain images snag and replay in her mind; the hazel of his eyes, the laughter lines which came and went with such ease.

'Well, you're a dark horse,' said Sharon. 'I thought you were looking a bit more gussied-up than usual. And it's because you've got a man!'

Kerry thought it might be the first time she had ever heard admiration in her friend's voice.

'Woah, steady on,' she retorted. 'If you mean I had time to change before I came out to meet you this time, then I suppose I'm more "gussied-up". Just because I'm wearing make-up doesn't mean I'm only doing it because I've got a boyfriend! And I haven't, anyway. We went to a pop quiz, we didn't elope to Gretna Green.'

But despite her protestations, Kerry realised that she did feel different. She never normally bothered with make-up – and yet now that Tim had told her she had a lovely smile, she'd suddenly felt that perhaps a spot of lippy wouldn't look ridiculous... It had taken her five cotton-wool pads, sitting in front of her mum's dressing table, scrubbing off previous uneven applications, but she had persisted. She guessed that "gussied-up" was Sharon's equivalent of a compliment, so perhaps her efforts had been worth it.

'So when are you seeing him again?'

Kerry basked in the unfamiliar novelty of being the focus of Sharon's attention. 'He said we should go to the quiz again next week, but perhaps that's a bit soon, I don't know.'

Sharon frowned. 'He's not married, is he?'

'No!' Kerry laughed. 'To be honest, Shaz, it's probably just going to be a friendship. He's new to the area and wanted to meet people. I'm not even sure I fancy him, and he's bound not to fancy me.'

Even though he told you that you had a lovely smile...

'What does he look like?'

Kerry shrugged, noting that Sharon hadn't contradicted her about Tim probably not fancying her. 'Average-looking. Bald, about five foot, er, eight or nine, slim, nicely dressed...'

Sharon lost interest altogether at that point. She only ever went on internet dates if the bloke's profile detailed a minimum height of six foot and a full head of hair. No wonder that she found it difficult to meet someone decent – her requirements were far too stringent. 'Well, keep me posted! Sounds like he'd at least be good for a shag if nothing else. You've been a born-again virgin for waaaaay too long. No offence.'

'None taken,' Kerry replied automatically. She certainly wasn't going to let on to Sharon that her virginity, far from being born again, was still in its original packaging with the labels on.

A couple entered the pub and took seats at the table next to theirs. They were unremarkable-looking; a tall guy who probably would just about have met Sharon's exacting standards, although his hair was sparse and greying, and a tiny slim blonde with short-cropped hair and a pixie face.

It took a few minutes before Kerry realised that when the couple kept looking in their direction, they were glancing across at her and whispering. Not at Sharon, at *her*.

She immediately felt that familiar sensation of deep discomfort and began running through a mental checklist of reasons they might stare at her instead of at the much more glamorous and noticeable Sharon. Obviously, everyone in the village knew her, and she did quite often get accosted in town as the local postie too, but this was usually accompanied by a jolly comment like Tabitha's, about hardly recognising her without her uniform on. Not the slightly mean display of unsubtle sniggering that was going on at the next table.

Wardrobe malfunction? Surely Sharon would have alerted her to anything like that, but she still checked that her shirt – cream silk rather than the usual plaid flannel – hadn't spontaneously developed two round holes out of which her breasts were unaccountably sticking.

Lipstick on her teeth? More likely, since she was so unused to wearing it, and the mask did a great job of smudging it. Squirming on her chair, she interrupted Sharon's diatribe about her noisy upstairs neighbours to ask, baring her teeth at her.

'No!' she said impatiently. 'Why are you asking that now?'

Kerry leaned forward. 'Don't look, but that couple behind you are talking about me.'

Of course Sharon immediately turned around and looked, so unsubtly that her poker-straight blonde hair whipped around her face and lashed her in the eye, making her blink in an even more obvious fashion.

'I said, *don't* look!'

'I'm sure they aren't,' she said dismissively and Kerry wanted to punch her arm.

'Actually, they are. I'm not paranoid.'

'You totally are. Well, why don't you ask them, then?'

Kerry blushed to the roots of her hair at the thought of confronting them. But then the woman caught her glance, held it and then, to Kerry's horror, actually stood up and walked over to their table.

'Kerry?'

'Ye-es...?'

'Don't you remember me?'

She looked properly at the woman for the first time and realised she did seem vaguely familiar.

'Um... sorry. I'm terrible with names. I do recognise you. Were we at school together?'

The woman grinned wolfishly and Kerry had a sudden stab of a flashback.

This woman had seen her naked.

Oh God, no. Surely it wasn't...

'It's me, Serena, don't you remember? Serena Jackson – although I'm Serena Mann now. Chris and I got married ten years ago. Took me ages but I finally managed to wear him down, haha!'

Christopher Mann. C & S. Chris and Serena. That postcard had been addressed to *them*. What were the chances of her running into them, only a few days after she'd seen that postcard?

Kerry immediately wanted to run out of the door, but her breathing had become so shallow she thought she might pass out if she tried any sudden moves.

Forcing herself to fill her lungs, she squinted over at the bloke, who gave her a small wave. Beth had got off with him, that night, the night of their mum's fiftieth. He had been so hot as a teenager, preppy and muscled with a thick glossy mane that he would theatrically toss, but now he was unrecognisable: a bland, middle-aged man with a paunch and greying thinning hair. She'd never have known it was him.

'Yes, of course. Wow, you two got married...?' Kerry tailed off. It felt miraculous that she'd managed to sound even halfway normal. Someone put 'Wish You Were Here' by Pink Floyd on the jukebox, and Kerry wished she were anywhere else. She also wished she hadn't asked. She did not want to ask any questions, lest it heralded the start of a conversation that would inevitably lead to the one place she definitely did not want any conversation to go, ever: *Hey, do you remember when...?*

And then it would all come flooding back, bursting out of the doors of her memory which had been firmly locked and barred for the past quarter century, until the other day.

Kerry wondered if they remembered.

'We went to uni in London, and we were still living up there when we got together,' Serena chirped.

I don't care. Please don't tell me your life story. Please go away.

Serena was wittering on about herself – Kerry remembered she had always tended to do that – 'moved back to Salisbury when the kids were born... *blah blah...*' but apart from the odd word, all Kerry heard was white noise. She tried to focus on Serena as a small child sitting with her in the story circle at the village school, not the teenager from that horrific, mortifying night. Back in primary school Serena had had ringworm and the skinniest legs Kerry had ever seen.

She remembered the hot shame of being in the pond and what happened when she came out, and it was as if she'd summoned it up, because although it was always there, lurking at the back of her consciousness, now it was tap-dancing centre stage in the spotlights. The night that had blighted her life.

Ripping up the postcard hadn't made any difference.

TWENTY-ONE

After bumping into Serena and Chris, the night lost what little appeal it had ever held. Feigning a headache, Kerry refused to allow Sharon to chivvy her into town for more wine and, in an attempt to mollify her, offered her a lift home even though the point of them meeting in the village had been so that Kerry could have a drink, for a change. This wasn't an entirely altruistic gesture, because otherwise Sharon would have had to wait another hour for the last bus, and Kerry couldn't bear to stay in the pub a moment longer.

Sharon was reluctant to curtail the evening, actually wondering aloud whether or not she could go back over to Serena and Chris's table and ask to join them – not remotely put off by the fact that she had never met them before.

When Kerry expressed horror at this idea Sharon eventually acquiesced, albeit sulkily, and allowed Kerry to drive her back to her flat. Although Kerry had drunk a couple of large glasses of wine, she decided she was probably teetering on, rather than tipping over, the limit. She would have forcibly dragged Sharon out of there rather than let her join Serena and Chris, and risk her finding out about The Incident.

Kerry and Sharon had been in the same year at both school and college, though not friendly back then, and Kerry had never plucked up the courage to ask her if she had seen one of the xeroxed photos of her that were briefly pinned up around the place. Chances were she had, or had heard about them before they got taken down – you'd remember something like that, Kerry was sure – but Sharon might not have known that she, Kerry, had been the subject. She wanted to find out, to put her mind at rest that nobody had really known it was her but was simultaneously too afraid to ask only to discover that everybody *had* known.

'Well, that was a fun night,' Sharon said, grumpily unclipping her seatbelt as Kerry pulled up outside her apartment block. 'Home by ten, practically sober. And I thought it was going to be such a good one, what with you making an effort to look like you might be on the pull, even though you've met someone now. Ironic, hey?'

'I'm never on the pull. I haven't met anybody. Plus, I don't think anyone in the entire history of eternity has ever pulled in the Cricketer's,' Kerry said wearily. 'And I'm sorry to be such a party pooper,' she added. 'It was just a bit of a shock, bumping into those two again like that, after all these years.'

'Why? What's the deal? Did she do something to you? You didn't seem at all happy to see her. I thought she was nice.'

Kerry bit her lip. Images strobed through her memory again, the cold dark pond, her flesh on display, cruel laughter in her ears, what those boys did... the horror. Fresh shame poured into her and settled like heavy cement.

'No big deal,' she lied. 'They went to the village school with me, and then we used to hang around a bit as teenagers. I lost touch with them after A levels. We weren't that friendly or anything. Beth used to fancy Chris.'

She tried to inject levity into her voice. 'Wish I'd taken a photo of him to show Beth – he looks so different. I'd never have recognised him. He was so gorgeous as a teenager.'

Sharon wrinkled her nose, trying to imagine it. 'Really?'

'I know, right?'

Sharon gathered up her bag from the floor of the car. 'OK, well, nice to see you, Kerry. Hope your head gets better soon.'

For a moment Kerry wondered if she was referring to her mental health, but then remembered that she'd told Sharon she had a headache.

'Thanks. And sorry again for cutting it short. I promise I'll try and be on better form next time.'

'You said that last time,' Sharon grumbled.

Kerry was about to tell her some – not all – of the reasons why she wasn't on good form. That even if she had taken a photo of Chris, she wasn't sure she'd ever get to show it to her sister because of the current tension between them. On tenterhooks – whatever they were – about whether Beth was still going to insist on selling.

But Sharon took her promise to be more lively next time as a dismissal and leaned across the handbrake to give her a quick hug before opening the passenger door.

'Well, you've saved me a bus fare, a hangover and about a thousand calories from the kebab I'd doubtless have bought when I was walking home from the bus, so I should be thanking you,' she said, hauling herself out of the car. She didn't sound grateful, though.

In the end, Kerry was glad to drive off, glad she hadn't confided in Sharon after all. She couldn't wait to get home, pour herself a huge gin and tonic, and play Solitaire till her eyes popped, to try and quash the unwelcome images that were currently front and centre in her head. She needed to block them out to save her sanity and, if she was honest, both the need and the images scared her a bit.

She gripped the steering wheel more tightly and forced

herself to concentrate on the road until she reached the outskirts of the village. Left by the war memorial, past the green, second right. She could have done it with her eyes closed. Through the open five-barred gate and on to the gravel drive.

Kerry got out and closed the car door quietly – sound really carried in a silent sleepy village, and she was used to trying not to disturb Mum when she got home. Tiptoeing across the drive to the annexe, it wasn't until she tried to put the wrong key in the door that she remembered that she had moved into the big house. She retraced her steps, fumbling with the same keys on the other doorstep.

Sometimes she shut her eyes and imagined herself standing in the same spot thirty years ago. The garage had still been Dad's darkroom back then. Three decades back she'd have been thirteen, before everything got difficult. Before she hated her body, before Dad died, before she ruined her life. She would stand there and transport herself back to when she and Beth played ponies together for hours on end; even though at thirteen she'd sworn Beth to secrecy about their games – she was getting far too old for all that horsey stuff by then. Mum would be cooking a roast in the kitchen. Their dog Cindy would have been barely out of puppyhood, gambolling around the driveway with her lead in her mouth as a heavy hint she wanted a walk across the fields. Dad would have been in the darkroom...

But then Kerry's nostalgic train of thought would stall, because she'd start wondering if Miss Smith had been in the darkroom with him. On the same rug she, Kerry, walked on every day; on the floor she had set foot on every time she got out of bed for the last few decades.

How could Dad have cheated on Mum with Miss Smith, on his own home territory?

This happened every time Kerry got stressed. Her thoughts always looped back to Miss Smith and those photographs in Dad's drawer. She supposed a psychologist would say that it was easier to think of Miss Smith and Dad's possible transgression than her own trauma.

Having decided this, Kerry thought there would never be any benefit to her having therapy. If she knew it already, what was the point of paying someone to tell her?

This reminded her: she still hadn't emailed Miss Smith. Every time she thought about it, she shuddered. She would though, definitely. Soon...

She let herself into the big house, went straight into the front room and slumped down on the sofa without bothering to switch on the lights. She could feel the bony springs under her bottom and concluded it really wasn't all that much better than the futon she had in her garage – in fact, the only thing it had going for it was that it reclined.

She'd love a new sofa. This one, like all their furniture, had been there since before Dad died. She'd be able to afford one – if Beth let her stay living here.

If.

Her phone beeped with a text, but she felt too low even to get a frisson from seeing Tim's name appear on the screen.

Hi Kerry! Sorry if it's a bit late to text. Wondered if you fancied meeting up for dinner next week? I heard there's a great Thai place in town. Thursday's good for me.

She decided to reply tomorrow with a polite rebuff.

TWENTY-TWO

Hi Tim, thanks for your text last night! Sorry for delay, just finished up my round for the day. Not sure I'm up for dinner but—

Kerry had fully intended to add something like, 'see you around', then had a last-minute change of heart. She felt less negative than she had the night before. They were becoming friends. She enjoyed Tim's company. Why cut off her nose to spite her face? It wasn't often that she met someone she liked enough to want to spend time with. So instead, she typed:

we could always go for a drink instead?

He replied so quickly she had a brief mental image of him having been staring at his phone screen continuously since last night, waiting for her reply. As if, she thought.

That would be great – but come on, let's have dinner! You know, 'Eat Out to Help Out' – I'd go as far as to say it's our civic duty!

This made her laugh, but she *was* sure about not wanting dinner. She'd feel far too nervous that she would tip pad thai into her lap or choke on a prawn cracker. Then there was the thorny issue of the bill —would they split it, or would she have the stress of him offering to pay because that really would make it a date, and then what? Sod that, she thought.

A couple of pints in the Fox would be great instead. And if we make it Thursday, we can do the pop quiz again, see if we can better our score!

Hopefully that sounded assertive enough, she thought. But when his next reply arrived, she realised it obviously hadn't been.

We could grab a bite first. Dinner would be on me, if that's what you're worried about!

Oh God, she thought. That's made it worse! Now he thinks I'm tight, or a scrounger. She was tempted to text back, *Let's just forget it then*, but managed to still her twitching fingers in time to compose a more tempered response:

Not at all. I just eat dinner super-early. Honestly, I'd prefer to have a drink and do the quiz. Thanks for the kind offer though.

Fortunately he seemed to get the message then, and they concluded the conversation by arranging to meet at seven on Thursday in the Fox and Goose.

Kerry didn't tell Sharon. She didn't want her to make a big fuss about it and, anyway, she had almost convinced herself that it would be a waste of time. She realised she couldn't even remember what Tim looked like, even though it was only a couple of days since their last rendezvous. Every time she tried to picture his face, she got a mental image of another bald, short guy, a bloke called Paddy from work, even though Paddy had black smoker's teeth and a squint. It took looking up Tim's Facebook profile picture to re-establish him in her mind.

That must mean something, she thought, that I can't even picture him. She decided to put it out of her mind. Although this did not stop her spending a couple of hours brushing up on her pop trivia, and buying a new dress on Amazon, making sure it came with free next-day delivery...

Thursday arrived so fast Kerry felt as if she'd tripped over it. Meeting Tim outside the same pub, him in his red baseball cap again, had a distinct *Groundhog Day* vibe to it, but it did feel a lot more relaxed this time.

He greeted her like an old friend and admired the new dress, a voluminous khaki cotton thing that doubtless would have made Beth shudder but in which Kerry felt comfortable and – dare she even think it – vaguely stylish. They seated themselves at the same table, the landlord remembered and wrote down their team name without them having to remind him, and – even better – they were reasonably confident that they'd got all ten questions correct in the Intros round, mostly due to Kerry's expertise. She had a few doubts as to whether one of them was The Clash or The Damned, but other than that, she felt they were doing well, both in the quiz and in their interactions. They were both looser and less formal with each other, and there was definitely more banter. Flirty banter too, if Kerry wasn't mistaken.

During the half-time break in the quiz, Tim jerked his thumb out of the window. 'Look. Isn't that great? I want to be doing that kind of stuff when I'm her age.'

She followed his gaze and saw a diminutive elderly lady in a flamboyant wine-red velvet dress and floppy felt hat standing alone across the square, singing something to a backing track that Kerry couldn't quite make out but which sounded like opera.

'Let's go and listen for a minute,' she said. 'The poor woman needs an audience.'

They left their jackets hanging on their chairs, and their quiz sheets and half-finished drinks on the table, and stepped outside into the balmy August evening. When Tim took her hand as they walked towards the singer, Kerry found she didn't mind. A tiny thrill like an electric shock went up her arm and she smiled.

The geriatric operatics got clearer the closer they got. 'She's actually pretty good,' Kerry said. 'That's from Fauré's *Requiem* – one of my favourites. I love choral music.'

'So do I!' exclaimed Tim. 'I never mention it because, well, it doesn't seem cool, but I do.'

He squeezed her hand and for a moment Kerry beamed and thought, *so is this what all the fuss is about?*

They stood together in front of the singer, letting the music wash over them. Kerry drank in the whole experience – the slightly quavery but heartfelt recitation, the tiny old lady's extraordinarily characterful face, lined and overly made up with bright pink lipstick a little outside the contours of her lips and too much powder, the balmy evening, lights twinkling in all the trees.

A sensation of burgeoning togetherness with Tim, the hint of a life that perhaps wasn't out of her reach after all, and that perhaps she did want... She looked at the singer, who did not appear to have anybody with her. A little two-wheeled trolley trailing bungee cords stood near her amp, implying she shifted her own gear, and Kerry wondered why she was doing it. There was no upturned hat for donations nor display of CDs for sale. It must be for the joy of it.

Kerry thought about her own life, and how much – if ever –

she had done anything in pursuit of her own joy. Never, until she'd staked her claim on the house.

'We'd better get back inside,' Tim said. 'Don't want to lose any chance of not being in the bottom three this time.'

Kerry laughed. 'All right, Mr Competitive.' She pulled a five-pound note out of her pocket and looked for somewhere safe to leave it, tucking it under a corner of the singer's amp. The singer smiled and nodded her thanks and they turned to leave, serenaded by a new aria, one that Kerry didn't recognise.

Halfway across the square, Tim stopped.

'What?' Kerry asked, looking back. 'Did you drop something?'

'No,' he said, turning to face her. He put his hands on her upper arms and squeezed gently. 'I just wanted to do this...' Leaning forward, he closed his eyes and kissed her.

Kerry was so shocked that she flinched and almost – almost! – pulled away, but the kiss was so tender and inno-cent that to her astonishment, she found herself automatically reciprocating. They were the same height and it felt like the most natural thing in the world to slide her arms around his waist and hug him to her as the kiss deepened. She didn't even care that they were outside, in a public place. They stayed like that for what felt like ages but was probably only a couple of minutes, before she extracted herself, laughing and blushing.

'Come on. We'll miss the start of part two.'

Her legs felt like jelly and her face was burning with plea-sure as they retook their seats just as the compere took up his microphone.

'Right, ladies and gentlemen, it's the picture round!'

Despite their promising early start, team Band on the Run's performance plummeted in the next couple of rounds, and by the penultimate one, they were once more at the bottom of the leader board.

'Yeah, but most of the other teams have at least four people in them,' Tim protested. 'We should have our points doubled since there's only two of us.'

'Do we have a sore loser in our midst?' Kerry asked, poking her forefinger playfully into his ribs. 'I'm going to get another drink – think I'll get a cab home tonight. What will you have?'

She did not recognise this version of herself, she thought as she pulled out her phone and navigated to the pub's drinks menu app; this flirty, light-hearted woman who was having a good enough time to go to the hassle and expense of cabs home and back to work tomorrow. But she liked her.

'Pint of Guinness, please,' Tim said. He reached under the table and gave her knee a squeeze, which made her smile.

Kerry was doing so much smiling that her cheeks were aching in an unfamiliar way.

After the third round of drinks arrived at the table, she asked Tim how work was going; how he felt about being back in Salisbury.

Tim took a long swig of his Guinness and wiped the froth off his top lip contemplatively. 'Hm. Only a couple of months in but I'm still finding it a bit weird. I don't know anybody outside work, apart from you. I need to get my act together and join a gym or something.'

She was stricken with the sudden pang that he had only kissed her because he didn't have any other social contacts. Her fear must have shown in her face because he suddenly leaned forward and grasped her hand. It was lovely that he was so tactile, she thought. To think she hadn't fancied him at first!

'But even if I knew a thousand people here, you'd still be the one I wanted to kiss,' he said, staring intently at her.

'I think that's the nicest thing anybody has ever said to me.' For a moment, she wanted to cry, but swallowed hard and tried to speak normally: 'So if you lived round here as a teenager, surely there are a few people from school you know still?'

'Not that I know of. Nobody that I want to see, anyway. Why – are you still in touch with old school friends?'

Kerry nodded, then shook her head. 'Yes – well, sort of. My friend Sharon was at school and college with me, but she doesn't really count because we weren't actually friends until she came to work at the Post Office. Most of my school friends moved up to London after A levels, and I lost touch with them. Not that there were that many. My sister was the sociable one.'

Talk of school and A levels, even though Kerry had insti- gated it herself, suddenly felt like treading on shaky ground. She was about to change the subject when Tim took another deep swig of his drink and said, 'I didn't have many either. I was such a nerdy little squirt as a teenager. And it didn't help that we lived out in a village.'

Alarm bells ringing, Kerry tried to keep her voice level. Lots of people lived out in villages, she reminded herself. 'Oh really? So did we. I still do. Which one?'

'Great Dunsmore.'

The room spun. It was a small village. They'd all got the bus into school and college together. He was only a year younger than her. She *must* have known him.

She gripped her slippery glass harder. 'Same.'

They stared at each other, puzzled. She could have sworn she'd never seen him before in her life, and she certainly didn't remember his name – and yet, something clunked into place. A familiarity about his eyes, his slightly crooked smile. 'You didn't go to the village school, did you?'

'No – we didn't move to the area till I was fifteen.'

Perhaps they used to get the same bus in?

'Did you use to hang around the green in summer?' he asked. 'There was a group of us. A bit of an oddball group, so you probably didn't.'

It was nice that he thought she *wouldn't* be in a group of oddballs. But – oh shit, this was beginning to feel way too close to home. What were the chances he was from the same village?

'I changed my surname when I left school,' he confessed. 'I was so sick of being bullied for it. I hated it, and I wanted a fresh start, so I picked my mum's maiden name and changed it via deed poll.'

Kerry coughed, feeling as if there was a shard of something sharp stuck in her throat. She didn't want to believe it, but suddenly she saw how he had been at fifteen or sixteen – tiny, the great mop of black curly hair and thick glasses successfully disguising him from the bald, contact lens-wearing adult he'd become.

'You were Timothy Alcock,' she said slowly.

He looked delighted. 'That's right! I mean, Alcock's the sort of name you can totally carry off if you're over six foot with muscles, but can you imagine the sort of stick I got, as a seven-stone weakling? It was horrific. Tim No-Cock, Tim Tiny-Cock... you name it.'

'Tim Alcock,' she mumbled, feeling sick. 'You complete *bastard*.'

His head snapped back as if she'd slapped him. She was tempted to.

'*What?*'

She pushed her chair back just as the compere switched on the quiz jingle to signify the resumption of the final round.

'You heard,' she said, scooping her handbag off the dusty floorboards. Catching a glimpse of her reflected face, distorted in an ornamental shiny brass jug on the windowsill, she had the flashing thought that she'd transformed in a second from a love-struck giggly teenager – the one she never was first time round – into a snake-haired Gorgon, hissing with fury and disappointment.

'I don't... What?' Tim looked utterly bewildered.

Kerry was so angry she could barely get the words out. She spat them into his ear, so nobody else would hear. Her voice shook with emotion.

'You took those Polaroids of me that night and photocopied them. How could you do that? You stuck them up around college. Do you have any idea of the damage that did to me? Still does? That was one of the worst things that ever happened to me! I never got over it, *never*. Well, now at least I can see why you have no friends. Don't ever contact me, ever again. You can go and screw yourself.'

Kerry barged her way out of the pub. Tears of rage and disappointment were streaming down her face and she almost tripped over the foot of a homeless person in a doorway of the next building along. The last thing she heard, over the homeless guy swearing at her, was the compere bellowing, 'and for a bonus point, which Scottish singer was mentored by Prince?'

Sheena Easton, she thought, immediately followed by another thought: *I wish I was dead.*

TWENTY-THREE

1994

Kerry hadn't even wanted to go and hang out with the others on the green on that meltingly hot night; the night of Mum's fiftieth. She was so bored with the little gang of them. They had all grown up in the same small clump of scattered villages, spread out over an untidy few miles of countryside as if some celestial hand had accidentally dropped a load of houses from a great height. So, by dint of geography alone, they had been thrown together in various primary school classrooms and secondary school buses since they were all about six years old. Once they hit adolescence it was just easier to sit around under a tree drinking White Lightning than have the faff of waiting for night buses back from town. Especially without any form of legal ID.

But that night, her mum had decided to have a party. A party! Dad had only been dead for a year. Mum kept trilling, 'Daddy would have insisted' that she celebrated and, Kerry supposed, she was allowed. It didn't feel right to her, though.

Kerry had stuck around, under duress, for the first hour or two, enduring Mum's friends asking the same questions over and over: 'How are you all *doing*?' (with the sympathetic head-tilt), 'How did the A levels go?' and 'Which unis are you applying to?'

The answer to the second one was 'Disastrously' and the last, 'None, because I haven't decided if I want to go,' which always led to an intake of breath and a shocked glance across at her mother, as if the interrogator wanted to rush straight over to her and say, 'Surely it can't be true? Kerry *might not go* to university?' As if the earth would tilt off its axis and the birds would all plummet out of the sky.

Beth was in her element, boasting about her predicted GCSE results and handing round sausage rolls with aplomb, but Kerry had never been keen on being on display and she detested having to make small talk. It was so hot that she just wanted to go and lie in a cold bath, but they had promised Mum they would help out, at least until the canapés had gone around.

The party was mostly in the garden, so she and Beth were rushing in and out of the kitchen with full trays of bite-sized things that Mum had spent all day making. Kerry had massive sweat stains under her arms and, when she caught a glance of her reflection in the mirror by the back door, she saw that her face was red and clashing horribly with her hair.

She was also getting steadily tipsier, having strategically placed several different glasses of punch along her route from kitchen to garden, and taken a gulp out of each one as she passed. It was so weird and horrible, seeing all Dad's friends there, but no Dad, especially because Mum seemed to be having an absolute blast, laughing too loudly and air-kissing everyone.

Her mood was rapidly deteriorating.

Her mum had commandeered several of the village pub's locals to man the barbecue, a motley crew with ancient Led Zeppelin T-shirts stretched taut across beer bellies, and she was flirting with them so determinedly that Kerry thought she was going to be sick. Beth caught the look of disgust on her face as she topped up one of her glasses from a massive jug of punch.

'Give Mum a break,' she said. 'She just misses Daddy, that's all.'

'She's got a funny way of showing it,' Kerry retorted, letting Beth fill her glass right to the top. A chunk of apple fell out of the jug and sploshed into her glass, spraying her white broderie anglaise blouse with pinkish punch. 'Oh bum, look at my top, I'll have to go and change. I'm out of here in a minute.'

'Where are you going?'

'Just over to the pond. Serena and that lot said they'd be there; nobody can be bothered to go into town tonight.'

'Can I come?'

Kerry shrugged. 'If you want.'

She had mixed feelings about Beth accompanying her. If she'd been going out in town, she'd have said a firm no, but the village crowd all knew Beth, so she wouldn't have to endure the usual looks of incredulity from strangers on learning they were sisters.

'Who else will be there?' Beth gazed into the middle distance and twisted one of her long curls around her finger.

Kerry rolled her eyes, knowing she meant which boys. 'What do you care? You haven't split up with Josh, have you?'

'Obviously not,' Beth said indignantly. 'I'm just asking.'

'I don't know. The usuals, I expect. Serena. Chris and Timothy, probably. Lee Carlton.'

'Chris is a laugh.' Beth brightened.

At that moment, Miss Smith walked up to them. At the best of times it had always given Kerry a lurch of discomfort to see her out of school mode, with a faceful of make-up, a tiny, short summer dress and her hair in a blonde flick that would have made a Charlie's Angel envious. She was ridiculously pretty. But since Kerry's discovery of the photographs, seeing her was nothing less than intolerable. Kerry felt ill.

'Hello, Miss Smith,' Beth chirped, standing to attention.

Miss Smith laughed, addressing them both even though Kerry had merely glowered at her. 'Oh, you two; I've told you, it's Anita when we're out of school! Which is always for you, Kerry, since you're at college. How did the exams go?'

Kerry felt herself blush scarlet. 'Fine,' she lied, not meeting Miss Smith's eyes. 'Anyway, got to go.'

Beth was gaping at Miss Smith like a goldfish, and Kerry supposed that because she still had her for history it was even weirder for her to see a teacher out of context like this. Or perhaps she was mortified and confused at how rude Kerry had just been to her. *Whatever*, Kerry thought, stomping back into the house and up to her bedroom.

Mum and Dad had known Miss Smith for years, and Kerry had overheard a couple of conversations pondering why she hadn't yet got married, since she was so pretty and funny and clever. She'd had a bloke at least up until last year, Kerry recalled – he'd been the sexy one on the coach trip to London with them. They might have broken up by the time of Dad's funeral though, because Miss Smith had been there on her own, and Kerry remembered her mum mentioning 'Anita's on-off gentleman friend'.

Funny how certain things stuck in your head, she thought, peering round the edge of the curtain at the party in the garden. There was no sign of a gentleman friend tonight. And now the sight of 'Anita' in Dad's photographs was going to be stuck in her head for the rest of her life. *Thanks, Miss Smith*, she thought savagely. She had a nerve, showing her face at their house, pretending to be all matey with Mum when all the time...

At that moment, someone turned the music up and the bassline from 'Car Wash' boomed around the garden.

'Ooh I love this song.' Kerry heard Miss Smith's high voice waft up to her. 'See you later, Beth!'

The woman spun on her high-heeled sandals and shimmied

over to Mum at the barbecue, grabbing her hands and pulling her over to a free section of lawn for a dance. Ugh, thought Kerry, watching them both gyrate and wiggle seductively. It was revolting.

Kerry dropped the edge of the curtain and changed the stained white blouse for her black UB40 T-shirt, trying to block out the mental image of Miss Smith naked. Then, as an afterthought, she swapped her flowery skirt for cut-off denim shorts. Chris Mann and Lee Carlton had recently gone quite Goth and she didn't want to lounge around with them looking like she'd dressed in her Sunday best. Peering intently at her face in the mirror on the wall, she applied some green foundation stuff that was supposed to tone down livid complexions. It did take the unbecoming flush away, but she realised she must have overdone it, because now she resembled someone with severe food poisoning. She ended up brushing so much blusher on her cheeks to cover it that she may as well have stuck with the original redness.

Peeking out of the window again, she saw Beth shouting in Mum's ear over the music, pointing in the direction of the village green and tapping her watch, probably to indicate they wouldn't be late.

Mum looked reluctant – Beth was only fifteen and Mum didn't approve of her hanging around with the older kids – but she was clearly too distracted with her party, now in full swing, to object. Kerry watched Beth kiss her cheek, then glance up and give her a double thumbs-up sign.

She smiled down at her sister. It was nice when they did stuff together. She vowed to do it more.

Beth was standing by the front door when Kerry came back down the stairs. A guest had foolishly but conveniently left a carrier bag with a few bottles of WKD in the entrance hall as their contribution to the party, so Kerry picked it up, suddenly registering the contrast between her new outfit and Beth's. Beth was in a strappy yellow sundress and flip-flops with her hair piled messily up on her head, like a teenaged Goldie Hawn. It instantly made Kerry want to go up and change again. She felt grungy and awkward next to Beth, which was possibly worse than the sensation of frumpiness she'd had in the skirt and top.

She dithered on the bottom stair, but then they heard a group of shrieking middle-aged women pile into the kitchen, laughing like hyenas, and it was enough to propel her out of the front door, Beth close on her heels.

'Good work, filching those,' Beth said, nodding at her clinking carrier bag. Her eyes were glazed.

Kerry grinned back. 'Thought we'd better scarper before anyone claims them. Are you pissed already?'

Beth tapped the side of her nose, annoyingly. 'Might be.'

'Well, go easy. Mum'll kill you if you end up puking everywhere.'

'If there's any puking, it'll be from you,' Beth retorted. 'I saw you necking that punch. And you're bright red. You only go that red when you're drunk.'

They went through the open five-bar gate and crossed the road. A few doors down, people were sitting at wooden tables outside the Cricketers' Arms, sipping pints and smoking, enjoying the hot summer's night. Music from Mum's party floated on warm air currents over the cottage roof and across to the green, another disco number, but not one Kerry recognised.

She ignored Beth's comment. 'There they are,' she said, pointing at the small, dark-clad group lolling on the grass on the far side of the pond. She felt sweaty and cross, trapped between two bad options; to stay at the party with Miss Smith, or hang out with the village idiots (as Dad christened them a couple of years back, after Lee Carlton was caught graffitiing the bus stop).

They sauntered across the dry, yellowing grass and around the edge of the pond, which looked cool and inviting. The gang glanced up with interest at their arrival – but Kerry knew this was because she had Beth in tow and not because they were pleased to see her.

'All right?' said Lee, who was rolling a joint, watched carefully by Timothy Alcock, who always looked as if he was studying his peers' behaviour for some kind of test on it later. Poor little Timothy still had the body and voice of a thirteen-year-old, even though he was in Year Twelve. He also had unfortunately thick glasses and a head of dark curly hair which sat like a wig on top of his skull. For some reason, he appeared to have two cameras on straps around his neck. His folks had only moved to the village a year or two ago, so she didn't know him as well as the others. He seemed inoffensive.

Unlike Lee. Lee was puny too, and also quite short, but in a far more wiry and edgy way. Kerry sort of fancied him a bit, at the same time as being scared of him. He had a tough streak that meant that he was always in trouble – he'd already had one brief spell in a juvenile detention centre, for persistent shoplifting.

She noticed he had a new tattoo on the back of his left wrist, a scabby horrible thing, clearly homemade and probably done with the point of a compass. Was it meant to be a nuclear missile, perhaps? She didn't like to ask in case it offended him. Or perhaps it was a penis. It was difficult to tell.

Lee had a mate with him, a boy Kerry didn't recognise. She thought he was introduced as Matt, but it turned out not to be, as she found out when she called him Matt about ten minutes later and he rolled his eyes and said, 'For fuck's sake, it's Mutt, OK?'

Mutt was quite spotty, with very small incisors, as if he'd never lost his baby teeth. Apart from that, he wasn't unattractive. Average height, skinny, like Lee. Kerry didn't dare ask why he was called Mutt. He didn't look any more stupid than most teenage boys. He had a surprisingly posh voice for someone who was mates with Lee.

Serena Jackson was sitting on her denim jacket a little way away at the edge of the pond, bare feet dunked into the water, sharing a cigarette with Christopher Mann. Beth shot straight over to join them. She knew Serena well, from a street dance class they went to after school, and Kerry knew she had a big crush on Chris because he was tall and dark and had swishy hair that flopped in his eyes.

Kerry had the choice of sitting with Lee, Mutt and Timothy, or going with Beth. She dithered for a moment, then noticed Timothy lift one of the cameras to his eye and begin to snap photos of, she assumed, the sunset reflected on the pond's surface.

'Are you doing photography A level?' she asked, still standing awkwardly.

Timothy nodded, without taking the viewfinder away from his eye.

'It's meant to be really hard,' she ploughed on. 'Is it hard?'

'Yeah.'

'Why have you got two cameras?'

He looked at her for the first time, witheringly, and gestured at the boxier one. 'This one's a Polaroid, so I can get an instant idea of whether the composition will work. If it does, then I take the actual shot with this one. Saves me having to develop any duff ones.'

Of course it was a Polaroid. Kerry felt embarrassed that she hadn't realised at first. He'd think she was an idiot who didn't know what a Polaroid camera was.

'My dad's hobby was photography too,' she offered, then mentally kicked herself. It was the sort of conversation that a ten-year-old would make.

Timothy grunted and she didn't know what else to say, or why she was even trying to impress this little shrimp of a boy. Beth was getting the WKD bottles out of the bag, and Kerry wanted to prevent her handing them round before she got the chance to nab one, so she used that as an excuse to slope over and sit with the girls and Chris instead.

'Let's have one.'

Kerry stretched out and whipped one away before Serena got her hands on it, even though she was already a bit drunk and didn't like WKD. Mentioning that her dad's hobby had been photography had reminded her yet again of Miss Smith naked, and the only sensible solution seemed to be to get more drunk.

There were only two bottles left. Beth kept one for herself, which meant that either Serena or Chris would have to go without. Serena glared at her as Chris casually grabbed the last one and flipped off the cap with the blade of a penknife.

'You'd better share that,' Serena said to Chris in a proprietorial manner.

'Might do,' he retorted, making a face at her.

'Don't worry, S'rena,' called Lee, who Kerry suspected fancied Serena. 'Got vodka over here.'

'Oh good,' Chris said, sliding up next to Beth and chinking his bottle against hers. 'All the more for us then.'

Beth giggled, put her head on his shoulder and twisted her face to simper up at him. He looked surprised and delighted.

My God, Kerry thought. The nerve of Beth. She herself would never, ever have the courage to do that to a boy she didn't know very well. Where had her sister got so much confidence from?

TWENTY-FOUR

2020

Kerry had to sit in the car taking deep breaths for about ten minutes until she felt composed enough to drive home, forcing herself to take a mental inventory of everything in her eyeline to try and stop reliving the nightmare of what had just happened. She'd read somewhere that it was a good strategy to help prevent a panic attack.

Air-freshener dangling from rear-view mirror.

Two kids in hoodies on bikes, circling menacingly in the car park.

Empty Costa coffee cup in her footwell.

An old couple holding hands as they walked slowly towards their car, neither of them looking alert enough to get behind the wheel.

At least she wouldn't have to pay for cabs home and to work the next morning.

But the sense of betrayal she felt was too strong to be distracted by what she could see, or to appreciate any positives. Her thoughts just kept turning back to Tim's shocked face as they both realised who the other was. Did he feel guilty? Embarrassed at being confronted? Both, probably, she thought.

Come on, Kerry, get it in perspective. It's a shock, but you'll get over it. Worse things happen at sea, as Dad used to say. She was being pathetic, getting so upset about something that happened over twenty-five years ago.

Yet it was more than that. It was the loss of someone she realised she had been thinking of as at the very least a potential new friend, in itself such a rarity in her small world and, since the kiss, possibly more. And it had all gone to shit with such breathtaking speed that she could only assume that there was just something about her, some sort of hidden inbuilt person-repellent. Self-pity flooded her, as if someone had tipped a bucket of it over her head.

He had seen her at her most vulnerable, and then exploited it for his own entertainment. Why would he do that? Why would anyone do such a thing? It was sick, and she hated him. It didn't matter that it was years ago; that he might have changed; that he might be mortified at his actions. If he was the sort of person who would even consider it, she wanted nothing to do with him, ever.

Kerry eventually managed to get herself together enough to start the engine, put the car in gear, disengage the handbrake and set off, although there was little else she remembered about getting back. She recalled stopping at the petrol station and picking up two bottles of wine and a pack of cigarettes, even though she hadn't smoked for years. She was astonished at the price of them, but at that moment the longing for alcohol and nicotine overwhelmed her. She'd probably have paid thirty quid for a single pack, if that was what it cost.

She drove through the open gate and parked carelessly outside the garage, hauling herself out of the car and heading for the front door of the big house. But at the last minute, she stopped and turned, as she had the other day when she felt distressed. She couldn't face being in there. It reminded her of coming back home after that night, soaking wet, shivering with shock and cold, creeping in to avoid the partygoers carousing in the back garden.

She wanted the comfort of her annexe, like a beaten rescue dog who only feels safe in a confined space. The irony of this didn't escape her. All this, trying to find Miss Smith and meeting Tim, had been to try and prove to Beth that she didn't imagine stuff, so that her claim on the big house would be more credible – and yet here she was, choosing her garage instead.

As soon as she got inside, she went to the miscellaneous drawer in the kitchen area and dug about in the ziplock bags, batteries and clingfilm rolls to find the lighter that she was sure was at the back somewhere. Fortunately it still worked, and she tore the cellophane off the pack and lit one before she'd even sat down.

The first hit of the cigarette made her so light-headed she thought she was going to fall over. She grabbed the edge of the kitchen counter to steady herself and took another puff. Almost pleasurable. It occurred to her belatedly that she could have gone down the e-cigarette route, but at that stage she didn't care. What did it matter if she got lung cancer? Nobody would miss her. She thought of how horrified Beth would be to see her smoking and took another defiant drag.

Unscrewing the wine, she poured over a third of the bottle into a half-pint glass. It was cold enough and cut through the unfamiliar sensation of a mouthful of smoke, so she downed at least half of it in one go.

Better.

Her phone buzzed in her back pocket so she pulled it out and saw that she had four unread texts and two missed calls from Tim. She couldn't face looking at the texts yet so she switched off the phone.

The first bottle of wine was empty within half an hour, and she'd smoked three cigarettes. She felt horrible; her lungs complaining, her head aching, and with an underlying sloshing nausea from the nicotine overdose. But feeling physically awful was a welcome relief from the emotional pain, and all the memories which were flooding back. The photos of her, her soft pale flesh on display to everyone. The photos of Miss Smith. Dad, yellow and shrunken, days before his death. Mum, being carried down the stairs for the last time.

Miss Smith. She *still* hadn't emailed her yet; she must do it. Obviously not now. Far too drunk right now, she thought.

She opened the second bottle and then, when all that was left was a puddle of dregs on its glass bottom, unearthed the small bottle of Icelandic liquor that Beth had once brought her back from Reykjavik from where it had been languishing unopened in her kitchen cupboard next to cans of tomatoes. Cracking the seal, she necked it straight from the bottle. It was pungent and herbal, coating her oesophagus as it slid down like alcoholic cough medicine, helping wipe her memory of the past four hours.

Kerry didn't remember anything else about that night except that the last time she had looked at the clock, she thought at first it said ten past ten before realising that in fact it was ten to two. After approximately thirty-seven games of online Solitaire, she eventually fell asleep fully clothed on the sofa, too wasted even to climb up the ladder to her mezzanine bed.

It was her bladder that awakened her again at four, pulsing in time with the pounding of her temples. It felt as if a badger had gone to sleep in her mouth – how much worse would it be once the hangover properly kicked in?

She went to the bathroom, had a wee, cleaned her teeth and knocked back three ibuprofen with a pint of water. Only an hour before she had to leave for work – was she really intending to go to work that day? She had to, she supposed. Too many others were on leave or off sick, and she couldn't text Nigel yet again pretending she was ill. He'd fire her. The job felt like all she had left.

She still couldn't face reading Tim's messages so she left the switched-off phone on the sofa. It had been down to five per cent battery anyway, so it would soon die. The lucky thing, she thought.

Tearing off her clothes, she climbed the ladder in her underwear, not bothering to change into pyjamas. It was such a relief to sink into bed, even though her head was spinning as well as throbbing, like some kind of complicated, malfunctioning engine that would imminently explode. Another half an hour's sleep was better than none.

It felt like no less than five minutes later when her clock radio alarm blared at her to tell her it was time to get up. Kerry inched herself gingerly up to a seated position, eyes still closed, clutching her head. She was strangely unable to prise open her eyelids for several more minutes – they felt as though they had been replaced by tiny bags of cement. Finally, the room stopped whirling long enough that she was just about able to crawl down the ladder, groaning and clinging on to its sides as if she were on the mast of a tall ship on a rolling sea, hunched over like a very old lady. After an enormous cup of black coffee with two sugars and a hot shower, she was finally able to stand almost upright without feeling like she was going to faint.

Kerry made it out to her car and into the driver's seat, even though the sound of the doors' locks popping open made her want to vomit. She plugged her phone into the lead attached to the cigarette lighter socket and switched it on, and it burst back into life just as she gingerly pulled out of her driveway. Her physical pain had almost obliterated the memory of the previous night – or perhaps her trauma had just forced her brain to forget it – but now a list of Tim's texts lit up her phone's screen and she couldn't resist pulling into the bus stop on the edge of the village to read them. There were four in all. She read the first, goosebumps breaking out over her body as she remembered the softness of his lips on hers, the way his hands had been firm on her waist as he'd pulled her towards him... It was a pang of what felt like loss.

> *Kerry, please come back. It wasn't what you think. Please let me explain. Tim x*

She let the phone drop into her lap. What a liar! It couldn't possibly have been anything else. He was just saying it as a ruse to get her to talk to him again. Rage coursed through her that he'd made all these memories swirl up in her, like muddy shallows when you walked through them. Like the shallows of the village pond...

She deleted all four of the texts without looking at the other three, blocked Tim's number and switched the phone off again.

TWENTY-FIVE

1994

Things got a little hazy after that. Kerry downed the sickly orange WKD and then Lee started handing round a huge bottle of value-brand vodka that he had filched from the top shelf of the corner shop in town. Apparently, he'd staked out the shop for ages, waiting for the owner to disappear into the back to make his move.

Kerry felt a drunken pang on hearing this – the shopkeeper was an elderly turbaned guy with an incredibly lively and complicated white beard, who was always really nice to her and Beth when they went in for sweets after school. Not enough of a pang not to take a huge chug of the vodka whenever it was passed to her, though.

When Lee, Chris, Mutt and Timothy got up and started messing around, racing each other across the green on their bikes, they left the vodka behind on the grass and Kerry kept stealing more and more gulps, knowing it was a bad idea to drink this much and long after she wanted any more.

Beth had followed the boys, and Kerry could hear her shrieking with affected laughter, encouraging them as they clowned around. She was all over Chris. It seemed that every time she turned to look at them, Beth's hand was on his arm or touching his bike handlebars.

Kerry was sweating profusely. 'Is it me, or is it just not getting any cooler?' she panted, having a mental image of neat vodka oozing from her pores. 'It's ten o'clock and it still feels like it's about eighty degrees!'

When she lay back on the grass, she felt the dry prickles of the stalks on her bare arms and legs. The blue-black sky was beginning to whirl above her.

'Stick your feet in the water,' said Lee, who had materialised from nowhere. He sat down next to her, which normally would have alarmed her considerably, but she was so drunk that she didn't think twice about it. 'It's right nice.'

What an excellent idea, she thought blearily, kicking off her sweat-dampened Converse and lowering her hot feet into the water. It felt freezing at first, but as her skin acclimatised, blissful coolness began to creep up her calves and through her veins.

'Aah, that's so lovely,' she agreed, rotating her ankles and enjoying the silken feel of the dark water against them.

'Isn't your sister going out with Josh Prettejohn?' Lee asked disapprovingly, taking a long drag of what she'd assumed was a roll-up but which, when he handed it to her and she inhaled, she realised was a joint.

She choked down the smoke, trying to suppress a coughing fit which led to a series of undignified snorting sounds, and nodded.

'She's all over Chris like a rash,' Lee said. 'She wants to watch herself. Serena won't be happy.'

Through her haze Kerry remembered that Serena really fancied Chris. Had done since about Year Five, but he seemed unmoved by her pointy-faced charms. Serena was petite, with thick blonde short hair that curved around her features like a picture frame, but not what you'd call pretty, no matter how much she fluttered her eyelashes and pouted.

'Beth's only messing around,' she said, wondering why Lee even cared. 'She won't do anything.'

'You'd better make sure she doesn't.'

Kerry was too wasted to figure out if this was a threat, but it was a pleasant feeling, to not care. Lee obviously fancied Serena. Or Beth. Or both, probably. However hard she tried to get Serena to like her, Kerry usually felt on edge and inadequate around her, and she had no idea why. It was actually kind of nice to have Beth as the reason for Serena's disapproval. She felt removed from the situation, an abstract onlooker.

Then, to her utter shock and delight, Lee carefully stubbed out the joint, flopped down next to her so that their bodies were touching and, before she could do anything other than react instinctively, leaned across and kissed her. It was so out of the blue that Kerry didn't have time to think about it, or worry if she had bad breath, or how to cope with his tongue immediately pushing its way into her mouth.

Her first kiss. A lustful thrill shot through her, even though Lee didn't smell too great, up close. But she liked it when he put his arm around her waist and squeezed her. Then he gently pushed her onto her back and rolled on top of her, grinding into her with something small but enthusiastic. *Oh my gosh, an actual penis!* She felt a bit overwhelmed, but not enough to want to stop, so she moaned, in what she hoped was an appealing way.

The warm prickly grass had started to whirl her around as if she was on a magic carpet, or the roundabout in the kids' play-ground. Kerry had to open her eyes to make it stop, and she found herself looking into Lee's. They were clear and green and she couldn't tear herself away from his gaze. At that moment, she experienced what it was like to be in love.

They kept kissing until time slowed down even more – she had no idea how long they'd been at it for. Eventually, she started getting cramp in her foot, and his body pushing against her started to feel quite painful even though she could tell how aroused she had become. She wanted him. Should she let him know? She felt so turned on that she'd have dragged him over to the nearest tree and sloughed off her virginity right then, if he'd given her just the smallest bit of encouragement.

Instead, he rolled off her and sat up.

'Want another smoke?' he grunted in his strange man-boy voice, extracting the now-bent remains of the joint from the back pocket of his jeans.

'Hey,' he said next, in that thick, choking voice people used when they spoke through a mouthful of smoke. 'Let's get in. I'm well hot too. C'mon, I dare you.'

The duck pond, they knew, was surprisingly deep, about ten foot or so. She'd never swum in it but people did, in summer, just to cool down.

In general, Kerry was so mortified by her body that she would rather have eaten earthworms than strip off and swim in a public place. It was sad, because she used to love swimming when she was a kid; she had been a real water baby. But all that stopped abruptly as soon as her breasts burst into their current full bloom and her hips began to swell sideways. Whenever they went on family summer holidays, Mum, Dad and Beth would be splashing happily around in the shallows while Kerry would be huddled fully dressed and glowering on a sunbed.

But nobody had ever suggested she go for a swim in a situation like this, and particularly never an actual boy; one who – at that moment – she fancied. Kerry just felt wild and rebellious. All she knew was that the water was calling her with velvety dark promises of coolness, and Lee's eyes were roaming over her body in a way that turned her on. His admiring looks made her feel that perhaps she wasn't so ugly after all.

Lee was already standing up and wriggling out of his jeans and T-shirt. Sod it, she thought, giggling now with him, enjoying their brief complicity as she pulled off her own T-shirt and then, after a moment's hesitation, her shorts and underwear. Fortunately, she was wearing nice knickers, and she was even gladder of this as Lee stripped off a pair of saggy grey Y-fronts, immediately cupping his hands over his privates. Then he paused and stared at her.

'Wow,' he said. 'Your tits are... immense.'

At first she assumed he meant 'immense' as a compliment – 'awesome' in teen-speak. Immense and awesome were interchangeable. Later, she realised he likely just meant that they were massive and was excited by the prospect of getting his grimy paws on them. He'd probably never touched any before.

But in her almost fugue state, Kerry wanted to roar with pride. *I am woman*, she thought, and it was a heady realisation. Not a girl. Her body was soft, pale and curvy, but the sky was dark now, and she had a vision of Lee getting a tantalising glimpse of her naked boobs and going wild with desire... She was enjoying the freedom from the absolute tyranny of her acute self-consciousness. It was like being a kid again, jumping around on a beach without a care in the world.

... oh God, she could hear the boys laughing in the distance. Where were the others, anyway? She'd actually forgotten about them. The village green was silent now, just the faint sounds of Mum's party music floating across, punctuated by the faint guffaws.

She almost chickened out again, but by then she was naked too and it was too late to do anything other than let Lee grab her hand and run into the dark water from the little gravelly beach section a few feet away.

The shock! It felt absolutely freezing after the warm shallows her toes had bathed in. The gravel quickly changed to mud, which sucked at their ankles. She had to swallow the impulse to scream – even in her drunken state, she knew the last thing she wanted was to draw anybody's attention – and, once she and Lee had waded in up to their thighs, they flung themselves forward until they were fully immersed.

At first, the cold made Kerry pant like a dog, but then gradually the shock began to wear off a little and the water embraced her like a smooth hug. Swimming around on her own for a couple of minutes felt incredible, and she wondered why she'd denied herself the sheer pleasure of this release for so long. Her world had shrunk to this dark pond, like being back in the womb; she was reduced to the very essence of her Kerry-ness. She even lay back in the water and spread her arms wide, feeling her hair caress her shoulders as she floated.

But then Lee swam up to her and hugged her body against his, sinewy and slippery like a fish and somehow no longer as pleasant – perhaps because the water had begun to sober her up and change her priorities.

She wanted a boyfriend, sure – but Lee Carlton most definitely was not boyfriend material. If she let him do what he clearly wanted, the most likely outcome would be that she'd be left with a reputation. Maybe even a teen pregnancy. And there was no way she intended to lose her virginity in the middle of the weedy village duck pond.

He grabbed her hand and placed it on his penis. Kerry snatched it away. He felt for it underwater and snatched at it again, guiding it back.

'No,' she said. His penis felt weird and warm and, surprisingly, in the freezing water, still hard.

'Ah, come on, Kerry,' he wheedled. 'How hot is this?'

Not very, she thought. And, literally, really not very. She was beginning to shiver. 'I'm getting cold,' she said. 'I'm going to get out. Sorry.'

His face changed then. Even though darkness had completely fallen by now, she saw it by the sly dappled grey of the moon and it scared her. Gone was the soppy Lee, whispering sweet nothings, with whom she'd been briefly acquainted. Now it felt more as if she had got into a pond containing a mean and hungry shark.

'Sorry,' she repeated, desperately trying to touch the sandy bottom of the pond, but they were still out in the middle. She turned and swam a few feet towards the bank and tried again. This time her feet got purchase on the bottom and she started to wade as quickly as she could. She heard Lee splashing up behind her and waded even faster – but his arm shot out, grabbing her elbow. Again, she shook it off, more panicked now.

'Get off me!'

'You know what you are? You're a little pricktease,' she heard him hiss. 'Like I'd want to shag *you*, anyway! I need my head testing, I do.'

Now it occurred to Kerry, in a way that it somehow hadn't on the way in, that she was about to climb out of the water. Stark naked. With people around, even though she couldn't see them.

She frantically scanned the copse of trees and all the bushes, knowing that the rest of them were out there somewhere: Chris and Beth, Serena, Timothy, Lee's friend – what was his name? Mutt. All of them. The silence and stillness made her paranoid that they were all hiding and watching. She waited for the peals of laughter as she began to emerge from the water, the warm night air on her cold skin, heading towards the pile of her clothes on the bank.

Lee suddenly put his fingers in his mouth and whistled, as if he was calling a dog. *Oh no, no, no please don't do that...* She was still up to her waist, waiting in horror for the whole gang to descend, but when she caught a dark flash of movement in a clump of trees next to the pond, she saw only Mutt appear. He must have been watching the whole time. Mortified, she ducked back down under the surface, turning away from him. She heard the rustle of his clothes being stripped off, and then a dirty laugh and a hasty splash. Unable to process what was happening, it was only when she felt the two boys each grab one of her arms that she realised exactly how much trouble she was in.

TWENTY-SIX

2020

Kerry felt sufficiently revived to pull over at the petrol station on the way into work and buy herself two doughnuts, baulking only slightly at the stomach-churning Barbie pinkness of the icing. She'd finished one before she was even back in the car, and the sugar rush propelled her the rest of the way through the rainy grey morning into the sorting office, where she polished off the second doughnut with a cup of vile office coffee. Something approaching normality was beginning to still her shaking hands as she sorted grimly, slotting the mail in silence, headphones on to repel any would-be conversationalist, listening to *The Dream of Gerontius* on her phone in an attempt to calm herself.

Only five minutes behind her usual schedule, Kerry loaded up the trolley and wheeled it out to her van, opening the back doors and transferring the bundled contents on to the interior shelves. The rain was coming down in stair rods now, driving cold into the back of Kerry's bare calves and down her neck. She zipped up her red coat and climbed into the van, shivering, glad that she had a rural round and didn't have to share transport with another postie as the urban postmen did. Although feeling slightly better, she was still in no fit state to make idle chitchat with anybody.

For a moment she wished it was still lockdown, everybody safe inside their houses and not likely to hijack her outside the pub to ask if she'd seen the shocking graffiti on the bus shelter, or that Doreen from number five was on crutches after falling off a kerb. If they did, she was worried that she might yell in their well-meaning faces: *Do I look like I care? I've got a hangover, leave me alone!* You couldn't really run away wearing a Royal Mail uniform with a large red satchel over your shoulder; it wouldn't be a good look.

Kerry executed a clumsy three-point turn and navigated the van to the open sorting office gates, briefly surprised that the normal rush-hour congestion was absent and the road was empty in both directions, before remembering the reason; roadworks were causing a diversion further into town.

Good, she thought, switching on the radio and accidentally jogging the volume control with the side of her hand, causing a horribly discordant modern piece by a string quartet to blast out at eardrum-shattering volume.

She flipped on the indicator and was starting to pull out to cross the road, simultaneously glancing down to re-tune the radio and turn it down, when a flash of bright yellow from the pavement to her right caught her eye. To her horror, she saw it was a small child in a bright yellow rain mac with the hood up, little more than a toddler, freewheeling on a tiny bike out of control down the hill towards her. The child's father was a good twenty yards behind, running and shouting for him to stop but the kid either wouldn't or couldn't.

He was almost upon Kerry before she realised that he was going much faster than she'd thought; that the little bike was on a direct collision trajectory with her van. She hesitated for a fatal second, wondering if she should pull out at speed but then realising there was a car coming the other way. In the panicked heat of the moment she opted instead to try and reverse, so that the miniature biker wouldn't plough straight into the side of her van.

Throwing the van into reverse, Kerry desperately spun the steering wheel and stamped on the accelerator, shooting back into the sorting office yard a split second before the child sailed past, red-wellied feet in the air, screaming in terror, a hair's breadth from unspeakable disaster.

But she had reversed so fast, in such panic, that she had not had time to check her rear-view mirror and hadn't seen that she was reversing right into another Post Office van, parked at the side of the yard. Nor had she put on her seatbelt yet – she had got into a bad habit of not pulling it on until she drove out of the yard, and today not even then as she'd been distracted by the radio.

The noise of the crash was horrific, amplified by the enclosed yard of the sorting office; a brain-shredding, panic-inducing screech of metal on metal as her little red van's rear end caved in and she was thrown back at full force against the seat, ricocheting forwards against the steering wheel and banging her nose, hard.

Faces appeared at windows of nearby offices, and Kerry's colleagues began to stream out of the yard's doors wearing various expressions from shock and concern to pursed-lip intrigue, primed to pass on the live-at-the-scene gossip.

It was Clarissa who dashed across the yard and yanked open Kerry's door. 'Kerry, my love, are you OK? Your nose is bleeding! Let's get you out.' She grasped her arm, waiting only briefly for Kerry's nod of confirmation that she was not badly hurt.

Kerry meekly allowed herself to be escorted from the van, so numb with shock that she could barely feel her feet, nor the clasp of Clarissa's tissue under her nose. All she could see were the appalled faces of her colleagues. Then, just to add to her mortification and the general confusion, the shocked father stormed into the yard and right up to her, screaming child under one arm and bicycle in the other.

'You could've killed him! You weren't looking, I saw you! You were fiddling with your radio when you pulled out! What is wrong with you? If there had been a scratch on my kid, I'd have you in jail! Where's your boss? I want to make a complaint.'

He was young and entitled-looking, in a tweed jacket that reminded Kerry of Lord Buckley's. She thought how long ago that lunchtime encounter felt, even though it was only a few weeks. If only she could be there right now, sitting in the sunshine eating sandwiches and looking at the view, not being yelled at in the rain with a crowd of fascinated onlookers. It helped, to try and mentally step out of her body. Her face was throbbing from the punch of the airbags. Where was Nasty Nige, anyway? It was unlike him to miss a drama, particularly one involving her humiliation and distress.

One of the postmen, Bill, squared up to the angry father. 'That's not what I saw,' he said, and Kerry wanted to kiss him. He was such a good guy. He'd been pounding the pavements for over thirty years, ruddy-faced, reliable and cheerful, just how a postman should be. 'Your kid was out of control and you know it – you were chasing him! It's only because Kerry reversed so fast that she avoided him crashing straight into her. It wasn't her fault at all, and I'm more than happy to provide a witness state-ment saying as much.'

A few more of her colleagues discreetly edged in next to Bill to form a sort of human shield around Kerry, a solid mass of red jackets. Kerry had a flash of a fanciful image that, if a drone were to be hovering above them capturing the moment, the red jackets would form a heart shape.

Don't be ridiculous, she thought, even though she felt briefly and immeasurably comforted by it, as she was by the

firmness of Clarissa's arm around her shoulders. Clarissa was
the first-aid rep, but Kerry knew that she'd have reacted the
same even if that role had belonged to someone else.

The show of solidarity took the wind out of the man's sails
and he immediately backed down, turned on his heel and
stomped back out of the yard, the sound of his wailing child
swallowed up by the rumble of a train passing on the bridge
nearby.

'Thank you, Bill,' Kerry mumbled through the now-sodden
tissue. Clarissa handed her another one. 'Thank God you
saw it.'

Bill scratched one of his chins. 'That's all right, my lovely,'
he said, before addressing the red-clad crowd. 'OK everyone,
show's over. Let's get back to work.'

Everybody trickled back inside and Clarissa led Kerry
straight into the staff lounge, pushing her onto one of the hard,
stained old sofas and kneeling in front of her.

'Let's have a look at that nose,' she said, gently pulling the
bloody tissues away from it. Fresh blood immediately streamed
down over Kerry's lips and chin and Clarissa handed her a wad
of kitchen towel. 'Tip your head forwards, lovie. How much
does it hurt?'

'A lot.' Kerry wanted to cry but it would only make her nose
even more stuffed up.

'I don't *think* it's broken,' Clarissa said, carefully exam-
ining it. 'It hasn't gone wonky. But if it still really hurts later,
or if it's really swollen and you can't breathe through it, you
should get yourself up to A&E for an X-ray. It can be hard to
tell at first. You should've had your seatbelt on,' she chided
mildly.

'Please don't lecture me,' Kerry whispered, tearing off
several sheets and scrunching them against her nostrils. 'I know.
I was just about to put it on.'

'I'll get you the icepack. And a nice cup of tea.' Clarissa

bustled about, putting on the kettle and extracting an ice pack from the tiny freezer compartment of the staff fridge.

Nigel stormed into the lounge, his face mottled and purple with outrage. 'What the effing hell have you done now, Kerry?' he demanded. 'Can't I even take a dump in peace without hearing all hell's broken loose and you've managed to write off not one but two vans? What is *wrong* with you?'

Clarissa folded her arms over her chest. Even though she was tiny, she managed to look intimidating and Nigel actually backed away a step or two.

'Nigel, for God's sake, can't you see she's hurt? It wasn't her fault. She reversed to avoid an out-of-control toddler coming down the hill on a tricycle!'

'If you could give us a minute, Clarissa,' Nigel replied coldly. 'I'd like to talk to Kerry in private.'

Clarissa touched Kerry's shoulder. 'Will you be OK, lovie? I'll be just out there if you need me.' She gestured towards their sorting frames without waiting for an answer, briefly visible through the lounge door as Nigel closed it behind her.

Kerry waited for Nigel to start shouting at her like the angry father had, but instead he leaned against the Formica table, lifting one meaty buttock to perch on the edge of it. The table was, as always, covered with crumbs, day-old copies of the *Sun* and numerous rings from coffee cups. Nobody ever took responsibility for cleaning it during the day.

'It's true,' she mumbled. 'If I hadn't gone backwards, the kid would have gone straight into me. I just reversed instinctively.'

There was an uncomfortably long silence and Kerry could almost see the cogs of Nigel's tiny brain slowly whirring.

'Thing is, Kerry,' he began. She noticed how he hadn't even asked if she was all right, if she needed medical attention. She knew this sly expression of old. He was up to something.

'... you've caused serious damage to two Royal Mail vehicles.'

She opened her mouth to retort, but he held up a hand, like a traffic cop.

'If that crash had happened on public land, like out on the street, I'd have had no choice but to call the police. But because nobody was hurt, and the damage was done on our property, I don't have to. Unless—'

He paused for dramatic effect.

'Unless what?' Kerry just wanted to lie down and go to sleep. Her nose was throbbing in time with her headache.

'Unless I suspect that a crime has been committed. Which I do.'

A crime? What the hell?

'Nigel, what are you on about? It was an accident. What – you think I did it on purpose?'

'No. But I think you was driving while over the legal alcohol limit, and I have every right to call the police and inform them of my suspicions so that they can breathalyse you.'

'I haven't had a drink!'

'Not today, maybe. But it don't take a genius to work out that you was caning it last night, probably well into the early hours.'

He pronounced 'probably' like 'prolly'.

'Kerry, you stink of booze! And this wasn't the first time, neither. You most likely are still drunk.'

'Oh my God, I'm not!'

Kerry's eyes filled with tears and she had to focus on the long-dead spider plant on the windowsill to stop herself breaking down completely. It had stopped raining and a watery sun streamed in, showing exactly how dirty the windows were. She would not lose it, not in front of Nasty Nige. She hardly ever cried – at least, she never used to before her mother died.

'I'm not drunk,' she repeated, but deep down she knew this was very unlikely to be true. The chances were that any breathalyser test would almost certainly show her as being over the limit. She decided to try grovelling.

'Nigel, please don't call the police; please. This is all traumatic enough as it is. I've had a car crash. My mum only died a couple of months ago. I've got all this family stuff going on... I'm not in a good place at the moment. Please don't make things worse for me. I promise I'll sort myself out...'

A sly smile crossed Nigel's lips and Kerry realised he was enjoying this.

'OK then,' he said. 'Here's what's gonna happen. I won't call them, but you and I know this job just isn't working out for you any more. You're going to write a letter of resignation right now, and I'll let you go on gardening leave from today until your notice period is up, and we'll say no more about it.'

Kerry flopped against the sofa's vinyl back, utterly flabbergasted, unable to believe what she was hearing. '*What?*'

Nigel repeated it and Kerry tried to let the words sink into her brain. Resign? Her job? He'd said it so casually, as if she were one of the eighteen-year-old seasonal temps they hired in every year to help cope with the Christmas rush.

'Nigel... I've been here for twenty-five years!'

He shrugged. 'Your choice. You quit, or I call the police right now.'

Even though every atom of her was willing self-control, Kerry couldn't help crying, tears rolling down her bruised face and blocking her already blocked and bloody nose, forcing her to breathe heavily through her mouth. 'But I don't want to quit!' *This job is my life,* she thought. 'You can't do this, Nigel, not without Colin, or at least someone from HR present!'

Nigel shook his head patiently, as if she was intentionally not understanding. 'It's off the record. Our little secret. You don't tell no one I made you leave, and I don't tell no one you was drinking. Honestly, Kerry, I'm saving you from yourself. You need to get a job where you don't need to drive, or something much worse will happen. Think of this as an intervention. Look, I'll even give you a reference.'

'Why do you hate me so much?' Her voice was tiny.

He gazed levelly at her and she saw the triumph in his piggy, pale-blue eyes. 'I wouldn't call it hate, Kerry, that's a bit strong. But you know we don't get on. I think it's time for a change, for both of us.'

Kerry knew that if she went straight to Colin, her union rep, to report this outrage it would be her word against Nigel's, and he was her line manager. They'd believe him, not her, and she'd only end up in the same situation but with a whole heap more aggravation.

'What about my *pension*?'

She couldn't believe this was happening.

Nigel smiled meanly. 'I'm not a complete monster, Kerry. I'll square it with HR that you get invalided out on enhanced health grounds.'

It sounded as if he'd already given it considerable thought, and today's incident had given him the green light to proceed.

'On what grounds? I'm not ill.'

'Oh, I think you are, Kerry.'

She watched him tap the side of his temple to demonstrate the nature of her 'illness'. It wouldn't have surprised her if he had twirled his finger round and round in the universal gesture for insanity – but he didn't need to. That tap made it quite clear what he thought. At that moment she had never detested anybody more.

'All you need to do is to get a letter from your doctor signing you off sick and confirming that you've gone for some kind of treatment. Depression, alcoholism, bereavement, whatever, I don't care. It's up to you. You get the letter, you get your pension. If not...'

He let the threat trail away, like a plane's vapour trail.

Kerry felt like her nose had stopped bleeding. Indeed, she

felt like the blood had stopped flowing through her entire body. She gingerly removed the wodges of tissues and placed them carefully on the table between them in a crimson crumpled pile. Nigel looked as if he was about to vomit and averted his eyes, glancing instead at his watch.

'So, you'll do it?'

Decide, just like that, after twenty-five years? She closed her eyes. Her whole adult life. Her career, her identity, her stability. What would she do? Who would she be? She had no qualifications, no self-confidence, nothing to offer anybody else.

She thought of her lovely round, how much she would miss the kindly old ladies waving out of their front windows or answering the door to her, unfailingly pleased to see her every day. Her lunchtime sandwich shared with the grazing sheep on Lord B's clover-studded land; chats with Clarissa in their frames about the latest Netflix drama; laughs with Bill in the tea room.

It would all be over. What would be the point of even continuing to exist? This was her entire *life*.

'Give me some time to think about it,' she said wearily.

Nigel headed for the door. 'I'll get Gavin to do your round. You can have half an hour to think about it, but no longer than that cos, if you say no, I need to get you breathalysed pronto. And anyway...' He was halfway out of the room when he looked back over his shoulder, not an ounce of compassion in his expression. '... I don't think you have a choice, do you?'

TWENTY-SEVEN

1994

Lee and Mutt held her arms so tightly that she could feel the different sizes of their respective fingertips pressing into each cold bicep, Lee's skinny and long, Mutt's chunkier. The two naked boys dragged her into the water again, like some weird midsummer ritual. Where was everyone else? Even in the terror of the moment, Kerry couldn't understand how they could be so alone. Surely Beth wouldn't have stayed away on their instructions?

She struggled as hard as she could to shake them off but, in a hellish parody of baptism, they seemed to share some kind of signal and simultaneously pushed her backwards, dunking her into the pond. It was so sudden that the algal water whooshed up her nose and down her throat, making her cough and splutter as they hauled her back up to standing. Mutt reached out and fondled her breast with his left hand, and Kerry wanted to rip both hand and breast off her body, leave them at the bottom of the pond. She coughed so much that she thought she was going to vomit, then tried to scream, but Lee slid behind her and clamped his forearm round her throat, shutting her mouth, making her choke. Both boys were laughing, low and quiet.

'You have first go,' Lee said, and for a moment Kerry thought he was talking to her. First go at what? Initially relieved when he started pushing her shoulders down because she could breathe properly again, she saw, in the silvery moonlight, that he was pushing her towards Mutt's erection.

Horrified, she started shaking her head violently from side to side, but Lee grasped each of her ears and then, when her face was level with *it*, he reached over the top of her head and pinched her nose between his fingers, forcing her to open her mouth. Mutt shoved his penis in, making her gag, unable to pull away because Lee had pressed himself up against her from behind. She could feel him, too, against the back of her head. Mutt began to move, groaning with pleasure. She started lashing out with her hands, splashing and hitting the surface of the water, making a high-pitched squealing noise like a kettle coming to the boil. Without any conscious thought, she bit down, and it was Mutt's turn to squeal.

'You bitch!'

He tore himself away from her, wading fast out of the pond, whimpering with pain, and Lee tried to pivot her by the shoulders. Was he crazy?

'I'll do exactly the same to you if you come anywhere near me with that pathetic little pencil dick,' she hissed, and Lee hesitated. That was all Kerry needed to be able to rip his hands off her shoulders and shove him away with all her might. He fell back into the water with a mighty splash and Kerry turned and headed for the bank of the pond as fast as she could, shaking with shock and cold.

That was when the darkness of the green was shattered by a sudden splintering white light. Lightning? No wonder it was humid. But then it came again, and again, and then, there it was: Serena's shrill laugh. They were back, and all looking. And someone – Timothy with the cameras – was taking photographs. She honestly didn't think things could have got any worse.

Panicking, she stumbled and almost sank back into the water herself. She didn't even have a towel to wrap herself in. What the hell had she been thinking? What was she going to do now?

Torn between staying in, with Lee still in there, and out, exposed, Kerry dithered for a second. But now that the others were back, surely there was no way that Lee would try anything else. Where was Beth? Why wasn't she helping?

Mutt had grabbed his clothes and vanished into the darkness, presumably not wishing to be seen naked by the gang. Kerry could hear laughs and jeers as Lee crashed angrily out of the water too, snarling 'Fuck off,' at the others as he cupped his hand back over his genitals and then covered himself with his shorts.

Mercifully alone in the pond, Kerry ducked back down in the water and crouched on the bottom, up to her neck, feeling soft cold mud squish between her toes and thinking she was just going to have to stay there for ever, or at least until they all went home. Gooseflesh swept up and down her body and her teeth began to chatter uncontrollably. Her jaw hurt and even after letting the murky pond water in, she still had a sour taste in her mouth.

Serena and the boys were still whooping and laughing, including Mutt and Lee now, both only too happy to deflect any embarrassment straight back onto her. Chris and Beth wandered over and joined the others, Beth's mouth a perfect circle of shock and astonishment at seeing Kerry on her own, submerged like a hippopotamus in the water. Her head swivelled between Kerry and the pile of her clothes on the bank, and Kerry knew Beth was trying to see if her underwear was there too.

Now all six of them were lined up on the grass, staring at her with a mixture of amusement, consternation and anger. They could have been at a zoo, standing next to the barrier of the hippo enclosure. Those evil bastard boys, looking as if they were as surprised to see her in there as the others were. Tears leaked hot from her eyes.

'Get out, Kerry, what are you doing?' Beth hollered. 'You'll freeze!'

Beth clearly couldn't get her head around what she was seeing – unsurprisingly, since she knew Kerry's abhorrence for being caught naked. Beth had never even seen her in her underwear at home, not since they got separate bedrooms when Kerry turned twelve. Kerry saw her glance again, even more incredulously, at the pile of clothes on the grass.

This was a nightmare. What was she going to do? There was absolutely no way she'd be able to get out with them all watching. She tried to telepathically implore Beth to make them all walk away, to protect her modesty, but of course it didn't work.

Kerry's whole body was shaking now, and she couldn't feel the mud between her toes any more. She couldn't feel anything at all in her hands and feet. Why was she so stupid? How could she have ever thought that letting Lee persuade her into the pond was a good idea?

She started to cry harder, warm tears now not just sliding down her face, but plopping into the water.

'I'll get you a towel,' Beth shouted, and started to run towards their house at a proper, all-out sprint. Relief flooded through Kerry. She had never loved her little sister more.

It felt as if Beth had been gone for half an hour, but it was probably only three or four minutes before she ran back – slightly more slowly, but still at a jog – a big bath towel over her arm.

She beckoned to Kerry impatiently. 'Come on, Kerry, stop messing around.'

But Kerry wasn't 'messing around'. She was frozen to the

spot with cold and embarrassment. She made an agonised face at Beth, gesturing towards the others.

'Right, you lot, show's over,' Beth barked. 'Give the girl some privacy! Chris – get them away, could you?'

Kerry had to admire her brass neck. The youngest of them all, she had no qualms in bossing everyone around and expecting them to obey her. Chris, presumably smitten, immediately dragged Lee, Mutt and Timothy back towards their bikes, which were lying on the grass over by the trees. Serena followed, but was looking back over her shoulder at Kerry, a sly, pleased expression on her face, as if she had won a competition that she hadn't realised she'd entered.

Still, Kerry was too cold and traumatised to worry about Serena at that moment. Beth angled herself between Kerry and the others and spread the bath towel wide to shield her as much as possible. 'Quick. Nobody's looking,' she urged.

Kerry whimpered. She didn't trust them all not to rush back, laughing.

'Tell them to go further,' she croaked.

'Oh for heaven's sake, just get out. You didn't worry about all this when you got in!'

There was a dog walker now, on the other side of the pond, taking an arthritic Scottie for its evening constitutional. Kerry's heart sank when she recognised the dog – its owner lived a few cottages away from them, an elderly widower who knew Mum. What if he told her? What if he told everyone? He'd stopped and was staring at her. Hopefully he wouldn't recognise her, she thought. Her heart was racing.

But at least the gang was a bit further away. She couldn't see them clearly, so surely they wouldn't be able to see her?

'Come *on*,' Beth hissed. Why was she being so unsympathetic, Kerry thought, before remembering that Beth was pretty drunk herself. Alcohol seemed to make her even more blunt.

Kerry took a deep breath and began to wade through the

water towards the shore, mud turning to sand to sharp stones that pricked her soles back to life. Water streamed off her as she dashed out, horribly conscious of her bottom and breasts wobbling as she ran towards Beth's outstretched arms and the safety of the towel's embrace.

But as she was almost there, more disaster struck. Clumsy with cold, shock and haste, she stumbled on unsteady legs and her ankle gave way beneath her.

She fell onto the grass, spread-eagled and humiliated. And immediately it came again, the camera's flash...

'Oh, Kerry!'

Beth ran to her and threw the towel over her – but not before Kerry heard a hoot of cruel laughter from the others. Of course they had all turned round to watch her undignified exit. For them, her fall was the icing on the cake of the evening's entertainment.

I want to die, Kerry thought as she lay there, her ankle throbbing, her flesh deathly cold. *I will never get over this, never.*

TWENTY-EIGHT

2020

Kerry survived a silent weekend on sleeping pills and in shock, seeing and speaking to no one, metaphorically licking her wounds. By Monday she supposed she would eventually have to get up and do some 'adulting' – much as she'd have preferred to stay there for ever. Her nose had ballooned rather than subsided, throbbing in time to the slightest movement, so she rang the doctor.

The doctors' surgery was still only reluctantly giving out appointments. You had to have a phone chat with the receptionist and then a video consultation first to determine whether or not you'd be allowed through the sterilised doors. Kerry couldn't face telling the receptionist that she needed a letter signing her off work in order to be able to claim her pension, so she pretended that her request for an appointment was solely because she'd had a car crash.

'I'm worried that it's broken,' she said, on Zoom, and one look at her black and purple eyes and swollen nose seemed to be enough to convince Dr Harkness to book her in for that afternoon.

Kerry drove slowly and carefully into town later, aching

from her heart up to the top of her head, but sober at least. The shock of Nigel forcing her to write her resignation letter had taken the stuffing out of her so thoroughly that when lovely Clarissa had driven her and her car home on Friday, Kerry had not been able to say a single word. Clarissa had offered to stay with her, but Kerry had gingerly shaken her head and hugged her wordlessly, before pointing her in the direction of the bus stop back into town and vanishing into the annexe.

Kerry arrived at the surgery to find all the chairs in the waiting room taped off across their arms like mini crime scenes, with just one or two left, marooned underneath bossy printed signs saying: STRICTLY FOR ELDERLY OR DISABLED PATIENTS. The heat and a strong smell of disinfectant was making her feel a bit dizzy, but since she was neither disabled nor elderly, she thought that she might get booted out if she sat down, so she leaned against the wall and waited. Her face mask was constricting her already-constricted breath and her armpits felt drenched with sudden sweat.

Last time she was in this doctors' surgery had been with her mum. Kerry thought of her apple-cheeked mother, the plump squashy bundle of her in her hairy wool checked coat and sensible shoes, smelling of hairspray and Imperial Leather soap. How could she just not be here any more? It seemed inconceivable.

The door opened and Dr Harkness stuck her coiffed head out. 'Kerry Tucker? Come on in.'

As Kerry walked into the room, tears clouded her eyes. Her head was swimming and her legs seemed to have no bones in them. The magnolia walls began to shimmer and turn black at the edges, and she must have wobbled noticeably because the doctor, moving more quickly than her stiff appearance implied she might, shoved a chair into the back of her knees and gently forced Kerry's head down into her lap.

'Oh dear, poor thing. We are in a bit of state, aren't we?' she said briskly, her cool hand pressing soothingly on Kerry's neck. Having her face down was making her nose feel even more blocked, so she took a few deep breaths and slowly raised her head. 'Sorry,' she said. 'Yes. It's been a very challenging week.'

Dr Harkness handed her a tissue but Kerry shook her head, gingerly. 'I can't blow my nose,' she said with a grimace. It sounded like *blow by dose.*

'So you had a fight with a steering wheel, you said?'

'Yeah. I had to reverse fast to avoid a kid that ran out in front of me, and I crashed one Post Office van into another. It happened on Friday morning and I got fired.'

'Oh goodness. I am so sorry.'

Dr Harkness took a seat behind her desk and regarded Kerry sympathetically. She was a beaky no-nonsense woman in her late fifties, whose rigid helmet of grey candyfloss hair meant that she would pass for someone ten years older. 'Let me know once you've stopped feeling dizzy and I'll do a few tests on you, check if that nose is broken. How long did it bleed for, at the time?'

Kerry shrugged. 'Um... not sure, really. Twenty minutes?'

'Any clear fluid from the nostrils since?'

Only when I've been crying, she thought, but shook her head. The movement made the room undulate.

'The faintness isn't a great sign, but your nose doesn't look crooked. I'll have a little feel in a moment. Breathing difficulties?'

'Well, it's still quite blocked.'

Dr Harkness gestured to Kerry to climb up on the examination coach and continued her interrogation, gently manipulating her head and neck and shining a torch up her nose. She eventually decided that Kerry probably hadn't broken anything, but should come back if the swelling hadn't gone down in a few more days.

Kerry was still prone, staring at the ceiling, which made it easier to make her request: 'Work is planning to invalid me out on enhanced health grounds and I need a doctor's letter signing me off sick,' she blurted, thinking that 'enhanced health grounds' made it sound like she was being sacked for being *too* healthy. To her surprise and embarrassment, she burst into tears. Once she started, she couldn't stop, and within minutes she was crying like a baby, the tears sliding sideways and being soaked up by the white protective paper on the couch.

'I'm so sorry,' she sobbed. 'Everything's just going wrong at the moment. My mum died. I've just lost the job I've had since I was eighteen. I'm going to lose the house I've lived in my whole life because my sister is insisting we sell it. Now we've fallen out and I'm drinking myself stupid on my own every night. I met a man I really liked, for literally the first time in my life, and it turns out he's the same guy who did something terrible to me as a teenager.' Her voice rose until she was almost wailing. 'Oh God, and my nose is so blocked.'

'Ah,' Dr Harkness said, levelly. 'Well, let's try and get to the bottom of this, shall we? My next patient has cancelled, so I have a bit of extra time. Tell me how often you drink, and how much?'

Fifteen minutes and several dozen questions later, red-eyed and subdued yet possibly feeling marginally better – it was hard to tell – Kerry left the surgery. In her hand was a prescription for antidepressants and a leaflet for the local chapter of Alcoholics Anonymous (which she screwed into a tiny ball and lobbed into the bin as soon as she stepped outside the surgery). Dr Harkness had also given her a referral for a course of six CBT sessions and the promise of a letter to the Royal Mail's HR department stating she was suffering from severe depression and not fit to work.

'Don't be afraid to ask for help, Kerry,' had been the doctor's parting words. 'And don't think that going to AA is any sort of sign of failure. What you've been through would test anybody to the limit.'

Dr Harkness had been really kind and understanding, despite her somewhat intimidating appearance. But, Kerry thought, there's no way I need to go to AA. I'm not an alcoholic! I'm just stressed. I'll get the antidepressants and that'll sort me out.

TWENTY-NINE

A middle-aged, lonely woman on – or about to go on – antidepressants. Fired from the job she's had for twenty-five years. A fight on her hands for the house which, whatever the outcome, would almost certainly result in further estrangement from her sister. And if she lost and the house had to be sold, she would also lose the only other home she'd ever known. She'd fallen out with Tim – or at least assumed she had, since she had blocked his email address and Facebook profile as well as his phone number – and with Beth. Parents – dead. Friends – basically one, Sharon, who she didn't even really like all that much, if she was honest...

All these thoughts were chugging in circles through Kerry's head like a toy goods train carrying a cargo of something particularly toxic. She had unburdened herself to the doctor in an attempt at catharsis but disappointingly, she realised that she did not feel any better. It was so irritating, feeling this low all the time.

To try and escape the negativity she went straight over to the big house when she got back, her nostrils tainted with the mingled tang of disinfectant and frustration. Despite Dr Harkness' words, having 'let it all out' only seemed to have increased her sense of failure and hollowness.

All she wanted to do was to sit on Mum's shabby reclining sofa in front of the big TV and binge-watch something while drinking herself stupid. If the medication was going to force her to cut down on the booze, she might as well have one last blow-out. She raided Mum's drinks cupboard, which yielded half a bottle of Hendrick's gin and an unopened bottle of tonic water.

Good old Mum, Kerry thought, mentally blowing her a kiss.

Pouring herself a large G&T, she turned off her mobile – not that anybody would be trying to ring her, she thought self-pity-ingly – and levered herself horizontal on the sofa, glass in one hand, TV remote in the other. She decided to watch random episodes of *Friends*, for no other reason than that there were millions to choose from and mindlessly stare at, and they wouldn't remotely add to her current emotional challenges.

As the familiar theme music struck up, and the first numbing welcome hit of alcohol slid down her gullet, she thought of Mum sitting in this very spot, with this very glass in her hand. Mum wouldn't have been watching *Friends* though, she was too cerebral for that. She'd probably have been watching a David Attenborough documentary, or *Mastermind* or *Question Time*.

Kerry smiled then, thinking of her mother watching *Master-mind*, firing off the answers often before the young contestants could open their mouths. Kerry herself had a question-answering average of one per episode – and that was usually one she thought she *might* know the answer to, not necessarily even the correct answer – whereas her mum seemed to know at least three quarters, apart from the science questions, when she'd just sigh sadly and say, 'Oof, we need your father for this one.'

Then Kerry's mind scrolled back further, to the same room, a smaller, squatter television in the corner but from the same vantage point. Beth and herself, still at primary school, squashed together with Mum and Dad on an even less comfortable sofa – a dark green scratchy fabric that she remembered as being like hessian, with thin, straight, highly polished wooden arms. Very 1970s. But they were all laughing, watching one of the programmes they adored: *The Generation Game, Morecambe and Wise, It's a Knockout!* Kerry had loved it when she got to sit next to her dad because he always put his arm round her and hugged her close, occasionally kissing the top of her head. His beard would tickle her forehead and she'd squirm with happiness.

She could not imagine ever feeling happy like that again. Perhaps that was just adulthood for you, though. Nobody warned you about it when you were a kid. Nobody ever said, 'Enjoy life while you can, because it all gets a hell of a lot harder once you grow up. And there may even come a time when nothing even seems worth it any more.'

Within minutes, her glass was empty. On *Friends*, Phoebe was playing her guitar badly and singing about a smelly cat, but Kerry wasn't finding it amusing yet. She pressed the side lever on the sofa and lowered her legs to the floor to go and top up her drink, bringing the bottles back with her so that she wouldn't have to get up next time. Idly, she wondered how the sofa recliner worked. Did it plug in? Run on batteries? She didn't want to wear out the mechanism, anyway. Easier if she just stayed there and poured her drinks in situ. Who needed ice?

After the third drink and the third episode, she was feeling safer. Drunk, obviously, but safe.

Kerry sank into the sofa's leathery embrace. She felt close to her family here, on this sofa, which still faintly smelled of her mother, a unique combination of hairspray, knitting wool and perfume. She didn't have to think about anything except whether or not Rachel and Ross were going to get together.

After the fourth drink, her safe feeling had morphed into a

weird kind of reckless glee. Hell, she didn't have to get up for work tomorrow, or ever again. At that moment, she revisited the ever-more tempting idea of becoming a proper, full-on hermit. Claim squatters' rights on the house, do all her shopping online and literally never go out again. Why not?

She laughed out loud, drowning out the laughter from the TV. She'd cut her own hair when it got in her eyes, never shave her legs, never bother with make-up, never have to prepare small talk in advance of going to a party she didn't want to be at. She would get rid of the landline and her mobile and just communicate through her laptop. Eat takeaways and Wotsits for breakfast; drink whatever she liked. Slot jigsaw pieces together, if she got bored of the television. Keep the lawn edges looking sharp – which would also constitute exercise.

Sounded bloody great, if you asked her. She'd get gossiped about in the village, undoubtedly, by the same rotund ladies with ham-hock forearms and wheeled shopping bags who used to stop her on her round and gossip to her about their neighbours; or by Kev in the corner shop, whose double chin was so enormous that it practically had its own postcode and yet who saw no irony in mentioning that Neil the pub landlord was 'piling on the pounds and looked terrible'. But it wouldn't matter what they said about her, because she'd never know, and what she didn't know couldn't hurt her. Someone else could deliver the mail to her house, but she'd make sure she always ducked out of sight so that her replacement couldn't report back that she'd gone feral. Beth would never go so far as to get bailiffs in, or anything radical like that. She'd come around, eventually, to having the rental income from the garage.

Kerry decided to forget what Beth had said about the garage being unrentable to anybody apart from her.

She felt a strange, initially unnameable craving which, once she concentrated on it, she realised was a yearning for nicotine. Could you order cigarettes via Deliveroo? Then she remembered she still had a few left in the pack she'd bought after Tim's bombshell. They were in the side pocket of her handbag. Hurrah!

Completely forgetting her earlier vow not to sully the big house with nicotine smells, she levered herself back up and weaved unsteadily over to her bag. Collecting matches and an empty coffee mug to use as an ashtray, she rested the objects on the arm of the sofa and settled herself back in.

There was a lot to be said for giving up on life. No pressure. No expectations. Kerry thought perhaps she'd just kept going for as long as she had because she knew how disappointed and worried Mum would be if she didn't.

After another couple of episodes of *Friends*, two more drinks and five cigarettes on an empty stomach, she had to admit that she was starting to feel a bit ill.

And there it was again, that strange yearning to be back in the annexe, her breeze-block nest of safety. She suddenly felt as if she was still disappointing Mum by getting drunk and smoking on her sofa. Not to mention losing her job and falling out with Beth. The eternal teenager. She'd be getting spots next.

Kerry staggered back across the driveway, overcome with an exhaustion both physical and existential after her bewildering assortment of recent emotions.

She barely had the energy to climb up the loft ladder before she crashed out in her clothes, falling into a deep sleep that was more akin to unconsciousness than slumber.

It felt like mere minutes after that when something woke her, something strange and out of place. She couldn't work out what it was at first. It felt like something supernatural – a miasma, or presence. A smell, an aura, a taste; nothing physical. A ghost? She sat up, alarmed and frightened. She'd never felt frightened in her garage before.

'Hello?' she called, in a tremulous voice.

Silence. Then, when she listened very hard, an odd sound coming from outside.

A crackling sound, a dragon's exhalation.

Then Kerry realised what the smell was.

'Oh no, no, no – *fire!*'

THIRTY

Sliding down the ladder, Kerry looked wildly around her, but all seemed normal inside the annexe, still and silent, as if it was holding its breath. No fire in here then, good. Perhaps it was a barn across the fields; that had been known to happen. Or perhaps she was imagining it? Better check, anyway. She shoved her feet into trainers and grabbed her mobile from the table, realising that she still felt drunk.

Kerry opened the door – and fell to her knees on the gravel. The big house was completely ablaze, orange flickering light at all the windows, like a Halloween pumpkin, thick smoke leaching through any available gaps and billowing out of the chimney. As she watched, as if they had been waiting for an audience, both the first-floor windows shattered triumphantly and simultaneously, with a horrifying whipcrack sound, flames shooting out into the cool night sky like someone had set them free to dance.

She tried to shout, but nothing came out. *My home! Our house!*

Even then, in the midst of the shock and panic, she thought, *Beth is going to kill me*. She must not have put out that last

cigarette properly. She tried to remember where it had been and
her heart sank further – the mug she was using as an ashtray
had been balanced on the arm of the sofa. If it had fallen, an
unextinguished cigarette could easily have rolled out and
ignited the bottom of the curtain.

Kerry pulled out her phone to dial 999 but as she did so she
could hear a sweep of sirens coming down the lane, so she put
the phone away and ran over to open the gate for them. Three
fire engines pulled up in a swirl of red lights, the first labori-
ously manoeuvring onto the driveway, narrowly squeezing in
between the gateposts and parking so close to her car that their
bumpers touched.

The second and third engines parked outside in the lane
and suddenly the place was alive with activity, men running
everywhere, unrolling hoses, barking commands. A burly
fireman ran over to her, clomping across the gravel in his rubber
wellies, and shouted in her face: 'Is anyone in there? Is this your
house?'

He had kind eyes and a white goatee beard sticking out over
the chinstrap of his helmet, the sort of man who would look
more at home in an artist's smock than a fireman's uniform.

She shook her head, then nodded, suddenly mute with the
horror. She had an urge to step into his arms and let him bear
her away somewhere safe where there were no fires. She
wanted him to whisper reassurances into her ears, *No, no, don't
worry, Beth will understand, accidents happen, as long as the
house is insured...*

Oh hell, she thought, the panic rising in her again. *Was* it
insured? Who had renewed the home insurance? When had it
run out, before Mum died, or afterwards and neither Beth nor
she had realised? Then she thought, thank God there wasn't a
cat. Or a lodger. Or *her!* She could so easily have gone up to the
spare bedroom to crash out. In fact, she wasn't sure why she
hadn't, given that she'd been sleeping over there on and off for

the past week or two. It was nothing short of a miracle that she'd decided to go back across to the garage. She'd probably be dead if she hadn't.

The fireman was shouting something else at her but there was so much of a din, with the fire and the hoses and water spraying in huge arcs at the windows, she couldn't make out what it was.

'There's definitely nobody inside?'

Kerry shook her head again, more firmly.

He leaned closer to her and gently took her elbow. 'Please step away. Let us get on with our job. Our fire officer will come and have a word with you in a little while, OK?'

'OK,' she said obediently, and turned away, towards the gate, heading in the direction of a police car's whirling blue light. She noticed that people were congregating on the green across the road, staring like zombies at her and the burning house, some in pyjamas and dressing gowns. What were they doing? Wasn't it the middle of the night? She realised she had no idea what time it was. These were people she knew, that she'd known for all her life no less – but not one of them approached her, even though they'd been friends of her parents', and she'd delivered their birthday cards, their bills, their insurance renewal requests. Instead, they moved slightly away as she came through the gate, even though she was nowhere near them, as if they thought she was contagious.

It cut through her shock, this brutal shunning, wounding her more than she would have thought possible. These were the people that she believed were her community, the 'leaves on her tree', the reason she'd stayed in the village so long. She was Kerry the Postie! She had a kind word for everyone, she always stopped to chat. Deep down, she'd always thought – hoped, at least – that the community might love her too. Not in an arrogant way, but in a way that gave her a place in the world, the sense of security she lacked in family and love. She was their postwoman, the continuity in their village lives for a quarter of a century. She had thought that meant something. But now, as she stood alone in the middle of the road outside and not one of them came forward to talk to her, she realised she must have been wrong.

Tears streamed unchecked down her cheeks as more villagers clustered on the green, staring as if they expected her to start juggling or doing cartwheels or something to entertain them. As if the sight of the crackling orange flames shooting out of the roof and windows of her house wasn't enough. Her childhood home, her inheritance, her memories of happier times.

There was Mrs Keneally, whose eldest daughter had had a sex change and who once told Kerry she was the 'only person round here who hasn't judged me'. She was on the green tutting and clutching hands with Irene Martin, whose first husband used to abuse her continually. A few years ago, when Kerry could no longer bear hearing Barry yell at Irene whenever she walked up the garden path, she'd slipped an envelope containing the number of the local women's refuge through their letterbox with their post. Irene told her that her note had given her the courage to confide in her brother, and he had come round and forcibly ejected the abusive Barry. 'I'd never have done it if I hadn't realised that it was getting obvious to everyone else,' Irene wept on Kerry's shoulder a few weeks later. 'I feel like a new woman!'

Now Irene and Patricia Keneally were just standing gawping silently at her, in a little huddle with Neil and Ginny from the pub, and Tom and Jean, the farmers. The thought that they must actually have climbed into their battered old Land Rover and driven here made Kerry want to go up and scream *get a life!* at them. At that moment, she hated them all.

There was enough of a crowd gathering now that two policemen were setting up a cordon and firmly gesturing to everyone to get behind it. Kerry wiped her burning eyes and approached the nearer officer – a slight, weedy-looking bespec-tacled man whose hat seemed far too big for him – tugging at his sleeve as if he was her infant-school teacher even though she was probably twice his age.

Kerry thought of her mum, always commenting how young the police were getting these days... *We all turn into our parents, in the end.*

'Hi,' she said, speaking close to his ear. 'This is my house... my mum's house. Well, actually, she just died, so it belongs to me and my sister. I live there.' She pointed at the garage.

He made a sympathetic face at her, turning the corners of his mouth down and tilting his head to one side. 'Right. I'm so sorry. This must be horrible for you.'

'I've had better nights,' she agreed.

Taking out a pencil and small notebook – didn't they have Notes apps on their phones these days, like everyone else? – he opened it at a blank page. 'Could I take your name, phone number and this address please, Miss...?'

Even in the midst of the trauma it didn't escape Kerry's notice that he assumed she was a Miss, not a Mrs.

'*Ms* Tucker. Kerry Tucker. 5B Barley Cottage, Main Street, SP5 7JT. The main house is number five, I'm 5B.'

He took a few more details, which she recited on autopilot, hoping she wasn't slurring her words. She wasn't entirely sure that she'd got the digits of her mobile number in the correct order. What if he breathalysed her?

'You'll have to repeat all this to the fire officer over there for his official report but – you weren't in the house when the fire broke out, were you?'

Kerry couldn't tell if he said this in an accusatory way or not, but assumed he did, because she was feeling so paranoid.

'No! Definitely not. I popped in earlier to, er, water the plants, but I was asleep in the garage – the annexe. The smell woke me up but I'm a heavy sleeper and by the time I realised, the fire had really taken hold. I don't know who called 999 but it wasn't me – the engines were already arriving before I got the chance. It must have been one of the neighbours.'

He wrote this down, although Kerry couldn't think why he needed to. Or why she'd lied about watering plants. Mum hadn't even had any houseplants. Her eyes were stinging badly from the biting smoke, so at least she could pretend she wasn't crying. The policeman's eyes were watering too, and when he wiped them, he left black sooty marks on his cheeks.

'So nobody is currently living there, no lodgers who happened to be away tonight?'

'No. Nobody else. I keep an eye on the place, obviously. Mum left it to me and my sister in her will. I'm hoping to move in soon, but my sister wants to sell, so we're just waiting for that to get sorted out.'

Kerry immediately cursed herself. What the hell did she say that for? Now he would think that Beth had a motive for burning the place down! And he did start scribbling even faster. What had she done?

As if he could read her mind, he said, 'Oh dear. Hopefully the brigade can save it, although I'd say it's not looking too good.'

They both stared in the direction of the house and Kerry saw the flames reflect orange in his glasses; felt them warm her cheeks. Despite jets of water from several hoses all directed at the roof, it was now fully alight too, the fire seeming to climb ever higher skywards, roaring and hissing at her. There would be no house left, that much was obvious.

The villagers were now corralled behind the police tape, muttering to themselves. The crowd seemed to have grown and Kerry's heart sank when she was sure she recognised Lee Carlton at the back, astride one of those bikes with ridiculously small wheels and low saddle, the current equivalent of an old

Raleigh Chopper. He was the last person she wanted to see. She scowled in his direction, even though he wasn't looking, and then looked twice and saw that it wasn't him at all, just a skinny teenager with a similar build.

Kerry felt like she was going mad; seeing things. She glanced at the house, half expecting to see her mum's stricken, beseeching face trapped at an upstairs window.

'Can't you get rid of them all?' she begged the policeman, gesturing over to the green. 'I can't bear that they're all staring, like my house burning down is free entertainment.'

He smiled sympathetically. 'I'll have a word,' he said.

'Can I go home? Back there, I mean.' She pointed at the garage again. 'I feel a bit shaky.'

'It's a shock,' he agreed. 'I'd say you could do with a cup of tea. But you shouldn't be in there, not until the fire's out. Just to be on the safe side. Fumes and suchlike. And like I said, you need a chat with the fire officer. I'll introduce you now. After that, is there anyone local you could go to?'

Kerry looked around doubtfully. If none of the assembled company even had the decency to come over and talk to her, she didn't think they'd welcome her bringing her sooty distress home with them. Not that she wanted to, anyway.

The policeman walked her across the drive towards a rotund fireman who was also writing in a notebook, the yellow reflective strips on his tunic and trousers flashing in the head-lights from the nearby fire engine.

Then, just as she thought things couldn't get any worse, she saw Beth ducking under the tape at the gate.

Who the hell had called *her*?

THIRTY-ONE

Beth ran across the driveway towards them, crying uncontrollably into her sleeve. When she saw Kerry standing with the policeman and fireman, her face collapsed with relief and she pulled her into a huge hug, the sort of hug she hadn't given her for years, not even when their mum died. The two men moved awkwardly away, deep in the sort of conversation that made Kerry feel anxious.

'Oh my God, Kerry, I thought you were in there! I thought I'd lost you!'

'How did you know about the fire?' Kerry asked, submitting guiltily to her embrace. Beth smelled wholesome in the gritty, smoky night air, of apple shampoo and some sort of expensive moisturiser. Kerry could see her sister's pyjama bottoms, tucked into Ugg boots, underneath her coat and thought it must be the first time Beth had ever left the house without carefully checking her appearance.

She immediately felt guilty, not only for the critical thought, but also at Beth's misguided sympathy. Beth wouldn't be hugging her when she found out Kerry had been smoking in the house, she thought miserably.

'Joy rang, really distressed. She said she'd seen you in there earlier; that you'd been staying there. She was the one who called the fire brigade.'

Joy was the next-door neighbour on one side, a bitter, unfriendly woman with one long wiry hair sticking out of a mole on her cheek. Mum used to say, 'This lovely village, with all these lovely people, and we have to end up with *Joy* as our neighbour?' Mum couldn't stand her. Dad had been more tolerant, but then, he wasn't the one to whom Joy constantly moaned about various transgressions by their family: balls over the fence, noise in the garden, bins occasionally not brought in... If ever someone had been given the wrong name, it was Joy. Dad used to call her Joyless.

Kerry always felt sorry for her, though; she'd been on her own for the last thirty years, since her husband died. Not that Kerry's cheery overtures when she delivered the post seemed to make any difference to Joy's mood. Kerry had always entertained a fear that she would end up the same. Existing, not living, gaining no pleasure at all out of life; just waiting to die.

Pretty much exactly how she felt right now.

Funny how it was easier to think about Joyless than about their house being burned to cinders.

'I did pop over earlier but thank God I decided I didn't want to stay there tonight. Lucky decision, hey?'

Beth gave her a small shake, then released her from the embrace. '*So* lucky. Believe it or not, I would hate to have lost you.'

Kerry managed a smile, then gave a sob. 'Think we've lost the house, though.'

'We don't know that yet, not for sure,' Beth said doubtfully.

At that exact moment there was an enormous crash, and the roof collapsed in a shower of sparks that made some of the onlookers scream, as if they were watching a particularly lively firework display.

Kerry grabbed Beth's hand. 'Can we sit in your car? Or go back to your place? The policeman told me not to go back to the garage. I don't want to be here. I can't breathe. But we have to talk to that fireman guy first, he's the one doing the report.' She had to talk loudly above the roar of the flames and the whooshing of the water jets.

The fire officer asked her, in a thick Wiltshire accent, all the same questions that the policeman had, reciting them from a laminated list on his clipboard. Kerry dutifully replied with the same not entirely truthful, answers, but this grilling was harder. When he asked her if she or anybody else smoked, she was grateful for the darkness hiding what would in daylight have probably been a blush scarlet enough to be visible from space.

'I haven't smoked for twenty years,' she said, with her fingers crossed in her coat pocket, mentally adding, *until I started again last week*. Oh hell, she thought, they'll know. They'll find evidence. Why did I lie? I'm an idiot... She realised that, had Beth not been standing at her elbow, she probably would have told the truth.

'Do you have any idea how the fire started?' she asked, in as innocent a voice as she could muster.

'We won't know for sure until it's out.' The fire officer gestured towards the front room, fully ablaze now, with a corner of his clipboard, 'But it looks like that's the seat of it. Were there a lot of things plugged in?'

Kerry pretended to think, although her head was spinning with panic. 'The TV – I'm afraid I never switched it off at the socket at nights. Should I have done? Mum's answerphone. Her old hi-fi but that hadn't been used for years. A couple of lamps... was there anything else, Beth?'

Beth was staring at the conflagration as if she was in a trance.

'Beth?'

She shook herself and exhaled hard. 'This is horrific. I just can't believe it. No, I can't think of anything else in the living room. Did you mention the DVD player?'

'The DVD player. Oh, and a little fan heater.'

The fire officer wrote that down too. He had that weirdly laborious style of handwriting some left-handed people had, wrist bent, knuckles pointing towards the top of the clipboard.

'Can we go now please?' Kerry shifted from foot to foot. Her head was pounding and she felt as dehydrated as if she'd been in a desert for ten days. 'I'm not feeling too good.'

He looked at her then, his eyes stunningly clear in his soot-blackened face. 'Let me write down your numbers. I'll give one of you a call when the report's done.' He unclipped a printed sheet from the clipboard and handed it to Kerry. 'Here's a list of what to do after a fire, who to call and so on. I'm afraid it's a bit of hassle, but this should help.'

'Thanks.' Kerry folded up the sheet and stuck it in her pocket. 'We'll get on to it tomorrow.'

They walked back towards the gate, every onlooker's eye still on them. Kerry felt a tiny bit better, noticing that none of the neighbours spoke to Beth either. Perhaps she *was* just being paranoid. People often struggled to know what to say in awkward or life-changing situations. She had never forgotten Mum crying at the kitchen table after Dad died, because two women she knew really well from choir had crossed the road to avoid speaking to her.

'They *blanked* me!' she'd sobbed. 'I thought they were my friends.'

At the time Kerry thought they must have been utter unfeeling bitches. Now, she realised emotions were not so black and white, and awkwardness had a lot to answer for.

Beth drove them back to her place in silence. It had begun to rain, which was good, Kerry supposed – although there would need to be biblical amounts of the stuff to make any sort of dent on the fire – and with every squeaky swish of the wipers

across the windscreen, she experienced a deepening sensation
of betrayal; that they were just driving away and leaving all
their memories to be razed to the ground. It wasn't like there
was anything they could have done to help, obviously. She knew
that. They would hardly have been allowed to turn the garden
hose on it, and it wouldn't have made any difference anyway.

It felt like there was so much to say that they just said nothing. Kerry couldn't stop thinking about all their family photos
still in the sitting room, gone for ever. Mum's clothes. The blan-
kets both Mum and her own mother, Kerry and Beth's granny,
had crocheted over the years. Irreplaceable memories. Kerry
wanted to joke, *Look at all the work we've saved ourselves,
clearing the place! No need for all those charity shop trips now!*
But the question 'too soon?' didn't even begin to cover it. She
could just imagine the look of utter disgust on Beth's face if she
had said it out loud.

This in turn made Kerry want to laugh, in a hysterical,
desperately not amusing way. Her lips must have twitched as
Beth glanced over because she broke the silence:

'What's so funny?'

'Actually, nothing. Nothing is funny, Beth. Nothing at all.'

'I can't believe it.'

Kerry shook her head. 'Nor can I. Thank God Mum wasn't
here to witness it. She'd have been devastated.'

Would they forget it all, she wondered, now that they had
no physical reminders, and no Mum to repeat the well-worn
family anecdotes? No more photographs of Dad, or their childhood birthday parties, or the glitter-covered, star-shaped
Christmas tree decorations that Beth and she had baked as
biscuits when they were four and six, and which had somehow
remained rock-hard for all these years? Kerry's heart hurt so
much at the thought that for a moment she couldn't breathe.

'Have you got any photographs of Dad?' she asked
brusquely, once she found her voice again. 'I'd meant to take

that one Mum had on the mantelpiece but I hadn't got round to it.'

'I'm sure I've got a couple somewhere.'

'Oh, Beth. All our photo albums. Our baby books.'

'I know.'

They got to Beth's house, creeping up the tessellated-tile driveway like burglars, and Beth turned the key silently in the lock.

'I don't want to wake Jitz,' she whispered. 'He's got an important meeting in the morning.'

Kerry was bemused. 'You didn't tell him you'd gone out, or that Mum's house is on fire? Don't you think he'd want to know?'

That was weird, she thought. Surely an event of this magnitude was worthy of informing your spouse? She had assumed the only reason Jitz hadn't come with Beth was because someone had to stay with the kids, not because he needed his beauty sleep.

But then, what did she know about relationships? Perhaps Beth was just a lot less selfish than she was.

Kerry had a sudden yearning to call Tim. Maybe because she was thinking about relationships, and that was another one she'd screwed up before it had even started.

No, she corrected herself, carefully. *He* screwed it up. I had a lucky escape.

'I texted him, in case he woke up and found me not there,' Beth explained, *sotto voce* and slightly crossly. 'He puts his phone on silent when he goes to bed.'

'Right.' Kerry followed Beth into the kitchen, noticing that her hands had started to shake. 'Can I have a brandy or something? I feel a bit sick all of a sudden.'

Beth switched on the lights in the kitchen, then gasped in

shock as she saw Kerry's bruises properly for the first time. 'Bloody hell, Kerry, what the hell's happened to your *face*? I thought it was soot or something when I first saw you.'

'I had a bit of a crash in the yard. I was heading out on my round, just pulling out, and had to reverse fast to avoid a toddler on a bike. I smashed into another van and bashed my nose on the steering wheel.'

Beth came up close to her and gawped at the swollen nose and two black eyes. 'Oh, Kerry.'

There it was again, Kerry thought, that tone of disappointment rather than sympathy.

'It's fine,' she said brusquely. 'I went to the doctor's; she doesn't think it's broken. So – what about that drink?'

'I'll put the kettle on for tea,' said Beth.

'I don't want a cup of tea. I need something stronger.'

Beth wouldn't look her in the eyes. 'I don't think that's a good idea, Kerry.'

'*What?*'

'You, er, stink of booze as it is. What were you doing this evening – I mean, last night?'

'Nothing!' Kerry said hotly, before she realised that this was a much worse answer than 'out having fun with friends' would have been. She might as well have said 'getting pissed on my own like the pathetic loser you think I am'.

'I was just feeling shaken up after the accident. I had a bit of a meltdown at the doctor's and so I had some wine to calm myself down.'

Beth took two mugs down from the cupboard and filled the kettle. Standing at the sink with her back to Kerry, she said, 'I know now isn't the time to discuss it, but Jitz and I feel that perhaps you need help. I'll take you to an AA meeting, if you like.'

Kerry was flabbergasted. Two people suggesting that, in one

day. What was wrong with everybody? 'AA? Don't be ridiculous, Beth, I'm not a bloody alcoholic!'

Beth didn't move, but in the reflection in the kitchen window over the sink, Kerry saw her eyebrows shoot up.

'Literally every time I've rung you in the evening recently, you've been drunk. Even on work nights. For the first couple of weeks after Mum died, I put it down to the stress of that, and lockdown, but you can't go on like this. I mean, if you'd been sober, you'd probably have smelled the smoke much sooner.'

In Kerry's still quite inebriated and shocked state, she gave a howl of outrage that Beth was blaming her for the fire – until she remembered that it probably *was* her fault. She'd never have smoked in there if she'd been sober.

She shut up again. She still had to break it to Beth that she'd been sacked for suspected drunk-driving.

'Shhhh!' Beth hissed. 'You'll wake everyone up.'

'I don't know how you can tell on the phone if I've had a drink,' Kerry said sulkily.

Beth threw teabags into the mugs and poured still-boiling water on top. 'God, Kerry, it's so obvious. You repeat yourself; you bang on about nothing; you go "errrrrrr" and "ummmm". It's why I've had to stop ringing you in the evenings. It's just impossible to get any sense out of you.'

So that was why Beth only seemed to call her at work these days? Wow. Kerry really hadn't had any idea it was obvious at all, let alone *that* obvious. It seemed only recently she'd been mentally deriding Sharon for repeating herself, and it turned out she was guilty of it too?

That was ironic. The biblical quote about taking a splinter out of your neighbour's eye when there was a plank in your own sprang to her mind. Not that it had ever made sense to her. Surely it was a good thing to take a splinter out of someone's eye, regardless of whether or not your own was impaired by a plank. As if you could fit a plank in your eye anyway...

Oh, she thought. Maybe I am still drunk.

'I don't drink *every* night,' she said defensively. 'And anyway, I'm definitely going to knock it on the head. The doctor gave me some antidepressants. Things have just been really difficult lately, with Mum, and work, and... the house.'

She'd been going to say 'you' but thought better of it.

She couldn't tell Beth she'd been fired, not tonight. Instead, she sat down on a kitchen chair and closed her stinging eyes.

THIRTY-TWO

Kerry had a very sleepless night in the single bed in the smallest of Beth and Jitz's spare rooms. 'Sorry, Kerry,' Beth had said as they headed upstairs, 'I wasn't expecting you and the king-size in the main spare isn't made up, you don't mind, do you?'

She didn't mind, not really, but it did seem fairly par for the course. And the single bed was one of those tiny, narrow, lumpy-mattressed ones. Kerry decided to see it as a sort of penance.

She was on tenterhooks all night waiting for the promised text update from the fire officer, whose name she'd instantly forgotten, but nothing arrived and eventually she dropped off as the sun was coming up. Perhaps he'd written her number down wrong. She and Beth would just have to go and see for themselves what the damage was.

She had a shower to rid herself of the clinging stink of smoke and stale wine and dressed in yesterday's sooty clothes before heading slowly downstairs, her head banging. She could hear the squawky noises of the kids rushing round getting ready for school, and Jitz's softer tones, exhorting them to remember book bags, PE kit and lunchboxes.

They looked up in surprise when she appeared in the doorway, and said an obedient 'Hi, Auntie Kerry' each, before disappearing upstairs, leaving their cereal bowls on the table.

Jitz gave her a quick hug and whispered, 'Beth decided not to tell them yet till we know what the score is. So sorry, Kerry, it's just awful.'

Kerry nodded and accepted the cup of coffee he proffered.

'Sugar?'

She shook her head. 'No thanks. Got any paracetamol?'

Beth bustled into the kitchen, looking a little pale but otherwise her usual immaculate self. She was wearing what looked like brand-new exercise gear; trainers and top in matching shades of salmon-pink, with coordinated patterned leggings that hugged her tight hips and bottom and showed off her ironing-board belly.

'Going to the gym?'

'Pilates at eleven,' she said, then looked meaningfully at her, 'provided we get everything done first.'

Kerry wondered what they needed to 'get done'. Presumably by this she meant 'examine the smouldering wreckage of our house and apportion blame.' She didn't know how Beth could think about going to a gym class under these circumstances.

She was not looking forward to the day.

'Work OK about you not coming in today?' Jitz enquired. 'I guess they have to be fairly understanding about this kind of crisis.'

Kerry muttered something noncommittal and buried her face in her coffee mug.

There was a lot of yelling from the stairs – Beth and Opal having a very vocal disagreement about the suitability of some shoes, it seemed – and they all traipsed back into the kitchen.

'Right, sorry to rush you, K, but we need to go.'

'Oh! OK.' Kerry downed the rest of her coffee and put on

her trainers – down at heel, scruffy, non-brand, in stark contrast to Beth's pristine pink Nikes. 'Bye, Jitz, see you soon.'

He waved all four of them off, and Kerry had a strange feeling that she was one of the kids, off to school, part of a family again, with a mum and dad. This was a feeling which was then amplified when Beth made her sit in the back with Opal, since 'Roddy gets car sick unless he can see out of the front windscreen'.

Roddy threw her a smug smile.

Opal grabbed Kerry's wrists and started arranging her arms at ninety-degree angles, palms facing. 'Right, Auntie Kerry, you put your hands like this, OK? I need to practice my cat's cradle.' She took a long loop of string out of her blazer pocket, hooked it around Kerry's obediently outstretched hands, and then made a loop around each of her wrists.

'Ah, cat's cradle,' Kerry said contemplatively. 'I haven't done that for decades. Remember we used to do it, Beth?'

It felt nice, doing something with Opal, feeling her small fingers brushing against her skin. Kerry couldn't remember her niece ever voluntarily touching her before.

Even better, she could see the side of Beth's cheek curve up into a smile at the question. 'I do,' Beth said. 'You were always better than me at it.'

Kerry saw them both as little girls, their heads touching, utterly focused on weaving the string over and under and round between each thumb and finger. If she narrowed her eyes into slits and looked at Opal, she could almost be Beth as a six-year-old again. The continuity of it felt ridiculously comforting.

Somehow she remembered what to do without being prompted, an ancient muscle memory kicking in as she pulled each wrist loop towards her with her middle finger, creating the first shape.

'Good, Auntie Kerry.' Opal deftly pinched each of the X-shapes and pulled them over the sides, manipulating the string into a new configuration. Kerry didn't have to be told the next stage either, and they worked in companionable silence for a few seconds, Opal's tongue sticking out with concentration, until they both ran out of steam as to what the next step was and the cat's cradle collapsed back into an untidy circle of string on the car's back seat.

'Let's try again!'

'Later, Opal, we're here,' said Beth, parking on the zigzag lines outside the kids' school and yanking on the handbrake.

'Are you allowed to park here?' Kerry asked.

'No, but we'll only be a sec,' Beth said, nipping out and chivvying Opal and Roddy onto the pavement, making sure they had their book bags and PE kits and art projects, bustling them in through the gates in a manner reminiscent of an army manoeuvre.

Kerry took the opportunity to get in the front passenger seat, noticing how many of the other parents glared at her and the illegally parked car. She wanted to call out of the window, 'It's nothing to do with me!' but then remembered she had more pressing issues to worry about and was tempted to run away and hide under the nearest hedge until Beth had gone.

Beth climbed back into the car, her face white and set, and Kerry realised she must be feeling just as nervous as she was about viewing the wreckage of their house.

'Let's do this, then,' Beth said, pressing a button to start the car and putting it in gear.

When did car engines start having on-off buttons? Kerry thought, opening her mouth to ask – but instead, what came out was not at all what she had intended, as if her subconscious had taken the reins and decided it had to be done:

'Beth, I've left my job.'

Beth slammed on the brakes at a set of traffic lights on the way out of town – unnecessarily as the lights were only now turning amber – causing cars behind them to do emergency stops and honk in irritation. '*What?*'

She turned to face Kerry, her expression one of distress and frustration. 'Kerry, not your job! Why? You love that job, it's all—'

'Yes, I know it's all I've got, no need to point it out. And I didn't want to leave, Nigel forced me into it.'

'Oh don't be ridiculous!'

Kerry noticed Beth hadn't even given her the chance to explain. '*Beth!*'

'What?'

'Listen to yourself, just for a moment! And you wonder why I get upset with you? Would you talk to any of your friends that way, tell them they were being *ridiculous* if they confided in you they'd been forced into leaving the job they loved?'

Beth had the grace to look sheepish as the lights turned to green and she pulled away. 'Sorry, K. You're right. I wouldn't. It's just...'

Kerry held up her hand. 'No. Don't say it. I don't want to get into another row with you. I'm letting you know the situation, if you'll just let me explain what happened without judgement. It was because of the accident.'

Kerry told her as much of the truth as she could bear to; the damage she'd caused to the two Royal Mail vehicles, Nigel's ultimatum about her resigning or – and she was about to come clean, but quailed at the thought of her sister's fresh censure and changed the bit about being breathalysed to, 'he said I'd have to pay damages for the vans out of my wages.'

She kicked herself. What was wrong with her? She'd been many things in her life, but never a liar.

'He reminded me that he's really good mates with my union rep, and that it would be better if I just resigned and went on gardening leave until my notice period's up. He said if I got a letter from my doctor, he'd make sure I was invalided out on ill-health grounds, so I'd still get my pension. So I did. I resigned. I didn't want to, but I couldn't face getting into a big row with him and the union and HR. It's all too much. I've had enough.'

Beth was lost for words, for once. They both stared rigidly ahead, Kerry looking at the bumper sticker on the car in front, which instructed, *Don't Touch Me, I'm Not THAT Sort of Car.* You didn't often see bumper stickers any more, she thought. They must have suddenly gone out of fashion at some point. Who'd have thought they were fashion items to start with?

'I am sorry. Nigel's a bastard. That's another huge life change. I suppose it's too soon for you to have thought about what you're going to do now... Are you going to appeal against it?'

'I don't know,' Kerry said, her voice cracking at the sympathy, finally, in Beth's tone. It felt strange and incomprehensible, as if Beth had suddenly started speaking in Urdu. 'I can't think about it at the moment. I wrote the resignation letter so I suppose I can't retract it.'

'No need to make a decision straight away. Just concentrate on getting better.'

Again with the implications of illness! Kerry gritted her teeth. 'I'm not ill. Even if Nigel implied that I was.'

'You said the doctor gave you antidepressants? You're being invalided out on health grounds. I'd say that makes you unwell.'

She didn't mention the drinking again, which was initially a relief. But then Kerry felt an overwhelming desire to come clean. It was as if she suddenly, finally, realised that there would be no hope of true reconciliation with Beth unless she started to be honest with her, about everything.

'Yeah. Actually...' She stared down at her bitten fingernails.
'What?'

It was so hard to say. 'Nigel threatened to call the police and have me breathalysed if I didn't resign. I wasn't drunk that day, but – I probably was still over the limit from the night before. So I agreed to write the letter.'

Kerry held her breath and waited for the censure, but none came.

'I'm so sorry, Kerry,' Beth merely repeated quietly, and tears sprang to Kerry's eyes.

They drove on in silence, through the suburbs and up the hill, the cathedral spire shrinking behind them. Kerry didn't need to turn around to see its position in the valley; she knew every inch of that drive in and out of town, having driven it most days for over twenty-five years. She had seen whole new estates go up on the route; identical little Toytown houses and streets too new to be on maps, causing problems for whichever poor postie had to deliver the proud new homeowners' mail.

Who would deliver the village post now? Kerry felt a pang of jealousy so sharp that she physically shifted in her seat. She could not bear the thought of seeing someone else do her route. And there was so much they would need to know! That they shouldn't deliver anything to Mrs Polkinghorne's address for her deceased brother because it made Mrs P too upset. That Donald O'Donnell's dog Boris was a sweetheart as long as you tossed him a treat before you tried to put anything through the letterbox. That the lock on the post box on the green was tricky to open unless you really persevered with it.

I'll never sit in Lord Buckley's kitchen having a fresh scone again, she thought. Or be able to sit in the sunshine on his estate in my lunch break.

Hopefully her replacement would be Bob or Clarissa, someone nice – although they were both happy with their current rounds. She couldn't see any reason they'd be persuaded to switch. Please God, she thought, let it be someone non-gossipy. All the villagers would ask where Kerry had gone and why she'd left, and she couldn't stand the prospect of them all speculating and whispering behind her back. It would most likely be someone new, which would be better, but there'd be nobody to show them the ropes.

Still, not her problem, she thought. She'd probably have to move away anyway.

Beth broke the silence as they approached the outskirts of the village.

'Right,' she said, and even the tone of her voice made Kerry feel back on steadier ground, like Beth was in charge and everything would be OK. 'I've typed up that list the fire officer guy gave us last night into my Notes app so I can tick things off as we do them. First, we need to see if there's anything we can salvage. Then call someone to come and board up the windows. Call the insurance company. Mum always used Saga, so it's bound to be them—'

Kerry interrupted, shoving her fingers underneath her thighs to stop them trembling. 'The policy will have got burned up. All the house documents were in her office. What if it wasn't Saga, how do we find out?'

Beth made an impatient face. 'I'm sure it would have been. We only need to give the details and explain the situation. It's not like Mum had the only copy, Kerry!'

'Could you do that? Ring the insurers? I'll call a builder to come and do the windows and bar the doors or whatever. You know I'm rubbish with the financial stuff.'

Kerry didn't want to admit that she could not face speaking to anyone from the insurance company, because she knew her voice would be dripping with guilt. She'd probably start apologising on the phone for causing the fire. It would better if Beth handled all that. If she, Kerry, had forgotten to renew the policy, or if the premiums hadn't been paid since Mum died, then Kerry did not want to have to be the one to break it to Beth.

'What if the policy had run out and neither of us renewed it?' she asked in a very small voice, as Beth parked on the verge outside their gate. They both unclipped their seatbelts and stared at each other. A few sheep in the field across the road came up to the fence and joined in with the staring. Kerry thought how tired Beth looked, even though she had 'put her face on' that morning for the school run.

'I don't know, Kerry. Let's hope to God one of us did. I don't remember doing it, not since Mum died.'

'Nor do I.'

'That might just be because it was still running. Do you remember which month she used to renew it?'

Kerry shook her head. Because their mother had kept her marbles intact right up to her sudden death and had been almost excruciatingly well organised, neither sister had power of attorney.

'I don't, either.'

Beth slipped easily out of the car, squeezing through a gap between the door and the fence of a size that Kerry would never have managed with any sort of grace. Rummaging about in her capacious handbag, she pulled out two pairs of brand-new gardening gloves and handed one to Kerry. 'Hope for the best, eh, or it doesn't bear thinking about.'

Kerry couldn't break it to her, not yet, that even if the policy *was* still current, once the cause of the fire was established and blame apportioned, there was no way the insurance would pay out. She pulled off the cardboard label to separate the gloves and slid them over her hands, slowly raising her eyes to the smouldering wreckage of their house. They were most likely going to lose everything either way.

Red and white tape stating FIRE AND RESCUE: DO NOT CROSS flapped across their five-barred gate. 'We can't go inside,' Kerry exclaimed, her knees weak at the sight in front of her. 'Look, it's still smoking. The fire's not out properly!'

Beth tutted. 'It is out. It's just steam, from the heat in the beams and all the water. A fireman mate of Jitz's told him that once. They aren't allowed to leave the property unless the fire is completely extinguished, and there's nobody here.'

'Are we even allowed in?'

'Yeah, it's our house. That tape's just to keep out the rubber-neckers, or the looters.'

They ducked under the tape, opened the gate and picked their way across the drive to the house, stepping over puddles of water and bits of debris strewn around, their faces white and set with shock, the smell of soot and old smoke already filling their noses.

'I don't know why they threw these out the window, it's not like we'll be able to use them again,' Kerry said, pointing at a mattress and several pillows lying near her car.

'They throw out anything flammable they can get to, to prevent it making the fire worse, and anything they think looks valuable.'

'Like this,' Kerry said, crouching down to pick up her mum's antique writing box lying on the ground. 'Oh, Beth – remember this? I think it was Granny Bailey's mum's – our great grand-mother. I haven't seen it for years, where was it?'

Beth traced a finger over the inlaid walnut lid, and the tip of her glove came away black.

'I think it was in her bedroom, under the bed. When Dad was alive it used to be on the bureau, didn't it? The firemen must have handed it out of the window, because it's not broken.'

'So at least we've got *something* of hers.'

'Looks like that's all, though.'

They gloomily surveyed the rest of the broken, sodden objects on the driveway.

'Why have they saved the little spare room TV and not Mum's expensive Toshiba?' It looked so incongruous, sitting neatly right outside where the front door had once been, as if it had come to visit.

'Because the fire started in the living room, that fireman said last night. Look, it's a shell. They wouldn't have been able to save anything from in there. Anything they did salvage is from the back of the house.'

'Oh. Yeah.' Kerry didn't think her heart could sink any further. 'So it is.'

THIRTY-THREE

Kerry decided to stay in the annexe that night. It had to be better than Beth's disapproval and lumpy spare mattress. Beth hadn't argued, merely said she would call her the next day, or as soon as the fire report came in. But she hugged her warmly when she left, and things felt different between them – although Kerry knew that this rapprochement was only likely to last until Beth saw the report...

There was an unopened bottle of wine in her fridge that Kerry had been looking forward to but the moment she grasped its cold, slippery neck and went to unscrew the lid, somewhat to her surprise, she found that the mere thought of it made her feel ill. Her brain immediately flooded with memories of the wine she'd drunk so much of the other night that she had smoked cigarettes and burned down her house. Snippets of Beth's words came back to her: 'Literally every time I ring you in the evening, you're drunk', and, 'We'll take you to an AA meeting'.

Had she really got that bad? Beth hadn't sounded remotely surprised when she'd admitted Nigel wanted to breathalyse her.

She put the wine straight into the bin unopened and made herself a cup of tea instead, which she sat on the sofa cradling, listening to Vaughan Williams' *Sea Symphony* at full volume. The music enveloped her, temporarily at least bearing her away from all her troubles, the swells and splashes of the music making her feel as if she was in a tiny boat on a vast, stormy ocean – and yet, somehow, that she was both safe and simultaneously at rock bottom. Alone, but not lonely; too exhausted to be stressed about it all. It was an interesting sensation, finding comfort in believing that things really could not get much worse.

She went to bed early and straight, for the first time in months. To her astonishment she slept better than she had done for years, waking around ten the next day, the smell of her charred history in her nostrils afresh. It seemed to be seeping under the door and through the window frames, penetrating everything in her garage – but it still felt better than waking up in Beth's spare room trying to pretend it hadn't happened at all.

She half climbed, half slid down the ladder from her platform bed and was shuffling across to fill the kettle when she saw a letter lying on the doormat. A proper letter with a handwritten address, the sort that would instantly have intrigued her when she'd been sorting the mail. Delivered by somebody who was not her, she thought, as she opened the curtains, her eyes intentionally downcast so that she did not have to look out of the window at the wreckage of the big house.

The memory of being at work made her eyes fill with a Pavlovian reaction of grief and shame, but she tried to quash the sense of loss. *No more Nasty Nige,* she reminded herself in a vain attempt to stem the self-pity. *Time for a change. Nothing lasts for ever.*

The letter was postmarked Salisbury but she had no idea who it could be from. It wasn't formal enough to be anything to do with the fire, or insurance. She felt torn between reading it and chucking it unopened in the bin; her old impulse to bury her head in the sand was rearing up strongly. But no, she thought. She wasn't that person any more. She confronted things! It was probably just one of Mum's friends sending an 'I'm Sorry You Burned Down Your House' card. If Hallmark made one.

She made herself a cup of tea, sat down on the sofa and slit open the envelope. It wasn't a card. It contained a folded cream sheet of good quality thick writing paper, the sort her parents would have approved of. The writing was small and neat and she flipped the letter over to see who it was from.

Tim.

Seeing his name at the bottom, with two kisses, gave her a strange frisson, although she didn't know if it was the dregs of desire or a fresh spark of sorrow. How had he found her address? She didn't think he'd have known it even when they were teenagers and he was living in the village.

Kerry felt torn between admiration at his persistence, and abhorrence at him trying to justify the unjustifiable. Being sixteen and stupid just didn't cut it, as far as she was concerned. She hesitated, then began to read:

Dear Kerry,

Just to say, I do understand why you don't want to speak to me, but I have to tell you something. You've blocked me on the phone and Facebook etc. so I've gone old school and written a real letter (must be the first in years! I had to remember how to do handwriting). But it's important that I tell you: I neither took nor distributed those photos of you that night, I swear. It was Chris Mann. He grabbed both my cameras off me and he took them. Lee was the one who photocopied the Polaroids and stuck them up around college. He always was a knob. I'm guessing he did it because you had enough sense not to put out for him, and he'd assumed he was on a promise. Please believe me. I remember that night so well, because I felt so sorry and mortified for you. But I didn't realise it was you when we met again.

I also realise it must have been a massive shock to discover that I'm the same Tim, and I'm concerned about you. Please at least let me know you're OK, even if you don't want to see me again. But I do wish we could talk. There's more to the story that you don't know – that night had a really big impact on me too. I'll tell you some other time, I hope.

I loved your company the other night, until it all went pear-shaped. I'd been really looking forward to seeing you again. I would very much like to see if this might go some-where. However, I understand that seeing anybody connected with that incident, even though it was all those years ago, would be pretty traumatic even now, so of course it's your deci-sion. I'll be very sad if you don't ever want to see me again, though. You are such easy company and fun to be around and I thought of you as someone who would soon become a friend and, after that lovely kiss, possibly more.

Finally, another confession: I went to the sorting office to ask for you and the man behind the counter told me you'd left. He wouldn't give me your address so I drove out to the village last week and asked around. The guy in the shop told me which house you lived in. Thought I'd better post this though rather than just turning up to deliver it. Don't want you to think I'm a mad stalker. But please call me.

Love, Tim xx

This was, Kerry had to admit, intriguing. How on earth could that night have had any effect on *Tim*, especially if he really hadn't been the one to take or distribute the photos? It didn't make sense.

It made her cringe to read that Tim remembered the night 'so well'. What did he remember, exactly? Her white arse lying on the ground? Her huge breasts bobbing around in the pond? Worse, had he seen her in between Lee and Mutt? She shuddered and tears blurred her vision. Partly because, regardless of what he'd seen that night, Tim really did seem to understand. Far more than Beth ever had.

Beth had never asked her if she was OK – which was fair enough at the time, when she'd only been fifteen herself – but not even once in all the intervening years. She had never mentioned it again and Kerry strongly suspected that this was because she had been almost as embarrassed as she was. She supposed though, to give Beth some credit, as far as she, Beth, was concerned, she had only witnessed Kerry's naked fall and that someone had taken photos. Beth didn't know what Lee and Mutt had made her do before that, and – as far as Kerry knew – she didn't seem to have been made aware of the photographs in college either. But given Beth's reaction to the pictures of Miss Smith, Kerry didn't think there was any point even mentioning it. Beth probably wouldn't believe her anyway.

Hang on, though – if what Tim said was true and it had been Chris who took the photos, then Beth surely *would* have witnessed it? She must have done, she and Chris were stuck together like glue that night.

Perhaps that was why Beth had never spoken of it again. Because she felt ashamed.

Kerry did not know how to process this. If Beth had seen it all and never mentioned anything, it would be... it was... a huge betrayal; the biggest yet. Like a secret Beth had sat on for years. She could have helped Kerry get over it! Or, better still, she could have intervened in the first place and smashed the camera out of Chris's hands. There was nothing Beth could have controlled or altered about what Lee and Mutt had done, Kerry supposed, although, at a worldly fifteen years old, Beth surely hadn't thought the boys had taken off all their clothes and got in the pond just to splash around with her?

She would have to bite the bullet and speak to her about it at some point. The thought of that, on top of everything else they had to sort out, made Kerry feel sick but, like the admission of being over the limit, she knew it would have to be done. Perhaps difficult conversations got easier the more of them you had? She wouldn't know; she'd always avoided them like the plague.

Until now, when she had nothing else to lose.

Glancing up, Kerry saw the still-smoking ruins of their house through the window, its roof completely gone; charred skeleton rafters, empty windows gaping, a heap of rubble and the blackened exterior walls were pretty much all that was left. It looked as if it had suffered a direct hit from a mortar rocket. Bile rose in her throat and she jumped up and closed the curtains again with shaking hands.

Switching on the light – fortunately the annexe was on a separate electrical system, otherwise she'd have no power at all – she turned back to the letter and re-read *You are such easy company and fun to be around.* Then she read the whole letter again from top to bottom. Eyes on the page, on Tim's words, meant that she didn't have to see the evidence of her destroyed family home because even with the curtains shut, it was still all around her, trapped in her nostrils, the sooty footprints on the floor, the black marks on all the towels. Every surface had a dark-grey film of dust, the likes of which Miss Haversham would have been proud of, even though the windows had all been closed since the fire.

You are such easy company and fun to be around. Her eyes kept rolling over that sentence, on a loop. Nobody had ever said this of her before, but for some reason she didn't doubt that he meant it. She didn't think he was *right*, of course, but she was so grateful to read that he thought it. It was something she could mentally file away and remind herself of, when needed.

Then she thought, *Chris Mann. Ugh.* She had sat in the pub

just a couple of weeks ago with him and Serena on the next table, the two of them loved up and flipping beermats on the edge, laughing conspiratorially together.

Chris was the last one of that group Kerry would have thought would take photos of a naked vulnerable teenage girl without her permission – apart from Tim, of course. Did he, Chris, feel remorse? Perhaps he barely even remembered. She found, somewhat to her surprise, that she did not feel any anger towards him; not specifically. They'd all been drunk. It was an idiotic teenage stunt, that was all. In her mind he was not nearly as culpable as Lee Carlton and his mate Mutt – especially Lee, for stealing and circulating the photos as well as for assaulting her.

Alongside the relief that it hadn't been Tim who took the photos after all, for the first time Kerry also felt a renewed deep, visceral hatred of Lee and Mutt for what they had done to her that night. Why hadn't she gone to the police? It had been sexual assault, without question. To think that she'd occasionally bumped into Lee over the years, and not punched him in the face! He made her feel physically sick.

Another thought came at her, from left field: if she had assumed wrongly all these years about who took the photographs of her, then could she have assumed wrongly about Dad and Miss Smith too? Emailing Miss Smith to try and find out suddenly shot to the top of her to-do list. *No more putting it off.* Maybe – just maybe – something positive could come out of all the still-smouldering trauma, and she could extinguish it for good; sticking around, like the firemen had to do, until it was completely out.

THIRTY-FOUR

Perhaps it was curiosity, perhaps loneliness and a yearning for a kind word and a gesture of comfort, but it was only a matter of hours before Kerry decided to ring Tim and apologise for jumping to conclusions. She hadn't spoken to anybody – apart from when Beth had rung, so much relief in her voice that it sang a song of jubilation down the phone, to tell her that their buildings and contents insurance was still in date so they'd be *fine*...

Kerry had stayed silent, unable to share Beth's happiness, having googled it to discover that insurance companies never paid out for house fires when there had been a smoker in the house, let alone if the fire had been caused by said smoker. It would have been less painful if the policy had actually lapsed. Beth would never speak to her again when she found out.

The official fire report was likely to arrive any day now.

Not that Kerry wanted to speak to Beth again anyway, not yet, after the discovery that it was Chris Mann who took the photos of her, and that Beth might have been able to stop him.

But, Kerry realised, she *did* really want to see Tim again, and if she didn't take this chance, she might never be able to.

That was the thing about being at rock bottom, she thought. Nothing left to lose – because even though Tim's letter had made it clear he wanted to see her too, she still fully anticipated rejection. What on earth did she have to offer anybody?

Yet when she dialled his number, she was astonished to discover he was delighted to hear from her. She lay back on her loft bed, uncomfortably warm with the skylight firmly closed against the smell of smoke, and felt her body relax, just a little bit.

'Kerry! You got my letter! Thank you so much for calling me, I've been so worried. So, how are you? Have you really left your job?'

Kerry found herself grinning up at the pine ceiling slats, the first time she'd smiled since Nigel had forced her to resign.

'Hi. Yes – long story, I'll tell you some time. But in the ongoing dramas of my life, leaving my job has been superseded by the fact that I managed to burn down my mum's house two days ago.'

'*What*? Are you OK?'

The concern in his voice made her throat constrict. 'Yes. I'm fine. I'd been living over in the house for a few weeks, but on a whim decided to sleep back in my annexe that night. Guess I've got some kind of guardian angel watching over me because I'd been in the house earlier...'

'Thank God for that. Is it salvageable? How did it start?'

Kerry hesitated. 'I don't think so, no. We're waiting for the fire report to find out the cause, but—'

Was she really going to tell him? Sod it, she thought. She was.

'Oh Tim, it's a nightmare. I'm sure I caused it because I'd been smoking in there. I was using a mug as an ashtray and I left it on the arm of the sofa, near the curtains – they think that was the room it started in.' Her voice wobbled. 'Even if it wasn't that, and the insurance company finds out, our policy will be invalidated. I looked it up.'

There was a pause on the line. 'I didn't know you smoked?'

'I don't... I mean, I hadn't done for years, and I definitely won't again. That night I stormed out on you, I bought some cigarettes on the way home, on a whim. Then when I lost my job, all I wanted to do was smoke and drink. I'm such an idiot.'

'You poor thing. That's awful. I feel like it's my fault!'

Kerry gave a huff of a laugh. 'It's definitely not your fault. But my sister's going to kill me when she finds out. That's both of our inheritances gone up in smoke. Literally.'

'You've basically had the worst week in the history of bad weeks, haven't you? What can I do to help? Would you like to go out for a drink tonight?'

And there it was again, Kerry thought, that tiny wave of revulsion at the mere word 'drink'. Her inadvertent aversion therapy was clearly still working. She cleared her throat. This next confession was almost harder to make than the one about smoking.

'I'd really like to see you, yes. But, er, could we do something that doesn't involve a pub, or alcohol? I've been overdoing it a bit lately – I'd never have had a cig in the house if I hadn't been drinking – so I've knocked it on the head. I don't *think* I'd be tempted just by being in a pub, because the idea of either smoking or drinking makes me want to puke at the moment, but I wouldn't want to risk being around other people doing it... is there something else we could do?'

'Sure,' Tim said easily, and Kerry felt so glad she had rung him. He hadn't shown any censure at either of her revelations. 'Look, it's a lovely summery day, why don't we go for a walk? Is there a tea room anywhere out your way? I could drive out to you, then we could walk and have a tea and scones, like a right pair of oldies. I'm owed a few hours in lieu.'

'That sounds really nice,' Kerry said shyly. 'There's a

National Trust house about three miles from here, they've got a cafe. Park on my drive, and don't be freaked out by the smoking wreckage.'

'I'll try not to be. OK. I'll bring my binoculars and a shooting stick, and wear something tweedy, since we're visiting a National Trust place. Pick you up at two? We have a *lot* to talk about.'

While she was waiting for Tim to arrive, she composed a Facebook message to Miss Smith – technically, Mrs Pickles now, but not to Kerry. She kept it fairly brief and didn't go into many details beyond saying that it would be lovely to chat to someone who knew her mum and dad, plus that she was in between jobs and available to meet pretty much whenever Miss Smith was free, if she'd like.

Before she could change her mind, she pressed Send. It would go into Miss Smith's 'Other' folder, but she just had to hope that it would be found quickly and not languish unread.

Then she went to get changed into something appropriate for both a walk in the country and a date – how strange, to be going on a date when her whole life had fallen apart – settling on a rarely worn short flowery number, with sturdy ankle boots to make it look less dressy. It was only as she was pressing a blusher brush into a pot of funny little bronze beads that Sharon had given her one birthday (Sharon! She supposed she should contact her and update her on everything – but then remembered that she was probably still flirting with waiters on a Mediterranean island somewhere; it could wait) that she was surprised to find that she was humming.

THIRTY-FIVE

Kerry saw Tim's face through the car windscreen – a nifty little dark-blue Audi, she noted with approval – at first beaming, when he saw her waving at him from outside the annexe front door, then paling as he pulled onto the gravel driveway and clocked the house. He steered carefully, avoiding the flapping tape she had taken off one side of the gate to let him through, and parked up next to a soggy king-size mattress that she hadn't been strong enough to drag out of sight.

'Shit,' he said, getting out and staring at the remains of the house. She was faintly relieved to observe that he wasn't actually wearing anything tweedy, nor did he have a shooting stick and binoculars – she'd been fairly certain he was joking, but it occurred to her afterwards that she didn't know him well enough to be certain.

'That's horrendous. And what's happened to you? You look like you've been ten rounds with Tyson Fury. Were you injured in the fire? Can I give you an illegal hug or should we stay socially distanced?'

'Illegal hug, please.'

He reached out and clasped her tightly, and it felt entirely natural for her to sink into his embrace, letting her head fall against his shoulder, like they had been friends for years.

'Not Tyson Fury or the fire but an airbag – as you said, it's not been a great week.' She looked up at the blackened wreckage of her family home, seeing it through Tim's eyes. 'Yeah, it's awful. I can't get my head around it. It all happened so fast.'

'And you've left your job too. I'm amazed you're still upright, under this tsunami of crap. How are you doing?'

Kerry stepped back so she could look him in the face. 'I don't know. Numb, I guess. Really worried about the insurance, and what that'll do to my relationship with my sister. And what it'll do to me too – I need that money more than ever now that I'm unemployed. But at least I still have somewhere to live.'

She gestured towards the annexe, speaking with a faux enthusiastic irony to cover her embarrassment at the humbleness of her abode. 'Home sweet home!'

Tim followed her gaze, scratching his head and frowning. 'You're not planning to stay living there, are you? With this view? And – not to be too blunt, you'll either have to have it torn down, or there'll have to be a massive rebuilding job. Either way, it'll be a building site here for a few weeks or months.'

Kerry gulped. She hadn't really thought it through. 'Well, I don't have anywhere else to go. There's no way I'd move in with Beth, even if she offered. Which she won't. Especially once she finds out I started the fire. Anyway, can we not talk about that? You ready to head straight out for a walk?'

She *really* hoped he was ready and wasn't going to ask to use the loo or anything. She didn't want him to see the inside of the garage – the outside was bad enough. To her relief, he nodded. 'Lead on,' he said. 'I didn't bring my walking poles but hopefully I'll manage without.'

Kerry laughed. 'You look pretty fit to me,' she said, then winced. Good grief, was she flirting? She, with her swollen nose, two black eyes and no prospects of anything apart from the dole queue?

But Tim didn't seem to think anything of it. 'I do go to the gym. You know, Lockwood, on the way into town?'

'I know where it is. I've never needed to join a gym, what with all the walking I do – did – every day. I guess maybe I should now, otherwise I'll turn into a blob.'

'It's a decent enough gym.'

They set off, heading through the village, Kerry donning huge black sunglasses to hide her bruised eyes. It was the first time she had set foot on the main street since she'd last done her round, only just under a week ago. It seemed like a lifetime – and it felt different. She saw all the cottages and houses as if for the first time, rather than just concentrating on their letterboxes as she used to. How had she never noticed that large empty birdcage through the window of Derek and Nigel's purple house (a house notable not only for being purple, but for having its kitchen in the front room)? Knowing the names of all the homeowners made Kerry somehow feel all the more voyeuristic.

'It's so strange, walking along here but not having a big satchel of post on my shoulder,' she said. 'I feel like I'm missing a limb.'

Tim said nothing but reached out and gave her hand a squeeze. As they passed the village shop, Kev spotted them through the window and, even though he was serving two customers – Martin and Sheila, from the Old Oast House, Kerry saw – he rushed outside. 'Kerry, love, how are you? I'm right sorry to hear about your lovely house. And I see your friend found you.'

He nodded at Tim then gave Kerry such a big hug that, as she was disappearing into his ample front, she found she couldn't tell him off for giving Tim her address last week. In fact, she couldn't be gladder that he had done.

Kev smelled of boiled ham, body odour and hair oil. Two

hugs in ten minutes, Kerry thought, at a time when nobody was meant to be hugging at all! Three in three days, if you counted Beth's from the night of the fire. Even with the risk of Covid, she could get to like it – although this one was also giving her a brief flashback to the van's airbag assault last week. 'Thanks, Kev.'

She extricated herself and came face to face with Sheila and Martin, who'd also come outside, pulling down their face masks to speak to her.

'Hello guys, how are you both?'

Sheila squeezed her arm and patted her cheek. She was a sprightly seventy-five-year-old who always dressed like a 1950s shorthand typist in neat pencil skirts and fitted jackets. Her white hair was piled on top of her head in a loose bun held together with a big tortoiseshell claw grip.

'Kerry, dear, I thought you'd moved away till I heard about your fire! We've got some young lad delivering our letters and I have to tell you, it's just not the same. Why have you left? He said you weren't coming back! I was ever so upset, wasn't I, Mart? Didn't I say, I'm ever so upset, what'll we do without our Kerry? And what about your lovely house? I'm so sorry for you, but I'm glad your poor mum wasn't alive to witness it, God bless her soul.'

Kerry smiled wanly, her lip trembling. All this attention felt both comforting and slightly overwhelming. 'Time for a change, I guess,' she said, unable to keep the tremor out of her voice.

'We'll all miss you terribly, dear,' Sheila said. 'Nice to see you out of your shorts and red T-shirt, though. You're such a pretty girl and that's a lovely dress, isn't it, Mart?'

Martin grunted in a noncommittal way and turned away to check his phone.

'Hardly a girl, Sheila,' Kerry said, although she felt hot with pleasure at a compliment about her appearance – even coming from Sheila, whose current suit, while nicely tailored, was made of a grey-and-pink shiny material that seemed familiar to Kerry. She had a feeling that her parents had had dining chairs uphol-stered in the same fabric in the 1980s. 'I'm forty-four next month.'

'Spring chicken!' Sheila crowed. 'Mine's September too, ninth. What date are you?'

'Twenty-third,' Kerry said, glancing at Tim, hoping he wasn't getting bored. But he just stood smiling at her.

'Well, you make sure this nice chap of yours does something special for you,' Sheila said flirtatiously. 'Have a nice walk!' Before Kerry could correct her, she had hustled Martin away with their brown paper bags of groceries.

'Sorry about that,' Kerry said to Tim, once Kev had gone back behind his counter, the shop doorbell clanging loudly in his wake.

'No need to apologise,' Tim replied. 'It was kind of sweet.'

They walked on down the main street. Passing the turning to the little cul-de-sac populated by Great Dunsmore's council houses, she braced herself for the sight of Lee Carlton out walking his mum's dog, but thankfully the street was empty.

Everyone they passed either gave her a cheery or sympa-thetic wave – presumably dependent on whether they'd heard about either her fire or her firing, or both – or stopped to briefly chat, and it took them ten minutes to complete the three-minute walk.

'Do you know literally everybody in this village?' Tim asked, after they had been forced to admire and discuss the hanging baskets of bright pink and red begonias outside Mrs Peabody's converted barn. The elderly Mrs Peabody had been spraying a garden hose on them, her stance like Sly Stallone wielding a machine gun, as she too commiserated with Kerry about the fire.

'I suppose I do. Although the problem with that is – every-body knows me.'

'I don't think that's a problem at all. I think it's really nice. People care about you, Kerry, it's obvious. You're such a big part of this community.'

Do they? she thought. Am I? Maybe I was – but what happens now, though?

After a couple of hundred metres the hotchpotch of houses lining the road came to an abrupt end. Kerry and Tim walked along a high-hedged lane cut into a dip between undulating stalks of pale yellow wheat on either side. Hidden sparrows sang enthusiastically from the hedgerows and a hawk wheeled lazily overhead, biding its time. The road was empty of traffic and people and, apart from the birds, there was such absolute silence that Kerry fancied she could hear the faint pulse of the hot sun on the crown of her head. She should have brought a hat.

'I haven't walked along here in decades,' Tim said. 'It's so pretty. I never appreciated it when I was a teenager. Obviously.'

Kerry glanced at him. His face was a little contorted behind his sunglasses, in a way that made her think he was working up to tell her something.

'We can talk about what happened,' she said. 'After that night, I mean. You won't upset me. I've got enough other things to be upset about at the moment.'

To her surprise, she realised that this was true. Curiosity had taken the upper hand and, besides, it was good to have something other than the fire to think about. She still couldn't guess how her assault in the pond, and the naked photos, could possibly have impacted on Tim's life too, but she liked him enough to want to find out.

'OK.'

Kerry saw him take a big breath. He wasn't looking at her but at his feet. 'So, like I said in my letter, that boy Chris nicked my Polaroid camera that night. He pinned me down on the green when you were still in the pond and ripped it from round my neck. It was him who took the photos, and then Lee and Mutt snatched them off him, copied them and put them up round college. Not me.'

'Yeah. I do believe you, honestly.'

'But there was more, for me, like I said. I couldn't believe what they'd done. As soon as I saw the photos up on the notice-boards and realised what they were, I went straight to the college head – do you remember him? Mr Whittaker? He had masses of nostril hair and a comb-over but he was a decent bloke.

'I explained what had happened, that the photos had been taken with my camera, without my permission. He asked me who'd done it and I dobbed them both in. Lee and Mutt, I mean. Chris was at a different school... I didn't realise that they would get expelled – to be honest, I just thought they'd get a warning or something. I also didn't realise that they would know it was me who shopped them. A couple of days later they were waiting for me when I got off the bus, and they beat me up pretty badly.'

Kerry stopped in her tracks. 'No!'

Tim kept walking, rubbing the back of his neck, and Kerry had to scurry after him, her mouth dry with shock. He continued to talk, without making eye contact with her, as if this was a monologue he had been rehearsing for months.

'It was bad, that first time, but it got worse. I had to go to A&E for stitches at least twice. Those boys made my life a misery for the next year; Lee, particularly. He didn't finish his A levels anywhere else; I think he got a job as a farmhand or some-thing, but basically he was just always around in the village, tormenting me. Mutt disappeared. I think his folks probably sent him back to the private school he'd done his GCSEs at. I don't remember seeing him again.

'But Lee Carlton... I couldn't escape him. There just seemed to be a constant stream of jeers whenever I went anywhere. Mostly here in the village, but he and his gang would get on the same bus as me into town and follow me around there too, calling me names – Tiny Tim, Smallcock, Tiny Cock, you get the picture – throwing shit at me; literally, a few times. Or they'd wait for me outside college. It was horrendous. It went on for months. I couldn't eat or sleep, couldn't concentrate. My grades went down the pan. My hair started falling out. I became a total introvert. My parents wanted to call the police and report him, but I wouldn't let them. I thought it would just make things worse. They were so worried for me – they both worked full time so couldn't be around for me after school. I'd get a lift in with Mum in the mornings, but I had to get home on my own.

'In the end I failed my A levels and had, to put it bluntly, a complete breakdown. I was ill for months and I only started to get better when my folks got me a bursary to a boarding school near Cambridge where nobody knew me and I could retake my exams in peace. I changed my name to Deyes, Mum's maiden name, cut all ties with my friends except my mate Johnny. I didn't even come home in the holidays. I stayed with my aunt in Cambridge and my parents came to visit whenever they could. I haven't ever been back to Great Dunsmore until a few days ago when I drove over here to try and find out which house you lived in.'

'I am so sorry, Tim. That's just terrible. I don't know what to say. Except – Lee Carlton; what an utter bastard... Weirdly enough, we just walked past his house. His mum's house now – I think he lives in town – but he's out here quite a bit, walking her horrible dog. Good thing we didn't see him. I honestly think I'd try and kick his head in after what you've just told me,' Kerry said with feeling.

'I'd join you. He wouldn't know what hit him.' Tim said it

jokingly but Kerry could see the effort his explanation had taken, in the curl of his fists and the clench of his teeth. Poor Tim.

She tried to process it. All those years she'd struggled with what happened, when all along Tim had probably had it worse. A great wave of shame crashed over her at the thought that she had always assumed he'd been her tormentor, when he'd been as much of a victim as she had. At least for the worst part of her ordeal she'd been wasted, and the memories were mercifully cloudy and nebulous, like a fever dream.

Kerry felt a sudden huge pang for him, the Timothy she remembered as a teenager, his baby-faced, guileless expression, the NHS glasses sliding down his nose. In her mind she recalled the arm of the glasses as having been repaired with a Band-Aid wrapped around it, but whether that was a real memory, or whether she was just mentally embellishing, she wasn't sure. He'd definitely been the type to have a sticking plaster fixing his glasses, though.

But her overriding feeling was that she wasn't alone. It was a heady and new sensation of comradeship, one which made her blurt out words she had never spoken before:

'It wasn't just the photos. He... Lee, I mean, and his mate... they did things to me that night. In the pond. They made me...'

She tailed off, gulping, and Tim stopped. He took her hand and they stood, staring into each other's eyes in the lane.

'I mean, it wasn't... they didn't... force me to go all the way exactly, but it was bad enough. It was terrible. I couldn't forget it, and then with the photos... I think that's why I've never...'

Could she admit it to Tim? If she did, he might think she was a freak and run for the hills. But the way he was looking so tenderly at her, and the utter understanding in his expression, made her think it would be OK. She'd already wrongly doubted him once; she knew she needed to give him a bit of credit.

'... had a proper relationship before,' she whispered, dropping her gaze to focus on a huge dandelion clock on the verge.

Tim didn't reply. He just took a step forward and wrapped his arms around her, holding her so tightly that it was the easiest thing in the world for Kerry to relax into his embrace. He smelled incredible, of shampoo and some earthy, mellow sort of aftershave.

They stood like that for a couple of minutes, until a car approached from behind and they pulled apart, laughing sheepishly as they flattened themselves against the hedgerow to allow it to pass.

Tim did not let go of her hand, though.

Walking on in silence, Kerry felt too overcome with emotion to do anything other than squeeze his hand, bursting with gratitude. She realised for the first time the true meaning of the word 'catharsis'.

When she could finally speak again, she asked, 'How does it feel, being back in the village now?'

A tractor chugged towards them and they waited for it to pass.

'Weirdly, it's been harder to tell you about it than to be here... In fact, you know, it's actually OK,' he said, raising his voice to be heard above the rumble of the tractor engine. It was towing a trailer, which shed and blew shreds of straw and dust in a whirl around their heads, making Kerry think of the dark crackle of the fire again.

It was constantly in her thoughts, the memory of its petrifying roar causing her knees to go weak. She could hear the blood suddenly pounding in her ears, a slow internal vibration that made her visualise the wheeze of bagpipes before the wailing starts, and had to focus hard on Tim's words to keep herself grounded.

'It was such a long time ago. I swore I'd never come back, but I didn't have a reason before. And now I do.'

He smiled at her and the terror subsided again.

He wasn't going to run for the hills.

'I'm so glad you told me,' she said impulsively. 'Because then I was able to tell you what happened to me that night. I've never told anyone before.'

'Reckon we're quits now, in the confessional stakes,' he said, reaching forwards and picking a small piece of straw out of her hair. 'Anyway, so that's why I had to really think twice about accepting a job in Salisbury, but my therapist – yeah, I'm still having counselling – thought that it would be "closure" for me.' He laughed. 'Actually, this is a whole lot more closure than I'd assumed – but that's got to be a good thing, right?'

'Too right,' said Kerry, pointing down a long driveway to a large square turreted house. 'Look, there's the place.'

The cafe was in the courtyard entrance of the small stately home and fortunately they did not need to be members to get either tea or the two vast slabs of Victoria sponge cake that Tim insisted on buying. They sat at a shady outside table surrounded by neat beds of flowering lavender and marigolds, a large rack of pot plants for sale behind them.

'I was so looking forward to keeping Mum's garden looking nice,' Kerry said wistfully. The cake was reminding her of her mother. 'She wanted me to, she told me all the time.'

Tim hesitated. 'Tell me to mind my own business, but do you know why she might not have put her wishes for you to live in the house in her will? It seems like such a glaring omission.'

'I know. And it's made things so terrible between me and Beth. I really don't understand it.'

'Perhaps she realised that it wasn't fair on Beth, to keep her from her half of the inheritance?'

Kerry narrowed her eyes. 'Yeah, but years ago Mum gave Beth the money for a big deposit on the house she and her first husband bought together. My understanding was that letting me live in the big house was her way of balancing the books.'

Tim shrugged, stirring sugar into his tea. 'It would have to have been a pretty massive deposit, if that was it.'

For a brief moment Kerry felt like snapping, *whose side are you on, anyway?* Then she realised that this was true. 'Maybe. But I still think it was rubbish of her not to have warned me.'

'Perhaps she didn't get the opportunity.' Tim's voice was gentle. 'So, have you and Beth discussed what you're going to do with the house, assuming you do get the insurance money?'

'We won't,' Kerry said glumly.

'Don't be so pessimistic. You don't know for sure you started the fire. Let's not assume the worst.'

She liked the collective 'let's', as if Tim was in it with her.

'OK. Well... I'm not an expert but I'm pretty sure it's too far gone to just repair. I suppose it'll have to be pulled down and a new one built on the same site. God. I really can't face that. Or we could sell the land for someone else to build on.'

She gulped and looked away, over at two parents showing their twin toddlers the plants for sale and telling them the Latin names. As if toddlers would care!

Tim followed her gaze. 'They'll be testing Tarquin and Jemima on all that later,' he said. 'Woe betide them if they get any wrong.'

Kerry grinned, but the sight of the sturdy little boy wriggling with boredom in his father's arms reminded her of the crash in the post office yard. Reminders of trauma everywhere. It must have shown in her face because Tim cleared his throat.

'Say no, if you think it's totally inappropriate...' he began, and Kerry wondered what he was going to ask. Become his sex slave? Come and work in his office? *Marry* him? She couldn't imagine.

'... I've just been thinking that it will be depressing for you, having to see your house in ruins every time you look out the window or step out the front door. And that's before it gets torn down or rebuilt or whatever...'

'Hmm,' Kerry said. She had been thinking the same. She wondered how soon the antidepressants would start to kick in, having taken her first one that morning, marvelling at the idea that one tiny little tablet could possibly make things seem less bleak.

'So I wondered if – if – no strings, of course, unless you want strings – you'd like to come and live with me? As a house-mate, I mean. You'd have your own bedroom. I wouldn't want much rent, just a contribution towards bills and so on.'

Kerry was so astonished that she couldn't think of a single response except an extremely ungrateful sounding, 'Oh! Where do you live?'

Then she gathered herself. 'Sorry, Tim, that was so rude. I mean, thank you! That's so kind of you to offer. Wow. That would be – I mean – I don't know what to say. I've literally never lived anywhere else, it would be... Can I think about it?'

Tim laughed. 'Of course. But you'd be doing me a favour. I've decided I'm not keen on living on my own. I was thinking of getting a lodger anyway, but I'd much prefer it to be someone I already know rather than risk some guy who bites his toenails and listens to heavy metal day and night.'

'How do you know I don't bite my toenails?'

He chuckled again, an easy, comforting sound.

A faint beep from Kerry's pocket alerted her to the arrival of a new Facebook message, so she pulled out her phone and took a glance, wincing in case it was news of the fire report – but when she saw who it was from, she gasped.

'What is it?'

She stopped and faced Tim, holding out the phone to him. 'I don't believe it. Miss Smith's replied to my message!' Then she realised that Tim didn't actually know why this was so important to her.

'If this confessional thing is a race between us, I think I'm about to take the lead,' she said, putting her phone face down on the table. She could look at the message in a moment. 'There's something else you might want to know, about the reason I was so keen to contact her in the first place...'

Kerry took a deep breath and told him the whole story: her dad's death; her parents' apparently blissfully happy marriage; the contact sheet in the drawer; Miss Smith reclining on the familiar rug; Beth's conviction that she was wrong; Kerry's desperation to prove she hadn't been mistaken.

Again, Tim did not let her down – although his eye did twitch slightly, at the mention of Miss Smith naked, which made Kerry grin to herself just for a second. He listened intently, his hand resting lightly on her knee, letting her talk. When she finished, he just said, 'Wow. That's – intense. It must have been so upsetting for you.'

Then he added, 'You know what? I think what you've done is incredible. Most people would have just given up and either blocked it out after all these years, or allowed themselves to be convinced they must have been mistaken after all. You're not letting yourself be forced into pretending it didn't happen, and you're ready to face the truth even if it's not what you want to hear. Good for you!'

Kerry blushed. She'd never thought of it like that. 'Thank you,' she said shyly. 'Anyway, yeah, I'm prepared for whatever the outcome is. I've spent the last twenty-six years assuming the worst about my lovely dad, and I really, really hope I'm proved wrong – but if I'm not, at least it won't be a shock. I don't want to upset Beth so I won't tell her if it does turn out Miss Smith and Dad were involved. But at least I'll know, one way or the other.'

Tim nodded, then gestured at her phone. 'Well, you'd better read the message then.'

.   .   .

Miss Smith had been very happy to hear from her. Miss Smith would love to meet her. Miss Smith would come to Salisbury; she could time it with an appointment with the chiropodist. Miss Smith commented on what a long time it had been! Miss Smith signed herself 'Anita' and appended her message with a kiss and smiley face. Miss Smith suggested this Saturday.

'Aargh!' Kerry said, having read it out loud to Tim as she jiggled her leg anxiously under the cafe table, causing the teacups to tremble. 'I'm going to meet Miss Smith again, in three days' time!'

'You really ought to stop calling her Miss Smith. It'll be Anita, now you're both adults.' Tim put his hand back under the table and gently stilled her knee.

'I know. But old habits die hard.' Kerry couldn't stop staring at the screen, but she stopped the jiggling. Tim's hand felt steady and she missed it as soon as he withdrew it.

She would finally *know*.

Lately, with all the other crap going on, the issue of whether Miss Smith and her dad had ever made the beast with two backs had unsurprisingly been pushed to the back of her mind, but now it all came flooding back, a welcome distraction from the anxiety over the fire, the job, the imminent insurance claim.

'Where are you going to meet her?'

'She doesn't mention that. I'll suggest the Museum Cafe in The Close, I think. We can sit outside if it's sunny.'

Tim looked wistful. 'Wow, you lucky thing. You're going to meet Miss Smith! Can I come?'

Kerry laughed at his comically smitten face. 'No you can't! Anyway, she's got to be pushing sixty now. Surely you wouldn't still fancy her?'

He shrugged. 'I looked at her Facebook profile pic after you told me her surname. She still looks pretty hot, for a sixty-year-old. I could be her toy boy...'

'She's married! And I need to have what might well be a

really awkward conversation with her, but if it goes well, who knows. Maybe we'll become best mates and she'll invite you on one of our nights out. She'll finally see you as more than little Timothy Alcock from her Year Ten history class.'

Tim threw a scrunched-up paper napkin at her and Kerry felt that unfamiliar sensation again, the one that took her a moment to identify. The one that, weirdly, under the circumstances, felt a lot like happiness.

THIRTY-SIX

Sitting at an outside table in the Museum Cafe a few days later, with the vast West Front of Salisbury Cathedral looming up in front of her, Kerry no longer felt happiness.

What she did feel was more akin to abject terror, and she was on the brink of tears already. She was ten minutes early, so she ordered a pot of tea, briefly wishing it was a pot of wine. But she hadn't had a drop of alcohol since the night of the fire, and on the whole, she still wasn't finding it as tricky as she'd thought she might.

Of course, there were moments that she craved it with every atom of her being, most notably when she'd been on the phone to the insurance company, who had rung the other day to update her. They had obtained an incident number and the report from the brigade but it had been 'inconclusive' and they were sending in their own loss adjustors to undertake a separate enquiry and test all the appliances. The next day Kerry had peeked out of a gap between her tightly drawn curtains and seen the two men in hard hats and hi-vis, one scribbling on a clipboard while the other wrestled with the padlock to take the boards off what had once been the front door. They had vanished into the dark, charred hallway, doubtless to discover the evidence of cigarettes in the living room and seal hers and Beth's fates...

Don't think about it, she instructed herself sternly. This was nerve-racking enough as it was.

The weather had recently changed and it was overcast; granite clouds swollen with about-to-fall rain. The sky matched the grey stone of the cathedral. Kerry hadn't brought an umbrella, and nor were there any over the tables, but she supposed they could move inside if it did start to pour.

She realised that she was muttering to herself when a couple of elderly tourists in matching cagoules both stared so hard at her that she blushed. Her hand was shaking as she poured her tea. *Hurry up, Miss Smith. Anita.*

On cue, a lone woman walked in, scanning the tables. She was petite, about five foot five, and Kerry had to do a double-take because in her memory, Miss Smith had always been really tall. She supposed it was because she hadn't finished growing herself, and Anita had become frozen in her mind as taller than her. But there was no mistaking her face. Kerry thought that, even if she hadn't seen her profile picture on Facebook, she'd still have recognised her anywhere.

She waved, and Anita broke out into a beam so wide and natural that for the first time, Kerry doubted that the naked photos could have been of her after all.

Anita rushed across, dumping her handbag on the grass next to the empty chair at her table and opening her arms to her. Kerry stood up awkwardly and allowed first the embrace, then to be held at arm's length and cheerfully scrutinised.

'Oh Kerry! How wonderful to see you again after all these years. You are the image of your mother!'

This took Kerry aback. Nobody had ever said it to her before.

'Really? I always thought Beth was the one that took after

her and I ended up with the least attractive features of both Mum and Dad.'

Anita laughed. 'Not at all. You look fabulous.'

Kerry noticed she hadn't flinched or blushed at the mention of Dad. Either the woman had a totally brass neck, or Kerry really had got the wrong end of the stick.

They sat down and Anita – Kerry was slowly beginning to get used to thinking of her by that name – beckoned a waitress across.

While she was ordering a peppermint tea and a chocolate brownie, Kerry studied her surreptitiously. She had aged brilliantly, it had to be said. Her hair was still thick and wavy, no longer blonde, but a lovely golden-auburn colour without a hint of grey. Definitely dyed, but expertly done. She did have plenty of laughter lines, and her chin was a tiny bit crepey, but her figure was still trim. Kerry thought how delighted she would be if she herself looked as good as that once she was approaching sixty.

The waitress wandered off and Anita's face turned serious. 'Kerry, I was so very sorry to hear about your mum's death. I feel terrible that I didn't know about it until after the funeral. We were on holiday anyway, so I couldn't have come – but I could have sent condolences to you and Beth. Poor Hilary!'

'How did you hear?' Kerry asked curiously.

Anita shook her head and her earrings whipped back and forth. They were lovely: three little purple crystal beads on the end of short lengths of delicate silver chain.

'I'm still in occasional contact with Mary Atkins from choir, remember her? She was a good friend of your mum's and she told me, last time we spoke on the phone. I felt a little bit cross that she hadn't let me know sooner. I could have sent a card to you girls.'

This felt a bit strange to Kerry. Miss Smith hadn't been in touch with Mum – or her and Beth – for years, as far as she knew, so why did she seem so upset? Perhaps she was overcompensating... Trying to make out they were better friends than they were, so Kerry wouldn't suspect anything had ever gone on between her and Dad? Kerry narrowed her eyes slightly. For the first time, Anita looked a little flustered and Kerry felt embarrassed, remembering too late that she had the absolute opposite of a poker face, and Anita could doubtless clearly see how suspiciously she was being regarded.

'I like your earrings,' she blurted, in an attempt to make Anita think that these were what she'd been glaring at.

'I made them!' she said, looking relieved. She whipped one out to show it to Kerry up close. 'I make most of my jewellery. I'll make you a pair if you like.'

'Oh – er – thank you.'

Kerry never wore dangly earrings like that, although they were pretty. They were more Beth's kind of thing.

'So, Kerry, it's been so long. I don't think I've seen you since your darling dad's funeral all those years ago.'

Darling Dad. Whose darling?

Anita looked a little misty-eyed. 'That was the saddest funeral I've ever been to. He was such a wonderful man. We all adored him, and he was taken so very young. Your poor mum. And you girls... your faces... it was heart-breaking.'

To Kerry's horror, her own eyes flooded with tears. Anita was mortified.

'Kerry, I'm so, so sorry! How tactless of me.'

Kerry sniffed and blew her nose on a paper napkin she plucked from a metal holder in the centre of the table. 'No, don't apologise. Gosh, it was twenty-six years ago, I ought to be over it by now! It's actually really nice to hear someone mention it.' She hesitated. 'Actually, I remember you from that day. You were in the choir and you were struggling during the "Hallelujah Chorus". I think it was your expression that made me cry hardest.'

It was Anita's turn to well up. 'Yes, I really was. It's such an emotive piece of music. I think of your dad every single time I hear it; have done ever since.'

Kerry took a deep breath. 'You and Dad were close, weren't you?'

Anita's head shot up, but she looked surprised rather than horrified. 'Well, yes – I was close to both your mum and dad. I saw a lot of Hilary after Ralph died, but I'm sorry to say that we lost touch once I got married and moved out to Trowbridge. They were – very kind to me, your folks.'

Kerry took a sip of her tea and tried to sound casual. 'In what way?'

If she was honest, she hadn't planned to jump in with the interrogation quite so early in the conversation, but it seemed naturally to have headed in that direction.

Anita gazed across The Close and up at the cathedral spire. She sounded as if she was choosing her words very carefully.

'A few years before I met my husband, I had a boyfriend who... wasn't very nice. Your folks were really supportive when we broke up. Especially your dad.'

Kerry waited, studying a tiny prickly black and yellow insect crawling across the tabletop, trying not to let Anita see how much she had invested in what followed. She hadn't intended to say anything but suddenly she couldn't wait any more and the words blurted out of her, the question she'd been dying to know the answer to for twenty-six years:

'It's just, I found naked photographs of you in Dad's drawer, and I've always really wanted to know why there were there.'

THIRTY-SEVEN

Kerry didn't know which of them was the more horrified. The words hung in the air above their table like poisoned darts paused in flight. She opened her mouth to apologise, then closed it again in case Anita took it as an excuse not to tell her. But Anita looked her full in the face, her expression full of mingled compassion and embarrassment.

'Oh *Kerry*. That must have been absolutely awful for you. Let me tell you how they came to be there.'

Exhaling hard, Kerry gazed over her shoulder with her eyes wide to prevent them filling with tears, focusing on the cathedral, its granite splendour and intricate carvings, imagining medieval stonemasons chipping away. It had taken thirty-eight years to build, far longer than she'd waited to find out what Miss Smith was about to tell her.

'It was only a few months before your dad passed away. I showed up at your house one day in a state – I'd never have done that if I'd known he was ill. He seemed fine then...'

Miss Smith seemed more distressed that she had burdened her folks with her own problems than with any admission of guilt, which was a good sign, Kerry thought. She tried to reassure her.

'We might not even have known at that point. We only found out about three months before he died.'

This was sort of true. She and Beth hadn't known, but Mum and Dad had been keeping it from them, like a shit sort of Christmas present that had been poorly hidden on the high shelf of a wardrobe. They'd been aware it was up there, its corners hanging over the edge, but it had never looked appealing enough to climb up and investigate. Muttered conversations that stopped when they walked into the room, Mum crying and not telling them why, Dad being uncharacteristically snappy or withdrawn...

'I hadn't wanted to go round, in case you or Beth saw me like that, but I knew your mum hadn't ever really approved of your dad setting me up with him; Jeff, I mean. I think she could tell he was trouble long before I ever figured it out. I was so naive... Anyway. I can't even remember why I went to see them that day, I mean, we weren't hugely close friends, just pals from choir. I suppose maybe I thought all my other friends would just say *I told you so*. My parents definitely wouldn't have been sympathetic. They'd have been disgusted if they'd found out I moved in with Jeff so soon, without even being engaged. They were very old-fashioned like that...'

Anita was blurting out the words, splurging them over the table in a way that made Kerry picture them slopping between its wooden slats, like confessional vomit.

This worried Kerry anew. Exactly how sympathetic had Dad been? Had this been the start of it? A consoling cuddle that had turned into something else? She wanted to say *Just spit it out! What happened?*

'Wasn't Mum in that day?'

Anita looked at Kerry then, puzzled. 'No, she was. She opened the front door. She said you girls were out doing something or other and I remember being really relieved, because I looked terrible. I was in floods of tears, wearing some ratty old tracksuit with a big greasy mark on the top, and my eyes were all red and puffy... I was so embarrassed.'

That would indeed have been a shock to her and Beth, Kerry thought. Miss Smith had always been immaculately turned out at school, neat blouses and court shoes, perfect hair and a particular shade of bright coral-pink lipstick Kerry could still remember. She was wearing a similar tone now, but more matte and subdued. Kerry could not imagine her in any sort of dishevelled state. No wonder Anita had remembered the stain on her tracksuit.

So, Mum had been there. This was a relief. Kerry felt a tiny bit less uneasy. Her emotions were see-sawing so much she felt almost vertiginous.

'Hilary gave me a big hug – I can still remember the feel of it even though I was mortified at the time. I almost ran away but she pulled me inside and sat me down in your kitchen. She made me a cup of tea with three sugars in it, and handed me a box of tissues...'

'Where was Dad?' Kerry was still trying to keep her voice casual.

'He was out in the garden – building a bonfire, or digging something, I think. I remember he left mud all over the floor when he came in the back door later.'

In one way, Kerry thought, it was kind of nice to be talking about Mum and Dad like this, even though the topic wasn't what Miss Smith would have preferred to discuss as if it was something that had only happened last week. She could so clearly picture Dad bursting in through the back door – he never could enter a room quietly. She imagined him pulling his tucked-in gardening trousers out of his socks and kicking off his wellies, clots of muddy earth flying out of the treads, leaving the boots flopped on their sides on the utility room floor like he always used to, probably calling out something like, 'Lunch ready, Hils? I could eat a scabby horse—' then breaking off when he saw Miss Smith crying at the kitchen table with, most likely, a wide-eyed 'oh, crikey!'

The imagined memory made Kerry smile. Poor Mum used to despair, because she and Beth would follow suit with their own footwear, and the utility room was always an untidy sea of discarded shoes and unpaired boots.

She felt a pang of nostalgia for her family, back when they were still whole. A lump came to her throat and she took a polite sip of tea, even though it had gone cold, and waited for Miss Smith to continue.

'I remember them asking what had happened. Ralph was looking sort of pained, and your mum was hugging me. Eventually I told them what Jeff had done...'

Kerry was still struggling to make a connection between Anita's ex, Jeff, and the naked photos on Dad's rug. She vaguely remembered Jeff, because he'd been ridiculously good-looking; a tall, suave, seventies-throwback who drove a yellow Triumph TR7, wore a caramel-coloured leather bomber jacket and let his hair grow down below his shoulders. She and Beth had commented on a few occasions how dishy he was, and – after that coach trip to London – how smitten Miss Smith clearly was.

He and Dad had met at camera club. Ah, Kerry thought – she'd forgotten that. Camera club... Dad obviously thought that Jeff and Anita would make a good couple so had persuaded Mum to have them both over to dinner.

It all started to come back to her. It had been love at first sight between the pair, her mum had told her. Well, lust, probably, for Jeff at least. Mum once told her that she and Dad had actually gone to bed in the end, leaving their guests canoodling downstairs after that first dinner party. Dad had to stagger downstairs in his tartan dressing gown at 3 a.m. and kick them out, clearing his throat loudly on the stairs to give them a moment to rearrange their clothing. Kerry remembered it now, because she been as surprised that Mum had told her about it as she had been at the thought of Miss Smith snogging someone on their sofa.

Her mother had also confided in Kerry about her reservations. At first glance they had seemed to be a match made in heaven – Anita had been so terribly pretty, with peachy porcelain skin, curly blonde hair, a lovely figure and huge blue eyes but her mum had said to her – (Kerry remembered the thrill of complicity she'd felt that Mum was gossiping, to her! About her history teacher no less!) – that it was a worry that Anita was a lot more square, although she'd probably used the word 'conservative', than Jeff.

Anita liked classical music and gardening, whereas Jeff was into West Coast rock, photography and smoking weed. Still, Mum supposed, the language of love trumped hobbies, and they did seem to really hit it off. That conversation stuck in Kerry's mind for a long time because the words 'smoking weed' seemed so strange coming from the mouth of her also-quite-square mother. How could she have forgotten all of that?

'I tried to break it off with him,' Anita said now. 'I'd tried a few times, but he always talked me round. But that time I was really sure. I told him to move all his stuff out.'

'Why did you want to break up with him?' Kerry immediately felt bad. 'Sorry – that was tactless. You don't have to tell me.'

'It's OK. It just wasn't working. I hadn't been happy with him for a few months. He wanted' – she hesitated – 'I mean, he had a really high sex drive. And he was really possessive. He insisted on seeing me every day. I was, you know, flattered at first, and so crazy about him. But then after a while it just got a bit much. I had so much marking to do in the evenings during term-time.'

Kerry imagined Anita sitting at the kitchen table trying to mark essays on the Reformation while Jeff relentlessly pestered her, lifting the red felt-tip pen out of her hand and sliding his fingers up her skirt. Poor Miss Smith. It confirmed Kerry's suspicions that life was much easier being single.

'Didn't he have a job?'

Anita shook her head. 'When we got together, he said he was between jobs after his boss at the printing works let him go, some kind of vendetta, Jeff said, because the guy was jealous. Or something. I mean, honestly, that doesn't even sound plausible, does it?'

'Not really,' Kerry agreed. By the sound of him, Jeff had probably slept with the boss's wife.

'He said he was applying for jobs, but I don't think he was. Then he started going on and on about moving in with me. I said I wasn't ready for that, it was too soon, but he just wouldn't shut up about it, so after a couple of months I let him.'

She sighed. 'It was actually really nice at first. You know, having a man around the place. Having someone to wake up with and cook for. Once I got used to the idea of, er, living in sin. That's how my parents would have thought of it anyway, God rest them, if I'd told them. Which I didn't. I rationalised it by thinking it didn't matter, because we would definitely be getting married sooner or later. I thought he was the love of my life...'

Her lip trembled at the memory. 'I did things,' she said quietly. 'Things that I've never done before and wouldn't ever do again. Things that made me feel... ashamed.'

Kerry had an idea, finally, of where this story might be going.

'Poor you,' she said, putting her hand on Anita's. Mum had probably done the same, she thought. It made her feel close to her mother.

'He'd moved out, that same day, I think. Went back to that

bungalow he was renting before he moved in with me. But... he left me this awful note, telling me what he was planning to do...'

'Do?'

'Yes. You see, one of the things he talked me into was, um, letting him take my picture. Naked.'

And there it was.

'Oh. Oh no.' Relief was slowly beginning to sweep over Kerry like a vast welcome puddle-splash in slow motion. Although why on earth had Dad let them use his studio?

'I didn't want to. I said no for months, but it was like the moving in thing; once he set his mind on something, he didn't stop till he got his own way. In the end he persuaded me, saying it was just something private, something for us, and that I should appreciate my body the way he did. He said I'd see it in a different light. That I should be a model... all that rubbish. And that it would help him "hone his craft". So I did it, although I felt really self-conscious and embarrassed. The pictures did turn out nicer than I'd thought, and they weren't... explicit. Just arty and titillating, you know, nothing pornographic. Well, you'd know, if you saw them.'

Kerry nodded, although she'd been so shocked to find them that she couldn't have commented on their artistic merits.

'In the note he told me he was going to enter the photos into all the local photographic competitions. He'd always had a real thing about winning competitions, and there were loads round here. Including the one the camera club ran, where they printed the winning entries in the *Salisbury Journal*.'

'Oh God. How awful. What a bastard! Would he really have done it?'

'Absolutely he would. I've got no doubt. And because they were really nice pictures, he probably would've won a prize and then literally everyone would have seen me nude in the paper! All my pupils. All the staff and parents. Someone would have complained to the board of governors, and I'd have lost my job.

My reputation. Everything! It was bad enough that I'd already lost him, and he'd turned nasty. I thought he was the one, and he was nothing but a horrible blackmailing...'

She ran out of steam.

'The *Journal* wouldn't have printed anything salacious, surely,' Kerry contributed, not really knowing what else to say.

Miss Smith managed a laugh. 'That's exactly what your mum said too. But he'd have made sure it was one of the more discreet arty ones, you know, a side view with just a hint of boob, something like that. He wasn't stupid. But I'd still have been recognisable. He'd *promised* he would never show them to anybody else. It still makes me go hot and cold when I think about it. If it hadn't been for your dad...'

'What did Dad do?' Kerry's voice was small and tight with a growing sense of relief.

'He went over to Jeff's and somehow got them back off him. Wouldn't take no for an answer. He offered to give them back to me but I asked him to destroy them. He told me he had done – there were about six contact sheets and loads of negatives – but I guess one of them must have just been left behind.'

THIRTY-EIGHT

Kerry couldn't speak. She stared at Miss Smith, completely overcome. Her gorgeous, loyal, wonderful dad, who she'd doubted for all those years. Why on earth hadn't she just asked her mum? Mum had known; she could have put Kerry's mind at rest in a second.

She felt absolutely terrible, and as guilty as if she'd slandered his name all over town for no reason. Eventually she whispered, 'I thought you must have been having an affair.'

Anita reached across the table and grabbed her hand, squeezing it fiercely. 'Oh darling, you poor thing. How long have you thought that? When did you find the photos?'

'Years ago. Not long after Dad died.'

Kerry broke down completely, burying her forehead in her crossed arms on the table, her shoulders shaking. Anita stroked her shoulder, bringing her mouth close to her ear so they couldn't be overheard – although the cafe was about to close, and all the outside tables were now empty apart from theirs. No one to overhear but the stone bishops, looking down from their perches on the West Front.

'No, no, Kerry, never. Your dad was totally devoted to your

mum. I was so envious of their relationship – but I'd never have done anything to jeopardise it. Never! And he wouldn't have let me anyway, even if I'd wanted to. They were the best couple. Seriously, they were rock-solid. I can't lie, I did fancy Ralph – but then, so did every single one of the sopranos. All the altos, too – and likely about half of the tenors, when I think about it! We used to giggle in the tea breaks about how gorgeous he was, and how lucky Hilary was. But we all knew he only had eyes for her. That's partly why I was so upset at the funeral. I just felt so sorry for Hilary that she'd had that incredible love and lost it. I remember thinking that if I ever found a man who adored me half as much as Ralph adored Hilary, I'd consider myself doing very well. Here, have a tissue.'

Kerry lifted up her head, and the little yellow and black insect was in her eyeline again, crawling valiantly past like a tiny Stickle Brick. Dad would have known what sort of bug it was. She missed him then, more than she had in years.

'I should just have asked Mum about it,' she said, sniffing unattractively and blowing her nose. A young waitress clearing the tables around them studiously looked away.

'But presumably you wanted to spare her feelings in case it turned out to be true and your dad *had* taken those photos?'

Kerry nodded miserably. 'I ripped up the contact sheet when I first saw it.'

'Well – it must be a relief to you too, to find out she already knew?'

'Yes.' It was, actually. A huge relief. Then a thought struck her. 'Wait – that rug, though? The rug that you – that the photos were taken on. It's still in the annexe. Did your boyfriend take the photos at our house?'

Old suspicions briefly began to swirl back, the muddy water of doubt clinging to Kerry's ankles. That rug was the reason that she was so sure Dad had to have been the photographer.

Anita frowned. 'The round shaggy green rug? No, that was

in my living room. I've still got it but it's in the spare room now. I keep meaning to get rid of it, it's probably a health hazard by now, it's that ancient.'

'It's a red rug,' Kerry persisted. 'Dad had it in his office.'

Anita laughed softly. 'Kerry, those photos were in black and white. I promise you, it was green. If you don't believe me, come over and I'll show it to you. It must just be a similar style rug – they were in fashion around that time. Habitat, I think it was from.'

The photos were black and white. Of course they were. Another incorrect assumption that had been moulded inside Kerry decades ago, fired in the kiln of her grief and suspicion until it was set solid.

'So that's why you wanted to meet me. To ask if Ralph and I had been having an affair?'

Kerry nodded. 'Basically, yes. Sorry.'

'No need to apologise! I wish you'd found me decades ago. I could have spared you all that worry and doubt.' Anita hesitated. 'Bloody Jeff. Horrible man. This is all his fault – and mine, for being gullible enough to let him talk me into taking the photos in the first place. I was too weak to say no, even though I wanted to. I thought he'd go off me if I didn't oblige. Ironic, since I dumped him a couple of months later anyway. At least I had the guts to do that. He caused nothing but pain. And I know your folks felt bad too, because it was them who introduced us in the first place.'

Anita poured herself another cup of tea and Kerry looked at her delicate hands, the big rock on the third finger. She hoped Glen Pickles had given Anita that sized diamond to show the world how much he loved her, how happy she made him, rather than because he wanted to flash some cash, like Jeff undoubtedly would have done.

Thank God Anita extricated herself from *him*.

Anita looked up again, the pain clear in her blue eyes. 'I was traumatised for years after that,' she admitted. 'Partly because someone I thought I loved had turned so nasty, and partly because I realised how foolish I'd been. I have no doubt that if your dad hadn't got the photos back, Jeff would've carried out his threat and entered them into competitions all around the place. I really could have lost my job, and my reputation. It still makes me go cold just thinking about it.'

Kerry gasped, unable to help it.

'What's the matter?' Concern etched itself at the corners of Anita's eyes.

'It's just...' Kerry found herself choking up again, '... actually, something similar happened to me, a few months later.'

'Oh goodness, no!' Anita sounded genuinely distressed. 'Kerry, what?'

'It wasn't anybody I knew well, and they didn't blackmail me, but—'

She took a deep breath, and told Anita what she'd told Tim the week before. She mentioned Mum's party – Anita interrupted briefly to say she remembered that hot summer night, dancing to disco records in the garden – then all the local teenagers congregating on the green. Timothy Alcock with his cameras. Lee Charlton snogging her and persuading her to skinny-dip. Her, drunk and stoned, agreeing. Changing her mind about wanting Lee, him turning nasty, her stuck in the pond while his mate got in and they forced her head into their vile crotches as they laughed and jeered. Beth running home to get her a towel, her coming out of the water and tripping over. The flash of the Polaroid. Then – fresh horror upon horror – the xeroxes on all the college noticeboards a few days later...

Kerry had to stop talking. Anita's face was tight with fury and sympathy.

'All this time, I assumed it had been Timothy Alcock,' Kerry said, once she could continue. 'I couldn't really understand it, except that I thought he must have been egged on by Lee.'

'I remember little Timmy Alcock,' Anita said. 'He was a sweet boy. Could he have been bullied into doing it?'

'He *was* bullied, but not into distributing the pictures. Another boy, Chris, who was on the green with us that night, nicked his camera and took the photos. Lee grabbed them off him, photocopied them and stuck them up round college because he was mad at me. Timothy – Tim – only told me a few days ago that he'd gone to the head and explained what had happened and who did it, and Lee got expelled. After that, he and his gang made Tim's life a misery. Bullied him so badly he messed up his A levels. He had to change his name and move away to make it stop. Said it really traumatised him.'

'Oh, poor lad,' said Anita. 'That's horribly unfair. So when did he tell you all this? Because presumably you didn't keep in touch, if you always thought it was him?'

Kerry gave her a watery smile. 'I didn't know he'd changed his name. It's thanks to you, actually, that I found out. I posted on the school's alumni Facebook page asking if anyone knew how to get in touch with you. He was the only one who replied – under the name Tim Deyes, so I never thought for a minute it was the same Timothy, and he looks really different now. I'd never have recognised him. A friend of his bumped into you in Trowbridge and relayed the conversation to Tim later, and it gave me enough information to find out your new surname.'

'Gosh,' Anita said. 'He must have a really good memory. I don't think I'd ever remember something about someone else that was mentioned in passing!'

Kerry grinned. 'Ah. That's because – and he'll probably kill me for telling you – Tim had an absolutely massive crush on you when you were his teacher. Still does, I reckon.'

Anita laughed and mimed fanning herself. 'I did suspect as much at the time. He did a lot of blushing and lurking around my desk after class, bless him. I always had a bit of a soft spot for him, actually.'

'He'll be overcome to hear it.' Kerry giggled and thought how unfamiliar a sound it was. She was experiencing another new emotion – levity. She had no idea who it was that first coined the expression 'a weight off your mind' but she literally felt several stone lighter, both in the wake of Anita's explanation of the photos and her own unburdening of the trauma she suffered that night by the pond.

She cleared her throat. 'Tim's actually just moved back to the area from London. We met up for a couple of drinks a while back, but I stormed off when I realised who he was. He's only just managed to get me to listen long enough for him to explain what really happened that night, and who'd been responsible for the photos, and now we're friends again. Funnily enough, he's just invited me to go and live with him; be his lodger.'

Anita raised an eyebrow. 'Were you looking for somewhere to live?'

'Long story, but the latest entry in the catalogue of disasters in my life is our house burning down. Well, Mum's house, which Beth and I now own. My annexe was OK, but I can't face living opposite the charred wreckage of my home, especially because I was about to move in.'

Kerry decided not to burden Anita with the sorry saga of her dispute with her sister. She'd already told her enough that the poor woman would have been able to write a convincing misery memoir about it.

'Good heavens, I am so sorry to hear that. What a trauma! Well, that seems like a kind suggestion of Tim's. Are you going to take him up on it?'

Kerry visualised Tim, his fond, intelligent eyes, his humour and generosity. 'I said I'd think about it. I have thought about it – and you know what? I am. I'm going to ring him up later and ask if the offer still stands.'

Funny how only a month ago she had vehemently asserted that she never wanted to live anywhere other than the annexe or the big house, she thought.

Nothing changes for years and years – and then suddenly everything changes at once.

THIRTY-NINE

'Beth! What are you doing here? Is everything OK?'

Kerry was alarmed to see Beth standing on Tim's front doorstep at ten thirty in the morning on a Wednesday, clutching a brown paper bag with a greasy stain spreading across it. It had to be the first time Beth had ever just 'popped in' unannounced – although of course in bygone days, she hadn't needed to. She used to come to visit their mum and Kerry had always crunched across the driveway to join them in the big house.

Oh no, thought Kerry, the fire report must be in. It had been due any day for the last week. But Beth didn't look angry or upset – in fact, she seemed to have lost the pinched look she had worn since the fire, and there was colour in her cheeks. Her auburn hair was perfectly blow-dried and she was in her customary immaculate workout gear.

'Everything's fine!' she said. 'I've been to the hairdresser, and it's only round the corner. I just wanted to come and see your new place. Can I come in? How are you settling in?'

Still bemused – and a little suspicious – Kerry held open the door to admit her. 'Good, thanks. What's in there?' She pointed at the bag, from which a delicious pastry smell was emanating.

'Croissants from the bakery!'

'*Croissants*? For who?'

'Us, of course, silly.'

OK, Kerry thought, things are getting really strange. She hadn't seen her sister consume anything containing trans fats since about 1995. 'I thought you didn't eat white carbs?'

Beth followed her through to Tim's small, neat kitchen and dumped the paper bag on the counter, revealing two huge, flaky pastries that immediately made Kerry's mouth water.

'I don't, normally, but I just couldn't resist. Once in a blue moon won't hurt! A little bit of what you fancy... as Mum used to say.'

'Wow.' Kerry scratched her head, thinking, Who are you and what have you done with my sister? 'I'll put the kettle on. Coffee or camomile tea?'

'Tea, please.' Beth pulled up a stool and sat down at the counter, looking around. 'Cute place he's got,' she said. Was that an admiring tone, Kerry wondered?

'Yeah, it's so nice,' she agreed, getting two plates from the cupboard. She'd had breakfast, a couple of hours ago, but there was always a little extra space for a fresh croissant. 'I'll tell him you thought so.'

'How are things going between you?'

Kerry paused, blushing. 'Slowly,' she said, 'but very well, I think. We really enjoy each other's company.'

Beth laughed, but not unkindly. 'Does he make your heart skip a beat?'

Kerry didn't have to think about this. 'Actually, yes he does,' she said, smiling. Her heart was jumping, even just thinking of Tim. Of how, when he got home from work, he'd give her a big hug as soon as he got through the door. Of how they would sit down and eat together, chatting ceaselessly about nothing and everything before giggling at some comedy on TV, kissing each other a tender goodnight and retreating to their respective bedrooms. Of how Kerry would fall asleep every night with a big secret smile on her face, thinking of how she couldn't wait to see him again first thing in the morning.

'Have you, you know...?'

Kerry knew exactly what Beth was asking. Her initial instinct was to shut down this line of questioning; to scowl and change the subject. But she found she didn't want to. Beth's enquiry didn't seem salacious or intrusive, just concerned.

'No, not yet,' she replied shyly. 'I'm not ready. But between you and me, I don't think it'll be all that much longer.'

Beth beamed. 'Ah, that's lovely, Kerry, I'm so chuffed. I know what a big deal it is for you.'

Kerry made the tea then pulled up the other stool and sat next to her sister, taking a big bite out of the croissant. 'Do you?' she asked curiously, with her mouth full.

She felt herself blush again and picked individual pastry flakes off her chest, for something to do.

'Well. I've always assumed I knew,' Beth said carefully, ripping the end off her own croissant and chewing it thoughtfully. 'I mean, because you never had a boyfriend or anything.'

So Beth had known, about that night on the green? Kerry gulped. Time to get a few answers.

'Funnily enough, I've been thinking about it a lot recently. You know who Tim is, don't you?'

Beth looked puzzled. 'What do you mean?'

'I didn't recognise him at first either. He grew up here too. Timmy Alcock. He's changed his name. But he was the boy with the cameras on the green that night, the night of Mum's fiftieth.'

Beth's mouth dropped open. 'No way! I'd never have realised. But it wasn't him who...?'

Kerry looked her right in the eye. 'Who did what, Beth? Took photos of me naked? No. I always thought it was, but it turns out that was your crush, Chris—'

She stopped herself before adding, *as you must have known, since you were there.* They were having a civil conversation and Kerry didn't want to change that. In fact, it suddenly occurred to her that perhaps, just perhaps, her own pass-agg defensiveness had had more than a small part to play in their arguments and disagreements over the years.

Beth did look shamefaced at the mention of Chris. 'I wish I could've stopped him, Kerry, I swear. I thought it was a horrible thing for him to do. I went right off him at that point. I felt so sorry for you.'

'Did you know what Lee and his mate did to me in the pond, right before Chris took the photos?'

Beth was silent for a moment and when she raised her eyes, they were full of compassion. 'Not exactly; not at the time,' she said carefully. 'But Serena hinted at a few things when I saw her at street dance, you know, asking if you were OK, and saying they'd been bang out of order.'

'You never asked me, Beth. You never once asked me if I was OK.'

To Kerry's astonishment, Beth gave a sob. 'I know,' she said, gripping Kerry's hand. 'I felt – still feel – terrible, but I just couldn't. I wanted to, honestly, it's not that I didn't care, I promise you. But – I don't know, it was like it was too big, too scary, and if I brought it up it kind of made it too real for me to cope with. I felt guilty that I hadn't stopped them. Then, the more time went on, the more impossible it got until in the end I convinced myself you were fine. It was so selfish of me. I am so sorry I wasn't there for you.' She paused. 'Did they... rape you?'

Kerry felt a tear run down her own cheek. 'No,' she said. 'They just tried to force me to give them blowjobs.'

'Vile, horrible boys.'

Kerry nodded. It was excruciating, to be discussing it with Beth after all these years, but so cathartic too. And yet – it wasn't the half of it, she thought. 'Lee and Mutt nicked the

Polaroids off Chris and photocopied them, then stuck them up around college, did you know that?'

'No,' Beth whispered, still crying. 'Oh my God, Kerry, you poor thing.'

'They weren't up for long, and you probably couldn't even tell they were of me. Tim complained to the head and got them all taken down straight away. He felt bad because they were taken with his camera, but then Lee made his life a misery after that, because he and Mutt got kicked out.'

Beth wiped her eyes. 'We should have talked about all this years ago,' she said. 'I'm not great at confronting things, even though I bet you think the opposite. I wasn't straight with Larry, when we were married. I wasn't straight with you. Jitz is so good for me, though. He doesn't let me get away with anything. So I think I'm slowly getting better at it. I'm trying, anyway. Losing Mum, then thinking I'd lost you in the fire – life is so short. It's made me realise I need to be better.'

This was a huge admission. Kerry couldn't speak for a few moments, then all her thoughts crowded into her brain at once; the will, her mum's wishes, the photos of Miss Smith, the insurance money...

'Thank you for saying that, Beth. I've really missed you. We just haven't connected, for so long, have we? I know that sometimes it's because I haven't been honest with you either, and other times that I've felt you don't believe me about certain things I've told you, and that's made me feel rubbish—'

Kerry hesitated, thinking about the insurance money and how they weren't going to get it, and how when she found out why, Beth would immediately have the moral high ground.

Dammit, she thought. I'm going to have to be straight with her now, otherwise this entire heart-to-heart will have been for nothing.

She reluctantly opened her mouth to admit she'd been smoking in the big house on the night of the fire – and as if by some kind of celestial miracle, Beth's mobile rang at that exact moment. Beth gave her an apologetic glance and picked it up. 'Hello? Yes, this is she...'

She listened for a few moments then a rueful smile spread across her face. 'Right, I see, yes that's good news, thank you.' Terminating the call, she turned back to Kerry. 'Guess what? That was the insurance company. The fire report's arrived – they emailed it to us too. The fire was started by that big old block connector Mum had by the TV, remember? There were too many plugs on it, and a spark caught fire and set the curtains alight. I kept telling her it was dangerous.'

The kitchen counter tilted beneath Kerry's hands and she closed her eyes for a moment, to try and absorb Beth's words. 'Overloaded plugs? Are they sure? Nothing else?'

Beth looked askance at her. 'What else would it be? No, just that. So the good news is that we'll get the insurance money; all of it. Are you OK, Kerry? You look really peculiar.'

FORTY

Kerry had to excuse herself, trying to do it discreetly and without alarming Beth. As soon as she left the room, she rushed upstairs to the bathroom where she locked the door and sat on the lid of the toilet, shaking, her head in her hands.

The fire hadn't been her fault! It was nothing to do with her! The relief was so overpowering that she thought she was going to faint, and it was a few moments before she could even lift her head without feeling dizzy. She focused on Tim's ornamental light pull, a little blue and white ceramic seahorse, bobbing about at the end of its string. Not. Her. Fault.

Thank you, God, she whispered. *Thank you.* It felt as though she had just had the most massive reprieve.

She splashed cold water on her face and went back downstairs to the kitchen, where she caught Beth red-handed, taking a bite of Kerry's barely touched croissant.

'Hah!' Kerry said. 'Gotcha!'

Beth laughed sheepishly. 'Sorry,' she said. 'Still hungry. Did an online spin class first thing this morning.'

'It's fine,' Kerry said, crossing the room and giving her sister a big hug. 'Finish it.'

Beth looked surprised but reciprocated the hug. They stayed there motionless for a moment, Beth's head on Kerry's shoulder, Kerry's arms around her sister's slender back. It felt so good, Kerry thought.

Eventually she pulled away. 'I've got something else to tell you,' she said, sitting down again. 'It's good news.'

'Oh yes?'

'Those photos of Miss Smith...'

Kerry caught the brief look of irritation that flashed across Beth's features and could see she was thinking, *Oh no, not this again...* But they were in a major spirit of détente, so Beth said nothing.

'I met up with her last week and asked her. They were of her.'

Beth gaped at her, and Kerry held up a palm in a conciliatory gesture.

'But – and this is the good news – Dad didn't take the photos. Miss Smith's – Anita's – ex boyfriend, do you remember, the one who came with her to London on that coach trip? *He* took them, then threatened to enter them into competitions when she tried to finish with him. He was a bastard. Daddy went round to his house and got them back off him when Anita told him and Mum what had happened. That's how come he had them.'

'Wow!' Beth's eyes were on stalks. 'Wow.' Then her shoulders sagged with relief. 'That's great, Kerry. I knew they couldn't have been having an affair!'

Kerry opened her mouth to protest that she couldn't possibly have known that for sure, and that she wished Beth could have believed her in the first place – then closed it again. It didn't matter now. All that mattered was the truth.

And speaking of the truth, Kerry thought, it was time to ask this, one last time: 'Beth? Speaking of Mum and Dad – well, Mum, anyway – I just keep wondering why she told me that I could stay living in the house and then didn't write it into her will. It doesn't make sense to me.'

She slid off her stool and went to refill the kettle for more tea. She heard Beth sigh behind her. 'I know. It doesn't make sense to me either. But I think it's worth remembering where both of us get our inability to confront things from. Mum was terrible at it too. I wonder if she told you that you'd get the house to live in, then realised that perhaps it wasn't the best solution for either of us, but didn't have the nerve to let you down in person? I know she wouldn't have done it maliciously. She loved you to bits, and whatever she did, it would one hundred per cent have been because she felt it was best for you.'

'She did only mention it that one time, literally years and years ago,' Kerry said slowly.

'Maybe she even forgot she'd said it,' Beth added. 'It's not that unlikely, you know what a sieve for a brain she had at times.'

'And I should have had the courage to ask her again. I couldn't, though. It just seemed so... greedy. Like I was waiting for her to pop her clogs.'

Beth laughed sadly. 'I know what you mean. Well. I think we should both promise to each other that we won't ignore things that need to be said any more, to each other, or to anybody else. Deal?'

She held up her mug of tepid camomile dregs and Kerry chinked her own against it.

'Deal.' Then she hesitated. 'OK Beth, so here's one more thing that needs to be said.'

Beth looked nervous. 'Yes?'

'I love you, and I love the kids and Jitz. I'd really like to be more a part of your lives, if that's OK with you.'

Beth reached up and affectionately cupped Kerry's cheeks in her palms.

'Yes, that's absolutely OK with me. I know I'm a pain in the ass sometimes, but I do love you too, big sis.'

FORTY-ONE

ONE MONTH LATER

'I can't hear the band,' Kerry said as they pulled into the grassy car park of the village hall. 'Are we late? And don't you think it's weird that Beth's band has a gig in this village? I thought they mostly played out Andover way. Why are there balloons outside?'

'Which question would you like me to answer first?' Tim asked, grinning. 'The balloons must be left over from some kids' party, I suppose. Now we're all allowed to have parties again, the backlog is probably huge.'

He put on the handbrake, switched off the engine and took Kerry's hand, turning his head to gaze at her. 'You look lovely, by the way. I'm sorry I didn't tell you before.'

Kerry reached over and kissed him, before brushing a speck of something off the shoulder of his smart burgundy button-down shirt. 'You're not so bad yourself. Although I'm really not sure why we got all dressed up just to see Beth's band.'

'Because you said she'll be dolled up to the nines and we don't want to look like grungy teenagers next to her? Because this is the first time in a year any of us has been for a proper night out with live music?'

'Ah yes, that'll be it,' Kerry said, as they exchanged knowing looks. She loved how quickly they had developed an effortless complicity, as if they could read one another's minds.

Tim had met Beth a few times now. Since Kerry and Beth's heart-to-heart on the day of the fire report, their relationship had turned a huge corner and now both she and Tim went over for weekly Sunday roasts together.

Kerry no longer felt outnumbered and intimidated by Beth and her family, and consequently was so much more relaxed around them all that even Opal had started talking to her normally and not like some mad old lady neighbour to whom she had been told to be polite. It was lovely.

Kerry and Beth had agreed that the house should be knocked down and the insurance money used to build a new one, which would immediately be sold and the money divided. Beth was delighted that she would definitely be getting her inheritance, and Kerry's relief that it hadn't been her cigarette that started the fire was so overwhelming that she was more than happy with the decision. She also found that, now the decision was out of her hands, she had no attachment to staying in the village after all.

She had been living in Tim's spare bedroom for a month and couldn't get over how easy and convenient life was, now that she didn't have to drive in and out of town every day nor prise open her eyelids at four thirty. It had been a godsend, helping her see that she wasn't tied to her annexe; that change, albeit one forced on her, was not to be feared the way she realised she always had.

Sharing a house with Tim had been a revelation. She'd always assumed that living with a man would involve untold indignities – pubes in the bath, awful stinks from the toilet, dishes in the sink... but Tim was as obsessively tidy as she was. He smelled amazing, always. He cooked delicious, healthy meals involving beetroot and pine nuts and all sorts of things Kerry had rarely encountered, which they ate on trays while binge-watching series on Netflix. They laughed together every day and she didn't feel any need to drink alcohol.

They kissed and hugged, often – but Kerry had still not yet shared his bed, and Tim, while making it clear how much he fancied her, was still not pressuring her to do so. She did want to, more and more every day, but she was determined not to rush into it. She was a forty-three-year-old virgin, for heaven's sake! Forty-four next week, she realised with a slight pang. It would be the first birthday she'd ever spent without the comforting presence of her mother; the carefully wrapped gift, the warm lemon cake, the scented kiss on the cheek. She was profoundly glad she wouldn't be in the annexe for it.

Still, being a virgin was undoubtedly embarrassing, but as with everything else, Tim seemed to completely take it in his stride. 'You're worth waiting for,' was all he ever said on the matter. 'Take your time.'

Tim was surreptitiously tapping out a message on his phone as they approached the quiet village hall.

'Who are you texting?' Kerry asked, intrigued. Tim had been behaving slightly oddly for a few weeks, now that she thought about it.

'Nobody,' he said, tucking the phone back into his pocket. 'Hold on, my shoelace is undone.' He sounded shifty as he bent to briskly re-knot the lace, but before Kerry could quiz him further, he had straightened up, grabbed her hand and marched her towards the double doors of the hall.

'Why are you being wei—' she began to say, but before she could finish the sentence, he had pushed open the doors and she didn't even have time to wonder why it was dark and silent inside, just for a moment, before the room exploded in a blur of light and sound:

'*Surprise!*'

FORTY-TWO

Kerry couldn't process it at all, not for almost a minute, as everyone she knew in the entire world – or so it seemed – was crowding around her, bumping elbows, in the new Covid version of a handshake, and slapping her on the back. Disco music blared through a big PA system on the stage and everybody talked louder to be heard above the thud of the bass. Unable to speak herself, Kerry tried to pick out individual sentences from the celebratory hubbub:

'Happy birthday, love!' Sheila from the village, wearing the same pink and grey shiny suit she'd had on last time Kerry saw her.

'Ha, we got you good, didn't we? You had no idea!' Jitz, giving her a side-hug.

'We couldn't let you go without a bit of a knees-up and thank goodness Boris is letting us have gatherings again otherwise this one would have been *very* small.' Clarissa, her hair freshly pinkened for the occasion, with a matching pink flowery full dress, as if she was about to break into a jive. 'The whole gang's here.'

She gestured towards a group near the bar who all waved enthusiastically at Kerry – all her Royal Mail colleagues, looking scrubbed and strange in their mufti. Everyone except Nasty Nige, she realised with relief. There was Bill, his wife and their postie son Kieran, the one who'd covered for her on her last leave; Gavin, Jacky, Pete, the young fella from accounts whose name she had already forgotten – and, it seemed, most of the villagers too. Kev, Neil and Ginny, Tom the farmer and his wife, Jonty the binman, all the pub regulars propping up a different bar for the night. Even Old Mrs Peabody and Joyless were sitting together at a table in face masks and Sunday best. Joyless even seemed to be smiling in her direction – although of course it was hard to tell under the mask.

'Auntie Kerry, look, me and Mum made the sign!' Opal was tugging at her hand and pointing towards the stage where a large banner was strung. It read *Happy Birthday and Happy Retirement, Kerry!* in wonky painted lettering, with misshapen flowers around the edges. Underneath it, several middle-aged men were tinkering with guitars and keyboards. Beth's band! Playing for her! Kerry couldn't believe it.

'It's lovely!' she said, blinking away astonished tears. The fact that her gardening leave had now officially been transmuted into early retirement, thanks to the letter from Dr Harkness, still hadn't properly sunk in. She missed the routine of her job but definitely not the ludicrously early starts.

'Happy birthday, dear Kerry,' said a soft voice in her ear, and she turned to see Anita at her elbow, next to a tall, smiling man in a suit. 'This is my husband, Glen.'

'Pleased to meet you, Kerry,' Glen said, proffering his elbow. 'Happy birthday!'

Kerry bumped funny bones with him. 'Thank you! I recognised you from your photo. I'm so happy that you're both here.' She turned to Tim, who was hovering at her side. 'I'm sure Tim is too,' she said slyly, and he blushed.

'Actually, it was me who invited them,' he said, and Kerry winked at him.

'Any excuse to contact Miss Smith,' she said quietly into his ear, digging him in the ribs and laughing. 'Did you invite *all* these people? Is that why you've been acting so weirdly recently?'

'I sort of did, but I had a lot of help,' he said. 'In fact, it was Clarissa who kicked it all off. She rang Beth and suggested you had a leaving do but we'd have to make it a surprise, otherwise you'd probably never have agreed to it. Then I thought we could make it a joint leaving and birthday party. I was a bit worried that you'd kill me, though.' He looked anxiously at her. 'You're not going to kill me, are you?'

Kerry hugged him, their bodies slotting into the now-familiar grooves. 'No. This is the nicest thing anyone's ever done for me. How did you get all the villagers here?'

'Clarissa photocopied an invitation and got it put through everyone's letterboxes. Great turnout, eh?'

She scanned the room anxiously. An open invitation wasn't ideal, what if—

Tim read her mind. 'Not *everyone*. I made sure Clarissa knew that it wasn't to go to Lee's mum, or to the Manns.'

Beth pushed her way through the crowd of well-wishers and pulled them apart. 'Let go of her, Tim, I want to wish my sister a happy birthday too.'

She was wearing the short gold dress that she'd bought on their shopping trip together – which seemed like a lifetime ago – and the metallic sequins scratched Kerry's bare forearms as they embraced.

'Thanks, Beth. This is... amazing. I can't believe it.' Even better, she thought, knowing that neither Chris, Serena nor Lee were going to turn up.

'You OK with it? I know you're a bit of a shrinking violet at the best of times.'

'Not any more, I've decided. New chapter, new me.'

Beth laughed. 'That's the spirit. And you know what? It suits you.' She put her mouth closer to Kerry's ear. '*Tim* suits you, too. We really like him.'

Tim had moved away and was chatting animatedly to Opal and Roddy.

'You're not the only one. So, what time are you on? Can't wait to see you.'

Beth glanced at the clock on the wall. 'Any time now! We have to finish by eleven. Can I get you a glass of fizz?' She hesitated, looking stricken. 'Oh – maybe not, I mean, it is your birthday bash, but—'

Kerry smiled. 'It's OK, sis. Coke's fine, please. It's so strange but I'm honestly not even tempted.'

Relief imprinted itself on Beth's features and Kerry thought how much like their mother she looked at that moment. 'Wish Mum could be here.'

'Me too. She'd be so pleased to see you this happy, so soon after... everything.' Beth's eyes filled.

'Well, I'm not sorted yet. But I feel better than I've done since she died. Anyway, you go and get ready to sing. I'll get primed to throw my knickers at you!'

Beth made a face, dabbing under her eyes. 'Oh God, please don't. I've seen your pants. Come on, let's fight our way to the bar.'

As they began to make their way across the hall, impeded by everyone stopping to bestow either birthday or retirement good wishes on Kerry, someone she didn't recognise caught her eye; a rake-thin woman in a coral-coloured dress tight enough that each of her ribs showed. She had calves so spindly that her legs looked like twigs. Her matching coral high heels seemed too big for her. Kerry was about to ask who it was when the man with her turned and she recognised his white hair and weather-beaten face. 'Happy birthday, young postie!'

'Lord Buckley! Gosh, hello.' Kerry felt like she should curtsy or something, but instead held out her elbow. Lord B reciprocated, then turned to the woman at his side. 'This is my better half, Fenella. Fenella, this is the woman of the hour.'

'Hello, birthday girl,' chirped Fenella in an unsurprisingly plummy voice. Up close, she had an angular yet friendly face. Nasty Nige would have called her a sixteen-sixty-two, Kerry thought; sixteen from the back, sixty-two from the front. But then, he always had been a sexist pig. So this must be the fourth Lady Buckley, she thought. She hadn't realised he had remarried after wife number three.

'Hello! Lovely to meet you. It's such an honour to have you here.'

'Don't be silly. We love a good party, don't we, Charles?'

'We do,' agreed Lord B.

Kerry couldn't believe that Clarissa had had the nerve to stick the invite in their post too – but then, it clearly hadn't been too outrageous a notion because here they both were, almost but not quite blending in. Lord B was sporting the standard-issue country-gent casual uniform of checked flannel shirt, brogues and mustard cords, even on this warm September night.

'Sorry to hear you've left the Royal Mail,' he said. 'And I heard on the grapevine that you've recently had a house fire. Frightfully sorry about that too. Did you get yourself a new job?'

'Not yet,' Kerry said, nodding thanks at Beth as she pressed a glass of Coke into her hand and shimmied off towards the stage. 'There's been so much admin and so on to do, sorting everything out after the fire. But I'm going to be looking around soon. I can't not work.'

Lord B and his wife exchanged glances. 'Interesting,' Fenella said, 'because as it happens...'

At that moment the band took to the stage, the lights went down and the background music fell silent. 'Good evening!' called a tall wiry guy in his fifties with statement sideburns.

'We're The Fluffinators, and we're here to entertain you, so let's see you all on the dance floor to celebrate Kerry's big night!'

A cheer went up as the drummer knocked his sticks together to count them in, and Kerry burst out laughing – mostly at the expression of discomfort that flitted across Beth's face when the band's name was announced. The Fluffinators? This was *hilarious*. No wonder Beth had never mentioned it. It must be the naffest band name in the history of bands. And why, if she was the singer, was she not the one introducing them? In fact she was standing slightly to the side of the stage, looking beautiful but surprisingly nervous behind a mic stand. Their opening number was 'All Over the World' by ELO. Again, surprising. But they were good, in time and funky, and people were already on the dance floor, months' worth of pent-up post-lockdown party spirit unleashed.

Kerry caught Tim's eye across the room, and they shared a moment of mutual hilarity as Tim mouthed *The Fluffinators?* at her and mimed clutching his sides.

Fenella and Lord B – Charles – were still standing with her, and Fenella leaned in closer to speak to her above the noise of the band. She smelled simultaneously of insanely expensive perfume and musty dog hair.

'As I was saying, we heard about your predicament with the fire, and that you're no longer our postie, and we wondered if we could help in any way. It might not be up your street, but we are about to advertise for a new housekeeper as our lovely Virginia is retiring.'

Kerry remembered Virginia from her regular visits to the Dunsmore House kitchens, a kind and plump grandmotherly type. For a moment she wondered what this had to do with her, Kerry, and why it might not be up her street – then she frowned.

'Wait – are you suggesting...?'

Charles and Fenella both nodded enthusiastically. 'Mornings only. Just admin, really, keeping the wheels well oiled. Nothing too challenging, we just want someone reliable, honest and friendly. So we thought you'd be perfect,' said Charles, braying slightly over the music.

Unable to process this new development, Kerry looked towards the stage. Beth had joined in on harmonies now. She was OK, Kerry thought, but not nearly the pop diva she'd assumed her sister would be on stage.

The Fluffinators – *ha!* That would never not be funny.

Kerry turned her attention back to the lord and lady, her head whirling with adrenaline. They were both beaming at her, as if she had already accepted a position she had just that second been offered, of a type that had never crossed her mind to do before. It felt a lot like when Tim had asked if she wanted to move in – the sort of thing that she would never have suggested herself, but which appeared undeniably appealing when someone else did, with such conviction that it was a good idea.

'Gosh,' she said, visualising the views from Dunsmore House. The rolling hills, the lush kitchen garden, the lawns speckled with ancient willow trees. The space and beauty, when she had imagined that any job she'd be lucky enough to get would involve her sitting at a grey melamine desk in a windowless cubicle somewhere depressing. 'That does actually sound up my street.'

'Splendid!' said Charles. 'Here's our card. Give Virginia a ring – she'll be expecting to hear from you – and you can pop over to see if you think it might be something you'd like to do. Right, we shall leave you to enjoy your party – must get back for the dogs. Have a super evening.'

As if they'd choreographed it, they both mimed air-kissing Kerry then turned and swept out of the hall, partygoers parting and turning to watch their progress in true serf versus lord of the manor style.

Tim was by her side again. 'What was that about? Who were the poshos?' he asked, gesturing to the business card in her hand.

Kerry blinked at it then put it carefully into the side pocket of her dress. 'That was Lord and Lady Buckley from Dunsmore House. They've only offered me a job as their new housekeeper!'

Tim laughed with delight. 'No way! Do you think you'll do it?'

Kerry shrugged. 'I don't know. Maybe. I'll definitely look into it though. Isn't it weird how suddenly people keep offering me stuff?'

'People? Stuff?' Tim affected a confused expression.

'OK – you, inviting me to move in. Them, offering me a job out of the blue.'

Tim took both her hands in his and turned her to face him. 'And can't you see the reason why it's not weird at all?' he asked, leaning his forehead against hers.

Kerry blushed and kissed him. 'Come on, let's go and dance,' she said. Just then, someone ran up to her, puffing, with a musclebound shorn-headed young man in tow.

'Kez! Sorry I'm late, babes, I had a last-minute nail emergency. Happy birthday! What's going on? I leave you alone for a few weeks and you've burned your house down, quit your job and shacked up with a bloke! Although I can talk – this is the reason I've been a bit quiet, this is my new man, Damian.'

'Hello, Sharon,' Kerry said, grinning at her. 'Tim, this is my friend Sharon. Nice to meet you, Damian.'

The four of them nodded at one another and sized each other up. Sharon stuck out her boobs and flicked her hair back. She was wearing a low-cut tight white vest and a black tube skirt with vertiginous heels.

'You must come round to dinner soon,' Tim said gravely.

'Lovely!' Sharon agreed, linking arms with Damian.

None of them could think of anything else to say, so after an excruciating few moments, Sharon gestured towards the bar. 'Let's go and get a drink, Dames. Do you think they have Prosecco? Kerry, catch you later darling, let's have a boogie, it's so exciting to be able to dance again! Did you know, Dames, I was once Junior National Disco Dance Champion?'

Tim and Kerry watched them go, Damian's trousers tight enough to give him a hernia, Sharon's manicured hand giving one of his grapefruit-tight buttocks a good squeeze.

'So that's the famous Sharon.'

'It is, bless her. Terrible fibber but means well. It's nice to see her looking happy, with a new man.'

'Like you.'

'Like me.'

The band launched into Stevie Wonder's 'Superstition', to which Beth's only contribution was shimmying about and banging a tambourine against her toned thigh. 'I really thought she was the lead singer,' Kerry said wonderingly. 'Funny, how easy it is for someone to give the wrong impression, when they want to.'

'That's one of the things I love about you,' Tim said as they headed for the dance floor. 'You never do that. In computing they used to call it WYSIWYG – what you see is what you get. That's why everyone's here. For you. Because they love you too.'

Surrounded by friends and family on the dance floor, Kerry let her eyes close and her feet move to the music, the words 'one of the things I love about you' thumping round her brain in time to the bass. She smiled and danced, raising her arms in the air, looking only ahead into a future that she realised she couldn't wait for.

Anita shimmied up to her and mirrored her movements.

Kerry beamed at her and they danced together, with Tim next to them looking like all his Christmases had come at once.

Miss Smith always did love to dance, Kerry thought, followed immediately by another reflection: So this is what it feels like to be complete.

EPILOGUE
1993

It was anathema to Ralph, the thought of stealing anything from anyone. But as he looked at the contact sheet of naked Anitas that Jeff was, almost shyly, proffering for his approval, such a rage bubbled up inside him that it took every ounce of composure not to show it. Could Jeff really not see the dull glint of shame in the poor woman's eyes? If he couldn't find a way to slip this sheet into his backpack, plus the envelope of negatives that he could see still in the briefcase, he thought he might actually have to punch Jeff and simply run away with them.

He was a dying man; what would Jeff do, punch him back?

As he examined the photographs with what he hoped was a dispassionate, professional eye, his mouth made all the right sounds: 'Ah, yes, goodness, excellent angles in this one, the way the crook of her knee and elbow are in such perfect symmetry...' but internally, he was in fierce debate with himself. Perhaps he should just confront Jeff, tell him straight that it was completely wrong of him to threaten Anita with making these pictures public? But that would mortify him, and might even get Anita into trouble with Jeff, who clearly had enough of a temper to have threatened her in the first place.

Clearing his throat, he decided to test the water a bit.

'You were lucky, that Anita was happy to be your model,' he said diffidently. 'I'd have thought that she might be worried, being a teacher and all.'

Jeff nodded, somewhat over-enthusiastically. 'She was well up for it.' He gave a slightly falsetto laugh. 'In fact, it was her idea. Said she'd always wanted to have some nice arty pics of herself, while she had a good enough body. She said she'd get one framed and look back at it when she's eighty, remind herself what she looked like in her prime.'

'Ah. I see.'

Ralph felt a swell of pity as he gazed at Anita's admittedly very lovely breasts. Her expression did not tally with that description at all. He wouldn't say she looked as if she'd been coerced, not exactly, but the look in her eyes was not just bashfulness. Unless his perspective had been skewed by the knowledge that Anita was deeply unhappy and frightened about the pictures and the effect that their circulation could have on her life? Could be, he thought. Perhaps it was only the threat of exposure that she was upset about; not the photos themselves.

Either way, he thought, she did not want them out in the world and that was absolutely reasonable and understandable. The photos were supposed to have been private, between her and Jeff.

Ralph felt fresh anger with Jeff for even showing them to him, even though it was a stroke of luck that he had and made his task easy. What a cad, he thought, the old-fashioned word seeming the most appropriate to describe the sort of a character Jeff's actions were showing him to be.

'Well, best make sure you keep them to yourself,' he said. 'Wouldn't be right, to go showing those around anywhere.'

Jeff frowned and chewed at the little triangle of facial hair just under his bottom lip. 'Actually, I was thinking of entering them into a comp or two. Nobody would know it's Anita. Anyway, she wouldn't mind.'

Ralph snorted. 'Anyone who knows Anita would immediately see that it's her! Have you asked her permission?'

'Oh yes,' Jeff said airily, although he wasn't meeting Ralph's eyes. 'She said it's fine.'

It was at that moment that Ralph thought he really *was* going to punch him. 'Gosh. That surprises me. She's always seemed pretty... shy.'

'Square, if you ask me. Anyway, she knows it's art. She's good as gold about it.'

You are a horrible, horrible man, thought Ralph. He watched as Jeff packed all the prints and contact sheets back into the briefcase, doubtless having sensed Ralph's disapproval.

Suddenly he just wanted to be back home with Hilary and the girls. He had so little time left, why on earth would he waste it with this creep? He did not want to wait until Jeff's bladder necessitated a trip to the bathroom and a clear coast. He wanted to go *now*.

He stood up, the black leather sofa making a farting sound under him. 'Well,' he said. 'Thanks for the drinks, Jeff, but I think I'll head off now.'

Jeff's eyebrows shot up. 'But I only just opened those beers.' He gestured at Ralph's untouched bottle.

Ralph shrugged. 'Drink 'em yourself.' He picked up his bike helmet and rammed it on his head. Then, without hesitating, he picked up the briefcase too.

'I'm taking this, and you're not going to stop me,' he said, his voice clear and firm. 'I won't allow you to do this to Anita. I made a grave error in judgement, setting you two up, because she is a lovely girl and you are a liar, a pervert and a bully.'

Jeff's expression scrolled through so many different emotions simultaneously that Ralph wished he had a camera at his eye taking thirty frames per second. It would have made a lovely study. Rage, guilt, embarrassment, defensiveness, sorrow all passed across Jeff's features like clouds across the sun. He squared up to Ralph, eyeing the briefcase.

'No,' was all he managed to say. 'You can't take that!'

'I'll get the briefcase back to you at some point,' Ralph said, then neatly sidestepped him and headed for the door. He braced himself for Jeff to follow him, even physically wrestle the case from his hands, but he heard a heavy sigh and the squeak of the black leather as Jeff flopped back onto the sofa, defeated. Not even someone of Jeff's dubious morality would attack a dying man.

There were some advantages to terminal illness, Ralph thought, as he put on his cycle clips, hung the handles of the briefcase over one handlebar and wobbled away into the dusk, permitting himself a small smile.

When he arrived back home, it was almost completely dark. He propped his bike against the garage wall and took the briefcase into his office, stuffing the contents so hastily into the bottom drawer of his photography chest that the paper envelope ripped and the photos spilled in willy-nilly. He shoved the wonky drawer shut with some effort, thinking that he'd take them out and burn them later, when the girls were at school, and he could ask Hilary to drop the empty briefcase back on Jeff's doorstep.

It turned out to be the last time Ralph ever went for a bike ride.

A week later, in an act that used up all the available strength he had that day, he burned all the photos – apart from one contact sheet that had been at the bottom of the pile and which he'd completely missed when he picked them up.

A week after that, the next time he opened the drawer, he discovered the left-behind sheet and lifted it out, permitting himself a lingering, guilty look at Anita's body. She was a beautiful woman, there was no denying it. But he had derived far more pleasure from overhearing her gratitude, when Hilary rang her up and told her that Ralph had 'sorted' it and the photographs were now burned, than he got from gazing at her naked form.

He was about to rip it into pieces when he heard the garage door open and Kerry's voice calling him. She always burst into his office, so he hastily shoved the contact sheet right to the bottom of the drawer.

Then he forgot about it entirely, in the self-absorbed, heart-breaking and painful business of dying.

A LETTER FROM LOUISE

Dear Reader,

I want to say a huge thank you for choosing to read *Kerry Tucker Learns to Live*. If you want to keep up to date with all my latest releases, just sign up at the following link. Your email address will never be shared and you can unsubscribe at any time.

www.bookouture.com/louise-voss

If you enjoyed *Kerry Tucker Learns to Live*, I would be very grateful if you could write a review. I'd love to hear what you think, and it makes such a difference helping new readers to discover one of my books for the first time. It's always really great to hear from my readers – you can get in touch on my Facebook page, Twitter or Insta, details below.

This one was pretty hard to write, for one reason and another. I'm sure that its main theme of isolation was inspired by the pandemic lockdowns, even though it's not technically a 'Covid novel'. In the book, lockdowns act as an accelerant to, rather than the cause of, Kerry's loneliness. I took inspiration for her feelings from a number of quarters; sadness at not having as close a relationship as I'd like with some of my few remaining relatives, periods in my life when I've felt like that too, as well as knowing that I have friends who have been through, or are still going through, something similar.

Feeling alone is a terrible scourge, even if you start to realise that your own patterns of behaviour may at least in part be what drives people away from getting or staying too close, as with Kerry. But everything turns out OK for Kerry in the end; she lays to rest all her ghosts and learns to appreciate her own worth. For me as the author – having of course not planned out what was going to happen, as per usual – this has been incredibly satisfying and, to my surprise, quite moving. I hope you feel the same.

If you are reading this and realising, as Kerry gradually does, that you are lonely too, please don't retreat into it. It's sadly so easy to do, and completely understandable. Although it is a daunting prospect, my advice (from my own past experience) is JOIN things, sports clubs, choirs, community projects – whatever's your bag. It's hard at first but you will meet other people in similar situations who may well become friends over time. And if you really can't face that, try www.samaritans.org or call them for a chat, any time, on 116 123.

Thanks for reading,

Louise Voss

facebook.com/louisevossauthor

twitter.com/LouiseVoss1

instagram.com/Louisevoss

ACKNOWLEDGEMENTS

Biggest thanks to my editor Ruth Tross for all her suggestions and encouragement. Writing a novel is never a piece of cake and we both nearly gave up on this one – but I'm so glad we didn't!

Thanks as ever to the awesome Phil Patterson, aka Agent Phil. So lovely having you on side.

Shout out to my fantastic Bournemouth Arts University creative writing group; Hugh, Sophie, Vikki, Moira, Amanda, Benedict, Nadine, Lara and Iva, all potential future bestsellers, IMHO. Each one of you is an inspiration and a pleasure to work with.

Huge thank you to Jackie Compton for your time and generosity in talking me through the life of a Royal Mail postwoman and answering my dozens of questions, all those months ago. Very much appreciated. Any inaccuracies about the life of a postie are of course my own mistakes.

Thanks too to Matt Skyme, Station Manager at Dorset & Wilts Fire & Rescue Service, for the long and super-helpful chat about post-house-fire procedure, and to Judy Burns for authentic GP advice. Also to Clarissa for inspiring the Clarissa in the book, and to Jitz for allowing me to borrow his name.

Thank you to copyeditor Jennie Ayres. Loved all your little comments in the margin, cheering Kerry on and commiserating with her traumas. And apologies for inflicting yet another terrible timeline on you! Think we sorted it out in the end.

Massive thank you to everybody on my Facebook author

page for the many hilarious suggestions of cheesy cover band names – reading over 180 of them was the best laugh I'd had in ages. The winning entry, *The Fluffinators*, came from Hayley 'Princess Peacock' Wright and, I thought, couldn't really be topped. Honourable mentions also go to Rachael Henshall (*Right Said Geoff*), Annie Manfield (*Tepid Fun*) and Derek Farrell (*Mike Du Vey and the Continental Quilts*). Ha ha!

Finally, loads of love to Ade for patient and constructive plot troubleshooting. And lots of cups of tea.

Printed in Great Britain
by Amazon